High praise for
M.A. LEVI
and 'FLAMES TO THE BEAST'

"Flames to the Beast was a wild ride. M.A. Levi created characters with depth and emotion you can connect with."
– Author, Tonya Coffey

"This was by far one of the best books I have ever read. It had me on the edge of my seat wondering what was going to happen next. The writing is flawless and made this book an even better read."
– Book Blog Critique, The Picky Digest

"'Flames to the Beast' is a kick-ass novel that centers around unrequited love, jealousy, revenge, possession, and a whole bunch of werewolves!"
-Author, Stephanie Flores

"An epic story of good versus evil. As the werewolves changed, I could almost feel my bones breaking along with them as my skin peeled away."
-Author, K.K. Watson

"There are so many facets that make the plot complex and mesmerizing.... The ending was both tragic and satisfying, a trait that I always equate to excellent storytelling."
–Book reviewer, Amy Winters

Tenth Anniversary Special Edition

ISBN-13: 978-0692793657
ISBN-10: 0692793658

FOR THE *BEASTS* WE HIDE,
THE *FLAMES* THAT FORGE US,
AND THE *LOVE* THAT *REFUSES TO DIE.*

M. A. LEVI
FLAMES TO THE BEAST

PROLOGUE

Original document predated:1100 A.D. England
Early Translation: First mark of Summer Solstice, 1400

Prophecy: Flames to the Beast

My brothers in Christ, hear me well. I have been blessed by a vision of divine influence. For more than a century, talk of vampirism and lycanthropy has haunted this village. A black shroud has settled over their meaning, ruling our reason and our fear for far too long. Hundreds of innocents have died, and their blood stains your hands. You are sheep led astray—obedient, mindless fools driven into a wild hunt for those you believe responsible for the murders and massacres of our children. And all the while, the truth stands directly beneath your blinded gaze.

We have seen their bodies drained of blood as life receded from their cold, graying flesh. Your leaders declared them dead. Yet when dawn spilled its comforting light upon our desecrated homes, those same children walked among us once more, renewed, animated by something not of God. Are you so brainless to believe the clergy of the devil when they proclaimed a miracle had taken place? Do you not see that their eyes have changed? Soulless black—or rolled white—undeniable proof of the corruption that now walks freely among us. Bastards—selling our children, our future, into the hands of Satan.

A soul traded for hammered coin to line your pockets. Blood money. The ones responsible for these wretched trespasses are the very figures you follow without questions. You fear what lurks within the darkest reaches of the forest—aye. But what of your towering meeting halls? Your gaudy castles perched upon our fair hills? You take comfort in the false security of the stone walls and brightly burning fires that illuminate their lairs.

They feed you lies, sending you to slaughter the very being who could protect us from them and their unholy necromancers. The demons within outgrow their decaying mortal casings, splitting free—and they murder our youth to extend their own wretched existence with the deaths of godly innocents.

Is what I claim unnatural to what you're forced to believe and do? Is it strange that your leaders groom their own successors—evil reborn—to carry on their studies and their rulings? Do not shield your eyes. Do not hide within ignorance. No longer remain mindless puppets in their designs, staining your souls with holy blood spilled for wicked ends. Free yourselves from their intentions and seek the Creator for redemption. Take seriously what I speak of. Embrace it as truth. Do not dismiss my words as the ravings of a madman. Hunger does not elude my senses, nor drink, nor plague. I am sound in what I say. I pray for your protection—and the protection of all humanity. They are at stake. I have no choice. The world's salvation comes when the divinity of man has been silently waiting for the day of revelation.

Heed my heavenly vision or let the repercussions be as they may. You may set fire to the grass, and watch it burn as it begins to ash—but the roots are still below the earth. Heaven and Hell will twist in a bloody war upon this world. Humanity will stand witness in awe as the world burns around them, the sky turning gold, the land beneath their feet blackened and dead. The clock turns. The pendulum swings. It's only a matter of time before it truly begins.

—Solomon,
Founder and First Master of the Holy Order of St. Michael

CHAPTER ONE
A MOMENT TOO LATE

Fortaleza, Brazil
January 23rd, 1881

Rushing down the narrow alleyway, Leonardo tore through the darkness in a blind panic. He stole frantic glances over his shoulder as he ran, never slowing, never daring to look ahead. He continued to run at his fastest pace, oblivious to the sleeping homeless man sprawled out on his back in the middle of the stone path. Leonardo didn't look ahead until it was too late. He stumbled forward when his bare foot slipped under the man's back, his heel striking bone as she stumbled forward and kicked hard into the old man's rib cage. The impact jolted the man awake with a strangled gasp. Bloodshot eyes bulged from a sunken, bearded face as he rolled onto his side, coughing violently. Each breath came ragged and shallow, his vision doubling and spinning as he struggled to focus. At last, through the blur, he found the silhouette of Leonardo. Knowing where to aim his words, the old man began to swear at him in slurred speech.

By then, Leonardo steadied his tall, lean body, bracing one hand against the jagged stone wall. Pain flared as the ridged surface tore into his palm. He dropped his arm, watching as the stark red of his blood stained the sandstone just as he expected it would.

"Jesus," Leonardo muttered with an exasperated sigh. If anyone from his clan was tracking him, it would be easier now. They would smell his blood on the walls, follow his path by the undeniable scent. He slowed to a hurried walk, forcing himself to steady his pace to avoid another accident. Leonardo clenched his bleeding hand and shoved it into the pocket of his trousers, already feeling the skin begin to knit itself back together.

His anger—long past its limit—turned sharp and focused on the man behind him. Leonardo cocked his head slightly and growled over his shoulder. "Drunken fuck. Get the hell out of the alley."

If he had time, he might have made an example of the man—pressed fear into the last fragments of life the old drunk had left. But Leonardo wouldn't waste what little time he had on someone like that.

His mood darkened further, settling into his features as the plan took shape. There were three men. Leonardo was going to kill them. The justification came easily. They were demon-possessed—humans beyond redemption. Their eyes were soulless black, sunken deep within narrow faces, and though their skin appeared flawless, they reeked of rot. He had seen the bodies they left behind, devoured and discarded along the outskirts of town. He knew who was responsible.

Leonardo would wait. He would strike at the precise moment when he could become their executioner. It had to work. Not only to end them—but to prove something to Eli.

The thought made his stomach tighten. Anxiety coiled beneath his resolve, but there was no room for hesitation. This was his one chance. When he got word where these demons would be residing tonight, he knew it was a sign. Redemption was near. He moved quickly then, the plan assembling itself with ruthless clarity. He knew exactly where to go—and what awaited him when he arrived. The men were lodging in a familiar tavern nestled in the city's slums. Leonardo knew the place well. The brothel hidden within its walls had once been his refuge, a residence for months at a time, where indulgence drowned out consequence. Tonight, it would serve a different purpose.

Leonardo was sweating profusely. He dragged the back of his hand across his brow just as pain struck his core from the inside out. He bent forward, twisting from the onslaught of trembling pain. He worked through the familiar suffering. With ragged breath, he gnashed his teeth together and willed his feet to keep moving. Time was against him in more ways than one. He shot a glance toward the sky. The moon hung low and full, bright and watchful, taunting him—close enough to touch. He felt its ancient power stirring his blood, calling him to surrender. He longed to succumb to it. It demanded transformation. Leonardo clenched his jaw harder, certain his teeth might shatter as he fought the beast clawing for release.

"Not yet," he growled, tearing his gaze from the moon's haunting pull. Even the heavens seemed determined to bar his path. More resolute than ever, Leonardo pressed on, pushing toward the outskirts and slums of the blooming city—before it was too late.

Blasting through the silence, crates crashed and wood splintered behind him as a black cat bolted through the alley, vanishing into the dark. Leonardo spun, paranoia flaring as he scanned the dreary surroundings. The lamps burned low tonight, their glow weakened by the wind, but moonlight spilled just enough illuminated across the stone. Then—a blur of shadow caught the corner of his eye. It tore down the narrow alley, followed by the sharp clack of boots striking stone, the echo growing louder with each step.

Leonardo broke into a full run. He turned hard into one alley, then another, weaving through the slums with instinctive precision. He wasn't far now. The brothel lay ahead. Relief surged when he spotted the oil lamp flickering above the tavern's back entrance in the distance. He could make it. He could transform. Even if someone was following him, they would be too late to stop what was coming.

A salty breeze rolled in from the Atlantic, churning around him and dragging with it the stench of mortals and animals long gone stale. His heightened senses amplified every foul note, and his stomach twisted violently. It wafted the putrid smells of mortals and animals that had sat stagnant a moment ago. Leonardo's heightened sense of smell amplified their horrific compounds and his stomach rolled. Leonardo bent forward again, clutching himself as bile burned at the back of his throat. His eyes glistened, a thin sheen coating them as they caught the firelight of the oil lamps—bright, unnatural. Every sound sharpened. Every movement aligned with terrifying precision under his heightened awareness. Leonardo didn't know how much longer he could fight the instinct to change.

He grunted, squeezing his eyes shut as radiating pain tore through him. He forced his concentration inward, wrestling his thoughts into order. After a moment, the agony dulled enough for him to move again—but it was costing him. Another crippling round of pain, Leonardo screamed through his gritted teeth. He recognized this stage. His muscles were tearing from the bones and tendons as they shaped into a distorted form. Violent spasms wracked him, ribs cracking as his feet locked him in place. His body convulsed as his feet rooted his body where it stood.

He needed to transform—but not yet. He couldn't arrive as a monster. Gnashing his teeth, he shoved forward through the pain, dragging his feet inch by inch. Frustration tore free as a roar ripped through his chest. "You will not win."

Blinding pain exploded through his nerves, striking his legs useless. The severity of his suffering churned his stomach into a violent spell of dry heaves wrenching his body as he collapsed to his hands and knees.

"No," he bellowed, choking as bile burned at the back of his throat. Fear surged—sharp and immediate. At any second, he expected hands to seize the back of his tunic and tear him down. The bile refused to rise further, leaving acid and blood pooled on his tongue. His mouth went dry, numb as he swallowed it back. This was the cost of denial. He was suffering by denying the moon its powerful ability. Bitterness clouded his heart as he nearly cursed Eli for forcing this life on him. But not tonight. Tonight, Leonardo chose. Not the clan. Not Roslyn. Not Eli.

Eli. The mighty clan leader. Leonardo mocked the thought and rose to his feet, forcing himself upright, stumbling into a half-hearted run. He scanned the alley again—but no one was there. A shaky breath escaped him, relief bordering on laughter. Delusion, he decided. Fever and pain conjuring ghosts where there were none. He pushed the thought aside and fixed his gaze forward, a fierce, burning purpose settling in his chest.

Son of a bitch. What choice was there for me? She wanted him, and I needed the rich bastard's money.

Leonardo leaned into the anger, using it to dull the pain enough to keep moving. Roslyn's name—once respected—had been dragged through scandal because of him. Sharp tongues in high society whispered and sneered and she was shunned for his shameless indulgences. It only worsened when the truth surfaced. They were broke. Creditors and gossipers alike spread word of how Leonardo had squandered the family fortune on his own excesses in the slums. His name became poison. No one would honor his word, no one would extend credit—not to him, not to anyone tied to him. So he turned to men who trafficked in darker dealings. In exchange for coin, Leonardo handed over the ownership papers to the family businesses. One by one, he sold their homesteads. Their heirlooms followed. Then the furniture. Their possessions were dragged into the street and sold beneath the open sky while strangers watched their disgrace unfold. When the final cabinet was gone, all that remained was the small townhouse they clung to like a last breath. It didn't last long. Day and night, creditors battered their door, demanding payment that would never come.

They fell even deeper into poverty—and closer to danger. Leonardo couldn't leave the house without being cornered in some nearby alley, muscled to the ground by hired thugs and beaten senseless. The last time, he'd been shot through the upper thigh, a blade dragged across his face as a final warning. Desperation hollowed him out. For a time, he had even considered selling Roslyn. The thought still made him sick. He knew what she was worth in the eyes of men like that. Young. Untouched. Beautiful. Men, even women willing to pay handsomely for her. He already line one up. But he couldn't do it. He couldn't condemn her to a life that would strip her soul bare, not after all she had already endured. He knew the kind of demented pleasure such men would demand, the damage they would leave behind. Disgusted with himself, anger curdled into self-loathing, and drink became his only companion. Still the memory lingered. A man named Keller Luis Costa had wanted her. He offered nearly three times what Leonardo had dared to ask.

Even now, revulsion twisted through Leonardo's gut at the memory of their meeting. He regretted opening the door. Regretted allowing that first—and only—encounter. Keller's smile surfaced in his mind, thin and revolting, exposing dull teeth that tapered to unnatural points.

The man's eager smile did nothing to ease Leonardo's unease. If anything, it hardened his resolve. The memory had burned itself into his mind, etched in merciless detail. Keller had thinning white hair, his brows so pale against his luminous skin the appeared nonexistent. His thin lips lightened as they stretched across sharp features when he introduced himself. Though close to Roslyn's age, Keller looked diseased—sunken-eyed, near death. His nose was sharply pointed, his eyes a washed-out blue that sloped unnaturally within his narrow face. There wasn't a blemish on his skin. His hands were smooth, his face waxy, almost translucent—marked by a sheen that spoke of long years hidden from the sun. Combined with his black attire, the effect cloaked him in something quietly vicious.

It was his eyes that betrayed him. Those pale, bluish-white orbs promised twisted desires and unnatural appetites. Leonardo remembered cutting him off mid-speech, shutting down the offer without hesitation. He told Keller plainly that he had changed his mind, and broke the exchange. Keller had pressed harder. Leonardo remained firm. His reasons were his own.

Keller had slammed his stout hand against the closing door. Color flared briefly beneath the pallid skin as his eyes turned even whiter, gums bared in a flash of wet, blood-red fury. His voice changed too. What had been smooth and measured dropped into a low, snarling demand—asking why. Leonardo stiffened, instinctively preparing to defend the doorway. He pressed his weight into the wood, silently praying Roslyn wouldn't descend the stairs during the confrontation. Slowly, he reached for the pistol tucked into the back of his trousers—a habit formed after hired thugs had put a bullet through his thigh. His finger had closed around the smooth steel of the trigger. Keeping the weapon hidden, he ordered Keller to leave.

Keller lunged, and Leonardo had drew the pistol in one swift motion and slammed the barrel against Keller's chest, centering it over his heart. A hard silence fell between them. Keller glanced down at the gun, then snapped his cold gaze back up. Murder flickered across his expression as logic warred with impulse. Slow, deliberately, he eased his stance—but the tremor in his hands betrayed his composure. He was furious. Venom filled his voice. "Watch your fucking back, snake," he hissed. "I *will* bury a blade in you."

Leonardo had clenched his jaw as his anxiety curdled into anger. "I like to see you try, bastard."

Keller answered with a tight smirk, turned from the porch and disappeared into the pouring summer rain. Leonardo slammed the door and locked it behind him as he ran the words of Keller's threat through his mind. That was the last he had ever saw him.

Hearing a metallic scrape against stone behind him, snapped Leonardo from his bitter thoughts. The aura around him shifted. He focused, honing his sensitive hearing, straining for the slightest irregularity—but the sound was gone. After a few tense moments, his attention drifted back to his plan. He stood before the tavern. From inside, the gruff voice of the owner carried through the walls—a loud portly Spaniard named Rico, bellowing a crude song about a woman's sexual conquests. The crowd roared with laughter, rowdy cheers from drunken men answered by the lusty cries of women on cue.

Leonardo curled his lips into something resembling a relaxed smile as he moved forward, ready to transform once inside. Then another sound intruded. Metallic. Jagged. Growing louder against the stone. Leonardo froze. Suddenly, hearing heavy boots swiftly running behind him again, he spun, muscles coiling as he prepared to strike.

"Quit fucking with me, goddamn you!" he thundered. The fanatical edge of his anger faded. No one was there. His mind raced, instinctively placing an unseen attacker within the shadows. He wasn't foolish enough to doubt his senses now. Someone was there—watching, testing him, playing with him, waiting for another moment to catch him off guard as they remained cloaked in the darkness. A prickling sensation crept across his skin as he coiled tighter, ready. The ocean breeze surged harder, teaching his long brown hair and tugging at his loose clothing. The air grew colder, sharper. The night itself felt altered—leaning toward something far more sinister. Leonardo tipped his head back and inhaled deeply, filling his lungs with the chill air while searching for the unseen figure. His nostrils flared as the smell of mortals, sex, and freshly spilled ale engulfed him. Within the dense mixture, he had caught the faint and familiar smell of iron and leather.

Leonardo's jade-green eyes flew open, flaring into glowing orbs as the nocturnal sheen caught them in the moonlight. He spun, lifting his gaze skyward. Keller stood above him—silent, unmoving—framed by the pale glow of the moon atop the tavern roof. Leonardo strained to make out his face, but Keller's features remained concealed beneath a billowing hood. Ebony armor clung tightly to his frame, dulled and dark enough to swallow the light and blend him seamlessly into the night. Leonardo's attention dropped to Keller's hands. Gloved fingers twitched near the black hilts of twin blades resting against his slender hips—murder waiting for permission.

Understanding struck with brutal clarity. Keller had followed him from the moment he left the clan. This was no chance encounter. This was revenge—long planned—and Leonardo had unknowingly led him straight to it. Regret bled into his fury as he locked his glowing gaze on the shadowed face above.

I started this. And it will end tonight. Leonardo snarled, baring clenched white teeth as he addressed the still silhouette. "So you've come to keep your promise," he hissed. "I take it you've been following me for some time. You know what I am now." Keller did not answer. Leonardo's lips curled. "Well equipped for a fight," he said softly. "Then allow me to become prepared as well."

He stopped resisting the Calling, and painfully and let it come forth. The pain surged as he surrendered to it— his breath getting shorter while his heart pounded harder within his chest. Spreading his arms outward, Leonardo took a mocking bow toward Keller, pressing his hand to his heart. When he straightened, a dark flash crossed his features. His gaze flickered briefly toward the full moon. As he looked up at him, a dark flash crossed his features. *Finally,* Leonardo thought as he braced himself for what was to come.

His eyes enlarged as the possessive moon wielded its ancient power over his yielding body. Still bent forward, Leonardo's torso twisted violently as bones began to break. Silver moonlight consumed his flesh, blood boiling as his skin thinned and stretched. His screams tore through the quiet alley—raw, echoing—as his human casing split apart under the force of the expanding. His bones began to puncture through his skin and blood ran down his mangled body in pouring rivulets.

He clawed at his clothing to free himself from the clinging material soaked with sweat and fresh blood. He fell to the ground holding himself up with his hands and knees while his screams became gurgled growls when his jaw broke, and his human features began to distort from the reformation of his skull. Leonardo could feel the grinding bones in his limbs and spine break only to elongate, mending to take shape into a massive creature. Twitching through the unbearable pain, chunks of his flesh fell from his body and into a black-crimson puddle. Fur darted over his tougher rejuvenating epithelium, completing the transformation.

Suddenly Leonardo realized the music and laughter from the once lively tavern had stopped. Leonardo remained on all fours, eyes fixed on the stone path as he dragged deep, unsteady breaths into his enlarged lungs. He shook his matted, sandy brown fur, shedding clinging scraps of flesh and blood, then rose onto his hind legs. Piercing screams echoed in his ears. Men and women spilled from the tavern, stumbling back in horror at the sight of a man transformed into a creature of legend. Leonardo turned—and saw the three men he had come to kill vanish into the chaos. Rage tore free from his chest as he threw back his head and howled. Laughter answered him.

Keller laughed from the roof of the tavern in pleasure at the sight of Leonardo's dismay. "Well," he said lightly, "you are the strangest combination of fool and genius." He tilted his head, studying Leonardo as though inspecting a specimen. "You may remember me as the sentimental man of wealth and moral virtue who wished to marry your darling sister," Keller continued. "But that was nearly a year ago, Leonardo."

He smiled. "I have waited a very long time to kill you. And now—" his gaze flicked toward the fleeing crowd, "I finally have cause."

Keller laughed again, delighted by the realization dawning in Leonardo's glowing eyes. "I am untouchable, wolf. Every word I speak is truth to my Masters—and to the thousands of knights *I* command." His voice hardened. "Tonight, I will kill you and name you the long-feared werewolf responsible for the slaughter here." He heard Leonardo growled. Keller ignored it.

"I will tell the Order you attacked in a frenzy—crazed with bloodlust and hate. That I did my duty. That it was me who protected the mortals." His smile turned thin, calculating. "And who would question me? The Order?" He scoffed softly. "No one would doubt me. Especially after your incredibly dramatic display here tonight."

Kellers's voice shifted—no longer gloating, but calculating and cold. "Although," he said softly, "there will be one doubting man." He saw Leonardo stiffened. "Your brother-in-law, Eli." Keller smiled. "He would question my word, wouldn't he? Along with his clan. All those children—ready to turn. Their parents would doubt me."

Leonardo snarled loudly at the implication. Fear surged sharp and sudden at the thought of Roslyn in Keller's reach, dread crashing back with brutal force. His heart thundered as he stepped forward, roaring his defiance, making it clear he would not stand down.

Keller laughed again—deep, pleased—as he paced the edge of the roof. "Oh, Leonardo," he said, almost fondly. "Tonight brings me such joy. I feel like celebrating just how profoundly foolish you are." He pressed his tongue to the roof of his mouth and clicked. In a mocking scolding tone, he shook his head in feigned disappointment before laughing at him again. "Slinking away from your clan just to transform in the heart of the city," Keller continued, voice click with amusement. "Hundreds of witnesses. Such a spectacular display." He flicked a brow as his voice took a sly undertone. "I can use this now." Keller's smile sharpened into something malicious. "Tonight, will be special. I'll do what I do best." He leaned forward slightly. "Struggle if you like—it will only heighten the pleasure when I skin you, demon."

Leonardo growled and snapped as he yelled in head. "You are far more a demon that I will ever be," he roared. "I've seen your soul—and it's blacker than any sin I've committed!"

Keller rolled his eyes as he slipped the hood from his head, pacing along the edge of the roof with casual amusement. "You know I can't understand you," he said lightly, "but I'm sure you said that you've repentance. Or perhaps a plea for death." Then his tone shifted. "Of course," Keller added, almost thoughtfully, there is the matter of your darling sister… Roslyn." His expression darkened with twisted desire. "She'll be the last," he said. "Being the commanding leader in my Order has it's privileges. I could keep her alive." His smile curved, slow and vile. "At least for a while. Until I've had my fill of her tight little body. Maybe I'll kill her while I'm getting off in her wet dripping pu—."

An ear-splitting howl ripped from Leonardo's chest as he surged forward. He launched from the alley, landing against the tavern's second story with a bone-shaking force. Claws sank into the thick wooden siding as he climbed with feral speed, hauling himself toward the rooftop. Steel rang above him. He could hear Keller taking his swords from their sheaths and his heeled boots stomped along the edge of the roof. Swords ready, Keller leaned forward to see the side of the building. Expecting to find Leonardo's massive form clawing upward. Nothing. Confusion flickered across Keller's face. He peered down into the alley below—saw nothing, heard nothing. "Where are you fucking bastard dog." Keller harshly whispered into the darkness.

A burst of hot breath breezed against the back of his neck. Spinning around, he saw Leonardo's green eyes blazing, fangs bared in a feral snarl. Before Keller could react, razor-sharp claws slashed across his face, carving gouging lines through unmarked flesh. Keller staggered back, barely avoiding the killing strike. In a fluid, desperate motion, he swung a blade across Leonardo's exposed chest. Forgetting his place on the edge of the roof he began to lose his balance as he stepped back. In reflex, Leonardo grabbed Keller's slender throat preventing his fall. With a savage twist, he spun and drove Keller downward, smashing his body through the slate roof.

Shards of red slate and splintering wood exploded from the impact. Keller crashed through the ceiling and slammed onto a wooden table on the second floor. Glass bottles exploded beneath him as air tore from his lungs in a sharp, hollow rush. Disoriented from the fall, he tried to focus his vision by looking through the vast hole in the ceiling. But the light from the burning oil lamps in the spacious room made it impossible to peer outward. Leonardo dropped through the opening. Keller rolled off the table just in time as Leonardo's massive body struck where he had been moments before. Keller scrambled upright, already reaching behind his shoulders. In one swift motion, he tore two daggers free from the crossed sheaths on his back and hurled them in rapid succession. Leonardo marched toward him. Swiftly, Leonardo dodged the first dagger with ease. The second struck an oil lamp behind him, shattering glass and igniting a burst of flames as it embedded in the wall. Keller threw two more, and Leonardo roared with pain as several had pierced through his chest and abdomen. The force drove him to his knees, blood spilling across the tavern floor.

Keller swelled with triumph as his opponent fell. He savored the sound of steel tearing through thick flesh, the wet impact of his blade biting deep. Fire crept along the walls where a shattered oil lamp spilled its flame, licking hungrily at the tossed blankets on the large wooden bed. The room brightened as the blaze spread, greedy and fast. Certain of his victory, Keller strode toward Leonardo. Then Leonardo rose. He stood, blocking the inferno's light, his massive form silhouetted against the flames. Teeth gnashing, he fixed Keller with a defiant glare and began pulling the daggers from his chest—one by one. Each blade fell to the floor with a dull clatter as blood streamed freely. But only for a moment.

As soon as the steel left his body, skin and fur knit together with unnatural speed. Straightening himself to stand on his feet, Leonardo looked more monstrous than before. More than eager to finish the quarrel as the victor, he howled an ear-piercing battle cry. Another howl answered in the far distance. His ears perked, and he turned to the sound. *Eli*. Pride overcame him. If he killed the betrayer—the Commander of the Holy Order—Eli would see his worth. Respect him. Owe *him* for once.

Keller tore his hands from his ears, rage boiling over as he screamed back, his voice raw and burning with fury hotter than the fire surrounding them. He dropped his hands and charged at Leonardo, catching him unaware with a dagger he had hidden in his boot. Together they entered the inferno. Flames devoured Leonardo's furred flesh as Keller's heated blade sank deep into the side of his skull. It was Leonardo's undoing. Gravity claimed his body while death reached for his soul, pulling him downward as memories of his life unfolded in slow, fractured motion. Fear and loss overwhelmed him as his spirit fought to remain within its shell for just a few moments more. Death tightened its grip tearing the veil apart.

Roslyn. The thought of his sister struck his heart with searing regret. He should have been better. A respected man of society—not someone who had squandered their fortune on indulgence and excess, leaving them penniless and vulnerable to the monsters. If he had been stronger, Eli would never have crossed her path. She would never have loved him. Eli wouldn't have made them into the beasts of the night.

And perhaps—he would still be alive to care for her now. *God forgive me.* With that final thought, death claimed him.

A smug satisfaction curled across Keller's face as he left the fallen werewolf to the flames. He slipped out through a shattered window just as the structure began to give way, landing hard on the street below. Pain ripped through his body in searing waves before fading into numbness. He vanished into the shadows, swallowed by the night before the fire could claim him as well. But Keller did not go far. He lingered nearby, watching the tavern burn—relishing every moment, knowing exactly who was trapped deep within the fire's heart.

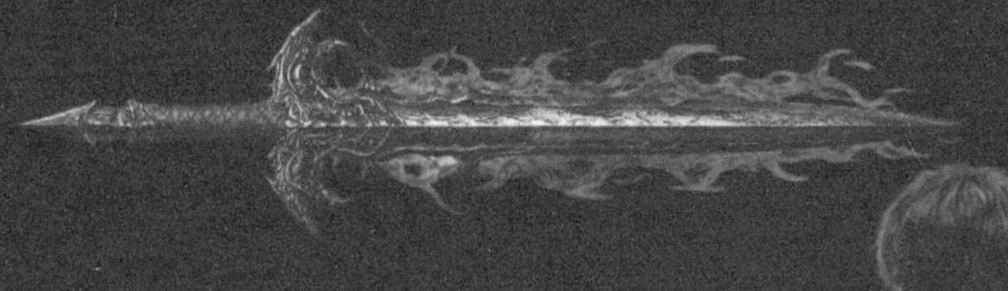

Eli caught Leonardo's blood on the stone walls and followed the scent without hesitation. As he raced past a drunkard sprawled along the alley, doubt flickered—had Leonardo bled deliberately to mislead him? Then came the howl. Rage, pain and terror fused into one sound—and Eli knew he was on the right path. He answered with a howl of his own, fury and dread tearing from his chest as he drove himself harder through the narrow streets.

Please, he prayed, sending word skyward as he burst into a wall of black smoke. The fire had swallowed the night. Swirling thick plumes spiraled upward, choking the moonlight and plunging the alley into suffocating darkness. The smoke burned Eli's eyes and seared his throat as it filled his lungs, but he pushed on—his black fur blending seamlessly into the smoke and shadows. He needed height.

With a powerful leap, Eli launched from the stone path onto the wall, then vaulted to the rooftop opposite, clearing the smoke in one fluid motion. From above, the tavern blazed like a dying star. Being clear from the smoke and able to see once more, Eli's enlarged black eyes mirrored the burning tavern. His heart seized as Leonardo's cries ripped through the roar of flame and collapsing timber. He sprinted across the rooftops, desperation fueling every stride, but the fire was moving too fast. Window's burst outward. The lower-level floor caved inward. The building groaned as it's structure gave way.

Leonardo's howls faded—swallowed by the thunderous crack of burning beams. The roof caved in. Fire exploded into the night, embers and debris hurled toward the heavens as smoke mushroomed upward in a towering column. Eli skidded to a halt, momentum throwing him onto his side.

Eli's heart sank into his stomach as it churned in revulsion. He was too late. Leonardo was dead. Eli became overwhelmed at the mixture of emotions that had reigned over him. He had failed. Eli closed his eyes while gathering enough breath. In a sharp cry, he released a haunting howl that echoed through the roars of the fires. After a few seconds, he slowly opened his eyes. A dull shine reflected from across the abyss and caught his eye as it darted into a nearby alley. Through the smoke and flame, he saw a tall, thin man clad in ebony leather armor standing on the other side of the fiery pit watching the building burn. He recognized the man at once. The Holy Order of St. Michael's Army Commander. Ash and blood streaked his scorched face, and his pale smoky eyes gleamed with victory as he watched the tavern burn. Eli moved closer, but made sure he stayed out of sight. He listened as Keller spoke—not to him, but to the fire.

"This is your fault, Leo. I warned you once," Keller said, his voice carrying. "It took a year, but I kept my word." He paused smiling. "Fire suited you better." Keller sneered. "I'll make one more promise. I will finish what you've started. No matter how long it takes or wherever I must go, I will kill Eli, and I will have Roslyn for myself. She'll become lowlier than your fucking whores. If you hadn't denied me, she would've been my wife, and you might have lived longer if you would've just given me her like I wanted. She should've been my wife. I asked for her hand before *he* came back. We could've been family!" Keller shouted violently.

Then, in a flash, he quickly cocked his head and raised his hand as if to settle his violent emotions. After a few seconds of composing himself, he continued to speak again. "Then once I've had enacted every torment, I can do to her, I will fuck her one more time. I will leave her still warm body to those that would do their worse to a corpse." In the far distance, he heard the chime of a church bell. He sneered. "A call to my brethren. Happy rotting in hell and taking my place, Leonardo." With that, Keller spat into the dirt and turned away, disappearing into the night.

Roslyn. Eli thought of his wife as the shock from the words radiated throughout his body. As Keller vanished, Eli took it as his signal to move. He launched himself from the rooftop, racing back toward his ancestral land—toward Roslyn and the gathered clan. A pack was a liability now. A single trap could wipe them all out. This was his failure.

If he had acted sooner—if he had understood who Keller truly was—Leonardo would never have become a Beast Blood. None of this would have happened. Eli snarled, forcing his thoughts forward as visions of Roslyn's death clawed at his mind. He shook them away and ran harder, faster—driven by fear, fury and the need to protect what remained. Before it was too late for them too.

CHAPTER TWO
ABROAD

THREE MONTHS LATER
MARCH 20TH, 1881

He knew they were looking at them again. He could feel their arrogant, suspicious gazes burrowing into his rugged face. If they only knew who he was—and saw the monster that lay beneath his skin—they would scatter in terror. And he would savor it. Eli studied the delicate faces of the wealthy mortals that surrounded him in the dining hall of the ship. He could hear their weak hearts beating, see the faint pulses pressing beneath their thin skin. The man seated beside him drew his attention most—an obese gentleman struggling to restrain himself from devouring the contents of his plate. With the faint scrape of his front teeth, the man took careful, measured bites from ta dainty fork. Eli snorted. A gentleman could never be savage. Not in public. Like Eli, they had to hide who they were. Behind closed doors, they could be anything they wanted. They were all monsters in waiting. Savages. Humans liked to pretend they were above such animal instincts, but it was a lie. The only difference between them lay in the degraded blood pumping through their veins—blood that kept them fragile, restrained, and weak.

As a child, he had heard the legends. His kind were once protectors of the mortals. The irony had never been lost on him. To protect them, they had to remain hidden. He loathed humans for what they pretended to be—and the freedoms they took for granted. *They* were the monsters of the night, not his kind. Eli would do what he's always done. Protect his own. His glare toward the surrounding mortals did not waver as his dark thought continued to churn.

"Please, Eli," his wife whispered. "Please don't look at them like that. "It's not their fault. They're innocent ones—and you're frightening them."

Eli looked at his wife. Her golden eyes glistened in the dull light of the dining hall, glassy as though tears hovered just beneath the surface. Her sun-kissed, oval face looked impossibly soft, fragile as fine powder. His gaze drifted to her lips—pink, stained with the red wine from their meal. On any other night, he would have leaned in, taken those lips within his, and sucked the lingering wine from them. He would've grabbed her by the throat and she would've melted into his hand. He would've gotten up from the table and she would've lead the way back to the room where he would worship every inch of her glorious body with his teeth, with his hands, tongue, plunging his cock in her soaking pussy until she begged for rest.

But this was not any other night. Everything had changed. What happened months ago had crept between them like a spreading disease. They were haunted by death—by the horrors of that night that replayed endlessly in their minds. Grief pressed down on them, heavy and suffocating. Their home engulfed in flames beneath the blackest sky he had ever known. Fire illuminated the night as it spread with ruthless speed. Mortals clad in ebony armor poured across the land, torches raised high. Dry grass caught and burned, waves of orange rolling through the forest. Smoke swallowed the moon, blotting it from the sky as darkness claimed the land.

His people scattered—from the woods to the fields—to in desperate attempts to escape the fire, only to be overtaken by another advancing wall of flame. Many alphas fought to protect the children from both the inferno and the mortals. Despite their efforts, most met their demise like Leonardo had. Fortunately, Roslyn had run to the coastline leading the survivors away from the blaze. That was where Eli found her—with the others huddle low in the hollow cliffs, the sea crashing below. He saw fear in their eyes as they looked to him for guidance. And he had none to give. All he could do was tell them to run—to scatter and seek refuge with nearby clans. Swift farewells followed as he and Roslyn fled the coast together. Despite her desperate pleas about her brother, Eli waited until the next morning to tell her the truth about Leonardo's death. Keller's name never crossed his lips. Not yet, at least.

Snapping to the present, he replied through gnashed teeth and harshly whispered in a tone lower than the humans could hear. "I can't help it. When I look at them, I see the faces of those that came to burn us out. The Order had betrayed our alliance because of your brother." His jaw tightened. "Our friends, their children who hadn't gone through the sickness yet; all are dead. You barely saved those that ran for safety. Thank God, they escaped." His voice dropped further, poisoned with bitterness. "If Leonardo weren't already gone, I would've crushed his windpipe myself."

Roslyn reached for him, grasping his hand in desperate attempt to ground him before he caused a scene. "Calm yourself, Eli. Please," she whispered, tears threatening to spill. "This isn't the time. Or the place." She swallowed. "Let's go to our cabin." Eli ignored her.

"He's lucky he's dead," he snapped, the restraint finally breaking. "He endangered us all. I warned him—again and again. What did he do? He defied common law. You wanted me to change him, and I listened. I shouldn't have—not without knowing his past." Eli's voice sharpened cruelly. "He should have died a mortal. Old. Gluttonous. If he'd stayed human—like these idiots—none of this would have happened."

Roslyn broke. "But he *is* dead, Eli!" she cried. "My brother, the only family I had left—is dead!" The tears she had fought spilled freely. Shame flushed her face as heads turned toward their table. She snatched the napkin from her lap and tossed it onto her plate, rising abruptly. Unable to face the watching mortals, Roslyn turned on her heel and fled the dining hall.

Left alone at the table, Eli slowly scanned the dining room Every gaze was fixed on him—mouths agape, eyes wide—as if he had sprouted three heads. Even through the haze of his anger, embarrassment crept in, shrinking him by inches. He leaned his head back with an exasperated sigh. He knew he fucked up.

He straightened, tossed his napkin onto the plate, and rose from his chair. The room followed him upward, eyes widening further as they took in his full stature. His black hair and dark eyes were unsettling enough—but it was his lean build and towering height that made him predatory. The once-noisy dining hall fell into uneasy silene. He looked all around him as the noisy room became silent.

I'll show you savage, he thought, irritation burning hot. Eli reached down and seized the salmon with his bare hand. He bit into the cooked, scaly head, tearing away a thick chunk of flesh with his teeth. Grease and juices ran down his chin and fingers as flakes of fish fell to the floor. He watched disgust rippling across their faces. He pushed the meat to the inside of his cheek to help him speak. "I suggest you fine folk kindly gorge yourselves with your meals while minding your own *fucking* business," He scorned with venom in his voice, and stormed out of the room throwing the decapitated salmon to the floor. He heard a few outraged gasps from the women. They derided him as they cupped the ears of their children from his obscene language.

Walking down the dimly lit corridor, Eli wiped the greasy residue from his chin with the back of his hand as he swallowed the last of the fish. His steps slowed as he reached their cabin. He hesitated when he heard soft sobs through the thick, wooden door. Eli pressed his furrowed forehead against it, shame sinking deep into his chest. He knew he had been cruel—especially to his mate, who was still drowning in grief. And worst of all, he knew he could not take the words back. He had failed her and his people as a Clan Master, but he would not fail her as a mate. Another sob escaped from the room, snapping him from his spiraling thoughts. He couldn't endure the sound of her pain any longer. He heard her sniffling breaths as she tried to compose herself.

He gripped the handle, turned the bolt, and slowly pushed the door open. He crept inside, moving carefully, unwilling to disturb such a fragile moment. It didn't matter. Roslyn had already heard him. He caught her gaze in the reflection of the standing mirror. Her golden-brown eyes were rimmed red, cheeks flushed beneath the tear-streaked skin. A sharp ache pierced his chest, their eyes locked.

For several heartbeats, they just stared at each other. Neither spoke. Roslyn looked at the floor and turned her back to him. She reached behind herself, fingers fumbling with the pearl-sized buttons lining the back of her dress. They slipped from her trembling hands, frustration mounted as she struggled to free herself from the heavy garment. Eli stepped forward instinctively to help.

She twisted away before he could touch her, her voice breaking sharp and raw. "Don't touch me. Don't you *dare* touch me, Eli! I... I... don't need your help. I can get the damn thing undone myself."

He dropped his hands to his side in restless defeat. He gritted his teeth and turned away, fighting the urge to throw something, to shout. Logic told him to leave it be, but fear of their uncertain future kept his anger simmering just beneath the surface. It had become impossible to say the words he needed to say. Whenever he tried, he found her already crying. And when the tears stopped silence took their place. The routine was suffocating. before he acted on the thought of losing his temper and throwing something. Eli sat heavily on the edge of the narrow bed and began to undress. At least the moon was new tonight—the Calling wouldn't tear them from the fragile isolation of the cabin. He gruffly pulled at his boots, his gaze drifting back to Roslyn despite himself. She finally had unhooked the small latches that held the dress tight against her petite, curving frame. He watched her carefully, trying—and failing—to read her thoughts. Stripped down to her worn petticoats, Roslyn dragged the thick fabric down her body.

As the fabric around her ankles, she stepped out of the silk ring. Relieved to be free from the confines of the dress, she could breathe better. She looked at the garment with disgust and kicked it aside toward the small trunk. Once they were off this accursed vessel and settled into whatever life awaited them, she vowed she would burn the dress—and take pleasure in watching it turn to ash. On the rare days she forced herself from the safety of the cabin, the emerald gown was always there. A constant reminder of death and loss. Of the night that shattered everything. Even its tightening fit felt accusatory, clinging to her body as though it knew her guilt. Day and night, anxiety gnawed at the secret she had meant to tell—yet continued to withhold. Fear closed its hot grip around her heart. She shook her head lightly, squeezed her eyes shut, and willed the sensation away.

Not now. She thought as she stole a glance at her mate in the mirror and felt desire rush over her as he unbuttoned his shirt, revealing his lean muscled body. Roslyn wasn't ready to submit to him. Not yet. With fierce determination, she turned her attention to the trivial task of taking down her hair. One by one, she removed the pins, releasing long brown curls that spilled down her hack in heavy waves. The thick strands cascaded in waves and brushed below her rounded ass. She felt a little better until she turned around. Eli sat in the shadowed corner of the cabin where the candlelight failed to reach. His dark features were carved in stillness, brooding and unreadable. Half undressed, she watched him peel back his shirt as his eyes stayed lock onto hers.

She could sense the predator beneath his skin—it paced in anger and irritation. Radiating from in in a way that would have made any other beta avert their gaze. Roslyn did not. She was his mate. His equal. Although it took everything in her not to submit to the unspoken command in his black eyes, yet she held his stare. Too much has already happened. And she sensed far more was yet to come. She knew he hadn't told her everything about that night. He'd offered only fragments of Leonardo's death, softened details of the Order's betrayal. But the truth lingered in his eyes—unspoken and heavy. She figured she was going to shut him out as well. If he could shut her out, then so could she. Roslyn drew in a shaky breath and began to form a sentence.

Eli interrupted her before she could release a single word. "Baby, I see that you're not going to wait till morning this time," he said quietly. "Good." He lifted his hand and flicked his fingers for her to come to him as he asked. "Will you sit down with me, please?" Eli saw her defiant gaze linger as she set the hairpins on the vanity. Wordlessly, she sat naked on the chair placed farthest from him as possible in their crowded cabin. The distance was intentional. She crossed her legs and then her arms over her breasts as she released a sigh of exasperation.

"I am fine right here for now, Eli." She said matter-of-factly, lifting her chin in defiance.

Under different circumstances, Eli might have found the situation almost amusing. Instead, irritation flickered across his expression. He exhaled sharply and pushed forward, his tone turning gruff. "When dawn comes our ship will dock in the southern part of

America. As you know, before we married, I traveled there to expand our export business." He paused, measuring his words. "The trip wasn't for nothing. The diamond transactions were successful. Very successful."

He watched her closely as he continued. "Our funds are already secured in American accounts—New York, especially. They'll remain active as long as the mine continues to operate. So, we are not without, love. Her brow creased. Our Brazilian accounts," Eli added, "are void. For now." He lifted a hand before she could interrupt. "Franz closed them." She nodded faintly at the name. "Franz—our accountant. Alpha of the Badido Clan," he reminded her. "He would've heard of what had happened to our estate. As a precaution measure, he would've closed everything with the fail-safe. He would've destroyed the record. Our names. Our identities." His voice hardened. "Our lives in Brazil no longer exist." Deafening silence pressed between them. Yet he could feel her sadness wash over his collected senses. "We'll build something new here, Ros." Eli said at last. "Something different."

Eli saw her thin eyebrows furrowed as she waited. "We have to blend in," he continued. "Live as mortals do. Quietly. No titles. No followers." His jaw tightened. "I am no longer a Clan Master. And you are no longer and Clan Mistress." The words carried weight. "Even our transformations will change," he added. They'll follow the same method we used on this damned ship." He sneered faintly, his distaste for the sea unmistakable. He was eager once again to be on land since he hated the sea. "Once we're on land, we'll use lakes and rivers until we reach our refuge."

Her voice cut in, sharp with concern. "Where is this refuge?"

Eli sighed before answering. "Michigan. When I was traveling by train from Boston to Chicago, I ended up there on accident," he explained. "A malfunction of the tracks forced a change in route. It turned out to be…fortunate." His tone remained subdued. "I met several influential people at the station as we waited. Lawyers. Agents. Businessmen." Then he hesitated—just long enough to gather his words. One man in particular, George Crownwelm." Eli said. "An agent I befriended quickly. He was kind enough to help translate the language as I ordered a meal at the restaurant. It also helped that he was a keeper of Moon-Blood as well when I needed to transform and didn't know where to go." Roslyn's eyes widened. Eli couldn't help the quiet chuckle that escaped him. "What?" he asked, arching a brow. "Did you think our kind existed only Brazil?"

She dropped her gaze, a small frown forming. "No. I assumed there were others everywhere." Her voice softened. "I just didn't expect a stranger to admit what he was so easily."

Eli softened his tone as he spoke, taking pity on her ignorance of a life she had never been born into—only made by his blood. "No. He didn't say anything outright, per se. When you've lived as one of us long enough, an instinct develops. You learn to recognize your own. A scent. A glint in their eye coloring. The way their teeth set. Like mine." He demonstrated by flashing her his straight white teeth and flicking his tongue over his slightly longer, but sharper canines. "See?" He asked, through his rolled tongue.

Roslyn snorted through her nose, amused by his explanation. "Yes, I see. Go on, Eli."

Seeing how she softened as they talked, Eli flashed her a wolfish grin as hope rushed into his chest. *This was good.* He thought as he continued. "Well, the same was for him as well. He had been around for over three hundred years. He knew what I was the moment we met. That night when the train was held up, George insisted I'd stay with him at his estate, where I could exist properly after transformation, even if for a night. He and his wife offered me hospitality. Trust followed." He hesitated. "I confided in him. My mother's immortality. My father's mortality. My truce with the Holy Order." Then, more quietly, "And you—about my reservations of subjecting you to a life of immortal suffering. He's the one that helped me understand that a life without you in it wasn't a life to ever be lived for me."

Roslyn sighed, "Eli." Tears sprang into her eyes, and she looked away from him as she gathered her composure. Her voice cracked as she said, "Well, I must thank him then when I see him. Does he know we are on our way?"

A shadow crossed his features, his brow furrowing as he reached the part he'd been leading up to. "This brings me to my next point." He exhaled. "The night we fled—when we boarded this ship—I wrote George a letter. I couldn't risk it passing through mortal hands or even a carrier raven from our distance. And I damn well couldn't deliver it myself. So, I sent Bonita." The words left his mouth too quickly—he knew it the instant her fury ignited.

"What?" she snapped. "*When*?" Eli remained silent, giving his answer without speaking at all. She could feel it down the bond.

"God, Eli," Roslyn breathed, horror overtaking her anger. "Tell me you didn't send her alone." She shot to her feet. "She's twelve. She's only just turned when they burned us out." Her mind conjured the image immediately—the dark-haired, blue-eyed girl walking miles on her own, carrying a message that could get her killed if intercepted. Panic seized her, and she began to pace the narrow cabin.

Eli spoke quickly. "They followed us. They approached me while you were dressing.

She dragged a hand down her face. "When?" Her voice shook. "Where was I?"

"It was after we broke into the tailor's shop," Eli said carefully, "when you found that emerald dress." He heard her scoff but pressed on. "She wanted to thank you—for saving her and her friend, Jose. They refused to leave unless they found some way to repay us."

Roslyn placed her hands on her hips, head bowed. "I can't believe you."

Eli tried to reason with her, but she seemed so out of character. "I didn't even here them approach, Ros. I wouldn't have agreed if I thought they weren't capable. She's the smartest. He's the fastest. Their skills surpassed the others—it was the only way to get the message to George." His voice tightened. "And they're no younger than we were when we fell in love."

Roslyn shut her eyes, dragging both hands down her face. She rubbed her temples, trying to soothe the building ache behind them. Her sigh was heavy when she finally spoke. "Love is not the same as death, Eli." Her voice was low but unwavering. "They are still children. I saved them to keep them out of danger—and you put them right back into it." She opened her eyes and looked at him fully. "If anything happens to them," she said quietly, "I will never forget it. And you will never forgive yourself."

Her composure cracked as violent possibilities flooded her mind. "What if they don't even know where to go?" Roslyn blurted. "What if they're captured by mortals—or lose the letter? What if George has moved? What if he's already in danger too?" Her voice wavered. "There are too many unknowns, Eli. Too many."
She dropped back into the chair and dragged both hands through her long brown hair in frustration. Leaning forward, elbows on her knees, head bowed, she spoke more quietly. "What did you write in the note?" she asked. "Did you tell them anything about us? About where we're going? This world isn't big enough for our kind to disappear forever. I'm afraid someday…it'll be too small to hide in."

Eli let out a sharp, humorless breath. His teeth clenched against his lower lip as he fought the emotions surging inside him. Candlelight caught in his dark eyes as they fixed on her naked figure. Lightly he shook his head in disappointment. "Do you really think I'm that careless?" he said lowly. "That I'd write our entire situation on a scrap of paper?" His tone sharpened. "Do you think I'm so incompetent that you can't trust me anymore?" He rose from his chair and took a step toward her. "Before we ever married, you were already a part of me," he said, voice tight. "I came back for you—even knowing what I am. Even knowing the danger my blood could bring you. Because I love you too much to ever let you go. And you waited for me too. Years we waited for each other, Roslyn." His words came harder now, raw with conviction.

"I have done nothing but keep you safe. That vow hasn't changed." His gaze locked onto hers. "You are my life-mate; Roslyn. Our bond will outlast death itself. If either of us were to face it, I would give my life before I'd let a mortal lay a hand on you." Silence hung heavy between them. "I need you to believe in me," he finished quietly. "Everything I've done—everything—has been for us. To keep us together. That's why we're on this ship. That's why we're still breathing."

He moved toward her without thinking, dropping to his knees at her side. His broad arms wrapped around her waist as he pressed his nose into her bare stomach, taking in a lung-full of her scent, before he laid kisses across her belly, trailing downward before he buried his face in the tuff of soft dark curls that veiled her pussy. Her cunt smelled so sweet, he wanted to taste her, but instead together they rose slowly to their feet. He felt her face settle against his chest, her breath uneven. Gradually, she stilled, resting her ear over the frantic beat of his heart as she leaned into him for support. With her even in his arms, all he could think of was Keller—dead. Keller's pale skin beneath his claws. Keller's corrupted blood coating his hands as he watched the life drain from his eyes. The evil within that man was beyond redemption, beyond mercy. And worst of all, it had marked Roslyn as its target. Keller had to be destroyed. The thought was so consuming that Eli barely registered her words.

"What did you say?" he asked quietly, pressing her warm, naked body against his.

Roslyn lifted her head from his chest and rested her hand against him instead. She eased away carefully, as though not to provoke rejection. Eli released her without resistance. She looked up at him. "I have never doubted you," she said softly. "Not your strength. Not your ability to protect us." Her voice faltered, then steadied. "Everything that happened was…unforeseen. And losing my brother shattered me. It felt like losing my parents all over again." She swallowed hard. "Then you pulled me away from our homeland without telling me everything. And I became…numb."

"I did tell you why, love." Eli started. "The Order sent—"

She shook her head. "No. Not that." Her gaze held his firmly. "The part you won't allow yourself to say. I see it in your eyes, Eli. Every time you look at me. There's something you're hiding."
The air between them thickened. "I'm asking you again," she said softly. "Why did we have to leave Brazil? We could've hidden there.

Joined another clan. Disappeared just as easily." Her voice dropped, raw but honest. "This silence between us isn't healing anything. It's only growing. And it isn't who we are." She paused. "If you don't trust me with the truth—the full truth…then everything between us will begin to rot. Nothing will be resolved. More will rise between us. We should be preparing for it together." Roslyn's golden-brown eyes searched his face, studying every flicker of emotion. She had shaped her words, carefully—hoping to draw out whatever he was still hiding. She was ready, if he was. Ready to match his honesty with her own. His lips pressed into a thin line. His gaze dulled, distant—locked in a battle she could not see. Hope stirred in her chest as she waited.

The words curled around his tongue and danced behind his clenched teeth. Could he tell her that Keller—her childhood friend—was the one who wanted them dead. Who betrayed her? Could he tell her that he had foreseen what would happen and ignored it? That he knew of their son growing in her belly. Although couldn't hear the flicker of its heart within her." The thought decided him. He would not insult her intelligence—but he would not tell her yet. Not now.

"There is more than I've told you," Eli said firmly. "I won't lie to you about that. But I will not disclose the rest until the time is right. And that time…is not now." The words landed cleanly.

Roslyn nodded as she felt a pang of rejection course through her. Her heart hardened where it had once softened. The truth she had been ready to confess sank back into silence. *I can keep secrets too, Eli.* Roslyn thought bitterly but accepted his answer for now. She swallowed it down and shifted instead to the question that still burned. "What did the note to George say?" she asked quietly, through the hurt beneath her voice was impossible to hide. Eli heard it—and allowed himself to faintest smirk. He knew her heart still ached for the children.

They were to tell him they were newly orphaned children of the Blood Santos," he explained. "They were to describe what happened to their parents. To our estate. To us." His voice was steady now. "I gave them strict instruction. Only a man named George Crownwhlm was to receive the message. It was coded," Eli said. "A single sentence that George would understand."

Roslyn leaned back into him for another embrace. She felt his hands trail over her bare back as they rubbed in a rhythm. Up and down. Down and up her spine. She relaxed into him. Her voice was barely above a whisper. "What was it?" She looked up at him.

Eli studied her face—every familiar line, every expression he had loved for years. He had known she was his from the moment they'd met. The plan had begun the night they fled Brazil. His voice was firm, "Flames to the Beast." Eli tucked his fingers beneath her chin when he saw the worry rise in her eyes. His thumb brushed beneath her lower lip—still faintly stained with wine—and a low sound stirred in his throat as awareness sharpened between them. His throbbing cock pressed into her through his trousers that hung on his hips. She was naked in his arms. His body responded instinctively, pressing her closer as he growled. "Let's have tonight, Ros. This moment. For us."

She studied his eyes for a breath, searching, then nodded—the tension inside her breaking like a dam at last. His mouth curved with relief before desire overtook him. Eli drew her firmly against him, one hand cradling the back of her head while the other exploring the curves of her body. His kiss was deep, unrestrained, claiming her mouth as she softened into him with a quiet sound of surrender. Her hands slid over his stomach, trembling as they worked open the fastening of his trousers. She seen the bulge of his hard cock outlined beneath the material. She tugged them enough to where they hung on his hips revealing the tuff of dark soft pubic hair and the definition of muscles of his pelvis. He had already broken their kiss as Eli gripped her peaked breast, playing with her pebbled nipple, pinching and pulling as he teased pain and pleasure throughout her body. His hot mouth clasped around her nipple sucking it hard as he lightly inflicted more pain as he nipped and sucked, flicked with his tongue in a tantalizing rhythm. She gripped the sides of his head, running her fingers through the black curls as she pressed him closer to her chest. More. She wanted so much more.

It was her undoing. "Fuck… my alpha." Roslyn gasped as she wrapped her legs around his waist, locking her ankles together as her arms clung to his broad back and shoulders. "God, I need you. Now." She rasped, choking on the pleasure that spun her senses.

Eli gripped her ass, his palms cradling, supporting her as he turned them around in the cabin towards the bed. Roslyn's foot smacked something off the table, as they turned, and it fell to the floor with a *thud*. Eli didn't bother looking as Roslyn announced it for him. "It's nothing. Keep going." That was all the encouragement Eli needed. He had laid her down on the soft down of the mattress. The thick pale duvet wrinkling beneath her as candlelight flickered across her skin. Her beautiful body curved and thick with muscle was on display for him. For a moment, he simply looked at her—at the trust in her eyes, at the vulnerability she offered him without hesitation. Her eyes were half-closed locked onto his as she opened her legs before him and locked her feet on his lips, her toes gripping the band of his pants to shimmy them the rest of the way down his hips. His massive cock sprang free. It's swollen head and veined shaft bobbed. She growled with pleasure at the sight.

"That was impressive," he said breathlessly as he stepped out of the pants that pooled around his ankles.

"Thank you," she replied quickly, "So are you. Impressive." She clarified as her thoughts scrambled to make a comprehensive sentence as she nodded toward his large endowment that even within his large hands wrapped around the shaft, just seemed to make it more notable to nearly the point of intimidating. He laughed as he pumped his cock with both hands, making the head more swollen. She was so tight, it ached. He was going to feel so glorious stretching her out. Her pussy clenched in anticipation. He barely touched her, and she was already soaked for him. Precum dripped from the tip, and without a second thought she quickly sat up and licked the salty droplet from the head. She heard him suck in his breath as her pink tongue swirled around it as she looked up at him.

Eli's face was flushed with desire. His dark eyes roamed over her as the muscles in his forearms and biceps flexed while he squeezed and pumped his engorged cock harder. She leaned forward again, bobbing her head, her tongue tracing the sensitive tip, gathering the salty taste of him with slow, tantalizing movements. She lapped away more of the precum before sealing her lips around the smooth, hard head and sucking briefly—only to release him again. When she stopped, she looked up at him through her lashes, a wicked smile curving her mouth.

"God damn, Ros." Eli growled, "You are my undoing."

"And you are mine," she moaned, leaning back on her elbows and shifting farther up the bed to accommodate his lean build and height. Her legs spread instinctively. She was more than ready. They needed this. It had been months since she felt him inside of her. Months since they had connected like this. At this point it felt like healing. Roslyn's fingers trailed down her taut stomach, lower, until they hovered between her thighs. Then, she shoved them deep within her before they pulled out, moving over her slicked cunt as she parted her fingers and spread the silken folds of her pussy open for him.

In the flickering candlelight, her arousal glistened, began rubbing the sensitive, swollen nub at the apex of her womanhood. Her slender hand that spread her open for him, moved to her breasts, rubbing her fingers over her hard nipples, squeezing their fullness. The hunger in her golden eyes—visible beneath thick lashes—was unmistakable. They were full of need and fire. Through the bond he could feel her, and it frenzied against his control. His eyes darkened with desire as his jaw clenched, and he pumped his cock harder. Twisting and squeezing the shaft.

"Please, baby. I'm craving you, Eli. Please." She pleaded, head falling back, revealing her throat in submission. "Fuck me."

Eli growled with pleasure as his control was unleashed. He grabbed her by the hips, and pulled her down, ass edged at the end of the bed. He positioned himself over her, pressing the engorged head of his cock into her dripping pussy. "*Fuck*... you are such a good girl," he rasped, praise threaded through his voice as he drove fully into her. Her sharp gasp cut through the air, and he sucked in a strained breath of his own, overwhelmed by the intensity of the sensation. He was utterly lost in it. He thrust his cock deep within her to the hilt again. She moaned, cavernous and feral. Her pussy clenched in reply—wet and tight—as it pulled at his cock, drawing him in more, deeper.

"You feel so *fucking* good," Eli crooned. He withdrew slowly before moving again, watching the way her body responded beneath him, the breathless sounds she made in answer. The connection between them felt raw, consuming, almost unbearable in its depth. Her hands continued their frantic rhythm, her body arching. as he pulled out his entire massive length and slammed into her again. The smell of sex filled his nostrils, and he took a deep shaky inhale. He couldn't get enough of it. It smelled primal—a sweet nectar that he wanted to bask in. Her fingers worked her clit as he filled her, stretching her with his girth and length. Another sound of pleasure ripped through her throat.

"More… harder, Eli," she rasped. His grip tightened at her hips, anchoring her there as the intensity between them surged. He plunged into her again and again, carrying them higher, closer to that fragile edge where everything else began to fall away, besides the complete earth-shattering pleasure that anchored them there.

The world beyond the cabin seemed to disappear—the grief, the weight of their losses, the looming future. All that remained was the fragile peace of being together, of choosing each other despite everything. They poured every unspoken emotion into the closeness between them, clinging to the only thing that still felt real. Their bonded love. Candlelight trembled along the walls, shadows flickering around their entwined forms. Eli braced himself above her, breath uneven, sweat gathering along his back and brow as the moment stretched tighter and tighter between them.

"Eli…I'm right…there." Roslyn cried, her voice breaking on a rush of breath as the intensity of her climax crested through her, leaving her shaking and desperate for him. She clawed into his back and wrapped her legs around his waist as she bucked against his pelvis, stimulating her clit as she cried out his name again. "Oh, god…Eli!" With a broken groan of his own, Eli followed her in crescendo, surrendering to the moment as the intensity overtook them both, their bodies falling together into the aftermath of shared release. Eli remained over her for a moment, his forehead resting gently against hers, grounding himself in the simple truth that she was still here. Still alive. Still his. He stayed there, unmoving, catching his breath while she clung to him, neither of them willing to disturb the sanctuary the moment offered—the fragile peace they had found in each other. Silence settled slowly around them, heavy but no longer suffocating. The only sounds were their breathing and the distant creak of the ship's timbers as it shifted across the dark water.

Roslyn's hands loosened at his shoulders, her fingers tracing slow, absent patterns across his back. "I will always love you," she whispered against his ear. He lifted his head from hers, and studied her face for a long moment. His hand found hers, fingers threading through his with quiet certainty. He kissed her forehead, then gently pinned her hand above her head, his gaze soft as he took in her beauty—the fierce soul that shone behind those golden eyes. "And I'll always love you."

Outside the cabin, the sea rolled on endlessly. Inside, something fragile yet necessary began to shift between them. It wasn't peace yet—but it was a beginning. A delicate thread of hope they both desperately needed to believe could still exist.

CHAPTER THREE
NEWLY ARRIVED

Florida

Rising from the depths of the ship's dark cabins, Eli and Roslyn made their way to the upper deck. The dull gray light of the morning and the steady drizzle offered far gloomier welcome than either had expected. The once-lively shipyard was cloaked in a shroud of thick fog, and the heavy humidity hung in the air, made worse by the absence of even the faintest breeze.

Despite the dreary weather, an overwhelming roar of activity rose from the busy port. Life abord *The Roscatta*, had dulled Roslyn's memory of how turbulent land could be. Compared to the chaos below, she felt an unexpected pang of regret—realizing she would miss the steady hush of the ocean and the gentle rock of the vessel she had once despised.

Suddenly, eager passengers pressed in behind her and Eli, leaving them no choice but to move with the current of bodies toward the docks. They flowed together down the splintered planks. Halfway to the protruding quay, Roslyn felt the wood dip beneath her feet as it bowed under the weight of the shuffling horde. Eli must have noticed her growing unease, because his voice dropped to a calm whisper beside her ear. "Be steady, my dear." She took solace in his words. The moment her boot touched solid ground, relief washed through Roslyn—followed closely by something she hadn't felt in a long time. She had not lost the ability to feel joy after all.

"Thank God," Eli murmured with quiet enthusiasm as his boots sank into the dirt. "We're finally on land again. I've never been happier to smell the sweet intoxicating scent of the earth. The endless sight of the ocean was beginning to feel like a prison."

Roslyn absorbed the unfamiliar landscape with cautious uncertainty. Her emotions churned and collided in her chest, sending nervous fluttering through her stomach. Instinctively, she brushed her fingertips over her flat belly, suppressing the unease before it could rise further. She needed a distraction. The coastline stretched wide before them, revealing four other ships anchored within the harbor. Two were massive—nearly twice the size of *The Roscatta*—while the remaining to smaller vessels were already departing, their sails unfurling as they slipped toward open water. She watched, mildly surprised, as each ship maneuvered with practiced precision into its allotted space. The bay itself seemed far too small to accommodate such traffic. She turned forward again—and stilled. A sudden surge of mortals pressed around them, moving fast and without regard. Instinct flared. Roslyn stepped closer to Eli, gripping his hand more tightly as the crowd swallowed them. She stayed near his side, careful not to lag behind, wary of losing herself in the bustling crowd. Free at last from the crush of the crowd, they stepped into the booming town.

Roslyn lifted her gaze, gradually acclimating to the bedlam. What had first sounded like overwhelming noise began to separate into distinct threads—layers of life unfolding all at once. She heard the distant whinny of horses, the recurring pounding of hammers against wood. A sudden burst of children's laughter and shrieks rang out behind her, making her flinch as a small group of them sprinted past. Her attention followed their path and settled on a gathering of women nearby. One, with a crown of curly blonde hair, had broken away from the group and gently swayed as she sang to her wailing infant. The others stood together in loose conversation, periodically glancing down to keep watch over their toddling children, who crouched in the dirt, fascinated by the insects and stones.

Eli felt the tension in Roslyn's grip and turned toward her. The look on her face—wide-eyed, uncertain, absorbing everything—was almost childlike. Her gaze darted from one scene to the next, captivated by every unfamiliar detail. He couldn't help the soft chuckle that escaped him. "Welcome to the state of Florida, my love," he said warmly. "It seems to be growing quickly. This port held only two ships at a time last year. Now, by the sound of all that construction…it's expanding."

"Florida," Roslyn repeated quietly, tasting the unaccustomed word as she shaped it beneath her breath.

Charmed by her childhood habit, Eli laughed more openly. "Getting a taste for it, Ros?"

Roslyn returned his lopsided smile with a bright, unguarded grin of her own. The expression stirred an old memory—of herself as an awkward, lanky girl seated beside him during lessons with their shared tutor. She had been painfully shy then. Whenever it was her turn to read aloud, she'd struggled to talk through the mumbling stutter she'd developed from her nerves.

Eli, older and endlessly amused, used to tease her gently about it—but he had always defended her fiercely if anyone else dared to comment. Determined to overcome the flaw, she had trained herself with discipline and patience. When Roslyn had to speak, she did so with calm poise and perfect pronunciation. In short order, she no longer had to practice as her confidence grew and the stuttering faded. Even so, the sporadic habit of repeating unacquainted words remained.

She smiled fondly at Eli and retorted smartly, "I believe it would be in my best interest to learn everything I can. It's the only way to blend into this world. I'd hate to betray our foreign roots simply because I failed to understand the language properly."

Eli's smile slowly faded. She was right—and the realization unsettled him. He had spent two years here already, long enough to understand the rhythms of American life. But Roslyn had never left her homeland until only months ago. Everything here was new to her. Every custom. Every word. Every danger. Time was not on their side. He needed to secure a future for her.

And your son, his brain added quietly, unwelcomed and insistent, threading doubt through the vision he refused to fully accept. Forcing aside his spiraling thoughts, Eli drew on a practiced mask of ease. A faint, crooked smile touched his mouth. He narrowed his eyes, pressing his tongue briefly to his cheek as he studied her.

"Terminology is important," he said perceptively, "but what of your accent? Our tutors trained us well—years of French, English, Spanish... we learned with impressive fluency. Still, we are Brazilian. It lives in our blood, and it shapes how we speak. When we use English, they will hear it. Portuguese is our native tongue—it will mark us." His tone sharpened subtly. "We must blend in. When the situation calls for it, we'll speak the language that best conceals us. For now, we'll use Spanish. It's common in these parts."

Roslyn nodded, but unease rolled through her in a sudden, violent wave. It made her feel as though danger lingered everywhere—an unseen presence stretching far beyond what she could comprehend. "You make a good point," she admitted, replying in Spanish. Then she hesitated, challenging him gently. "But if they remain in Brazil… they couldn't possibly find us. The world is too large for mortals to hunt us across it. Even those men."

Eli held her gaze, expression carefully blank. His lips pressed together in a thin line. He wasn't going to tell her of the man that aided the Order—or what they were capable of. "Humor me, Ros."

Frustration flickered through her. She exhaled, conceding for now. She might be newly turned, but she was neither fragile nor foolish—and she intended to prove that to him. "Very well," she said, lifting her chin. "What would you have me do?"

"Listen carefully to those around you," Eli said. "Even within this country, the Southerners speak differently from those in the North. When people mention where they're from, their speech often betrays them. Can you truly blend in? Can you shape your voice as though you were born here?" He had no doubt she would rise to the challenge. Still, he needed to be certain. A time will come when he's not going to be at her side. In this dangerous world, she will need to adapt—become resourceful, disappear into crowds, and, if necessary, build an entirely new identity.

Roslyn considered his words carefully. Her attention shifted to a couple strolling leisurely nearby. She observed their refined posture, the subtle polish in the movements. Then she listened—truly listened—to the cadence of their voices. The rhythm. The inflection. It came more easily than she expected. After a moment, she shifted her tone and repeated a line the woman had just said, now speaking in lightly twanged English: "My dear sir, I don't require you handling my *assets* in public, no matter how subtle you believe yourself to be."

Eli let out a low chuckle. Relief followed quickly—she had captured the sound remarkably well, though she would still need practice. A proud, faintly amused smile softened his features as he continued speaking to her in Spanish.

"Well, I'll be damned." Eli said with a faint grin. "You have proven me wrong, my wife. Quite the little master of disguise. Tell me—is *Roslyn* even your real name?" A quiet comfort stirred beneath the humor, easing only a fraction of the unrest coiled inside of him. His thoughts never ceased their relentless spiral. The journey north, the dangers waiting ahead, the decision to invoke the coded prophecy—it had set far more into motion than Roslyn yet knew. An army would gather. War had already begun. Just like he was instructed to do. She was unprepared and he needed her ready. She needed the instincts she had not yet learned to trust, for the darker truths of the blood they carried. What happened in Brazil had only been the first glimpse of how merciless this world could be.

Roslyn, unaware of the storm behind his eyes, blushed at his praise. She dipped her head with a shy smile, her free hand tracing a gentle path along his arm. "You make sport of me—but I'm glad I can still impress you." Her gaze lifted, lingering along the line of his unshaven jaw before meeting his steady black eyes. Sunlight caught in his dark, tousled hair, giving it the sheen of raven feathers. His bronze skin and timeless features still had the power to leave her breathless. He was her protector. Her anchor. The love she trusted above all else. He looked at her again, and her heart fluttered wildly as memories of the night before surfaced unbidden. She caught the faint curve of a smirk at his lips before watching them part, as though he were about to speak. But she didn't need to hear what he had to say since their bond hummed with shared emotion. He was thinking of last night too.

The sunlight broke through the clouds and bathed them and dreary settings. Eli's breath hitched. She stared at him with open affection. Something in his chest swelled painfully at the sight. In the gentle warmth of the sun, her beauty struck him with unexpected force. For a fleeting moment, it felt as though the world had never burned. As though screams and fire belonged to another life entirely. As of now it only seemed like a distant nightmare. He savored the fragile illusion of peace, knowing it would vanish the moment he let it go.

Slowly, he exhaled, watching the sunlight thread through her deep brown hair, Each curling strand glowed like spun caramel as it fell over her shoulders, Her honey-colored eyes caught the light and turned to molten gold as they held his. Without realizing it, he stopped in the middle of the street while carriages and passersby flowed around them. He lifted his hand, fingers brushing gently through her hair before settling at the nape of her neck. Her eyes drifted closed, her head tilting instinctively toward him. He smiled faintly—and obliged.

Softly he brushed his lips against hers, back and forth, before he kissed her deeply. For a heartbeat, the world vanished. When he finally pulled back, he rested his forehead against hers, voice low and sincere. Eli parted their kiss slowly as he pressed his forehead to hers. "You never need to impress me," his deep voice, baritone with the spike of lust that sparked like electrostatic between them—unseen, but felt. "It is I who must spend my life earning your heart—for it is worth more than my own."

Roslyn's chest swelled with emotion at the sincerity of his words. For a moment, she was speechless. She swallowed the tight knot of feeling that rose in her throat—then seized his face and kissed him fiercely laughter spilling from her in bright delight. She looped her arm through his, eager to keep moving before the tears gathering in her eyes could fall. A shift of subject followed—less an attempt to distract him than to steady herself. "Tell me—where are we going now?"

And there it goes, he thought. Reality returning like a blade to the chest. The fragile illusion of peace dissolved once more. He released a slow breath, disappointment threading through him as the weight of their situation settled again. He inclined his head in the direction they were heading. "To the large corral and stables," he said. A faint smirk tugged at his mouth. "The owner must be older than humanly possible by now."

She studied him curiously. "Is he a *loup-garou* as well?"

Eli let out a hardy laugh. "No—God, no. He's what he was born to be, and that's how it's staying." He saw Roslyn's confusion, but he couldn't explain Bucky correctly. Bucky was not someone who could be explained without doing him injustice. "You'll understand," Eli said simply. "Once you meet him."

Roslyn answered his assurance with a knowing smirk. "I'm certain I will." As they passed the tall windows of a large brick building, she caught their reflection in the glass. Painted in bold letters across the pane were the words: At Shores End Inn.

"Theres an inn, Eli," she said with hopeful interest. "It looked like it might be a lovely place to stay. We could…continue"

He followed her gaze but kept them moving. "I'm sure it is, but we're not staying at the inn. Given our circumstances, it wouldn't be wise to linger in one place too long." He gestured ahead. "We're going straight to the stables. Last year, I had the pleasure of meeting a man named Mr. Bucky Johnson—"

Roslyn's chuckle interrupted him. She laughed softly at the name. "Bucky," she repeated. "That's his nickname, I presume?"

"Nope," Eli said with a grin. "According to him, his uncle was the only doctor for miles around and helped his mother through a brutal labor. Two full days, he said. When he was finally born, his uncle noticed his front teeth were already in—fully visible. Strange enough that he supposedly declared, 'Well, he's got buck teeth already.' The name stuck. His parents liked it enough to make it official."

Roslyn listened, amused, her sharp eyes bright with interest. "Two days?" she said in awe. "My God. With a story like that—and a name like Bucky—I imagine he must be quite the character. Likely unforgettable."

Eli nodded. "He is. Took a liking to me—so much that he offered me the opportunity to purchase one of his horses. A rarity, given his reputation in the carriage business. I had no need for a horse then, but I do now. I intend to buy his fastest one…assuming he's still there and that he even remembers me." A corner of his mouth twitched as he added, "When I saw him last, he was covered in dirt from head to toe, smelled like pure horse shit, and dressed in little more than scraps of clothing. He was too old to be working even then, but refuses to stop—and won't accept help from anyone."

He shook his head faintly, amused by the memory. "I once watched one of his hired men try to help him lift a bale of straw. Bucky went red with fury at the 'offense' and unleashed a storm of profanity I've never heard cleverly used in all my years—a strange, creative combination of words I'm fairly certain no one else has ever assembled before. The poor worker walked away looking mortified."

Eli glanced at her with mock solemnity. "So brace yourself for whatever may come out of this man's mouth. He's as honest as a saint…with the tongue of a well-traveled sailor."

Roslyn smirked, "I must say that it seems you actually have a fondness for mortals after all."

Eli snorted and added in quickly. "This one I actually like." As they approached the stables, she could smell the stronger scent of horse manure and rotting hay. "Do you think someone else manages the business now?" she asked.

Eli shook his head. "If he's not sick or dead, I doubt it. He deals with all his customers first-hand. Being an abrasive and overly talkative person, he feels his presence is beneficial to the business. Perhaps that stubbornness is why he's lived as long as he has." He glanced ahead and the stables came fully into view. "And here we are. Let's see what he has to offer."

They entered through the open doors of the white-washed timber building. Inside, the stable was tidy and well kept—so much so that even the floors appeared freshly swept and scrubbed. The familiar scents of a barn greeted them at once, but the harsher odors were softened by sweeter notes of leather, soap and polished wood. As they moved farther inside, they took in the impressive rows of horse stalls lining both walls, leaving a long, open aisle through the center of the barn.

Wrought iron gas lamps were fastened to support beams overhead, casting a dim, amber glow. Several workers stood atop unsteady ladders, struggling to unlatch the ceiling windows. One by one, square panels sung open on their hinges, allowing beams of sunlight to pour into the spacious interior. Suddenly, a sharp, high-pitched whinny erupted from the stall beside Roslyn. She startled and jumped, colliding lightly with Eli.

A raspy cackle of laughter followed her startled gasp. Both Eli and Roslyn turned toward the sound. An old man stood a short distance away, swiping mud-caked hands against his trouser leg. Eli saw him instantly. Roslyn studied the grinning figure before them. He matched what she had imagined…though somehow exceeded it. Where'd she'd expected this wisps of silver hair, he instead possessed a full man of thick, wild white strands that fell in loose waves over his shoulders. His toothless grin consumed most of his narrow face, and his large, milky-blue eyes blinked rapidly beneath overgrown brows, as though trying to keep them from obstructing his view. Despite his age, his body showed no frailty. His skin—scarred, weathered, and bronzed from years of labor under the sun—told the true story of his life.

Roslyn found herself smiling back at him. There was an unmistakable warmth in the man, something immediately endearing. Even his rough, raspy drawl carried an easy cheerfulness.

"No need t' be clutchin' them skirts, chère. That's just Ruccus bein' Ruccus again," the old man drawled with a crooked grin. "Meaner than a swamp gator with a toothache, that one. I swear on my mama's grave, he *waits* for the right moment to scare the sin clean outta good folks." He shook his head, white hair swaying. "Did it to me once. Made me hit me head once on one of the damn lamps. I was bent over fetchin' him a bucket full of water—bein' kind, mind you—when he let out a confounded screeching whore sound. More like the devil's own rooster. Then, *bang*! The bastard kicked me. Sent me flyin' straight into one of them lamps." He tapped his temple. "Had a knot on my head big as an orange and the water all over the floor. And that large ass made a noise as if he was laughin' at me. Just stood there, starin' at me with them smug eyes like he'd done something clever."

Bucky let out a gravelly laugh, then paused suddenly realizing himself. "Well now, look at me ramblin' like I'm talkin' to the chickens instead of company." He wiped his hands on his trousers out of habit, then thought better of it when he noticed Roslyn. With a gentler smile, he inclined his head respectfully to her. "Name's Bucky Harold Johnson. Folks round here just call me Bucky. Been keepin' these horses fed, brushed, and loved longer than most folks been alive." He turned to Eli instead, thrusting his hand out with a grin. "So tell me, what can this old swamp fool do for you fine pair this mornin'? You lookin' for a horse? A carriage? A miracle?" He chuckled. "I promise you two outta three. We got a whole lot to choose from."

Eli smiled and clasped his hand firmly, and spoke to him in nearly fine English. He had masked his accent well. "All we need is a horse, Mr. Johnson. But it's good to see you again. Looks like you're still thriving."

Bucky barked a laugh. "Thrivin'? Lord, son, I'm runnin' on spite, stubbornness, and bad coffee—but I reckon it's keepin' me upright." For a brief moment, Bucky's toothless grin faltered. He squinted at Eli, looking him up and down, then his milky eyes widened in sudden recognition. "Mercy me and magnolias…" he declared. "Well, slap my ass into running— the Ox has returned!" He jabbed a finger toward Eli, delighted. "Never could forget a man like you, Ox. Big as a barn beam, tall as sin, and look like you could lift my fattest horse clean over your head with one arm. You near talked my ear clean off last spring, ramblin' 'bout everythin' under this beautiful sun of ours." He waved a dismissive hand with a chuckle. "And don't go fussin' with titled. I ain't my daddy. You just call me Bucky, yeah. But to be honest I forgot your name."

Eli laughed, ignoring giving his name again, and glanced at Roslyn, who watched with a demure smile. Bucky caught to look immediately—the kind of look a man only wore for the woman he belonged to. "Well now," Bucky drawled, eyes twinkling, "I see you brung yourself a woman this time. And by the looks o' that rock she's wearing on her dainty hand, I'd reckon she is your wife."

Roslyn stepped forward at the mention of her, offering only a polite smile. She said nothing, but her attention remained fixed on Bucky, quietly amused—and genuinely fascinated. His manner of speaking was strange and brash, yet threaded with unmistakable warmth. She could see now why Eli had enjoyed this man's company. It would be hard not to. Eli took her and gently tugged her closer. "This is my wife—Maggie."

Confusion washed away her smile as she shot a look at Eli and was about to comment—but his gaze met hers with silent insistence. Don't. Understanding came swiftly. Roslyn's brow furrowed, but she forced her expression back into place. She turned toward Bucky with a practiced smile. Still furrowing her brow, she forced a wide grin for their companion's sake. "It's a pleasure to meet you, Mr. Joh— I mean, Bucky. My name is Maggie San—"

"Mackley." Eli cut in smoothly—though a shade too firmly. "Maggie Mackley. Remember, honey. You're a Mackley now." His jaw flexed as he held her gaze, tension pulsing beneath the words. Roslyn held his stare for a beat longer, then nodded almost imperceptibly. "Of course. New names. New lives." She turned back to Bucky, her smile softer now. It's a pleasure to meet you. It must be the lingering effects of seasickness causing me to forget my new last name. And this Florida heat..." She lifted a hand faintly toward her temple. "The humidity is rather distracting." The last part, at least, wasn't a lie. A wave of nausea lingered in her stomach, a faint dizziness behind her eyes. She doubted it was only the rising heat.

Bucky beamed at her, his toothless grin bright with approval, then shifted his attention to Eli. "We'll I'll be," he said warmly. "Mercy me and magnolias, son, you went and married yourself a fine one. Strong and sturdy. Girl like that could handle an Ox-sized husband and still have breath left to laugh about it." He chuckled, clearly pleased with himself. "Pretty as a sunrise over the march and sweeter'n honeyed wine," he added with a wink toward Roslyn. "You done real good, boy. Ain't nothin' worse than marryin' a woman who ages into a hurricane with legs. That kind'll have you wishin' 'till death do you part' came a whole lot sooner."

"That works both ways," Roslyn said as she raised her chin and cast a side-eyed glance toward Eli who looked highly amused.

"And she's got a sharp mouth. Lord, love her!" Bucky's laugh turned into a rough coughing fit. He braced himself against a stall post until he caught his breath, then waved them forward. "Come on now," he said, recovering quickly. "Let's get this young lady outta the heat and into my office where there's cool water and a chair that won't try to steal your soul." He jerked a thumb down the aisle. "Then you can tell me what bring you back my way."

He slapped Eli firmly on the back, the sound echoing through the barn. "Last time you were here, Ox, I promised you first pick of my horses if you ever came back needin' one. And I don't offer that to just anybody. In my younger days, I'd have punched a man clean in the mouth for even askin'. He squinted up at Eli with a fond, crooked grin. "But you didn't ask. You just talked to an old fool, givin' him the time of day. And I took a likin' to you."

Then he turned back to Roslyn with a playful bow of his head. "And now that you got yourself a wife, I'll make it better. Any horse on the lot—on me. That sound fair to them pretty ears of yours, Miss Maggie?"

"I'd say that's a mighty fine offer. Thank you." Eli said warmly, glancing at Roslyn with a small smile as he heard her shy agreement.

"Well, good then! Mercy me and magnolias, let's get yourself a horse." He waved them forward again. "Now, let's get you a horse! I'll introduce you to Little Bit, first."

Eli breathed easier. He'd been quietly praying the old, eccentric man would remember him. The last thing he wanted was to steal from Bucky—or worse, do anything that might shock the man's fragile heart into failure. Bucky didn't deserve that kind of fate. They need to remain nearly invisible. Discreet. Newly arrived strangers drew attention, and attention meant danger. Horseback was their safest option. Plenty of people still traveled that way, even in the more developed parts of the country. A single rider on a common road would raise no suspicions. A quiet trail would vanish with time. He didn't yet have a perfect plan—but his purpose was clear. Leave no trace. Stay unseen. Survive long enough for the right moment to reveal himself.

CHAPTER FOUR
WAITING

George Crownwelm slouched in his favorite chair, nursing a goblet of whiskey as rain lashed relentlessly against the parlor window. He tried to peer beyond the watery streaks that distorted the glass, but all he could make out were blurred silhouettes of the Northern Michigan wilderness. Not that it mattered. There was little worth seeing—towering oaks stood bare beneath remnants of melting snow, and everything else lay dead or dormant. He took another drink from his nearly empty glass.

Thunder rolled through the heavens as the wind battered the walls of his ancestral tri-level home. A jagged bolt of lightning split the sky, banishing the shows from the room before darkness reclaimed it. The violence of the storm mirrored the unrest twisting in his gut. The intensity of the morning storm matched his disquieting thoughts. He lifted the goblet and took a longer drink, eyes fixed on the dwindling level of amber liquid.

When the children had arrived with Eli's message, George learned the unthinkable: the Order had emerged from hiding and slaughtered a clan—Eli's clan. The ancient truce, upheld for centuries between Beast Blood and Order alike, had been shattered.

Just like he said it would, George thought bitterly and drank again. *But why?* George wondered again—and knew the answer was something only Eli could give him. He turned the events over in his mind, replaying every detail until they burred together in a restless storm of memory. He could still hear Bonita's small, trembling voice recounting the horrors they had endured. An older boy had stood beside her, filling in the details she couldn't bear to finish. When they were done, she pressed a hastily scribbled note into his hand.

Their accusations were grave—to grave to dismiss. Still, instinct demanded proof. When he unfolded the paper, the faint, but unmistakable scent of Eli lingered in the fibers of the page. That alone confirmed everything.

Half an hour earlier, George had returned from town, securing refuge for the children with a traveling clan of Romanian Gypsies. Fortune had favored them—the small caravan had arrived days ago and he caught them before they left. He prayed the children would finally find safety there, far from the reach of the Order.

Lightning flashed again, bleaching the room in harsh white before thunder followed with a violent crack. George exhaled slowly and dragged a hand down his face, exhaustion weighing heavy on his bones. A decision loomed before him. He could call the leaders together. Summon the clans. Prepare for war. But he hesitated. What unfolded now would shape the fate of their kind. It was a bitter irony: humans feared the Beast Bloods—creatures, stronger, faster, and longer lived—yet it was the humans who hunted, who burned, who slaughtered. And still, the Beast Bloods refused to retaliate against the innocent. Mercy was woven into their nature. Because of that mercy, many had died.

"George? Are you okay, love? Morning hasn't fully broken the night—why are you drinkin' again?"

He turned to see his wife, Sheryl, emerge from the shadows of the foyer. She stepped through the threshold already dressed for the day in her new scarlet velvet gown. Her silver hair had been coiled into a long braid, loose whisps escaping to curl at her temples. Her icy blue eyes glistened in the dim light as they caught the faint gray of dawn.

He forced a lazy smirk and looked back at his glass. In the corner of his eye, he watched as Sheryl moved gracefully to stand beside his chair, her gentle chastisement lingering in his ears. "I rarely drink, love. Thus, when I do, it is when I most need it." He scoffed quietly. "I woke up needing it."

"The children—and the news they brought last night—was nerve-racking." Sheryl said softly. "But you were referring to the nightmares, weren't you?"

George's voice turned grim. "Any day now, Eli and Roslyn will arrive here, and I do not know what to expect. The Order attacked Eli's clan. They burned his people until only a few remained, including them." He turned from her sympathetic gaze to stare out the window once more, his expression hollow. "There were children. Not even transformed. Murdered. Most of them younger than the two who came here with the note and the news." His voice lowered, thickened. "Their story was devastating. It will remain etched into my mind forever. My thoughts—memories twisted their suffering into nightmares that plagued me. I saw mangled bodies nailed to crosses—just as the Order likes to do to us, claiming it will cleanse our sin. Then they set the crosses on fire, the wind catching it and spreading it across the land. But the landscape changed. It became our home. Our people. The fire was here. Consuming everything. Humans and werewolves alike slaughtered. Lighting flickered across the sky, thunder cracking close behind. On cue, George lifted the glass and drank again.

"Oh, my sweet Georgie." Sheryl moved to the arm of the chair, lifting her abundant skirts as she settled onto his lap, curling into him. "Shush. Calm yourself, my darling." She wrapped her arms around his neck and rested her forehead against his. "Just like this storm, this too shall pass." Her voice was soothing as her long fingers combed gently through his disheveled hair.

He sighed, feeling marginally steadier, yet his voice remained grim when he spoke with his eyes closed. "No, it will not just pass. It will destroy. What will remain with the momentous change?" His brow furrowed as he squeezed his eyes tighter. "*Flames to the Beast*. That was what he wrote. Eli plans on waging war against them. He's not the first one to try to do so. But it feels different this time. It feels…*fated*."

Careful not to knock the drink from his grasp, Sheryl wiggled against him to find a swaddling comfort in his embrace. Her voice betrayed her uncertainty. "What do you want to do?" She asked softly, conflicted. "We have finally found peace here. We have lived undetected for decades. What of our people? We would be inviting the devil to our door if we allowed them to remain."

His eyes were strained with a forlorn look as he stared out the window. "I don't know." His voice followed with the weight of pent-up emotion. "Many will die on both sides, but once the flames wither to embers in ash, will our secret become known to the world? Then what? Will it only be a matter of time before we are hunted next since they would already be this far north?" His jaw tightened. "Aren't you tired of running?" He knew that something greater than the storm outside was stirring in the air. And when it finally gathered, it would be catastrophic.

"Send them away, George." Sheryl said softly as she kissed his temple. "Its not our war. We paid our dues."

George switched the glass from one hand to the other and downed the rest of the whiskey. His heart thundered as fury and resolve twisted together in his chest. He shook his head. "We're already in danger. There will never be true peace so long as the Order thrives. And you never know who among us belongs to them—until they arrive in the middle of the night with torches in their hands. I've seen it." George looked at his empty glass; his choice was clear. "We will stand with them. It's the right thing to do. Eli is an Elder. A friend. We are bound not only by blood, but by leadership—by duty. We are responsible for protecting our people…and humanity as well. The only choice is to fight. To die trying. Or we will all burn regardless." He drew in a sharp breath, forcing control over his anger. "I'm sorry for raising my voice. This is…hard today."

Sheryl was not offended by his raised voice—but truth of his words unsettled her. Still, her sympathy did not falter. She understood his pain. The worry and fear that consumed him. He had lost so much a lifetime ago at the hand of the Order. "I will stand by you, my George. Your choice is clear." She searched his face. "When do you send word?"

He exhaled slowly. "I don't. I feel it," he tapped his finger against his chest, "Here. There is more to this than what he told the children—or what they told me. He will be here within weeks. Perhaps sooner. And once he arrives, it will take no time at all to send word to the other clans." His jaw flexed. "If I knew where they were…how close… I would go to them myself." He exhaled sharply. "I fucking hate waiting. It's the cruelest part of uncertainty."

"But we must wait," Sheryl said calmly. "We live as we always have—until we are given reason not to."

He nodded and kissed the crown of her head as he tightened his arms around her. Together they sat in silence, gazing through the hazed window as the storm slowly dwindled to a gentle, lingering rain.

CHAPTER FIVE
THE SEEKER

April 1st, 1881

Keller's boots echoed through the hallway as he stormed to the door of the Seeker's chamber. Lining the passage, elaborate candelabras of twisted iron held dripping white candles. Their flickering flame carved light into the shadows and reflected across the polished marble floor. As he neared the entrance, he recoiled, cringing in disgust at the entwined stench of blessed incense and spent wax. The realization struck instantly—the entryway had been hallowed. The holy presence scraped against his senses, sour and invasive. He sneered at the sacred musk as he wrenched the door open.

"Seeker!" Keller boomed as he stepped inside. A wave of blue smoke slammed into him. He staggered, instantly swallowed by the swirling haze, coughing violently as the acrid fumes burned his lungs. Through watering eyes, he noticed silver canisters hanging above the doorway, each one smoldering with consecrated herbs—designed to saturate the chamber with holy smoke. Irritation flared hot in his chest. He drew a sharp breath through the burn and shouted again louder this time.

"Seeker, your superior requires your services!" A sharp crackle snapped through the room. Keller turned toward the sound. The fire in the stone hearth flared, its heat pushing back the chill of the underground chamber. Aside from a few scattered candles, the hearth provided most of the light. It cracked again, a burst of sparks leaping upward.

Keller watched he forking tongues of flame and felt unease curl in his chest. He could not recall much of the battle with Leonardo—but he remembered the fire. He remembered his victory. And he remembered how narrowly he had escaped being consumed by it. Without thinking, he lifted his hand to the left side of his face. Beneath his fingertips lay the bubbled, scarred deformity of melted flesh. His pride would not allow him to look upon his reflection—but he knew the truth. He had become a monstrosity. The self-pity lasted only a heartbeat before rage overtook it. Keller tore his hand from his face and snarled, "Seeker!" Kicking over piles of books that were stacked and scattered across the floor, he moved farther into the room.

"I heard you the first time you shouted."

The voice came from behind him—low, deep, touched with a lazy drawl. A man stepped out of the shadows. Keller turned sharply. He didn't even try to restrain his disappointment. Never, before this moment, had he seen the prestigious, intelligent Seeker. Keller felt cheated from what the master's encouraged one to believe the man would be. He'd expected more than what reality portrayed: a shaggy, bearded man short in stature with small hands and thick chubby fingers who stood there looking bored while wrapping his naked body in a crimson robe of silk. Yet despite the unimpressive form, something about him unsettled Keller. The man's placid expression lingered beneath steely blue eyes. Then, slowly, his mouth dipped into a frown, his thick brows lowering in quiet irritation.

"A private man such as myself is not above flattery. However, standing there with your mouth agape while my cock is exposed calls for a sword to your throat—especially while breaking into my chambers wasn't cause enough for that enough." The Seeker's voice was dry, unbothered, keenly aware that he was being judged yet again for what he was. A dwarf.

Keller bristled. Furious that a man of lesser stature had dared to speak to him with such authority, he snapped back, "Another remark like that and I will slice your belly open where you stand."

Unmoved by the threat, the Seeker merely shrugged and crossed to the table. He poured himself a drink infuriating calm, lifting the jeweled goblet to eye level as though Keller were nothing more than a passing inconvenience. His bored expression lingered. Unimpressed.

Keller's anger flared again at the man's defiance, and once more he reached for the authority his rank offered him. "I am Keller Luis Costa the Commanding Assassin in league with the Holy Order of Saint—."

The Seeker snorted into his cup, laughing openly. Keller gritted his teeth, jaw clenched and his nose curled up in his anger. He barked, "Why did you not come the first time I summoned you?"

The Seeker's lips curled into a slow smirk, amusement dancing behind thick lashes. He heard the faint patter of approaching footsteps from the concealed bedchamber. Turning his head, two scantly clothed women emerged from the shadows and moved to his side. With obvious smugness, he looked back to Keller and lifted his hands in silent demonstration of what had occupied his attention. His tongue, however, did not remain still for long.

"Who's to say I hadn't come several times already," he drawled, "while you were ranting like a lunatic." He took another sip from his goblet, unbothered. "It is the middle of the night. You are an intruder, regardless of what gaudy title you cling to. And when the blessed incense failed to kill you, I gathered you had no intent to murder me. So, as I had the time…" His gaze flicked lazily toward the women. "I was occupied."

He tilted his head slightly, eyes sharpening. "These are my quarters, my women—I would think it is my right to finish a well-earned climax." Angry at the stranger's haughty ego, the Seeker became slanderous as he mocked him. His smirk deepened, "Surely, a man so…impressive would not deny his cock the housing of beautiful women. Then again, I could be mistaken. It would not be the first time a powerful man concealed his preference to plowing his cock deep inside another man. Don't get me wrong. I approve. Love is love, isn't it? Never be ashamed, Commander." Seeker gave him a quick wink.

Keller hissed in a sharp breath, feeling exposed in a way no one should have perceived. He hastily unsheathed his sword and flicked the fine point under the Seeker's chin. In a flash, two swords pressed into his throat. Cold steel pressed against his throat from both sides—the women had produced weapons of their own. The tips bit into the scarred flesh as his neck, drawing the faint sting of blood.

Fearlessly, Keller did not flinch. He stared into the green eyes of the identical women, noting with certainty that they were twins. He cut his gaze back to the Seeker. The urge to drive his blade through the man's throat surged violently within him—nearly impossible to restrain. He gnashed his teeth together as he studied the Seeker's expression: not fear, not surprise, but cold intellect. Confidence. The look of someone who carried secrets unknown to anyone else. Keller jolted forward on instinct. The pressure of the swords increased immediately. Pain flared, and warm blood traced down the pulse of his throat. He stilled. Slowly, carefully, Keller removed his weapon from the Seeker's jawline. He returned it to its sheath without making a single abrupt movement. Only then did the women lower their weapons, though they remained positioned protectively, bodies tense and ready.

The Seeker studied him for a moment before speaking again. "That's the way of it sometimes, isn't it?" he said mildly. "When you point outward—whether it be an accusing finger or a deadly sword—two more will answer. Ready to accuse. Ready to kill. Sometimes both in the same breath." His gaze flicked toward the women, a faint smile touching his mouth, before returning to Keller. "I find there is a certain beauty in fine blades… and in loyal company. A pleasing combination. " He commanded the women, slapping the ass of the twin that stood to his right, "Rest easy, my ladies. This man has come to make use of my gifts, not to meet his end tonight. He serves the Order, after all." His tone sharpened subtly. "And the Order would be nothing without *me*." In unison, they replied in a soft tone of duty and compassion. "Yes, Seeker Raven."

Raven moved toward Keller and places a stout guiding hand between his shoulders. Together they crossed to the pair of overstuffed chairs near the grand fireplace. Starting with Keller's seat first, lifting away the thick, dust-laden books he had been reading earlier and setting them aside. "Here. Sit." Raven commanded simply before turning to prepare his own chair.

He watched as Raven arranged several of the books beside the matching golden chair—stacking them with precise care. Then, with calm composure, Raven stepped onto the stack as though it were purpose-built stool and eased himself into the seat with practiced dignity.

"Well done," Keller said with mockery edging his tone.

Raven did not rise to the bait. His gaze remained fixed on the fire as he replied evenly, "When you are born into a world built for giants, you learn to adapt. You learn how to fit within it." He shifted slightly, the firelight dancing across his features. "In time, people stop seeing what you lack and begin seeing what you provide. And rarely is it knowledge they seem from me. More often, they want what they cannot have—lost lovers, stolen power, impossible desires." His voice cooled. "Greed and revenge drive nearly every soul that comes to my door. And the vast majority of them…" His mouth curved faintly. "Are fools."

Keller glared at Raven for his judgmental scorn, and began to study his weathered face. He searched for weakness. Raven, however, seemed lost in distant thought, his gaze unfocused as he stared back. Shifting in his seat under the scrutiny, Keller clipped, "And what is it you desire," he asked scathingly, "that makes you above the petty wants of others?"

A faint smile touched Raven's mouth as he recognized he had struck another nerve. His gaze lingered on Keller with renewed attention. The commander's face bore the unmistakable evidence of fire. Flesh had healed where it had no right. His left eye had mended together when the skin from his cheek molded to his brow, distorting the natural line of his eye. The eyelid itself slanted unnaturally, as though forced into place. Hardened folds of scar tissue rippled across the side of his face and down along his neck. The rest of the burn and color distorted skin was hidden by the light black traditional armor he wore. Where his left nostril should have been, there remained only a dark hollow, puckering faintly with each shallow breath.

Keller caught the weight of Raven's observation and turned away sharply, jaw tightening. He hissed, "What are you staring at, freak?"

Raven snorted and still observed just a few moments longer. The right side of Keller's mouth had fused into a twisted seam of scar tissue, the shape uneven and warped. The texture reminded Raven of wax melted too close to flame—layered, distorted, forever altered. At last, Raven answered, lifting a hand vaguely toward the surrounding chaos of books. "I seek knowledge." His voice was simple. Certain. "I surround myself with texts of every kind—histories, myths, forgotten doctrines. Even the manuscripts of scholars and priests litter these floors."

Keller's temper flared. "Spare me your feigned humility," he spat, "I see you surround yourself in luxury and excess. Your *greed* is no different from mine."

Finally breaking, Raven's deep voice rose, cutting cleanly through the air. "I care nothing for riches, material indulgences, or the devotion of a single woman. Wealth comes easily. Objects deteriorate, break, and are endlessly replaceable. And I have never lacked for companionship when I keep my company in fine sorts." The humor faded as his voice returned to something colder. Deeper. "This world keeps growing. New life forms spring forth from all over the world, and I crave to understand it. New life, new languages, new forms of existence rise constantly across its surface—and I hunger to understand them all. Knowledge is the only pursuit that remains meaningful when you have outlived everything else." He leaned back slightly, gaze distant. "Even a statue would desire change if it possessed a soul. Stagnation becomes its own prison. Immortality loses its pleasure and after time it's a stoic blur when all lands bleed together, when everything becomes familiar and when nothing remains new." Raven's eyes locked with Keller's. He saw the shift immediately.

Keller bolted forward, hands gripping the arms of his chair. "Immortal?" he demanded. "What are you? Do you not know the marks on my armor and what they stand for?" Rage overtook him. He stood abruptly, hand flying to the silver hilt of his sword.

Raven's patience finally snapped. "What kind?" His voice thundered. "And what are *you*, Commander? Human?" The women instantly raised their weapons, bodies poised to cross the short distance and kill on command. Raven cut them a sharp look and lifted his hand. "Enough. I am unharmed. There is no *real* threat here. Not yet." The women obeyed at once. He leaned slightly forward. "I know of your marks, Commander. Who do you think taught the master's their meaning in the first place? In this room, you are neither above nor beneath me. For I am *human*, just as you are."

A pause lingered. The last statement held a meaning Keller didn't understand and as he was about to remark, Raven continued to speak. "The difference is this: you will one day know the release of death. I will not. Now, you can see yourself out of my fucking chambers."

Keller shook his head slowly. A creeping fog tugged at the edges of his mind—an encroaching darkness that ebbed and surged, threatening to consume his thoughts. He shook it off again and cleared his throat. He needed Raven to tell him where to go. But first, he needed to hear the man's story—before he decided to whether to kill him. "Then tell me, Raven," Keller said quietly. "How does a human become immortal…without the influence of evil?"

Raven studied his fingernails with feigned disinterest, though fury though fury simmered beneath the surface. Something about this stranger unsettled him. Keller was too volatile, too restless. His mouth twitched as though words fought to escape, and at times, his eyes seemed to shift in color—subtly altered, unfamiliar. Raven did not understand why the blessed incense had failed to affect him. But he intended to discover the reason. He decided he would keep the man here a while longer.

"I see no reason to share my past with you," Raven said flatly. "But if it will hasten your departure…then why the hell not." His voice steadied as he continued. "My mother was a countess—and a Wiccan priestess of righteous devotion. My father was a wealthy and powerful man, one whom even the King of our homeland owed debts to." He continued fluidly. "They tried for years to have a child. Stillbirths. Miscarriages. Loss after loss. He paused as emotion flashed in his eyes, giving them a watery shine of disdain. Not from hurt, but from disgust. "You can imagine their euphoria when I took a breath breathed and cried. When I survived beyond my first year, they believed me consecrated." His expression darkened. "For the first five years of my life, they were loving. Gentle. Affectionate. Yet they always sensed something…different about me. Something wrong in the proportions of my small, developing body. Deep down, they knew what I was long before they admitted it aloud." His voice was stoic as if he was recalling a tale he read from one of his many books. No emotion, apart from the look in his eye, came forth when he recalled his story. "By my tenth birthday, time had revealed the truth to my father—I would not grow further. And to him, that meant I was not the son he had envisioned." A bitter edge entered his words, though he did his best to bite it back. "He felt cheated. Ashamed. My existence became an affront to the future he had crafted in his mind." Raven's jaw tightened. "Bitterness turned to cruelty. And cruelty to hatred. In time…he came to loathe me."

Raven watched Keller's pupil's dilate small to large and small again. The white-blue irises holding edges of black that rimmed like ink cast in water. Shadows and swirls threatened to pool into the color. Raven knew exactly lay within the commander that was listening just as eagerly to him speak. He continued forward with his tale.

"Our so-called bonding often took the same form: he drank himself senseless while he beat me. His words cut deeper than the flogging belt—which more often missed than struck. Then for his own twisted comfort, he would console me afterward. Guilt and shame were added to the gifted toys. Bribes—insurance against the unfathomable possibility that I might tell my mother who inflicted the wounds. It was not long after that a single night reshaped everything. My father was drunk and started to assemble his weapons and hunting dogs. He was going to rid the world of another monstrosity, only if I could outrun his hunting dogs." Raven continued evenly until it tightened and cracked with the emotion that threatened behind his carefully bricked composure.

"My mother, of course, had intervened and stood outside my chamber doors. Loving my mother dearly, he pleaded to her that another would take my place. He confessed his infidelity to have another heir and revealed a bastard child had been born that night. Since the whore's son was born bigger than I, my father claimed the child was… acceptable. Not crippled. My mother was furious. Heartbroken. She ordered him from the castle and called for the guards who held her loyalty." He exhaled slowly.

"In desperation, my father blamed me for everything that had gone wrong. He claimed the creature he had made must be destroyed." Raven's gaze drifted to the fire. "I heard the shouting. My mother's cries. The sound of the struggle outside my chamber." A paused lingered. "Fear rooted me in place. I hid beneath my bed and did not move." His voice lowered. "My father entered my chamber. He found me. He dragged me out."

Silence stretched for a breath as he saw the inky black swirls in Keller's eyes began to absorb the rest of the color. No longer was the Commander in control of his body and consciousness. Something else stood present and silent under the vessel that was Keller. "He drew a dagger and drove it into my chest." Raven's eyes did not waver. "There were tears in his eyes as he did it. He whispered an apology as though regret could sanctify the act. In his pious mind, murder wrapped in repentance was enough to absolve him.".

I screamed, expecting pain—but there was none. I bled, expecting my clothes to be soaked crimson—but I had healed instead. The dagger was torn from my chest, and the wound had already closed. I had not weakened. I had not died. My father's eyes widened in terror. He called me a devil's spawn and fled. By then, the guards had arrived. They saw what he had done. Shock and revulsion crossed their faces as my mother commanded them to seize her deranged husband. That night he left, and we never saw him again. I suspect my mother had him executed…or did it herself." Raven's gaze drifted briefly before returning. "We returned to my mother's homeland, where my grandparents sheltered us. Years later, she confessed the truth." His voice softened almost imperceptibly. "When I was a newborn, she experienced a vision—of me exactly as I am now. A dwarf. Alive. Gifted. Afraid of my father's response, she placed a spell of immortality upon me." His expression darkened as a breath passed and his eyes lowered to his folded hands. "I am grateful for every moment of her sacrifice. Because the spell did not come without cause. When the debt came due…she paid with her life."

The room seemed to hold its breath. The tense silence was broken by the snaps of burning wood inside the hearth. Within the stillness, Keller mauled over what Raven had expressed. Dark vigor and skepticism stirred behind his eyes. "If you're truly immortal," he said at last, "then why did your women attempt to kill me when I raised my blade to your throat?"

Raven's skin prickled. The fine hairs along his arms lifted as unease surged through him—triggered by the sudden, unnatural depth in Keller's voice. It no longer sounded entirely like the man before him. Raven found himself wondering who was truly speaking now. Who might be using Keller's mouth like a puppet. He kept his composure. "They are sworn to protect me," Raven said evenly, "even with full knowledge of my immortality. They do not take threats lightly. I care for them—and they protect what is mine." His gaze sharpened. "Now. What do you seek? I will not ask again?"

"I seek a woman." Keller answered plainly.

For the first time since their encounter, Raven barked a brief laugh. "Don't we all," he remarked dryly, "when our beds grow cold and we're hard with want."

Keller's inner creature ignored the remark, and pressed further. "The sister of a man I killed several months ago," he continued, "was a werewolf."

Raven replied again as he nodded his head. He became eager. The creature was beginning to feel comfortable to release its secrets. "I understand," he said. "Beast Bloods pose no true threat to us humans—yet you killed him."

Once again, Keller spoke as though Raven's words were irrelevant. His tone wavered—controlled, but fragile around the edges. Nervously, he lied in half-truth. "As you well know, my oath is to protect mortals from the evils that prey upon humanity. Werewolves have become part of those evils." He drew a slow, shallow breath. "Months ago, I was in Fortaleza. I heard the screams of children and ran to intervene. The scene was already horrific. A werewolf had attacked a man in the middle of the city. I was too late to save him—but I managed to protect the children." His voice tightened as he cocked his head and swallowed hard. Raven could hear his women behind them shifting, whispering their concern to each other as they watched Keller closely seeing glimpses of the creature that was hidden beneath.

"Once the rest of the children were safe, I pursued the creature," Keller said. "I killed him with a flaming arrow. It was only after..." He faltered. A tremor rippled through him. Small muscle ticks jerked along his neck, tugging his head briefly to see the left. He forced himself to continue. "I knew he had to die for what he'd done... but I did not know he was my friend's older and estranged brother. Leonardo." His jaw clenched as his black eyes watered in mock brokenness. "My heart shattered when I saw his body lying there."

His voice changed just as quickly back to the monotone, placid emotion. "Regardless, my purpose here aligns with oath and duty. As painful it is, I seek the location of Eli and Roslyn Santos. The other primaries believe he's been attacking humans and corrupting them. That he is turning innocent mortals into demonic creatures and attacking our people. They fled their home after setting his ablaze to erase evidence of their practices" His soulless gaze locked onto Raven. "I need their trail. Their refuge. So, I can stop them."

Keller waited in tense silence as Raven's gaze drifted inward, lost in thought. Seconds passed. Raven exhaled slowly, then shook his head once. Rising from his chair, he stepped onto the stacked books and crossed swiftly to the towering bookshelf that spanned the wall. His stubby fingers moved with certainty among the leather-bound volumes on the fifth shelf. He selected a thin book bound in black leather and a binding deep blood-red thread. He opened it immediately, flipping through its pages with practiced speed. His pace slowed as he found the passage he sought. Reading softly under his breath, Raven turned and made his way toward his chair. Raven read aloud.

"Corrupted were the angels of heaven when they tasted the blood of a demon hidden within human flesh. Their white wings molted as purity gave way to rot. Their souls fell from the grace of Lord and descended into darkness, drawn beneath Lucifer's influence. In mercy toward their fallen brethren, the angels would wait with them until the last trace of purity faded from their hearts. After the final stage of their sinister metamorphosis, a blessed blade was driven deep into the throat, and the hard was staked with obsidian. Black tar bled upon the earth, marking the presence of the transformation.

Keller's creature hissed in blasphemy, cringing in disgust revealing pointed jagged teeth that were normal moments ago. "I didn't ask you to seek knowledge for me out of a fucking book."

Raven's head snapped up, irritation flashing. He lifted a finger in warning. "Patience. I am not finished." He returned to the text. "Unaware of what lurked among them, humanity was soon overrun by foul creatures. Chaos consumed the simple world. Witnessing the suffering below, angelic warriors descended to earth. Demons began hiding Unable to distinguish corrupted souls from the innocent, the angels were forbidden to strike. Michael, the warrior angel, gathered the six remaining archangels before the Creator. He humbly sought permission to enact an idea that had come to him while watching the world from above. The Creator granted it.

Time—a superficial construct within the realm of God—ceased when the angels searched the earth for suitable mortals. When they had chosen, the Blood Ritual was enacted. Two orders of warriors were formed, each tasted with strengthening their numbers to destroy the impostors while preserving the innocent. One was forged of equal portions of wolf's blood, man's blood and angelic blood. They became the Beast Bloods. The other was forged from years of select breeding: Angelic blood, demonic blood, and the blood of man. They became the Blood Tasters. United, they were created to protect fragile humanity and to destroy the wicked.

"This is preposterous! What does this have to do with me?" The creature seathed as he tapped Keller's fingers against the chair growing irritated further.

Raven's finger slid further down the page. "In their intricate design, Beast Bloods bore hallowed grace within their immortal bloodlines. Unless coaxed through deliberate creation, they are impervious to Lucifer's corruption unless the bloodline be tainted with demonic blood creating an abomination that will bring down nations." Keller's expression had gone blank—but beneath it, something darker stirred. Panic crept subtly into his features. The evidence unraveled his story thread by thread. Raven watched the commander's eyes shift, searching for an answer. None came. Raven's suspicion hardened into fury.

"Solomon," he said quietly, "the first visionary before me, foretold a prophecy. *Flames to the Beast*." Raven closed the book with soft finality. "The world dismissed him as mad—rambling of folklore and fairy tales." His gaze sharpened, locking onto Keller. "Everyone dismissed him…except me." Raven leaned forward slightly, staring into the soulless black eyes that reflected the room back within them. He held Keller's gaze with quiet, knowing intensity, and sneered. "I know what you want with Roslyn…demon."

Panic seized Keller as the black from his eyes receded and the white-blue irises returned to their full shade. "What trickery are you casting, Seeker?" He lurched to rise, but Raven hurled the book into his chest, catching him off guard. Keller fumbled for it and fell back into the chair. Before he could recover, Raven surged forward, gripping Keller by the head and pressing his thumbs into his eyes. The women moved in a blur. They seized Keller's thrashing hands and pinned them to his sides. Restrained, he shouted and bucked violently, struggling to throw Raven and the women off him. Raven's voice thundered through the chamber.

"You think you could lie to me? I exist to seek the truth. I uncover desire. By my judgement alone, I grant or deny what is asked of me. I separate the wicked from the righteous! That is why they call me the Seeker." Raven sputtered a quick prayer in Arch-angelic, and he tore his thumbs away. Keller's eyes flew open wide back to the black orbs they were moments ago. The room began to tremble. The fire in the great hearth roared higher. Candle flames surged violently along every wick. Without hesitation, Raven pressed his forehead against Keller's. And in a violent rush, knowledge tore from Keller's eyes into Raven's tranced gaze.

Raven screamed, gritting his teeth as his body trembled from the pain of transference piercing into his eyes. The truth flooded him. A lonely, orphaned boy. Living in alleyways. Abandoned. Time fractured. A young girl shows kindness. The girl named Roslyn. Her presence lingering far too deeply in Keller's mind. His desire twisting into something unhealthy, obsessive. The voices of many strewn into one. Delusional fantasies of her body. He saw the multitude of paid whores who looked like weak comparisons to the woman he craved, and Keller's heaving body poised in authoritative positions as his cruelty reigned. Time splintered again, flashing forward. The deal was made with Leonardo before his rejection. News breaks about Eli and Roslyn's nuptials. Maddness breaks the frail mind, and then a dark whisper entered the void.

Something new appeared to him. Raven saw a man talking with a demon hunched over a chalice. Blood. There had been so much blood on the ground spilling from an altar and a stone basin. The scene flashed, and the world was in flames. Buildings fell by the weight of the stars. Screams tearing through the sky. Then there was darkness.

Raven tore himself from the connection and staggered backward, tripping over the small stack of books. He crashed to the floor. Thoughts not his own clawed through his mind—dark, twisted emotions, and foreign intent, something foul spreading beneath his skin. A sickness churned in his gut, leaving him with the overwhelming urge to vomit. On his hands and knees, Raven braced himself against the waves of revulsion and cast a glance toward Keller's unconscious body. His voice was breathless, yet resolute. "He's compromised the reformation of the Order. There are others. She carries the chosen bloodline to come. That's what the demon wants her for. Keller is a vessel just like in the days of Solomon." He coughed sharply, bile rising and burning the back of his throat. A bitter edge crept into his voice. "I should kill you. But it is not my right. That fate belongs to another." He turned to the women, voice now sharp with command. "Remove that vile man from here. Give him a small amount of oleander milk to keep him unconscious—it will not kill him, unfortunately. Use the cover of the night to transport him back to the city."

He pushed himself upright, steadier now. "We abandon this place tonight. If he returns, he will find nothing but darkness." His eyes burned with purpose. "I must prepare a carrier bird. I have letters to write." He turned to walk away into the shadowed hallway of his small underground estate. "The prophecy is entering its final days."

CHAPTER SIX
HIDING WITHIN

"Wake up, Keller.... Keller... wake up." A distant, luring whisper reached him, tugging him from unconsciousness. His body hovered in the strange in-between—neither fully asleep nor fully awake. As awareness returned in broken fragments, he realized he was lying flat on his stomach, his face turned sideways against gritty earth. Something crawled across his tingling hand. Feeling the brush of furry legs, he twitched his fingers against the heated ground. It tickled his hand again. Slowly, he opened his eyes. Wary of the sun's blinding light, he kept them narrowed to thin slits. Even so, the dominating light pierced through his lashes, forcing them shut as the brightness burned. Grains of sand crusted along his eyelashes fell into his eyes, intensifying the sting. He blinked rapidly, struggling to clear both sand and sunlight from his vision. Through his blurred vision he saw a spider resting atop of his hand—orange and black, furred and dangerous.

"You're almost awake," the voice urged, more eagerly now.

Leave me alone whoever you are, he thought, believing he had spoken aloud—only to realize his voice had not yet returned. Then the voice thundered inside his skull: "Get up!" Keller jolted violently sending the spider scurrying away. He grimaced as he turned his dirt-caked face to the side and coughed, expelling clumps of sand from his mouth. His throat burned with dryness. He dragged his tongue along the inside of his cheeks, trying to gather moisture, but only stirred more grit. The bitter aftertaste of oleander milk still lingered beneath the grime. His mind churned, fragments of memory surfacing through a thick, hazy fog.

The Seeker…he drugged me, Keller realized. He rolled onto his back and threw an arm over his eyes to shield them from the mid-day sun. He immediately regretted the movement. Blood surged to his head, pounding violently against his skull, as though his brain might split against its own cage. Keller groaned as he clenched his eyes shut again.

The nameless voice returned—gentler now, almost kind. It echoed, sounding if there were hundreds of voices talking in unison making one clear voice. "Let me ease your pain."

The pressure in Keller's head faded. A strange calm settled over him. His body felt numb. Still. Unnaturally placid. Slowly, unease crept in. No one had touched him. No blade. No potion. No hand. "How did you remove my pain, traveler? I felt nothing." He asked suspiciously.

The voice answered smoothly, evading the question. "Lower your arm. Open your eyes. I will shield you from the sun. The pain is gone. You are safe." A pause came for a heart beat as the voice coaxed, "Trust me."

"I trust no one." Keller snorted in bitterness as he obeyed cautiously, attuned to every nuance of the unseen voice. The traveler's words carried a strange accent—one he could not place, nor trace to any known land. His arm dropped heavily to his side as he gave a small shake of his head, trying to dispel the lingering fog of the drug. He opened his eyes. The pain was gone. Just as promised. He felt cooler. The heat baking him within his armor was removed as if the rays were indeed blocked by an unseen cover. Above him, the sky stretched in a vast expanse of powder blue—endless, almost heavenly in its breadth. Feeling better, he turned his head to the side, searching for the one who had awakened him. No one. He snapped his gaze to the opposite direction. Still no one. Keller surged to his feet and seized his sword, relieved to find it still secured to his belt. His eyes swept the landscape. He knew exactly where he was.

"That bastard," Keller hissed. He stood just beyond the town of Fortaleza, caught between civilization and the dense reach of the jungle. A single dirt road cut through the open land, stretching from the city's edge toward the encroaching brush. Aside from scattered crops, low shrubs, and the remains of a small abandoned ruin, the field lay empty.

"You're looking for me, aren't you?" the regal voice said. "Finally ready to pledge your gratitude to your rescuer? If so, you won't find me out there."

Keller spun in place, scanning the open field—but again no one was there. "Don't play these games with me!" Keller shouted. "Do you know who I am?"

The voice lowered to a whisper as if it sounded deep within his ears, "I know you more than you think, Keller."

Keller's eyes widened. Understanding struck like a blade. He dropped his sword to the ground and gripped his head with his hands. "You're inside of me," he rasped. "Speaking inside my mind." His breath came faster. "Did the Seeker do this? Is this what happened? I will kill that dwarf once he tells me how to rid myself of you."

The voice laughed softly. "You cannot rid yourself of me, Keller. I have been with you far longer than you realize. We are bound through a blood pact. Since you were a small child, dying of fever and disease. I grew with you. I endured with you. I lived through you." Its tone deepened, darker now. "Within the shadow of your body, I remained dormant for many years. Hidden within. Waiting. Until last night—when the Seeker's power disturbed the balance between us. We are both separate and entwined. You can hear me because you are aware of me now." Another soft laugh. "I helped you survive. I shaped you. I strengthened you. I made you what you are today" The words lingered. "A killer. A fighter. A man to be feared and respected."

Keller gripped his head. "I don't understand how this is possible."

"Many times I revealed myself," the voice replied calmly. "But you never remembered. Each time I took control, your mind forgot."

The loss of control ignited Keller's fury. "You're the devil!" he snarled. "We're going back to the Seeker." His legs suddenly weakened beneath him. His knees buckled, and he collapsed to the ground. Thousands of high-pitched screaming and cries rang throughout his skull disorienting him. Slumped forward, he pressed his palm hard against his eyes, disbelief crashing through him in relentless waves. He shut his eyes tightly, fighting to contain the chaos surging in his mind. He waited. The voice of many returned, low and gentle—a dark murmur above the disturbing cries of torment.

"You have many questions, Keller. Where shall I begin."

"Don't fuck with me," Keller snarled. "I demand answers—from Raven!" His voice rose to a roar, veins-standing stark along his neck.

"Then waste your hours returning to his cave," the voice replied coolly. "He will not be there. He knew you would come back seeking to use my power against him. That is why his whores left you here by the ruin that accesses the Order's lairs."

"Our Father, who—." Keller began, attempting to recite the Lord's prayer. The voice laughed, dark and knowing. "You stopped believing long ago, Keller. You cannot hide from me. I know everything about you. You know nothing about me." The voice sneered, "And I find it…fascinating, the lengths you are willing to go to for *her*. The one who still holds your heart."

Keller's head snapped up. The hardness in his expression faltered at the mention of her. His gaze went distant, fixed on nothing. His stomach drop as his skin prickled with fear. He tried to detour the thoughts away. "Who?" he whispered, fear threading the question.

"Roslyn," the voice affirmed.

Realization followed swiftly. His jaw tightened as heartbreak pounded in his chest. "Why do you speak her name?" he growled. "What did you do, demon?"

Sinister laughter followed his question before, another echoed reply filled his skull, "It's what *you* did. You finally broke…*you* brought fire and death to the city of Fortaleza. *You* killed for Roslyn. *You* went to the Seeker to set things right. I watched your thoughts twist and fester for years. I watched the darkness grow. She belongs to you. Doesn't she, boy?"

"No. I didn't," Keller pleaded scanning his thoughts for bits and pieces of truth that confirmed nor denied what the demon said.

The demon cut him off. A chilling note of pleasure threaded through its words. "My delight was boundless when *you* killed Leonardo. Pride tore through me. Roslyn belongs to you now more than ever." The voice shifted suddenly—no longer triumphant, but smooth. Persuasive. Dangerous. "Yes, your Roslyn." Its words coiled around him. "You were never able to control your obsession. I saw every desire you buried—her body, her love, the life you believed she owed you." A cruel edge sharpened the next words. "You built your future around those fantasies. But you never accounted for the truth: that you became deadly to her." The voice pressed closer. "That is what terrifies you most. Not that you killed—but that you *enjoyed it*. That you relished every moment of becoming what you are." Its tone turned merciless. "You betrayed her kind as she betrayed your love. You will betray the Holy Order of Saint Michael. And I will grant *her* to you."

Keller's restraint shattered. "No!" he roared. "You spew poison!" He tried to rise again, but collapsed to the ground again, fingers digging deep into the cracked earth.

"Betrayal is dark," the demon murmured. "Twisted. Seductive. It conceals truth while unleashing desire, feeding the craving buried in the deepest part of your soul. And I am your soul." Keller's resolve began to rise against it—and the presence sensed it. The demon grew louder, sharper inside his skull. "Stubborn fool, Look at you! You are a deformed mortal, born of incest. An orphan child who grew into a killer. A monster to the very people he swore to protect in the reformation of the Holy Order."

Keller barred his teeth and screamed at the earth, the familiar insult cutting deeper than any blade. Years of torment flashed through his mind. The older boys at the orphanage—where he had spent much of his adolescence—had called him a freak. They would surround him in a circle, strike him with their fists, tear at his clothes, and kick him until he passed out from pain. They would leave him broken and bleeding in the alley dirt, laughing as they walked away, chanting their cruel names after him. Fury trembled through his body. Lips quivered as his scream echoed raw and unrestrained. With his eyes squeezed shut, another vision seized him. A face. Rotting flesh. Unholy. Hollow, lifeless eyes. It stared at him in silence—then its features twisted, crinkling into a savage snarl that revealed uneven rows of jagged fangs. It was so many teeth that swirled down its gullet.

Keller knew, without a doubt, that the demon had allowed him this glimpse. Shattered, he sobbed into the earth. His breath came ragged and broken. Through clenched teeth, he finally forced the question into the air. "Who are you?"

"I have had many names, Keller. You can call me Master. Yes, I like that." The demon stated.

"I will not call you anything of the sort." Keller snarled. "I will be nothing to you—nothing of yours, demon." His voice shook with fury. "I have reached a crossroads, and you offer me no reason to remain. I am a heartbeat away from dragging this blade across my throat and ending the cursed existence for both of us."

Keller lunged for his sword, wrapping his hand around the scorching metal. He welcomed the burn against his flesh as he lifted the blade to his neck, pressing its heated edge to his scarred throat.

"No!" The demon shrieked.

Keller's hand began to tremble. Then—against his will—it was slammed violently into the earth as a stronger forced seized control. "You cannot control me!" he roared. He fought desperately, straining to raise the blade again. His planted hand ground into the sand as he struggled. Blisters burst beneath the friction of his grip, blood seeping around the dark hilt of the sword. He could feel it clearly now. The demon was fighting him just as fiercely.

"In the years I have resided within your body, I have come to…care for you," the voice said quietly. "You are my protector, as I am yours." The demon's conviction sharpened. "The day you first saw Roslyn—I had already saved you before she ever reached you. It was I, Keller. They lured you into that alley with promises of friendship. They hurt you. Weakened you. Betrayed you." The words pressed heavier. "I made them weep. I took control of your body while you lay unconscious. I stood you back upon your feet. And I ensured that every single one reaped exactly what they had sown."

The demon flashed the memory in Keller's mind,— the events unfolded. Keller watched as his younger self lay motionless in the alley while three boys walked away from their beaten prey. Then he saw it: the child version of himself rising slowly from the ground. He was still bleeding. Still broken. But something else moved behind his eyes. Fury coated the boy's blackened gaze. With a speed that rivaled the demons Keller would one day hunt, the child launched forward. He seized the largest boy by the shoulder and spun him around. His thin arms—once fragile—now held unnatural strength as he lifted the heavier boy off the ground. The other two attackers froze in horror. The look on their faces—shock, terror, disbelief—felt gratifying to the boy Keller had been. Their look of horror was gratifying in Keller's young eyes. The demon spoke through him then, his voice deep and grating as it spilled from the child's mouth. *Your time has come.*

The boy dangling in the air began to soil himself. The stench of urine filled the alley. The demon laughed through Keller's lips and hurled the boy several feet away. The child struck the ground hard—still alive, but shattered and unresponsive. Keller's demonic eyes landed on the other two. They could not move. Fear rooted them to the spot. The demon used Keller's body to make swift work of them. He left them alive—but broken. Scarred. Ruined. And somewhere deep within the boy Keller had been, there had been a terrible, dangerous satisfaction. Once the demon hears the pattern of footsteps coming around the street, the demon had released control.

"Roslyn… she found me. Not had saved me." Keller murmured as he watched the memory unfold. He saw her kneeling beside him, her voice frantic was she called for her father. Her hands moved carefully over him, checking his limbs, searching for his wounds. Her empathy was too pure for what he was. Her father arrived moments later. His gaze swept the alley, taking in Keller's broken form—and the four injured boys. The memory bled to white.

Keller's vision snapped to the present. He couldn't deny the truth of what the demon had shown him. His fingers slackened around the sword's hilt. The blade slipped free and clanged against the ground.

"You were born for me, Keller. We are a pact."

"You saved me that day." A dangerous warmth stirred in his chest—an unfamiliar satisfaction, a rush of power he did not want to acknowledge. "When I awoke that day," he continued, voice lower, raw with emotion, "Roslyn's face filled my vision. I thought she was an angel. I remember believing I had died—that I had finally reached my Maker's side."

The demon laughed a low chortle. Keller drew a slow breath. "And I devoted myself to her. I loved her from that day. She was my only friend. My only love. I would leave flowers beneath her window—freshly picked, still wet with morning dew. I loved her from afar, comforted her after her parents died as I sat beneath that same window and we talked until dawn. She was the light within my darkness." His jaw tightened. His voice softened and pained. His expression darkened. And I lost her... to him." Keller slowly pushed himself to his feet. Standing tall, he closed his eyes and centered focus—listening for the demon's presence once more.

The demon answered gently, his voice shifting into something almost tender—soothing Keller the way a parent might soothe their distressed child. "Now you see the truth." The demon's voice dark and silky, soothed him. "My poor orphan, whose own parents didn't want you, but I did. I've always wanted you." Its words pressed deeper, deliberate and cruel. "It was never enough, was it? She could not love you as you wanted her to. I felt your sorrow each time she rejected you." Its voice became scathing, sharpened as it hissed. "And still, she kept you bound to her like a puppet on an invisible string. She loved another. And she used you." The accusation landed with precision. Then the demon whispered. "I can make that change."

Keller stilled. Every word the demon had spoken so far had proven true. The memories. The visions. The past. He saw it all. It could no longer be denied. Keller said brokenly. "Even you cannot turn back time, demon."

"Now, that I am awakened fully within you. I can give us what we both want. I just need your cooperation and your body."

Keller nodded, considering what the demon was saying. Inside, something shifted. His greed warred against what remained of his conscience—light and dark colliding in a brutal internal struggle. He felt the balance tipping. Slowly. Inevitably. Perhaps…he had always been a creature meant for shadow and death. The deal was sealed when he asked, "What is your prize?"

The demon's answer came without hesitation—hungry. "Sharing this body with your mortal soul limits my power. I can only control it for brief moments before you return, leaving me to weaken in the dark while I recover. "I want a body of my own. Your body. You have already done the work for me." Its tone became possessive as it hissed more of its demands. "You lead a powerful force. The Ebony Knights. I want command over them. "They possess something I require. And once it belongs to me…" Its voice lowered, reverent with ambition. "There will be no limits to what I can become."

Keller understood at once why the demon desired his body. The Order had guarded a singular artifact for thousands of years, sealed within a consecrated vault. Its existence was known only to those initiated into the Order by a Master. Even then, without taking the sacred blood oath, no one could ever breach the vault. "You want the Spear of Destiny," Keller said slowly, "because the blood of Christ still lingers upon its steel. Why?"

The demon evaded his question, responding instead with a contemptuous snarl. "What does it matter what I do with my prize when you have Roslyn keeping your cock occupied?"

Keller bristled at the crude remark, unease churning violently within him. "What will happen to me?"

The demon replied glibly, "There is a way that I can give you Eli's body—after you take his life, of course."

"How?" Keller demanded.

The demon snapped, irritated, finally growing impatient with Keller's ceaseless questions. "Do not kill him with fire. His body would be useless to you. There is a ritual that can empower your blade. Once consecrated, it will take his life the moment the steel tastes his blood. You would simply step into the space left behind. Take over his body. His life. Enjoying everything he is. But for this, we will need the aid of an occultist to perform the rite. Fortunately, she is closer to Eli and Roslyn than you imagine."

Keller's stomach tightened. He realized, with a chill, that part of him had already begun to accept the plan—and knew the demon could sense it. "How do you know all of this?" he asked again.

"Necromancers and demons. Demons and necromancers. Even you understand the truth of it—where witched gather, creatures of the abyss are drawn. Their power creates fractures in the veil. Openings that never fully close. "The witch I speak of is…exceptional. She does not wield her knowledge often—but when she does, the impact ripples across the world. Even Lucifer has felt it." A faint, dark satisfaction colored his tone. "I have heard whispered that long ago, a demon once bargained with her…in exchange for blood."

Keller rubbed his chin as he calculated what the demon had told him. "We would have to take the sword to her then."

"No…" the demon remarked again almost breathless. "There is one closer than you think that can do that. Right here in the Order. Master Sebastion. Your adoptive father's sealed room. I shall teach you how to wield the small power in you."

"Then let's go." He snapped his gaze toward the crumbling remains of the old building and strode toward the ruin. In one swift motion, he drew a concealed dagger from his boot and sliced two crossing lines into his calloused palm. The blood welled as he crouched low, balanced on the pads of his feet, scanning the ground. Keller Searched for the stone etched with overlapping crosses. After a moment, he found the weather-worn markings. Without hesitation, he pressed his bleeding hand against the stone and whispered a small prayer in Latin.

The ground began to tremble. Stones at the center of the pile grated against one another, shifting, rotating, then sinking slowly into the earth. Keller withdrew his hand. The imprint of a bloodied cross remained smeared across the doubled carvings. As the stones fully parted, a dark opening revealed itself. Keller leaned forward and peered into the exposed passage—a deep hole with narrow stone steps spiraling downward into the underground tunnels. He knew where they would lead. The caverns beneath the church. Keller descended the steps and disappeared into the darkness. His voice echoed firm and final as he talked to the demon with his mind, "*I will not address you as Master. But given our arrangement as… friends. I will call you John.*" The demon hissed as if to protest and then a deep growl sounded. Keller began to recognize the emotions that he shared with the demon as a feeling of reluctant acceptance washed over him, flooding as strong as any emotion he had felt before.

CHAPTER SEVEN
AN ARMY REMAINS

Traveling underground toward Fortaleza, Keller moved through a maze of dimly lit tunnels. As he made his way toward the bowels of the great church, he remembered the first time he had seen the structure. The massive edifice had stood for thousands of years, unchanged at the heart of the ever-evolving city. The tunnels had been constructed long after the first Primary established the Order beneath the church. Aboveground, discreet double crosses marked the hidden entrances—simple, easily overlooked. It was one of the main reasons their community—and their army—had endured in secrecy for so long.

Keller couldn't help smirking. People were so easily deceived by surface appearances. They never searched for deeper meaning—never questioned the true purpose behind anything. They never saw the deeper purpose of anything. Humanity had always been blind to its own selfishness. They didn't think twice of the beggar on the street or where the whore they had fucked ended up that night. That's why no one ever found the hidden entry point in a pile of stones in an open field. Things can slip by those who are unobservant in a world full of secrets. He hoped those that walked the caverns beneath the church were as unperceptive as those that roamed above them.

Several feet of earth separated them from the outside world. Faintly, he could hear the stirrings of the city above him echo throughout the corridor. They reverberated through the canals and tunnels, distorting into low, groaning bellows that created the eerie illusion of other men moving through the halls. However, Keller knew he was alone—sort of. The demon remained silent since their agreement earlier that morning. Yet Keller was keenly aware that his thoughts—and even his body—were no longer entirely his own. Not until the task was finished.

His anxiety spiked as he reflected on his current course of action. He was preparing to betray the only family he had ever known.

As a child, he had devoured stories of heroes—of adventures, knights and men of honor who saved the day and won the girl. An orphan with nothing, he had longed for that life with aching intensity. He wanted purpose. Status. Wealth. Honor. A name that meant something. That dream became reality when his adoptive father brough him into the Order. They gave him everything he had ever wanted—but not without cost. The training had been brutal. Endless. Merciless. The experiments worse. They had burned away his fingerprints. Filed and reshaped his teeth with their grotesque machines. Pain beyond endurance. Yet he survived it all. Endured every torment. Held onto his sanity for one reason only: the future he believed awaited him with Roslyn. To be worthy of her. To earn her. To deserve her. In time, the Order had elevated him. Pulled him from the barracks. Given him command. Named him a leader. A hero. And still it had not been enough. Roslyn had remained his final obsession. His final desire. Until she rejected him—when he asked for her hand. She had been sweet with him. Gentle. She held his hand, met his gaze, and told him she would always love him as a sister would a brother. That he was no more than her dearest friend. John flooded Keller's mind with memories now—showing how he had tried, in Keller's stead, to secure Roslyn through Leonardo's deal. Even then, they had been forbidden. Banned. Shut out completely.

"*No longer do you have to pretend to be the hero,*" John's voice lingered over the memory as surfaced unbidden—every failed attempt to purge Roslyn from his mind over the past year. By day, he forced discipline. Control. Distance. But when night fell, she invaded his dreams with cruel persistence. John would awaken then, restless, unsettled, consumed by a hunger that could never fully satisfy. More than once, John took over, seeking distraction in the arms of willing women and men. Bodies offered in the dark, meant to dull the ache. It never lasted. They were shadows. Echoes. Nothing more. None of them were Roslyn.

"They were never worthy of you. Those sluts of Adam would've never understood you. Never loved you the way your Roslyn could."

"You're right," Keller murmured under his breath. The words tasted like surrender. "If I am not meant to have her as the hero," Keller said, bitter anger tightening his chest, "then I will have her as the villain I was always meant to become." Silence followed—heavy and approving. Keller felt it. John agreed.

That determination made his stride longer, his back a little straighter and his muscles more taught. As he turned a bend in the tunnel, the detailed painting of Christ's crucifixion on the brick wall at the end of the tunnel came into view. A massive, intricate depiction of Christ nailed to the cross dominated the brickwork at the corridor's end. Keller approached slowly, as he had done countless times before. He stopped before it. He cranked his neck to stare at the poetic image and furrowed his brow. Strangely, Keller studied the artwork with a new awareness—one that unsettled him. With striking contrast to the stormy background of the painting, Keller saw Christ's frail body perched on the cross. Sadly, it was for all mortal life to judge. The unknown artist of this depiction had painted Christ's torso to slump forward, while his head rested against his shoulder with his sorrowful eyes starring toward something unknown in the sky. The painting was morbid and made Keller uncomfortable.

Breaking contact with the picture, he blinked. Within seconds the eyes of Christ changed their direction. The once somber blue-green eyes were burning directly into him. A piercing and gut-sinking tension thundered hard in his chest. The feeling was deeper than symbolism, and heavier than guilt. This was a moment of reckoning. He knew what stood before him. He had reached the final threshold. Keller knew his options; enter the caverns as a brother of the Holy Order or as its adversary. Quickly he cast his eyes away from Christ to ease the sudden discomfort of the shame he felt.

A whisper coiled through his mind. "You're so close, don't back away now," John murmured silkily. "Not when Roslyn waits."

Keller heard John hurriedly replace the residing guilt with renewed anger. Forcefully he implanted his choice before the image of

Christ. He snarled to the painting as he kept his eyes away from Christ's sorrowful gaze. "Foe." He shot his eyes to stare defiantly into the face of the thin man, but his eyes weren't cast at Keller anymore. He quickly became alarmed at the swift change in Christ's gaze. He had denied the son. The shift was immediate and definite: denunciation. He knew whatever heavenly influence he had was no longer existent. He had made his choice knowing the ties were going to become severed. Turning sharply, Keller noticed the ceremonial dagger mounted beside the painting. Its blade caught the dim light, glinting with an ominous promise. In one smooth motion, he wrenched it free from its dowels. As he did, faint Latin script shimmered in a dull white light into existence above the mural. He lifted his gaze, reading the words slightly.

Keller could feel John pressing against the back of his skull. His control grabbed at Keller's sight and took over long enough to read them, but it was Keller who said it aloud. "The Wounds of Christ."

Keller's sight was returned to him. Quickly, he pricked his finger with the dagger, gritting his teeth from the slight affliction. He dropped the blade to the ground and replied, "Stigmata." Rightly he proceeded to place his bleeding finger over certain parts of the painting. In his blood, Keller put crosses over the thorn rimmed forehead of Christ as well as the nailed wrists and feet. Then, he made a mark on Christ's side. Finally, the last blood cross rested over the heart. It depicted where he truly bled for all humanity, and they'd wound him. Once Keller had finished, his stark red blood soaked into the painting, disappearing. The stone wall groaned. With a deep, ancient creak, it began to swing inward, revealing a hidden chamber beyond.

Keller crossed the threshold into the vast domed hall. His gaze lifted immediately to the sight before him: the Order Masters, clad in their customary long black robes, stood in a tight circle around a massive, polished oak table set in the center of the room. Above them, an iron chandelier hung low, its presence heavy and severe. Their voices clashed in heated argument—sharp, raised, uncontrolled. Keller had never witnessed such disorder among the Maters. He needed to hear every word—their argument centered on him.

"Describe everything to me. Now," John demanded, frustration sharp in his voice. He hated being blind to the physical world.

Irritated by the intrusion, Keller replied through his mind, his thoughts edged with warning. "We're in the Chamber of Doors. Every wall is lined with identical doors—each one leading to different rooms. Some open into other tunnel systems throughout the sanctuary. Every door bears a specific marking, so no one becomes lost." He paused, focusing his gaze on the chamber around him. "The floor dips low at the center. Wide stones steps ring the basin, leading down a massive oak table where the Masters gather for council—like they are now." His patience thinned, "Now, be silent. I need to hear why the Order Masters are shouting." Keller could feel himself going numb and growing angrier as his sight slowly faded to darkness. "Don't even think about trying to take control, Keller snapped inwardly. "I will expose you to the High Master myself and end this." The pressure vanished instantly. His sight returned and his body was his own again.

John became eerily calm as he got the last word in until he went silent once again. "*Soon, Keller. Soon we will be equals.*"

Keller snorted internally, dismissing the words. He no longer cared what the demon promised. At last, he turned his full attention to the chamber. Twenty men stood gathered in heated dispute, their raised voices echoing through the domed room. Keller remained in the shadows, silent and watchful.

"What do you propose we do, Sebastian?" Percy demanded. "We sent scouts in every direction. They returned with nothing—no trace of him within a three-hundred-mile span. If he had been captured, there would have been signs. Evidence. Something." He shook his head, fury sharpening his voice. "No. He his tracks deliberately. He did not want to be found. He knew he would be forced to answer for abusing his power. He betrayed us." Percy, a middle-aged man with graying light brown hair and fiery green eyes, bellowed with conviction.

"He didn't betray us, Percy," Arilo said quietly. The blind man was advanced in age and known throughout the Order for his compassion. Yet compassion had not always been his nature. A lifetime steeped in bloodshed, brutality, and indulgence had carved wisdom into him near the end of his life.

Percy did not allow the defense to stand. "Keller seized control of the Knights and slaughtered an entire, powerful werewolf clan!" he snapped. "You know what the means. They will answer with prophecy. War will come between their kind and ours." He slammed his palm against the table. "No. I say it again—we send our strongest to find Keller and kill him. Then we make peace with the clans." His gaze hardened. "We send Jeremih."

Sebastian darted up from his throne of silver and black, both hands slamming against the table. The sharp crack echoed through the chamber, cutting cleanly through the noise. An echoing slap sounded throughout the room accompanied with his furious shouting. "I will not make assumptions," he thundered. "I know the evidence that stands against him. The testimonies of terrified citizens burying their dead are enough to paint a grim picture. But that is what *may* have happened—not what we know to be true." His gaze swept across the gathered Masters. "The cause of this tragedy remains unclear. And until we understand it fully, it would be reckless to condemn him." His voice lowered, sharpened with authority. "It would be wise, gentlemen, to honor the law of trial before we move to assassinate a man who had not yet been proven guilty."

Keller listened intently, a sly smirk tugging at his lips at the loyalty in his adopted father's defense. Once, he had been a cold, hungry adolescent with nowhere to call home—desperate for comfort, for safety, for survival. He needed money, and he needed it quickly. For two weeks, he had slept in the alley behind a jewelry shop, watching the owner each day, studying the old man's routines until he believed he had learned enough to steal from him. The night he finally acted, lock picks trembling in his fingers, a deep, stern voice cut through the darkness.

"Stop."

Keller had froze. He dropped the tools at once, convinced he had been caught and that prison—or worse—awaited him. He did not know then that the voice belonged to Sebastian. He only knew fear compelled obedience. But instead of punishment, Sebastian offered him warmth. Food. Shelter. Purpose. A life of duty. Keller accepted. He had little choice. Refusal would have meant prison—or the slow death he had already been living. Within the hour, Sebastian escorted him back to the orphanage and formally claimed him as his son.

Overtime, Keller became Sebastian's apprentice in the skills of enchantment. Yet he struggled to focus on the tedious nature of the craft. Sebastian soon recognized the fury coiled beneath the boy's surface and chose not to suppress it—but to shape it. Noticing Keller's underlying aggression, Sebastian thought it would be best to make such a flaw useful. He sent Keller to Gawain for warrior training. Through the years of back-breaking hardships, Keller excelled beyond his peers and had gained ultimate leadership. That was the day he looked at Sebastian's soft brown eyes and saw a father's pride. Through tears and a quick hug, Sebastian proclaimed he had become like a son to him, and God had offered him the chance to be a father again. Keller found acceptance. But he knew if it wasn't for Sebastian the others might've killed him long ago. The memory faded. Keller's faint smile disappeared as the argument around the table began again.

I hope you've found a better falsehood for them than you did for the Seeker," John whispered, its voice sliding through Keller's mind like a blade to provoke.

"I didn't need you then, and I don't need you now." Keller lied through his clenched jaw as he scurried for something credible to say to them. He forced his focus outward, scrambling to construct something believable—something flawless. Because within the Order, deception was a death sentence. And once you belonged to them…there was only one way out. Death.

"Percy is right, Sebastian. And yet… Sebastian speaks truth as well." Alejandro chimed in looking at the men that appropriately sat on opposite sides of the table.

"How diplomatically convenient of you, Alejandro." Simon said snidely.

"I'm being reasonable," Alejandro insisted, clearly weary of the prolonged dispute. He turned fully toward Sebastian. "We have waited nearly three months for Keller's return. He has not come. The possibilities are few: he is dead, he had been captured…or is he guilty of the crime." Silence fell heavier around the table. Alejandro continued, voice steady. "If he fled out of guilt, then he is a coward and does not deserve the dignity of a trial. He abandoned the very men he persuaded to follow him—men who now lie buried because of his actions. We are under a reformation of what we once were. We need to appoint a new leader to command the knights—should war come," Alejandro continued. "We must prepare for the possibility that the Beast Bloods will refuse to see the truth that Master Raven has been purging the order for the past decade. There's too much history. They won't see that we are not responsible for this catastrophe. That it was the act of a rogue within our ranks."

He watched Sebastian carefully. The white of the older man's eyes had begun to redden with strain and grief. Alejandro pitied him—but as a neutral voice among the Masters, he could not afford bias. Still, when he spoke again, his tone softened. "We all know Keller was among our finest. But there has always been something we overlooked within him. And he now broke the cardinal rule. He shattered alliances with the Santos clan. He caused civilian deaths through reckless violence. And he cost us many of our most valuable men as they acted mindlessly under his control." His gaze swept the table. "We cannot remain divided over this. I propose we vote—allow the tally to settle the matter once and for all." A murmur of agreement rippled around the chamber. Several of the Masters nodded. Even Sebastion, after a long, rigid pause, released a quiet breath and inclined his head in reluctant consent.

Alehandro straightened. "All those in favor of assassinating the corrupted—"

From the shadows at the outer edge of the room, Keller stepped forward, descending the shallow steps into the chandelier's glow. His boots echoed against the stone as he entered the light. He walked down the steps further into the light. "No need to vote on my life just yet, gentlemen, Keller said smoothly. "I've come to explain my absence…and to stake my claim." Silence detonated across the chamber. One by one, the Masters took in his appearance. The deformity. The scars. Gasps filled the room. The warped remnants of fire's cruelty etched into his flesh and fraying clothing. Keller stood unmoving beneath the chandelier, fully aware that the harsh illumination did nothing to soften what he had become.

Sebastian spoke first. Horror lined his features as shock shot through his voice. "Keller… look at you. Your face. What happened, son?"

Keller descended into the center of the chamber and claimed an empty chair from the circle around the table. He sat with controlled composure before answering. "Deformed by the fire in the tavern," he said evenly. "I battled the creature and defeated it. I escaped—but not without cost. When the flames took hold of its fur, the fire spread too quickly. I was caught in it."

"Then you are confessing to your crimes," Vaughn stated thinking it was going to be as simple as that.

Keller turned his gaze to the balding elder—a man blind in one eye, standing as close to death as Simon himself. Then he swept his eyes across the gathered men. "I confess that I killed a werewolf," he said, "But not an ordinary one. This creature was unnatural. Deformed. Corrupted by Satan himself. The way he stood, the way he moved—everything about him reeked of higher evil. Even his eyes burned blood-red. This was no mortal beast." It was a careful lie, woven with fragments of truth from prophecy. And with the Seeker currently gone, there was no one left to contradict him. Yet, he saw the Masters share glances at each other before looking back at him. Keller felt prickles along his skin and shifted slightly in his seat, careful to make it look like a subtle adjustment of nonchalance.

Gable's face drained of color. Fear flickered openly in his hazel eyes, but Keller suspected it wasn't from what he said. "Do you know what…whom you are describing, boy?" he asked quickly. His sagging face and jowls wiggling as he looked around to the others once more.

Keller met the burly redhead's stare without hesitation. "Yes," he said defiantly. "I understand the weight of my words. I've studied the limited records we possess about such creatures. But this one was different—even from the abomination we already fear. This is way I sought out the Seeker. I have just returned from his caverns. I needed to what I had killed. What I had witnessed." He lifted his chin slightly, voice steady. "My actions were justified. The Seeker confirmed what I feared—the time of preparation has begun. The werewolf I killed was the first of its bloodline to be tainted with demonic corruption."

Percy surged to his feet, fury exploding across his features. He slammed his fist against the table. "Liar!"

All eyes snapped to Percy. Keller felt the familiar rush of fury rise in his chest. He forced it down, carefully. If his temper slipped—or worse, if John surfaced—it would expose everything. For now, the demon remained silent, and Keller clung to that fragile mercy. He turned to Percy slowly. "Do you doubt me?" Keller asked, his voice cool and edged with warning. "Do you doubt the Seeker's vision of truth?" Keller gritted feeling the tick in his neck muscle I am out on the battlefields while you sit on your fat fucking ass and grow placid in your hall—"

Percy didn't back away from Keller's powerful augury. "Do you think you're the only one who's gone to see the Seeker about this matter," he shot back. "I am the Master of Coven research and Other Monstrosities. My division studies demons, rouge witches, and corrupted Blood Tasters—the very creatures *your* units are trained to hunt, boy!" He spat with malevolence foaming at the mouth.

Keller's jaw tightened. He met Percy's stare with open hostility. "And you're point?" he asked, hating every bit of the man he addressed.

"I will kill him first," John whispered through Keller's mind, the deep echoed voice blocked what Percy was saying. Keller shook his head to clear the demon's voice away.

Percy's face flushed with anger. "Don't shake your head at me, boy!" He raved. "The Beast Blood you speak of will mark the start of an unnatural Armageddon if it is not stopped. For years, I've traveled to Raven's chambers to study the texts on the subject to help change the direction of what the Order once was." He stepped forward slightly, voice growing more intense. "The kin of a Truer Sin will be chosen to be Lucifer's werewolf when the time comes to fruition, it will be born. Linked through blood, through time—and God alone knows what else will bind it. There will only ever be one demonic werewolf. And there will be signs. Many signs. Signs meant to prepare us for its arrival."

His gaze locked onto Keller as he drove his point further. "That is why our new alliances with the clans mattered. That is why their survival was vital. And yet, for months none of the signs have manifested. Not one. Until now." A cold smile touched Percy's lips. "The Seeker has tried—many times—to locate this creature through me. And he saw nothing. Nothing at all. Then again, he could see through *you*."

Silence thickened the chamber.

"Why is that, Keller?" Percy pressed. "Is your story truth…or merely a convenient lie to absolve yourself of responsibility." He gestured broadly to the council. "You bring no proof. No evidence in the Seeker's hand. And we are expected to accept it blindly?" His tone sharpened to contempt. "Why on earth would I believe your words against my knowledge?" Percy's smug features excelled through his cocky evidence. "Why should I believe you over this letter," Percy pulled out a letter from his robes, the black wax seal of a Raven—The Seeker's mark—broken. "Why should I believe your testimony over my knowledge?" Percy addressed the council. "A letter, gentlemen, arriving last night of what had happened when Keller visited him." Percy slammed down the parchment on the table as he cast his burning gaze at Keller. "A warning in Raven's own hand. Marked and sealed."

Keller studied the men around him. Their stern, weathered faced held judgment—every one of them—expect Sebastian, whose expression was filled with worry and quiet grief. Unbidden, the image of Christ's painted eyes flashed through Keller's mind. He shook it away.

John's voice slithered softly through his thoughts again. *Let me kill them for you, vessel. The time has come.*

"No," Keller said sharply—aloud.

Sebastion stiffened. "No… what, Keller?" he asked gently as he placed a hand on Keller's arm. Sebastian pulled it back suddenly, gripping it with the other hand as if that brief moment of contact had wounded him somehow. He stared at Keller's odd movements, suspecting something in him had changed. Concerned tightened his features.

John hissed. *He knows I'm with you. He has to die.*

Keller lowered his gaze, fixing on the grooves etched into the table. He could not afford to meet their eyes. Not yet. Not like this. He gathered himself carefully before speaking again. "I did not know I was expected to return with a letter pinned to my chest like a drooling simpleton," he hissed. "No—you do not have to trust my words over your knowledge." He finally lifted his gaze, locking it intentionally onto Percy. "But I do ask you to have faith in them. Faith, Percy." His brow arched slightly. His tone sharpened. Is that not the truest virtue the Lord teaches us to hold to in time of uncertainty?"

"Even Judas sat at the feet of Christ listening to his words before his greed overcame him," Percy said coldly. "So, tell me, Keller—what did you betray us for?"

Sebastian couldn't take it anymore. Fear clenched around his lungs, tight and merciless. His old heart thundered in his ears as if it might burst. Before Keller—or anyone—could answer, Sebastion slammed his voice into the room. "Enough!" he shouted. "This is getting ridiculous. We could sit here all day debating whether he speaks truth or lies, and in the end it will still be his words against…ours—" he looked at Keller as he said the last part, pain welling in his large eyes. He swallowed down his emotion and continued. "While we tear ourselves in half." He drew in a hard breath, forcing steadiness that would come. "We cannot be divided like this. Not now. He is here, and he will not die today."

He defends you even though he knows what you are, vessel. The demon whispered. Keller didn't reply. He was still as a statue as emotion rooted him in the moment as he watched Sebastion defend the honor he no longer had.

Sebastion pointed a finger toward Keller as if anchoring the room to that single face. "He has given an answer for his action. The prophecy was written long before any of us drew breath—yet who is to say prophecy cannot shift, the way all things shift with time?" His voice cracked with conviction. "Keller says he killed a corrupted werewolf." Sebastion's eyes burned as the looked at the Masters. "I believe him."

Grant—a middle-aged man with bronze skin and large sunken eyes of turquoise—lifted a hand, firm and controlled. "Sebastian, calm yourself," he said. "Your emotions are overworking your heart." His gaze sharpened, but his voice was pleading. "Use logic, my friend. You believe him for biased reasons. You have always looked at him as was Malik."

Sebastian felt the old wound tear open at the mention of his dead son. Anger, regret and grief struck his chest all at once, a crushing wave that fed the fire already burning inside him. His face flushed red, features tightening as his jowls trembled with raw emotion.

"I believe him." Sebastion growled, voice rough with pain, "because he is our brother. The Commander *you* all had seen fit to lead. He took the Blood Oath. What reason—of all the men in this room—would he have to lie to us?" His voice broke slightly on the last word. "To me." He looked at them all pointedly, daring any of them to challenge him. "May God strike me dead," Sebastian thundered, "if he is the devil in disguise."

In a violent instant, the iron chandelier tore loose from the stone ceiling and crashed down onto the wooden table. The men scattered from their seats, diving for cover as the impact exploded outward. Splinters of oak, shards of twisted metal, and hot candle wax burst through the air. Several ducked low, arms raised over their heads as debris rained down around them. When the echo of the crash finally faded, a heavy silence followed. Their eyes slowly adjusted to the sudden loss of the main light. The remaining wall torches and smaller ceiling fixtures still burned, casting flickering illumination across the ruined chamber. One by one, the men lifted themselves from the floor—shaken, but unharmed. They began to look around. And then they saw it. Shock spread across their faces in a silent wave.

Alejandro was the first to speak. He drew in a sharp breath, horror draining the color from his face. "Master Sebastian," he whispered. His gaze flicked toward Keller, and the rest of the men followed his eyes—only to recoil, tearing their attention away from the sight. "God took his life," Alejandro said hoarsely, "to show us the truth."

Keller was the last to rise. He pushed himself to his feet slowly, then stilled when Alejandro's words registered. The men stood scattered around the wreckage, their gazes locked onto him—hard, accusing, unmoving. His stomach dropped. He turned toward the devastation at the chamber's center. Sebastion. Metal and splintered wood had impaled his body at brutal angles. Shards of the shattered table pierced through cloth and flesh alike, while the twisted iron of the fallen chandelier crushed his chest beneath its weight. Blood pooled darkly beneath him, soaking into the ruined floor. Keller's breath left him all at once.

Percy's voice rose in a shout. "Seize him—!"

But the command never reached Keller. Sound vanished. All he could hear was a high-pitched ringing screaming inside his skull. The world blurred at its edges. He had seen death before. He had caused death before. But never someone who had loved him. Never the man who had called him *son*. He wanted to look away from Sebastian's eyes—lifeless, open, and fixed on him with something that looked too much like sorrow. He couldn't bring himself to tear his eyes away from him. Sebastian's white hair was matted with cooled wax and darkening blood from the metal stake that pierced through his skull. The contrast struck Keller with sickening clarity. Blood in the snow. The once-flushed warmth of the man he had called father had drained to a ghostly pallor. Blood pooled around his shattered body, spreading outward in a glistening halo.

They're coming for you. John snarled inside his mind. *Let me do it, Keller.*

Keller did not move. Did not speak.

Keller! John shrieked. *Look up. Say the words. Let me kill them! Do it for Roslyn!*"

Slowly—too slowly—Keller lifted his head. A dozen men surged toward him, weapons raised, faces twisted with rage and horror. Something inside him finally broke.

"Kill them all." Keller whispered. The words felt distant. Detached. Like they belonged to someone else. A cold numbness spread through him as his consciousness slipped backward—receding, dissolving—while something darker surged forward to claim what remained. The world vanished in a flood of black. Keller no longer saw. No longer felt. No longer existed. He surrendered to the void. And for the first time…he did not resist.

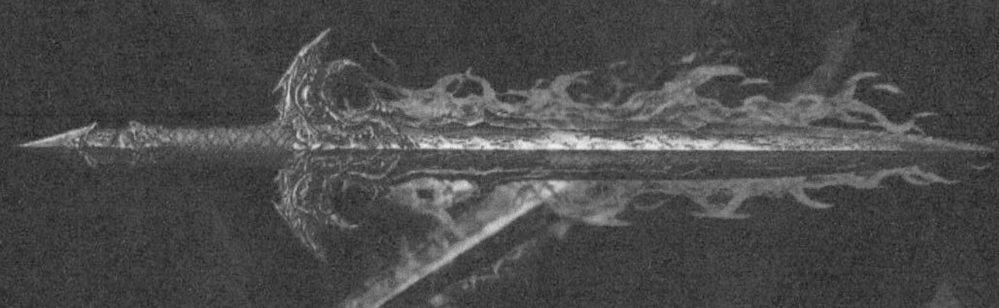

Slowly, Keller returned to himself, reclaiming control of his body. Slumped forward, he felt the cold stone wall pressed against his back. He opened his eyes and lifted his head, trying to remember where John had left him. He blinked sluggishly. His vision swam and doubled, like a man deep in drink. Nausea rolled through him. His stomach lurched from the strain his body had endured. He twisted to the side just in time, bile rising in his throat. His body shuddered as he vomited onto the ground beside him. The sour stench turned his stomach again, forcing dry heaves until nothing remained.

John finally spoke, his voice thin and drained, like a whisper dragged from dying lungs. "Our kind does this to yours when you let us in. Resistance makes it painful. You did not resist me. So, it will pass quickly."

Keller listened to John until the fog finally cleared from his senses. He realized he was back where he had first entered the chamber. He let his head fall against the cold stone wall and took in the scene before him. Bodies lay scattered across the room. One rested near his feet. He recognized Grant at once. Blood streaked his face, and his neck twisted at a grotesque angle. Even from where he sat, Keller could smell it—the metallic tang of blood thick in the air. The stench of death clung to the chamber. He felt nothing. No remorse. No emotion. Only hollow numbness. Then a sharp crack split the silence as flesh and cloth ripped. A corpse slipped from one of the smaller chandeliers and struck the floor with a heavy thud.

"So this is what remains after your chaos. Blood and gore." John's strange chuckle echoed in Keller's mind before he continued. "Well, the Masters are gone. The Seeker is nowhere to be found. You, me, and an army of ten-thousand remain. Our enemies are fewer, thanks to you, my friend. But one question lingers—Sebastin was the necromancer that I relied upon, and God, in His vengeance, took him from me. Who now will curse the blade?

"You've accepted me. You are now a necromancer. A vessel through which the shade may thrive. Our powers flows through your blood. Take us to his chambers and use his materials. We will perform the rites ourselves. There is no need to hide what we are any longer. You and I now rule this place. The Masters of the Holy Order of St. Michael are head, and we live to command as we see fit." John released his strength into Keller in a blazing surge. "The irony of evil thriving beneath holy ground. No mortal can touch you now."

Keller groaned as pain shot through his body, like lightening racing along his veins. He finished against the invasion, muscles tightening from the shock. Then it settled. Power. A new darkness wrapped around him like velvet. Heavy. Invincible. Intoxicating. Not a trace of weakness remained. Keller rose slowly to his feet, lifting his hands before him. The wounds that once marked them were gone. They looked unchanged—yet he knew they were not. They were weapons now. Beyond his fingers, his gaze fell upon Percy's corpse hanging over the high walk. Keller had despised the man for years—his piety, his smugness, the comfort of his soft life. Keller studied his hand again. Then Percy."

Do it. You know you can. John urged.

Keller's fingers sparked. Silvery-blue arcs of energy danced across his skin. He turned his hand, watching the current gather. Rolling his wrist, he cupped his palm as the electricity condensed into a glowing sphere. With a flick, he sent the charge into Percy's body. The surge ignited the black robes at once. Flames crawled across the corpse as the scent of burning flesh and scorched blood filled the chamber. Keller laughed—low and dark.

"If heaven would not have me, then I will make the angels kneel. I will spread hellfire to those who oppose me." Satisfied, he nudged the burning body over the ledge with his boot. It tumbled down the steps below. A twisted smile pulled at his lips. "Now," he said, "we can leave."

CHAPTER EIGHT
CURSING THE BLADE

Keller knew exactly where to go and along the way he left his mark. Fire cascaded up the tapestries of the Saints as he strode down the corridors, flames blooming in his wake like blasphemous offering. Doors burst open before he ever touched them, iron twisting and shrieking under the quiet command of his mind. He did not rush. He savored it. Power did not corrupt him. It simply removed what was weak. It answered him. He tested it with idle curiosity at first—a flicker of flame here, a cackle of electricity there—but the thrill quickly shifted into something darker. Something indulgent. The world bent too easily. Nothing resisted him. Nothing denied him. The realization settled deep in his bones. He was no longer part of this world. He was something above it.

In a violent burst of splintering wood, Keller forced open the doors to Sabastian's old chamber. Darkness pooled inside the room, thick and undisturbed. It did not hinder him. He could see perfectly. A smile touched his lips. "I see power comes with courtesies," he drawled.

"Darkness will become your daylight," John said, his voice slick with reverence. "And light will be your night. A costly exchange…the same one Lucifer paid when he fell from grace."

Keller stepped onto the wooden floor. The movement of his boot crossed the threshold, the chamber responded. Symbols awakened along the walls in a slow ripple, like a creature stirring from sleep. From floor to ceiling they glowed in cold silver-blue, etched in perfect sequence. Their light did not warm the room—it bled through it. They pulsed. Breathing. Waiting. Power traveled through the markings in faint surges, as though something inside them strained to fully awaken but lacked a final spark. Keller turned slowly in the center of the chamber. The room was circular, the ceiling rising high above him like the inside of a cathedral built for forgotten gods. Even the overhead beams were carved with sigils, layered upon older symbols worn faint with age. He felt it then. Belonging. "There are strange markings everywhere," Keller murmured. They seemed familiar somehow.

"The chamber is powered by you," John said, his voice threaded with memory. "The current in your blood must be fed into it. Once it drinks from you, it will shape itself to your will." He sounded almost nostalgic—as though he had stood in a room like this centuries ago. The air thickened. Energy churned beneath the floorboards like a storm waiting for command. Keller stepped toward the nearest sigil. It called to him. He could feel it—a silent pull beneath his ribs. Curiosity eclipsed caution. He dragged his fingertips across the carved symbol. The silvery-blue glow flickered. Then it bled into a deep, smoldering red. Heat surged instantly. The mark scorched his skin.

"Ah—" Keller hissed, jerking his hand back as the bur bit deep. "What the hell?" The room was already moving. The symbols began to rotate, shifting and whirling as if the walls themselves were massive gears turning in a divine mechanism. Sigils slid past one another locking into new sequences, rearranging in patterns older than language. The chamber was recalibrating. For him. The rotation quickened. Symbols aligned. Then—they ignited white-hot. The darkness shattered under a flood of blinding light.

Watch out! John roared, sudden fear cracking through his voice.

Before Keller could demand an explanation, the chamber answered for him. A hollow resonance rolled through the room. Deep. Ancient Bone-shaking. It swelled into a chorus—thousands of voices layered in the ragged octave, as if the dead themselves had found a hymn. Keller clamped his hands over his ears. The sound crawled inside his skull. "What is happening?" he shouted through the distortion.

John snapped, urgency cutting sharp. *Get us out! Shield yourself. Now!*

Keller didn't question it. Instinct took over. He lunged from the conjuring room, slamming himself against the corridor wall. He squeezed his eyes shut and turned his face away from the doorway just as heaven answered. A pillar of white-gold radiance detonated from the chamber. Not light. Judgment. It devoured everything it touched. The sigils. The books. The ritual space. All erased beneath holy brilliance. The blast surged outward, flooding the bedchamber like a rising sun. Only the consecrated stone walls held it back, drinking the radiance before it could spread further. But the heat—the heat was divine fire. It scalded the stone. It scorched the air. Keller felt his scarred skin sear. The left side of his face burned as if pressed to the sun itself. The undersides of his hands blistered beneath the holy glare. Still—he pressed himself harder against the wall. He would not yield. He would not kneel. Through gritted teeth, he endured the pain in silence, defiant even in suffering. Then—silence. The radiance withdrew as suddenly as it had come. The chorus died. Only the scent of charred air remained.

Through narrowed lids, Keller noticed the darkness return. He opened his eyes slowly. Everything the light had touched was gone. It was erased. Fine gray ash traced ghostly outlines where objects had once stood. A chair. A table. A stock of books. Their shadows remained like memories carved into dust. Keller's jaw tightened. If he had lingered one breath longer, he would be nothing more than a smear on stone…a nameless stain fading with time. The thought did not frighten him. It irritated him. He pushed away from the heated wall and studied the conjuring room. Strangely, it had reset symbols intact, chamber whole, as if the destruction had been swallowed and undone. Cautiously, he stepped inside again. He tapped the floor with his boot, testing, hunting for some hidden mechanism. A low growl rippled through his mind.

Imbecile. John's voice cracked like a whip. *It was not gears or switches. Those symbols are scripture-bound wards. You touched one.*" Keller's gaze slid away. *When a demonic presence awakens them, they answer with judgement*, John continued, his tone tightening despite himself. "*That was the killing light. The light of God. Do you truly believe your new tricks make you immortal?"* The air thickened as John's presence coiled around Keller's thoughts. *I could wrap my essence around your heart this very moment,* he hissed, *and feel it burst inside your chest.*

Irritation slid beneath his calm like a blade. "Do not threaten me for knowledge I was never given. You led me here. Do not pretend otherwise."

Johns laugh was dark, sinister as it curled through his mind. The echo hissed like blackened vapor. *Free will, Keller. You chose this. You denied your God. You let me tear through your precious Order. You stepped into my world with open eyes. You will submit to me, necromancer.*

Silence followed, but Keller did not recoil at the shift in John's voice. Pain he could always endure. Submission was another matter. Instead, a slow smile tugged at the ruined side of his mouth. "Yet you didn't," he said calmly. *Necromancer.* Keller rolled the word in his thoughts like wine on his tongue. It no longer tasted bitter. It tasted…inevitable. "This is exactly why you cannot kill me," he murmured. "A king is far more useful alive than a corpse." His blackened eye lifted toward the glowing symbols. "So you must need me alive."

For the first time since the blast, John had no immediate reply. Then Keller felt it. The flicker of hesitation. It pleased him. The silence that followed was wrong. Too clean. Too empty. Keller lowered his hands slowly. The sting still pulsed beneath his skin, but the pain no longer ruled him. John did not speak. For the first time since their bond formed, he was quiet. Keller snorted, muttering. "Lost your tongue?"

He felt John tighten inside him—rage coiling as the agony struck. His heart clenched as if an unseen hand squeezed it. His left arm went dead. Breath vanished. Keller dropped to his knees, fingers digging into the stone as panic flickered through him. His vision swam. He clawed at his chest a broken gasp escaping. "D-don't…kill… us…" For one fragile moment, he understood how easily life could still leave him. Then Jogn released him. Air ripped back into his lungs, hot and stinging. Keller inhaled sharply, choking on the influx of air and his fury. Slowly, he lifted his head. And his gasping became laughter. Low.

Hoarse. Darkly amused. "This is how gods argue," he stated. "By gripping each other's hearts."

He rose unsteadily to his feet, wiping blood from his lip with the back of his hand. His pale eyes gleamed now with an awakening of madness. "If I must become your monster…I will at least be a magnificent one." The illusion of dominance cracked, refined. Trepidation replaced his earlier arrogance, but it made him alert.

"Do not ever do that again," Keller said quietly, the softness more threatening than a shout. His voice carried the weight of a man learning where the blade truly hovered.

John's voice thundered through his skull, but his voice lacked its usual velvet confidence. *Do not confuse my patience with dependence. That was not meant for mortals to survive.*

Keller rolled his scorched wrist, testing the healing flesh. "It seems I did."

John spoke again, lower. *That was not a warning. That was a cleansing.* The word lingered like poison. *They tried to wipe the chamber from existence…and you with it.*

Keller let out a breath that almost sounded like a laugh. "Then Heaven should try harder." A ripple of unease moved through John's presence. Keller could *feel* it now—the subtle tightening in his mind, the cautious withdrawal.

Angels do not strike unless something threatens the balance. John boomed.

Keller finally turned toward the ruined doorway, eyes dark and with growing hunger. "Good." His voice dropped, short and harsh. "Let them fear me."

If Heaven has seen you…then Hell will soon crown you. John said silkily through his mind.

"What now?" he asked, gaze drifting along the walls. Symbols spiraled in strange sequences, older than any script he knew. "They look older than hieroglyphics." He moved toward the center of the center of the chamber, steps measured, controlled. He would not appear uncertain again.

"They are letters of the Archangels," John said. "Blessed spell work. Protection runes. When touched by something unholy, they answer." A dark chuckle followed. "They answered you."

"Keller's jaw tightened. John's laughter turned cruel. "I taste your fear now, Keller. Delicious." He purred. "As I told you—channel your power through the room. It will shape itself your will. But it requires blood. Are you so afraid I must perform the necromancy myself?"

Paranoia curled in his gut, but he masked it beneath steel composer. If John intended betrayal, Keller would at least see it coming. but Keller strangled it before it reached his face. "No," he snapped. Then, more controlled, "This is my body. My rite. I will not be a spectator inside my own flesh."

"Then kneel. Bow. Lay down your weapon." John shouted his command.

His pale gaze lifted, glinting with something new—something colder. "If I must kneel," Keller muttered, "it will be the last time I ever do." Keller slowly dropped to his knees as he unlatched the sword from its black, leather sheath. The movement felt ceremonial—a vow being rewritten. The blade whispered as it slid free, cold steel grazing his palm. He angled his hand outward, careful, respectful as though handling something alive. For a moment, he simply looked at it. His weapon—a former symbol of righteousness. The pommel bore a roaring dragon's head, sculpted in intricate detail. Its sapphire eyes shimmered with archangelic blessings, once meant to protect, to guide, to judge the wicked. Now their blue fire reflected in Keller's pale gaze like a memory that no longer belonged to him. The dragon's wings curved outward to form the guard, poised as if ready to strike. The blade arched in a wicked curve like a tail mid-snap, etched with fine scales. Twin rows of tiny, serrated spikes lined its edges—a design mean not only to kill, but to ruin what it touched. A weapon of judgement. Or of damnation. The difference no longer mattered.

Keller set the sword upon the ground with care, almost tenderness, as one might lay a crown at the feet of a darker throne. His voice, when it came, was calm. Empty of doubt. Empty of regret. "Done."

John's voice slid through Keller's mind like silk. "Cut your hand with the dagger at your boot. Feed the circle. Blood binds stronger than prayer ever could. Spread a single circle of blood around you and the sword. Then create five, connecting points to the ring. Then form an outer ring, connecting the points." A vision followed—a perfect design. John restrained his excitement. Everything was aligning to easily. The Truer Sin had chosen well. Keller was pride, hunger wounded devotion—a man already half-fallen before the first drop of blood touched the floor. A vessel shaped by obsession. A weapon disguised a believer.

Keller withdrew the dagger from his boot and studied the thing edge for a breath. Once, he would've hesitated. Now he did not. He dragged the tip slowly from the base of his finger toward his wrist. Pain flared, bright and intimate. He welcomed it with a groan of pleasure as he closed his eyes and flexed his hand. Thick crimson welled into his palm. Beautiful. Alive. He lifted his hand and let the blood fall. Each drop struck the floor with a soft, rhythmic patter, like a heartbeat outside his body. Still kneeling, he rotated, tracing the circle around himself and the dragon-blade. His free hand followed, spreading the blood into a smooth arc. Warm and sticky. Then the five points were made, connected. At last was the outer ring. A sigil of ascension. The moment the design completed, the blood began to crawl along the lines on its own—threading through the pattern like veins awakening. Keller watched with quiet awe as the wound on his palm sealed itself, flesh knitting together as though it had never opened. He flexed his fingers slowly. Power stirred beneath his skin, restless and eager. Electricity prickled along his nerves. His fingertips twitched, sparks dancing faintly in their wake. A dark smile ghosted across his lips. He wasn't afraid. He was…hungry. Hungry for more pain. More power.

John's voice coiled through him, smooth and self-assured. "Can you feel it, vessel? Feel the influence? The symbol's sealed. Stand in the center. Raise the blade. Claim what is yours. The power that will correct every injustice done to you."

Keller moved to the circle's heart. He lifted the dragon-blade slowly above his head, like a king raising a crown. Energy thrummed through his veins, heavy and alive. Not borrowed. Earned. His pupils widened until his eyes became endless black. The world dimmed around him as if the light itself bent away from his presence. The floor pulsed beneath his boots. Once. Twice. Then in rapid succession—matching the violent rhythm of his heart. The sigils flared brighter, feeding on him, drinking him in. Silvery-blue currents coursed along his body, crawling over his arms like living threads. Lightning snapped from the blade, striking the walls with feral hunger. Keller did not flinch. He reveled in it. His lips parted and words spilled out in something ancient. Something that sounded like it had been buried beneath creation itself. Deep in the smallest corner of his mind, Keller understood. He was not merely being used. He had opened the door. He had invited the dark to sit beside him. A puppet does not smile when the strings tighten. Keller did. His boots lifted from the floor. He rose slowly, suspended within the blood-marked circle, cloak swaying as if underwater. He looked down at the world beneath him with a strange calm—like a man already saying farewell to who he had been.

Power flooded through his veins. Hot. Devouring. It was an ecstasy that surpassed anything he'd ever experienced. For a fleeting moment, he wondered if this was how gods were born. Then the last fragment of light inside him flickered…and went out. Darkness welcomed him home. A thunderous boom split the chamber. The air turned heavy—ancient. Lucifer snarled through Keller's mouth, but the voice did not belong to mortal lungs. It reverberated through stone, through bone, through his soul.

"Blood of my blood…Bleed upon the holy ground. Boiling in my hellfire. Bear my mark." The sigils trembled. "Let the sealed earth awaken. Let the blade drink. Pierce their hearts. Gather the souls, my champion. Now…it begins."

The presence inside him was too vast to stay contained. It pressed against Keller's flesh like a god trying to wear a mortal skin. Then—gone. Lucifer withdrew as swiftly as a storm receding from the sky. For a heartbeat, Keller was empty. No thought. No will. Just a hollow vessel collapsing onto cold stone. His body struck the floor with a sickening thud. His eyes rolled white, showing nothing of the man inside.

John surged forward instantly, seizing the vacancy like a starving beast. Adrenaline flooded Keller's limbs as John forced the body upright. A roar tore from his throat—raw, feral, inhuman. His lips peeled back into a monstrous grin, revealing sharp teeth not meant for men. The sword was ripped from the floor and driven down again—hard—into the heart of the pentagram. The symbols flared violently. Light and shadow twisted together. The hum returned, deeper now. The room knew a greatest of evil had touched it. And it answered. A violent clash of angelic radiance erupted against the demonic force inside Keller's body. Light repelled darkness in a vicious surge, forcing its way outward. A protective sphere formed around Keller, the sword, and the blood-marked pentagram. It expanded like a second sun, humming with divine resistance. The sigils blazed white-hot, pressing against the barrier in relentless waves. Heaven pushed. Hell defied. The chamber quaked under the strain. Still gripping the hilt, John watched the dragon's sapphire eyes dim. Their brilliant blue faded to glassy translucence—the archangelic blessing unraveling before his gaze. A breath of silver smoke spilled from the dragon's carved mouth. The sword exhaled holiness and inhaled blood.

The pentagram drained into the blade as if the steel itself thirsted. Crimson veins crawled upward along the engraved scales. Burgundy stained the once-silver mental. The dragon's eyes filled last, flooding red until nothing else remained. The blessing died and the curse took root. The blade was reborn and the necromancer was restored. John tore the sword free from the floor. Victory flashed across his expression—sharp and feral—but it was short-lived. His control over Keller's body flickered. He was weakening. The hum grew louder now into a Harold chanting. A misstep now would mean annihilation. He bolted from the chamber, driving Keller's body at inhuman speed through Sebastian's abandoned quarters and into the winding corridors. Behind him, the divine barrier collapsed. The angelic force imploded inward—then detonated. Light erupted brighter than a thousand suns, blasting through consecrated stone as if it were dust. Walls fractured. Scared foundations screamed. The Order's sanctuary was being purged. John burst into the high chamber just as cracks splintered across the ceiling. Beams of heavenly light spread through widening fissures. Stones were raining down. Mortar split. The holy ground itself rejected what had been done beneath it.

His strength faltered. Keller's legs buckled. Then John saw it—a rupture above. A wound in the world. The open sky. Clutching the cursed blade to his chest, he gathered the last of his power. Keller's knees bent, coiled like a spring. Then he launched them upward. The ground shattered beneath the force. Debris chased them skyward as John wove a failing shield against falling ruin. His roar tore through Keller's throat as he fought to maintain control. They burst from the earth in a spray of dirt and stone. Keller's body crashed onto the surface with brutal force. John's presence wavered, thinning like smoke in wind. He pulled the blade close, savoring its pulse—its new, dark heartbeat. Above them, the sky burned orange with dusk. His vision dimmed and darkness crept in. With the last of his strength, he laughed manically, as he was receding into the void where Keller's soul was being transformed.

CHAPTER NINE
RUNNING ALONG THE COAST

May 18th, 1881

Riding their chosen steed, Maximous, they cut through the Indiana woodland like a shadow tearing across the earth. Only the rhythmic thunder of hooves and the wild drum of Eli's heart filled the night. The forest thickened, swallowing them in darkness. Branches whispered past them, leaves shuddering in their wake. The moon hung thin and pale overhead, barely daring to witness their flight. Eli kept one arm firm around Roslyn's waist. The horse ran hard beneath them, muscles straining, breath steaming in the cold night air. Still, he felt every quaver in her body—the tension she tried so carefully to hide. As shadows lengthened across the land, Eli had driven Maximous harder, the stallion's hooves tearing through dry earth and fallen leaves alike as they searched for water. Hope turned to silent prayers. Prayers to panic. Panic to dread. Until the scent of water found them. Relief struck like lightning then.

Now the moon climbed higher into the ink-black sky, silver and merciless. The lake was close—only miles away now—but the moon did not care for distance. For the past hour, the beast inside him had clawed at his ribs, demanding release as they raced toward the shore. Fear gripped his throat that they wouldn't make it in time. But he would rather break his own bones than frighten her with his own worry. Together on horse top, they painfully fought against the calling of the moon. It demanded them to change their flesh to fur as their bodies unwillingly bent to comply. However, their wills swayed the impulse from becoming fully transformed. So, they lingered within a limbo, mangled between human and beast.

"Go," he commanded, harsh and sharp. Eli gritted his teeth as he pushed the horse harder. Knowing the lake was on other side of the woods, their breakneck speed had only increased and had to get to the it before it was too late. Eli leaned closer to Roslyn, his voice lower near her ear. "We're almost there," he promised.

"Eli…hurry," Roslyn's voice came small. Fragile. Breaking. "The moon is breaking me." She lurched forward over the saddle horn as the change seized her. A sharp crack sounded beneath his hands. Then another. Fire rolled through her abdomen like molten iron. Her ribs began to break outward one by one as they made room for her expanding lungs. Her fingers dug into the leather. Her breath hitched in shallow gasps. She tried to scream—but pain stole the sound from her throat, leaving only thin, wounded squeaks.

Eli's grip tightened instinctively. Terror coiled in his chest. Not yet. Not before the water. "Stay with me," he said low and steady despite the fear sharpening inside him. "Just a little longer, Roslyn. I've got you." Eli caught the collar of her dress before his strength entirely gave out. He pulled her upright, saving her from slipping from the saddle and becoming trampled by Maximous. Her small frame convulsed against him. He drew her back to his chest, anchoring her there, one powerful arm braced under her waist while his leg secured hers against the horse's flank. His heart twisted painfully at her suffering. "I know, love," he said empathically near her temple. "Only moments more. Stay with me." He urged further, pressing a brief kiss into her hair like a vow rather than comfort. If pain could be carried, he would have taken every ounce of it from her body into his own.

She leaned back his broad chest, which rose in shallow, controlled breaths. Slowly, he realized she was matching her breathing to his—borrowing his calm to steady her breaking body. Even through the pounding of her heart against his arm, he felt the rhythm begin to settle. A silent trust. A shared survival. Eli swallowed hard. He only needed to get her to the water. Just a little farther. Pain rippled through his body. His broken leg strained uselessly in the stirrup, his mangled hand barely able to grip the rains as his spine shifted beneath his skin with a sickening pull. The change was coming whether he welcomed it or not. He forced himself not to look to closely at Roslyn—but he couldn't stop seeing it. Her nose broken and bloodied. The delicate tips of elongated ears piercing through strands of shedding hair. One side of her skull dented inward were bone fought to reshape itself. She was mid-change. So was he. They were both trapped between man and beast. And when the moon reached its throne at the peak of the sky, their will would no longer matter.

"Stay with me, little wolf. Don't let the moon take you yet." To keep from screaming through the agony, Eli gnashed his teeth together until his jaw threatened to break. His vision blurred, the world smearing at the edges as pain dragged his focus away from the path. He shook his head sharply, forcing clarity. Then he saw it. A massive fallen oak sprawled across their path like a grave marker. Too close. Too sudden. Maximous wouldn't correct himself in time. The stallion would crash, snap a leg, and send them all tumbling. A death sentence for the horse. Possibly for Roslyn. Eli refused that fate. With a raw shout, he snapped the reins one-handed. *Crack!* The leather snapped through the air beside Maximous's ears. The stallion surged forward in alarm. "Hold to me, little wolf." Eli locked an arm around Roslyn's waist, pulling her firmly against him as he braced "Jump, Maximous!"

The proud stallion surged and cleared the fallen oak in a powerful, fluid leap. Eli's body lifted with the motion, then settled back into the saddle as Maximous landed in full stride. Only then did Eli realize he had been holding his breath. He exhaled slowly. "Good boy," he said, voice rough with gratitude. Maximous answered with a pleased snort. Eli titled his gaze skyward, searching for the moon through the canopy. Branches tangled overhead, shielding them from its relentless pull. For a moment, it was mercy. His eyes flicked between the narrowing path and the fractured glimpses of starlight above. The higher the moon climbed, the less time they had. As the forest began to thin, silver beams of moonlight pierced through the trees, striping the ground in pale light. The path brightened. Maximous tossed his head, grateful for the sight over instinct. Eli stroked his neck once in silent praise. Eli breathed a quiet prayer of thanks for the animal beneath him. Bucky had nearly refused to part with the horse, but in the end, even he had seen the urgency. Maximous was no ordinary mount. The trees thinned at last. Blurring trunks gave away to open air, and through the clearing Eli caught sight of glittering water stretching into darkness. Then came the pale shimmer of damp, silver sand lining the shore of Lake Michigan. Relief struck him like a prayer answered. Above the swaying water, the moon loomed large and swollen, nearing it cruel peak. Its light spilled across the lake in ribbons, as if beckoning them closer—like a long-awaited relative welcome them home.

"Roslyn," Eli breathed, voice tight with hope. "We've made it. Look—the water. Just ahead. Only seconds more." Deliverance lived in that water. In its cold mercy was salvation. The lake mirrored the cloudless sky so perfectly it looked endless—a silver world between earth and heaven. Too perfect. Too fragile. Eli eased the reigns guiding Maximous down from a breakneck sprint to a hard gallop. Every heartbeat mattered now. Every stride was borrowed time.

Roslyn saw Maximous's bobbing head break through the last wall of trees. The moment he stepped into the clearing, the world opened wide—water and shoreline stretching threefold before them like a promised sanctuary. A brisk wind curled around their bodies, cool and inviting, coaxing them to linger when they had no time to spare. Gentle waves sighed against the sand in a steady rhythm, blending with the endless chorus of crickets, frogs, and whining mosquitoes hidden in the brush. The lake caught the moonlight and shattered it into a thousand sparks—diamonds scattered across black velvet. For a fleeting heartbeat, it felt like paradise. Rosyn ached to sink into that water. To let it cradle her. To let the cold steal the fire tearing through her bones. Then the pain struck again. Sharp. Merciless. It twisted through her leg like a blade. Her muscles contorted as bone strained beneath skin. She bit down hard, trapping her scream behind clenched teeth until it quaked through her jaw. Eli felt it down the bond before he saw it.

"What's happening, Ros?" Fear cracked in his voice. He pulled Maximous to a halt and quickly tied the reins to a low branch. He tore another strip from his dirt-stained tunic and gently tired it over Maximous's eyes. The stallion snorted but remained steady. Eli knew the animal would panic and cause too much noise at the sight of their transformation if left uncovered.

Eager to be free from the saddle and the tormenting pain, she tried removing herself from on top of Maximous. "Eli, my leg—put me down. Now. I can't bear it another second." Desperation cracked her voice. She tried to slide from the horse's back, but her body betrayed her, collapsing under the strain.

Eli's gaze dropped to her leg. The bone pressed grotesquely against her skin—not pierced through, but close enough to turn his stomach with anger. He's seen Roslyn shift countless times now, but tonight. Tonight, the transformation felt like a punishment because they waited too long. It angered him to see her like this.

"I'll carry you to the water. Between us we have one good leg left." A humorless breath escaped him. Eli knew horses were easily skittish and had to keep the steed calm, especially when they transformed. Hurriedly, he looked at the moon and saw it inching even closer to high-rise. They were nearly out of time. Working fast, Eli reached for Roslyn with his unbroken hand. He gathered the fabric at the back of her dress and lifted her into his arms. Pain exploded through him. A sickening crack split the air as a bone broke in Eli's shoulder. His arm gave way mid-motion.

"Goddamn it," he gritted through his gnashed teeth. He lost his grip. Roslyn slipped from his hold. Roslyn felt the support of Eli's strength faltered. The world tilted. She felt herself. and she felt herself falling. Frantic, her fingers clawed for anything—cloth, flesh, the saddle. Her grip caught his leg. Her other hand latched onto the waistband of his trousers. They collapsed together. Sand rushing up to meet them. A tangled head of broken bodies and ragged breath.

Pushing through the blurring pain that his head pulsed with now, Eli fought through the agony as the skin along his arms began to split. "We have to move. Roslyn, the water is right there, baby. Just a few feet more." His voice was calm, but there was enough quake in his tone to make it sound like a command and a plea.

"I can't walk," Roslyn cried, rolling onto her back, moonlight bathed her tear-streaked face. The change surged through her veins like lightning. Her bones pulsed. Her muscles twisted. Her will began to fracture beneath the moon's call. "Try," Eli urged as he pulled her up against him, but she fell. "Please…try, Ros." He pressed. He knew this pain. He had lived it since childhood—the agony of waiting too long, of resisting the inevitable. But Roslyn had not. Her mind was still human enough to fear what her body already understood.

Without further thought, he forced himself upright. Eli balanced on his one good leg, and he steadied on his feet. Feeling his bones shift and splinter even worse now since they were fully in moonlight, the other dragged uselessly behind him. He dug his foot in the sand, putting all his weight on his unbroken leg and bent to lift her into his arms. A scream clawed up his throat, but he controlled it. Controlled the pain by pushing it down and focusing on the task. "Arms around my neck," he commanded softly as he wrapped her limp arms around him. Obedient to his directive, Roslyn did as he asked. She held onto him as hard as she could, which was hardly a grasping hold since she was so weak.

He limped. Toward the lake. Each step left like walking on splintered glass. Each breath tasted of iron as his gums began to bleed and his teeth began to loosen to make way for the fangs that were ready to push through. Each step was a small victory as they edge closer to the water. He moved on for her. He watched her pale face glisten with sweat and small tears in her flesh that welled in thin lines of blood. Her eyes were squeezed shut, lashes wet with tears, jaw trembling as she endured the breaking of her own bones. Then came the sound again. A wet, internal snap. Then another. Eli's teeth ground together as his jaw began to loosen under the shift. Dry sand gave way to firmer soil. Then to wet, pulling silt that tried to drag him down. But he didn't stop. He waded forward. Water climbed his legs. His waist. His ribs. Cold salvation wrapped around them. He lifted his eyes to the sky. The moon had reached its throne. Full. Unforgiving. Absolute. "Roslyn," he whispered, forehead touching hers, "hold your breath." Relief and dread struck him in the same heartbeat. Then he plunged them both beneath the freezing water. Moonlight speared through the lake's surface, silver beams reaching down to claim them. It wrapped around their bodies like divine summons.

Fish scattered at their intrusion, darting away as the water itself seemed to recoil from what was about to be born in the depths. Roslyn released Eli's neck. Her fingers slipped from him as the first violent tremor gripped her body. She drifted backward, suspended in the dark water, her chestnut-brown curls floating like a halo around her face. Her cotton gown waved around, both afloat and suspended. She began to jolt in sharp twitches. Then came the first snap. Her body jolted again. Then another. And another. Eli watched helplessly as he stood paralyzed at the bottom of the lake transforming as she floated above him. Her bones reshaped beneath her skin. Her spine arched unnaturally, vertebrae pressing outward until one tore through the fragile barrier of flesh. A silent scream rippled through the water. Her spine curved and broke through the bottom of her back, puncturing through thin skin. Rapidly, muscles, tendons, and skin took life. In a twisting mold, they surrounded the exposed bones that created her beastly shape.

Then his turn came. Torment detonated in his skull. Eli released a choking scream as his jaw cracked wide beyond its natural limit, splitting at the corner as his face thrust forward. A snout burst through, fur already sprouting along its length. Pushing through Eli's head, a fur covered snout snarled and snapped. His human skin peeled away in ghostly ribbons, drifting like shed parchment into the water. The desquamation revealed thick black fur, sleek and alive. Their bodies thrashed in the water—a storm of blood, tattered fabric, and breaking flesh. Then suddenly, the thrashing stopped. Stillness came and they were transformed. Crimson unfurled around their bodies like ink in water. Moonlight filtered through it, turning the red into something almost beautiful. Almost holy. Slowly, the current carried the blood away as the fish began to nip at their dispensed flesh and muscle. What remained below the surface were no longer two broken humans—but two beasts, newly born beneath the gaze of the moon.

Turning beneath the water, Eli caught a flash of white in the darkness. Roslyn. Her resplendent white fur shimmered in the filtered moonlight like a spirit gliding through the depths. She looked toward him—her pale brilliance beside his shadowed black coat. Their eyes held. No words. Just knowing. He gave a subtle nod. *Rise.* Roslyn began swimming toward the surface whereas Eli pressed his clawed paws into the silty bottom and ascended. Together they rose. The lake released them like a secret. They emerged from the surface as creatures reborn—tall, silent, sovereign beneath the moon. Water streamed from their fur in silver ribbons as they stepped onto the shore. Roslyn's gaze shifted to Maximous. The stallion paced in tight half-circles, muscles tense, nostrils flaring. The reigns kept him bound to a small radius of safety. He didn't like the blindfold much.

She flicked her golden eyes toward her mate. Her voice reached Eli's mind, warm, filled with gratitude and breathless. "Thank you for not letting me break."

Eli's reply rolled through her thoughts, deep and steady. "*You are my world. I am your shield. There was never another ending for us.*" He stepped close, instinct guiding him more than reason. He pulled her into him, nuzzling into the curve of her neck, breathing in the scent that was uniquely Roslyn beneath the wolf. His hands lingered at her waist—then he felt it. A flutter. His body stilled

Roslyn felt the shift of his growing alarm. "*What's wrong?*"

Taken back, he focused past the sound of the waves…past the drum of her heart…and there it was. Another rhythm. Small and fragile. Alive. "*I can hear him now,*" was all he was able to manage to say as he looked at her. The words left him in a stunned whisper. He pulled back as if struck. His eyes dropped to her stomach—still slender, still her—and yet now impossibly different knowing that his son lived. His gaze lifted to hers, wide with awe. It was surreal to hear his son's heartbeat at last.

Roslyn stood perfectly still, though every muscle in her body coiled tight beneath her white fur. Once, she feared time. Now time had caught her. Five months. Five silent, secrets months. She held Eli's gaze without flinching, though a thousand thoughts stormed behind her golden eyes. She wondered which truth he would see first—the woman before him or the life she carried. She slowly shook her head in denial, but in surrender.

Eli's thoughts came strained, hesitant. "*I've known,*" He confessed to her. If it wasn't for the vision he had, he knew the moment her scent changed. Their son was growing. The promise written in fate.

"*How*?" She asked incredulously.

"*The night before we fled Brazil…we laid together as husband and wife.*" His gaze softened with memory, but his dark eyes glistened—haunted by the other memories that came forward. "*Your scent changed after conception—sweeter, more earthy. I noticed it while we were on the ship. It's gotten stronger every night since.*" His voice deepened, but it did edge with hurt. "*Why didn't you tell me? And Please don't lie to me, Roslyn. Your eyes never learned how.*" He stepped closer, searching her face. "*Five months is more than enough time for life to take root. I felt every shift inside of you. I didn't know if it was going to live since I hadn't heard a beat until now, but you could. The very moment it started thumping. You could hear it.*" Hurt seeped heavy into his next question. "*Did you truly think I wasn't paying attention? To everything that is you?*"

She looked away from him. Head hung low. "*If you already know, then why didn't you say anything*?" She spoke softly, but the strain beneath was clear. She did not want a fight. Not tonight. Not with the moon still humming in her blood and guilt coiled in her chest.

Eli finally broke and snapped at her. Teeth clicking together. "*Because I needed to hear it from you.*" His voice cut low and sharp. "*Truth sounds different when it's spoken, Roslyn. It becomes real.*"

Roslyn lifted her gaze to his towering frame. His black fur still glistened from the lake, drying in the cool air. Those ebony, unwavering eyes pinned her in place. She held his stare, refusing to back down though guilt clawed at her ribs. Then her truth surfaced in a roar of defiance. Her brow furrowed. Her spine was straightened. Her guilt hardened into resolve. She released a sharp breath through her snout, and snapped back. "I will speak when you do, Eli." Her golden eyes flashed. "*Tell me the truth about my brother's death. Tell me why we are in the middle of nowhere, running from who, exactly. You say the Order, but there is so much more. I may be new to your world, but I am not the fragile human you still see me as. Blood of your blood, Eli. We are one. We are blood-bound. Mated.*"

Hating the tabled turned on him, Eli released a guttural growl that built into a full, frustrated roar. The sound ripped across the shoreline. Maximous whinnied sharply in alarm, stomping the sand. Eli's gaze snapped back to Roslyn. She stood poised and alert—waiting, watching, demanding truth without another word. He felt it then. The weight of it. She carried his child. His blood. And suddenly every enemy had a face. Keller's face. His shoulders sagged. The anger drained into memory. Into something heavier. Regret.

"*The night he died…*" his voice lowered, "*I tracked him by blood.*" *He looked past her, seeing the past instead.* "*He'd cut his hands somehow. Left prints along the alley ways. At first, I thought it was a trick. A diversion.*" His jaw clenched. "*Then I heard the howl.*" His eyes darkened. "*It wasn't a call, but it was a warning. By then smoke filled the alley. Thick. Black. It took all I had not to choke, but I howled back, but he never answered again.*" He exhaled slowly. "*I climbed to the rooftops to escape the smoke. By the time I reached the building…it was already burning. Leonardo died in that fire.*" Eli's black eyes fixed on hers.

Roslyn saw it instantly. Felt it through the bond that he had mostly closed off until now. Now, there was only truth. His thoughts bled into hers, and the visions followed—smoke, fire, falling beams, the taste of ash. Eli spoke quietly. The memory weighed every word. "*I thought I was alone...but someone else was there.*" He growled as he barred his teeth. "*I saw him. The Commander of the Holy Order of St. Michael. His face…*" Eli swallowed. "*The fire had ruined it. Melted it into something unrecognizable. But he didn't scream in pain nor did he run far. He watched…and he spoke to Leonardo as if making some fucked up promise. He spoke to his body…not like a stranger. Like a man who believed he had been wronged.*"

Roslyn's pulse hammered. Her breath turned shallow. Questions clawed at her throat, but she forced herself to stay silent. If she spoke, she might fracture the memory—and she needed to see all of it. Eli's gaze flicked to her, something like dread darkening his eyes. The vision began to dim. He was going to end it.

"*No,*" she breathed, "*Show me.*" She demanded. Eli hesitated as he wrestled with his thoughts. With a reluctant sigh, he opened the memory again and let it flow through their bond. The alley reformed around them. Smoke choked the air. Embers drifted like dying stars.

Roslyn watched the commander run into the narrow passage. She saw Eli leap from the rooftop, shadowing him in silence.

"Ros," Eli's voice threaded through the memory, "brace yourself. *What he said….it wasn't right.*"

She was lost to the world around her now, living inside the memory. She was in her human form standing next to Eli in the memory. The commander stopped before the inferno. He did not speak to the flames. He spoke to her brother. To the body burning within. His voice was low. Calm. Reverent in a way that made her skin crawl. He stepped closer to the blaze, eyes reflecting the fire like molten gold.

"*This was your fault, Leo…It took a year, but I kept my word….No matter how long it takes or wherever I must go, I will kill Eli and I will have Roslyn for myself…you would've lived longer if you would've just given me her like I wanted….I will leave her still warm body to those…*"

Roslyn's stomach twisted violently. Her breath hitched. Her blood ran cold. Those were the words of a man staking claim. Her skin prickled with the sensation of being watched…chosen…owned. A revolting dread slithered through her veins. She felt stripped bare by his intent, as though his voice had reached through time to brush a finger along her flesh. He knew her, but not as a person—as a possession. The commander shifted. Turned. Firelight revealed the ruin of his face—bloody, warped, made monstrous by flame and obsession alike. Her breath snagged. Her voice trembled into the memory. "*Is that—*"

Eli cut her off, answering. "*Keller.*" The name fell between them like a stone. "Your childhood friend. The one you had spoke of, the one I never met—not once. I didn't know the Order's commander and your friend—that they were the same man… until that night." The night seemed to fall silent around them. Wind brushed through their fur. The next words came slower. "He waited. He watched. And when the moment was right…he killed your brother. He's been watching us. All this time. Waiting."

The alley faded, but Keller's vow did not. It echoed inside her like a curse. *I will have Roslyn.* Her body shivered. Her lungs refused to fill as shock bound her in the moment. This had never been about the

Order or the power they have. It had always been about her. Her voice came out hollow. "*He didn't just kill my brother.*" She swallowed hard. "*He was clearing the path to me.*" Fear settled deep in her bones—not for herself, but for everyone tied to her heart. For her unborn child. For Eli. For all the people he killed and will kill for in her name. Because Keller was no longer the wounded boy she once saved. He was a man who made vows to the dead—And meant to keep them.

It all made sense now. Roslyn felt her world shift. Her legs gave out. She collapsed onto the sand. It took a darker shade, and everything seemed even more foreign than what it already was. Roslyn looked to the damp sand as she swallowed a lump of bile. Feeling guilty for being the reason of her brother's death.

"*He killed my brother. My blood…*" A long, broken, haunted howl tore from her chest. "*I saved his life, Eli.*" Fury edged her voice as it boomed in him mind. "*And he repaid me with betrayal because he couldn't make me his.*" She bit out scathingly, claws digging into the damp sand. "*He was just a boy when I found him. Bloodied and half-dead.*" Her eyes unfocused, lost in memory. "*He barely spoke to me at first, but he would watch me like I was something…I don't know…like something warm in a cold world.*"

Her gaze dropped. "*We became friends. Real friends.*" The wind lifted strands of her pale fur. "*He used to sneak away from the orphanage just to see me. He didn't like other people around us because he trusted no one. So, I kept him separate…it was always just us.*" Her voice darkened as the pieces began to fall further into place. "*Then we grew older. And something in him changed. I didn't fear him then, but my instincts told me not to be alone with him.*" Her golden eyes glistened. "*When he confessed his feelings, I refused him.*" She finally looked at Eli. "*I told him my heart was already yours.*" Her voice cracked. "*He had smile. He said he understood.*" A tear slipped free. "I believed him." Her gaze drifted to the water. "*I never imagined he'd spill my brother's blood…or hunt us like prey.*" She looked at Eli, torn between denial and truth. But deep in her soul—acceptance already lived with fear. "*And our child grows…lives. It's strong.*"

Sitting down onto the sand. He leaned forward, elbows on his knees, massive clawed hands bracing his bowed head. The moonlight shimmered across the lake. Its serenity mocking the storm inside him. He breathed. Once. Twice. Regaining control the way a warrior does before battle. When he finally spoke his voice was steady. Eli turned his head slowly, his black eyes settling on her. For a moment, he said nothing. Then his words filled her mind. "*I don't know what I'm supposed to feel.*" His voice was low. Rough. "*A part of me wants joy. I know I should feel it…but I don't. All I feel is numb. And tired.*" His gaze drifted back to the water. "*There's a madman building an army to hunt us. I don't know when he'll strike. Or where. Only that he will. All to claim you. To spill blood for pride and obsession.*" A bitter breath escaped him. His jaw tightened. "*I fear for our lives before, but now—Now I fear for our child too.*" He looked away, disgust curling his lip. "*That night…I ran. Ran like a coward.*" His voice dropped to a growl. "*I could've killed him. I should have. That failure has stalked me every night since.*" Then he turned back to her, intensity burning in his gaze. "*But I chose you. I needed to make sure you were safe. I chose your life. Our future.*" Eli's voice hardened to steel. "*When the battle comes…you will run. You will hide. Somewhere far from here. Our child will need you. Even if it means leaving me behind. Do you understand me?*"

Roslyn's gaze snapped to him, panic rising in her voice. "*No.*" The word cut sharp into his mind. She dragged herself across the sand toward him, ignoring the ache still simmering in her bones. "*I will not leave you.*" Her golden eyes burned with defiance. "*I didn't choose this life to survive it without you.*"

Eli exhaled slowly, dragging his hands down his face. "*This isn't about choice anymore.*" His voice had shifted—firm and immoveable. "*It's about survival.*" He lowered his hands and looked at her fully. "*You're carrying a Beast Blood child now. That changes everything.*" He moved closer, his tone quiet but heavier. "*Our children aren't raised like mortals. They feel the moon. They feel and see…everything, differently. You shouldn't have to do that alone.*" He brushed his hands along the side of her face. He hesitated. For the first time, uncertainty flickered in his eyes. "*Roslyn…if I fall—*" He forced the words out. "*You run. You do not come back for me. If I survive, I will find you and our child again. You do not look for revenge.*" He placed his forehead against hers as his voice lowered into something almost pleading. "*You live.*"

"*Don't you dare say that.*" Roslyn's voice cut sharp, but it trembled at the edges. "*Don't speak of endings when we still breathe.*" Her gaze softened as it lifted to the moonlight. "*Until life itself is stripped from the earth, there's hope.*" A quieter breath followed. "*I feel it…here.*" She pressed a clawed hand gently over her stomach. "*Our child is hope, Eli. A different kind. A stronger kind.*"

Eli studied her eyes. They still held light. Still held belief. Too much belief for the world they lived in. A faint ache stirred in his chest—not from the transformation, but from the knowledge she had yet to learn how cruel fate could be. She was not ready for that truth. Not tonight. He exhaled slowly, letting the tension leave him for the first time in hours. Some things did not need to be spoken twice. The rest would come with time—and blood. So instead, he leaned forward and nudged her temple with his nose, a quiet wolfish gesture of affection. A moment of normalcy. A moment of almost-peace. Then her stomach betrayed her with a low growl. His ears flicked. A faint smirk tugged at his muzzle. "*You and our little hope are hungry.*"

Roslyn huffed a soft breath. "*Starving, actually.*"

Eli's gaze drifted over the lake. The moon now hung lower, brushing its reflection across the water like spilled silver. Stars shimmered in the slow-moving waves, and in the distance a lighthouse turned its patient eye across the dark. On its second sweep, an idea surfaced. "*When we entered the water, fish scattered everywhere,*" he said quietly. "*Trout, I think. I can catch enough for us.*"

Roslyn's ears twitched with interest. "*Anything sounds good,*" she said. "*But I should learn to hunt below the water too… not just on land.*" A future-minded thought. A mother-minded thought.

A faint warmth touched Eli's voice. "*I'd be glad to teach you, my dear.*" He rose and extended his hand. She placed hers in his without hesitation. His grip was steady. Grounding. A silent promise. When she stood, she caught him looking at her stomach. It was wonder. The kind that comes from realizing something exists beyond war and vengeance. Her breath caught. His gaze lifted to hers.
A small nod passed between them—a conversation without words.

"*Come into the water with me,*" Eli murmured. His voice was tight, thick with emotion he refused to show. Because he could hear it again. That second heartbeat. Strong. Persistent. And though he would never say it aloud, the thought lingered: *I may not live to watch you grow. But I will make sure you have a world to live in."*

CHAPTER TEN
WITH THE LIGHT OF DAWN

As the night surrendered to daybreak, the sky churned with the pale colors of sunrise. Like a tiny spark of flame on kindling, a brilliant orange hue burst forth from the horizon. It stretched higher and higher, until the heaven's were swathed in a golden glow. In the Sun's wake the earth began to warm, warding the last remnants of the night's chill. The shifting elements thickened the lingering fog, turning it whiter, heavier—a veil draped over the shoreline. Despite the dense haze, Harriet and Anne kept to their daily routine. Side by side, they guided their sturdy horses along the wide stretch of beach.

Usually, their rides were filled with laughter and idle gossip, but today stewing silence walked beside them. Falling back into childish habits, the two women exchanged sharp glances as they rode side by side. Harriet narrowed her cobalt eyes at Anne, holding the stare until Anne finally looked her way. The moment their gazes met, Harriet sniffed and tossed her chin high, her rounded nose pointed proudly toward the sky.

Anne rolled her brown eyes with an exaggerated groan. In retaliation, she stuck out her tongue and scrunched her face into a mocking expression.

Harriet caught it and bristled in irritation. Enough so that she broke her vow of silence and shouted to the thin, curly brown-haired woman. "This is ridiculous," she barked. "We're too old to keep doing this shit. We're acting like bratty children."

Anne scoffed. "Speak for yourself. You started it, Harriet." Her brows knit together, creasing her forehead in indignation.

Harriet rolled her eyes in exasperation, her voice snapping like a whip with pent-up vexation. "Dammit, Anne, I told you I had a bad feeling about riding today. I didn't want to go, but you had to be so damn stubborn and go out into the fog. So, I followed. And now we're completely lost in the cursed fog." She gestured at the white haze around them. "That makes *you* the fool here."

Any other time Anne would've had a lighter heart and found their bickering endearing. But she was too upset—too obstinate to push it aside this time. She gasped, "The audacity," and jerked her head toward Harriet, glare blazing. She saw her friend's large, furred cap that had covered most of her humble features. Only one slanted blue eye peeked at her from under the lopsided brim. "I am not!" Anne snapped. "And stop calling me names you—you….spinster hag!"

Harriet snorted. "I've had more men flutter these old skirts even now than you ever did in your youth." She laughed, then added with wicked satisfaction, "That's why you're angry. You're in a dry spell." She leaned closer and muttered, "A twenty-year dry spell."

Anne straightened immediately, lifting her chin with offended dignity as she huffed. "You have not. Liar," she shot back.

Harriet answered with another sharp glance.

Anne exhaled hard through her nose. "Harriet, I'm nearly eighty years old and perfectly capable of riding to the border and back without *your* company or your *feelings*." Anne ignored the scoff and flicked the reigns and trotted onward.

Harriet flicked the reigns as well. Her old stallion didn't like being pushed around and whinnied in protest but clogged on. "Don't ignore me," Harriet exclaimed. "You know damn well that my 'feelings' are always true. Go with your gut, they say, and I do. By doing so, I have saved you a few times from encountering some bad situations.

Remember last Winter?" She tightened her mouth and raised her eyebrows as her eyes stared steadily at Anne.

Anne rolled her eyes. She hated it when her friend mentioned those crooks. She hadn't known they were masquerading as hired men from the board. In truth, they'd been wanted thieves and murderers across several cities. If Harriet hadn't barged past her with a shotgun in hand, they would've overpowered her. One blast she dropped a man to his knees. The second shot had robbed the other of his pride entirely. Ever since that day, they kept three loaded shotguns and plenty of shells close by.

Anne muttered defensively as she waved a dismissive hand, "How was I supposed to know about those men?"

"Well, you weren't meant to know, sweetie. That's why God gave you me—your greatest and most beautiful friend all these years." A broad smile spread across her wrinkled face. "I'm here to save you from yourself."

Anne barked out a laughter. Some of the tightness in her shoulders eased, if only a little. It was typical of Harriet to smooth over arguments with that smug, self-righteous charm of hers. Irritating—but effective. It was a ridiculous tactic to relieve an argument in a humorous manner. She sobered some and finally asked, "And why do you suppose you had one of your famous gut feelings today? Did the tides turn and the winds suddenly cast in the wrong direction?"

Harriet smiled, but she genuinely pressed her lips together in a confounding look as she thought for a moment. Then, she said with a shrug, "I'm not so sure as of now, but the day is still young. Something always shows itself."

Her gaze drifted across their surroundings. To the left, shadowed trees loomed through the thinning mist. To the right, Lake Michigan glittered beneath the rising sun. The horizon burned in fiery oranges and golds and lightening hues of blue, the water reflecting it like a painted canvas. "Looks like the fog's finally lifting," she said with a relieved sigh.

Anne snorted. "Good. I was tired of feeling like something might burst from it and snatch us clean off our saddles. That damn book you wanted to read had me all sorts of spooked." She chuckled and leaned forward, stroking the mane of her mare, Magenta, who suddenly seemed to be a bit restless and her ears perked and flicked around.

Harriet snorted, laughter bubbling out of her. She knew exactly what Anne was hinting at—they had spent the last weeks of winter reading *The Man-Wolf* by the fire. Through her snickers, she said, "Dear God, Anne. I hope you brough a silver bullet and a string of garlic. Vampires are rumored to roam the Indiana woods too, you know."

Anne replied smartly, casting her a sly look. "Oh, I used my last silver bullet on that hairy captain you were snogging last month. As for the garlic? I'm saving that for the next poor bloke you drag home."

Their laughter rang out across the beach—bright and careless, until Magenta, normally docile as a lamb, reared in sudden panic. Her hooves thrashed the air. Anne screamed in fear certain she would be thrown. But she leaned low over the mare's neck, gripping tight, swearing and trying to calm the startled creature.

A flicker of fast movement caught Harriet's eye. She glanced down and saw it. A woman's body lay sprawled in the sand beneath Magenta's shadow, screaming as she looked up at them. Harriet's scream ripped across the shoreline.

Eli and Roslyn—naked in their human forms— jolted awake at the shrill whinny of a horse and the piercing scream of a woman. Roslyn's eyes flew open just in time to see massive hooves descending toward her head. She cried out and scrambled, but the sand dragged at her limbs. She wasn't fast enough. Eli reacted first. He lunged, catching her by the waist and rolling her over his body as the horse's hooves slammed into the ground where her skull had been a heartbeat earlier. Sand burst around them in a gritty spray.

"Get behind me, Roslyn!" Eli yelled. She didn't hesitate. Still gripping her hand, he rose to his feet and pulled her close behind his larger frame, placing himself between her and the mounted riders. His eyes never left them. His posture said what words didn't—one wrong move and he would become the beast again.

"Thank God…she's alive," Harriet breathed, clutching her chest as her pulse steadied. The mares were quickly settled, and both women stared in stunned silence at the sight before them—a naked man shielding an equally naked woman with the stance of a warrior. Panicked, the shock was evident upon their faces, and for a long moment, no one spoke.

Harriet looked at Anne as she sat in disbelief, turning all shades of red at the sight they were witnessing. Anne didn't look back at Harriet though. She was squinting, studying the pair more carefully, trying to observe them without gawking. The man's coal-colored eyes looked between the two women as he stood there in silence. The young man was exceptionally built with corded muscle like that of a lumberjack, and he did nothing to hide his cock that was surprisingly well hung and girthy in its current flaccid state. The woman was beautiful. Her chestnut curls hid her breasts and trailed down her stomach. She was curvy, thick with toned muscle as well. She looked like Venus. Her golden eyes seemed to shine in the light like amber specs. They were young. Striking even. Their features carried an exotic sharpness that marked them outsiders. Not locals. Not travelers she recognized.

Calmly, cautiously, she addressed the man. "Forgive the intrusion. We didn't mean to interrupt your, ahh…rendezvous." She gestured lightly between herself and Harriet. "We couldn't see you through the fog."

She finished speaking, and the strangers hadn't responded to her inquiry. Anne noticed it then—the tension in their shoulder's, the predatory stillness in the man's stance, the way the woman watched from behind him like a cornered animal. They were afraid. It was the kind of fear that bites first.

Almost like animals, she thought—and immediately dismissed the notion as foolish fancy. Still the feeling lingered. Carefully reading the tension between them, Anne spoke again, her tone gentler now. "Well…be that as it may," she said, "do you require help?" Her eyes flicked over them. "You're both without clothing, and I see none nearby. The morning air is cold enough to bite." She nodded toward the inland stretch beyond the dunes. "We live about an hour from here. Perhaps less on horseback.

"Harriet turned sharply toward her, eyes wide. "What are you doing, Anne?" she hissed.

Anne didn't look away from the man. "Listening to *my* gut," she replied quickly. The strangers understood her. She saw it in the subtle shift of them. It was the slightest easing of his shoulders, the way his stance loosened by a fraction. Not safe. Not trusting. But deciding. He was measuring them. Judging whether she was a threat…or a mercy. *They've been through something,* she thought as a feeling of validation bloomed in her stomach.

Eli studied the two overdressed elderly women with guarded suspicion. His gaze moved over them in measured passes, searching the smallest fracture in their composure—a twitch, a false breath, a scent of deceit. Nothing. Their eyes had only widened in startled fear before settling. Their heartbeats were quick, but not the frantic rhythm of liars. No malice clung to their scent. No hidden threat lingered beneath their words. They were innocent. Uninvolved. Safe. That did not mean he could afford to be.

He cast a brief glance toward Roslyn, a silent reassurance—*I have this.* To the women, it might have looked like acknowledgement of her presence. To Roslyn, it was a promise. Then he turned back and spoke, his English precise and controlled. "Yes, you came just in time. My wife and I were in danger," he said evenly. "But you just frightened them off and scared us in the process as we were forced to stay naked and laying down."

Harriet scanned the areas looking for anything amiss. "How so, stranger? Robbers?"

Anne sniffed and muttered, "The bandits must be back. Chicago's a breeding ground for crime, I tell you."

Eli did not correct them. A lie filled in by assumptions was sometimes more believable than one told outright. He gave them a premise, and they filled in the blanks making the lie fluid and complete. Eli nodded, slipping seamlessly into the story they spun together. His expression was slightly softer now, relaxed, but his eyes were cold and distant as if the memory still stung. "Yes," he said quietly. "Two men held us at gunpoint. They forced us to remove our clothes and jewelry. Took everything. His jaw flexed. "Until you arrived, one had the reins of our horse, and the other had us on the ground. They were ready to kill us." The lie came so smoothly, so grimly, that even he could almost taste its truth.

Harriet's brows pinched as she pieced it together. "They must've bolted when the heard us. And in the fog, you wouldn't see where they ran."

Eli gave a slight nod—not confirming nor denying, but just enough for it to remain believable.

Harriet's attention shifted to Roslyn. Her voice softened. "Then, I'm glad we arrived when we did. Do you live around here?"

Roslyn remained quiet, clutching Eli's arm. Her silence read as shock to the women. Only Eli felt the tension in her grip—the instinct to flee, and the effort it took to remain still. Eli answered truthfully—or close enough to earn their sympathy. He needed to get Roslyn somewhere warm and out of the cover of day for a moment. Since their other set of stolen clothes are now shredded at the bottom of the lake, some essentials are needed.

"We have no real home here," he said evenly. "We're visitors…passing through to go visit family. "If you lovely ladies would be so kind, my wife and I could use some clothing and a possible map. I could repay you in kind. I can provide some labor. Help you with some tasks you need worked on. Cutting wood perhaps for your fire?"

Both women nearly squealed in delight as they moved off their horses at a speed that was impressive for their age. "Here, we can help you," Anne said quickly. She swung a nimble leg over her saddle and dismounted.

Harriet was already down off her mare, shrugging off her heavy fur-lined coat. She stepped toward Roslyn, holding it out with gentle insistence. "You poor, frightened thing," she said warmly. "Here. Take my jacket. I've enough layers to survive this chill. You have nothing now. The nerve of those people, leaving you children out here. I hope horrible despair comes to those ungodly creations."

Roslyn hesitated only a heartbeat before accepting. The coat dwarfed her frame, but the warmth sank deep into her trembling skin. "Thank you, she said softly, voice barely above a whisper. Taking the coat, she felt genuine gratitude towards the women. Even if it is at the expense of them admiring her mate as he chops wood for their fires. Before she could say more, Harriet stepped forward and wrapped her in a firm, motherly embrace. Roslyn gasped in surprise and Eli flicked his head in alarm. She looked at Eli and spoke through the invisible tether that synced their thoughts. "*I'm just surprised, that's all.*" She saw him relax as a small smile touched the corners of his mouth.

"All will be now love," Harriet sighed as she gave her one more comforting, squeezing hug. And for a moment, Roslyn allowed herself to believe it and hugged the woman back.

Anne followed Harriet's example and removed her own coat—though with far less composure. A rosy flush climbed her old, wrinkled cheeks as she very deliberately looked anywhere but directly at Eli. He was far too handsome for comfort, and she was far too old to notice.

"Dry spell…" Harriet said in a teasing whisper that wasn't really a whisper at all.

Clearing her throat, she thrust the coat toward him. In a rushed breath, Anne spoke while she pointedly looked into his black almond-shaped eyes. "Here you are, young man. Let's make you decent again. No need to go stirring Miss Harriet's old heart with your naked glory. It's been quite an age when she's seen a man built like you." She said with tongue in cheek.

Eli laughed. "I'm well aware," he said to Anne while looking at Harriet, flashing her a wolfish grin. He didn't know why, but it was rather fun teasing these two women. "I am sorry for our indecency and what it does to your heart, Miss Harriet."

Harriet shot Anne a scandalized look, though a blush betrayed her. He puffed out her cheeks in offense. "Oh, bollocks," she huffed, swinging herself back into her saddle. Once settled, she spoke briskly. "Wrap yourselves up tight and gather your horse. Follow us. We will take you to the lighthouse that we live in and manage together. We'll see you clothed—ill-fitting, perhaps, but decent. And we have food enough for travelers. We'll send you onward safely wherever you're bound. What are your names, dears?"

Eli was a pillar of smooth calm and strength, he stood before her adjusting the coat more snug around her, clasping together some of the round ivory buttons Harriet had missed. He smiled warmly at her as he spoke through the mental connection. "*Use false names.*" Then he straightened, voice carrying again. "I'm confident you can give them our names, love, while I ready Maximous for travel."

Anne inclined her head. "Of course." She followed Eli with her eyes before their blue stare locked onto Roslyn, whose smile faltered for a nervous heartbeat before her eyes cast downward. A blush warmed her cheeks.

Roslyn managed another soft smile, clutching the coat tighter around herself. Her voice cracked. She cleared her throat gently.

"I'm Sarah. My husband is Frank."

"*Frank?*" Eli's voice invaded her head again, loud and obviously displeased with the name she had given him. "*I don't even look like a Frank.*" He muttered.

Roslyn couldn't help but to smile, but did so toward the older woman, masking the other round of banter she had currently going on with her mate. "*And I look like a Maggie?*" she retorted with tease in her tone. "*You know lying never came naturally to me. It was the first name I could think of.*"

"*I just don't understand how—*" Eli stopped. Suprise flooded the bond. The aura was bleak and distant in a way she recognized. Something was wrong. Her brow creased in silence, but as she turned around to look at him, Eli was already guiding Maximous beside her and extended a hand. Roslyn took it. She looked up at him, the unspoken question lingering in her eyes. He gave the slightest shake of his head and answered her with a thin, grim smile. A wall had come down behind his eyes. He was concealing something. She knew it as surely as she knew the rhythm of his heartbeat.

With practiced ease, he lifted her onto the saddle and settled her in front of him as he had countless times before. The familiarity steadied her more than the coat around her shoulders. Then his voice cut through the morning air, low and firm. "Let's go."

Harriet and Anne exchanged a quick glance—subtle, but not missed—before urging their horses forward to lead the way.

Eli gave a light tug on Maximous's reins, allowing the old women to lead. Roslyn leaned back into him, just enough to feel the solid warmth of his chest. Heat bled through the layers between them, raising goosebumps along her skin. She nestled closer, the fur coat bunching beneath her chin and the hood covered over far enough so only her eyes peeked out. She whispered under her breath, careful the women couldn't hear. "Divine timing, wouldn't you say?"

"Mm-hmm." Eli replied. His tone was quiet but edged with steel.

She could feel the irritation bristling through the bond like sparks of static. "You could at least pretend to be grateful."

He bent forward, lips near her ear, his voice a low growl. "I *am* grateful you're alive. Because if that horse had crushed you, I'd have ripped it's throat out with my fucking teeth."

Roslyn's mouth fell open as she came to the horse's defense, "It wasn't the mare's fault. It was horribly foggy this morning."

"Max would've noticed you, let alone smelled you, and stopped long before that mare did." Eli replied curtly. As if on cue, Maximous gave a proud whinny.

Roslyn shot the stallion a glare, "*You* stay out of it." She scratched behind his ears anyway, earning a pleased snort.

Eli straightened, but he kept his voice low. "I don't need more people remembering our faces."

"Well," Roslyn chuckled, "if it helps, I think these two will forget about me completely and only remember you."

"Yeah," His tone was dry. "As Frank. Tomorrow I'm someone else." Then he added begrudgingly, "But today…today, I am Frank."

Roslyn huffed a quiet laugh and leaned back into him again. A heartbeat passed as his voice filled her ear again. This time it was dark, sultry and low. "The world can forget my name a thousand times, Ros…as along as it never forgets you're mine." His breath ghosted along her skin. "And since fate robbed me of you this morning… when I get you alone again. I will savor, devour every fucking inch of you until you forget how to breathe."

Excitement fluttered low in her belly at the promise. She lifted her gaze to him. His mouth hovered inches from hers—soft, sculpted and dangerously tempting. His intoxicating scent of earth and oaky musk swirled in the heat between them, thickening the air. The pull between them burned with barely controlled desire. Before she could think better of it, she leaned in and kissed the corner of his mouth.

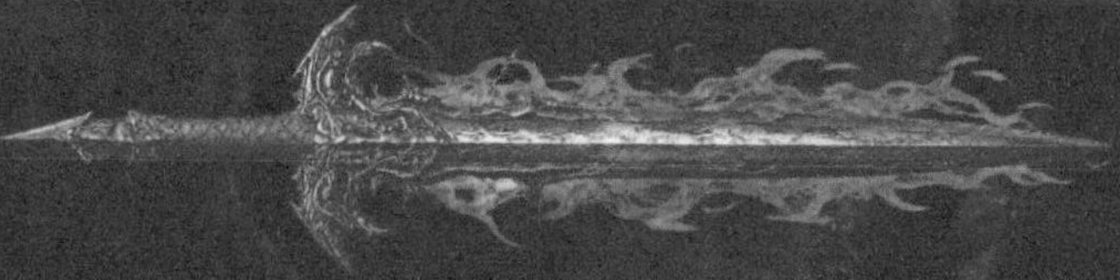

Eli's mouth claimed hers in seconds. The instant the door was shut and she turned, he had her pinned against it. His large hand wrapped around her slender throat, thumb resting beneath her chin, adding just enough pressure with a firm squeeze to command her attention. Her lashes fluttered as her gaze bore hot into his. She melted for him. He felt her surrender ripple through her body as her spine softened against the wood. With her chin lifted, her lips were his. Consuming her taste with fierce hunger, his tongue darted into her just enough to tease and deepened the kiss.

After a few moments more, a low sound rumbled from his chest as he broke the kiss with a soft snap of breath. "I want to hear you fall apart for me, love. I want to ruin every shred of composure you have and call it worship. Do you understand me, Ros? Every sound you make tonight belongs to me."

Roslyn fluttered her eyes open slightly as they closed again reaching and wrapping her arms around his neck. "But Anne and Harriet. They will hear—"

Eli cut her off, his grip firmed even more. "Every. Single. Sound. Do you understand me?"

His voice was rawer than she'd ever heard—stripped of armor, stripped of distance. It made her eyes open, not in fear, but in awe. She searched his gaze and found it there—the blaze of lust, yes, but beneath it something deeper. Love. Fierce and undeniable. There was so much love between them that was unmistakable, but tonight his dazzling dark eyes held also a mixture of forlorn sadness and desolation. A vulnerability that he hardly ever exposes even to her. This was more than just love. This moment was a sanctuary. It was sacred and it could be as timeless as they wanted, forever how long they could drag their time out in this room, they would be in a moment of perpetual bliss—or at least that was the illusion.

Without breaking eye contact, she gently removed his fingers from around her throat. She slowly slid his hand, open palm to rest on her cheek. Roslyn raised her hand and placed it along his jaw. Her thumb rubbing the stubble that had long since filled in. Her voice cracked the silence between them. "If loving me makes you vulnerable, then let the world fear the man who has something worth losing." Her gaze burned into his, "I chose this danger, Eli. I choose *you*. Let the world come for us—it will find me standing at your side."

Eli's eyes flared, darkening as they locked onto hers. Wordlessly, he slipped the furred hood from his head of dark, disheveled curls that were damp with sweat and lake water. He took a deep breath in, chest heaving as his jaw set tight. Slowly, deliberately, he began unbuttoning his coat, never once breaking eye contact. Roslyn watched every measured movement as if spellbound. Her breath deepened, each inhale heavier than the last. His gaze held her still, pinned into place as she watched every movement. He was so beautiful. He was captivating. With every button freed, more of him revealed itself—the sculpted planes of muscle beneath damp skin, the heat of him barely contained behind the fabric.

When the final button slipped loose, he sank to one knee. Then the other. Roslyn's breath hitched. The room suddenly felt too small, too warm, full of him. The coat slid from his shoulders, down his arms, whispered across his skin before pooling around his feet. He knelt before her, but nothing about him felt small. The position only made the moment more vulnerable. A predator choosing submission. His large muscular naked body hunched. His voice was a low growl. "You are under my skin, in my veins…" He reached out to grab the bottom hem of her coat and pulled her close to him.

Roslyn moved from the bathroom door as she stepped before him. She looked down at him and reached out and ran her fingers through his thick curls, watching the silky strands slide through her slender fingers. Dragging her hand back to the nape of his neck and repeat. She saw his eyes blink close as he took pleasure from her hands teasing his hair. She gripped his hair lightly and Eli's gaze burned as it dragged over her, slow and claiming. Like he was memorizing her. Like he was starving. His hands slid up her calves, unhurried, thumbs pressing into her warm skin as if testing whether she was real. Whether this moment would be stolen back. His voice dropped to a rough whisper. "You have no idea what you do to me." His eyes lifted to hers, dark with want, devotion, and a hunger that had nothing to do with flesh and everything to do with *her*.

Roslyn's pulse fluttered wildly. Her body became alive with his touch. He was unraveling her piece by piece. Eli's thumbs traced small, burning circles against her calf, grounding himself in her touch. He looked up at her through dark lashes, eyes molten with devotion and ruin.

He lifted her slender leg, and hooked it over his shoulder. She balanced herself by grabbing onto his shoulder, and steadying on her other leg. He murmured into her soft skin, "If the world ends tomorrow," he said quietly, "let it end knowing I worshiped you like my last prayer." The air between them thickened—heavy with want, with love, with the fragile awareness that time was never promised to them. His lips brushed her knee, feather-light. Nuzzling the inside of her thigh, heat from his nostrils trailed toward her slickened pussy causing a delicious shiver to quake throughout her body.

"That's it…" A faint smile curved his mouth. "Such a good fucking girl." He planted a kiss near her knee. Then another soft kiss inched higher. And another. His hands cradled her ass in his hands and he pressed her closer, inhaling her sweet, mouth-watering scent of her arousal. He buried himself deep in the apex of her cunt. The tip of his nose, putting pressure on her clit as he inhaled her sweet, delicious scent like she was the very air keeping him alive. The intimacy of it ripped a gasp from her lips, her fingers tangling in his curls as she held him there.

His voice was rough velvet against her skin. "Tremble for me," he rasped as the fine dark brown hairs on her pussy tickled his lips as she settled further onto his shoulders. Thrusting her pelvis, Roslyn began to grind so sweet against his mouth. She wrapped her leg tighter around his back. Gripping his head as she began to slowly rock as his hot tongue swirled between her lips. A shiver rolled through, her body moving on him. The slow beat between them turned molten, each breath, each touch drawing her further under. He didn't rush. He didn't look away. Looking up at her, she looked down at him, catching the way his eyes were a lit with a hunger for her and pride that she was riding his face. He tasted her like a vow he intended to keep.

"Oh my god," she whimpered as she arched her back. Her head fell backward in surrender to the pleasure he edged in her. His tongue felt like sin, and she was on her way to redemption. Each flick with the tip of his tongue on her sensitive clit sent stars exploding throughout her body as she rocked harder. Rolling her hips and matching thrusts to match the rhythm of Eli's thick, wide tongue as he licked, flicked and sucked.

"God, you are so fucking good at that." Roslyn cried as her fingernails bit into his scalp as she held him in place. He promised he would devour her and he was fulfilling that very promise to the core. She was lost in pleasure. The tip of his tongue found her over and over again as he sucked on her clit, swirling around the swollen nub before he flicked it. The world beyond that room dissolved—no fear, no Keller, no war—only heat and heartbeat and the way he held her like she was both his salvation and his downfall. She moved against him like she was trying to outrun the world itself, like every bitter memory could be burned away in the friction between their bodies.

Her fingers dragged along his shoulders, leaving faint crescent as she climbed higher on the tide he built.

"Don't stop, Eli." Roslyn begged nearly breathlessly. Her hands fumbled at the buttons of the fur coat, urgency replacing patience. One by one they gave away until the heavy garment loosened and slipped opened. Cool air rushed her flushed skin, a sharp contrast to the fire coiling within her body. A sigh of relief flooded her body as the fur lapels fell open exposing her breasts and her belly. The cool air kissed her nipples, adding to the carnal pleasure as they tightened further, causing enough pain to push her even closer to the edge. With one hand gripping the back of Eli's head, another worked her breast as she raised the mound to her own mouth and she licked her nipple before pinching and rolling it between her thumb and fingers. A cry escaped her lips as another shudder burst through. She was so tight, it hurt Eli pushed her to the point of no return. Every touch only reminded her how alive she felt in this moment—how desperately she wanted him, this, the now. Her breathing turned uneven, her body swaying on the fine line between earth and the heavens.

"Do it, Roslyn. Fucking wreck me, baby." Eli begged between his ragged, muffled breath before he dipped his head and licked. Roslyn swung her other leg over his shoulder and gripped his head between her thighs. She could feel Eli adjust and support her weight as he gripped her ass with his arms, hands splayed on across her back. He drew her closer, his focus entirely on her, on the way her body answered his, on the silent language only they shared. She shifted, trusting his strength as he steadied her, his hands firm and reverent at her back and hips, holding her as if she were something precious and breakable all at once. The world narrowed to breath, warmth and the electric pull between them. Desire tempered by love, urgency softened by the knowledge that time with each other was never guaranteed. She threaded her fingers into his hair to stay anchored to him to his moment as her pussy tightened one last time before a cry ripped from her throat. Her head swung back and her body quaked from the climax that burst hot in waves throughout her body.

Eli lapped up her climax as she flooded around his mouth, dragging out her pleasure, sending her crashing and rising, crashing and rising over and over. Roslyn's chest heaved as she choked on the air that threatened to burst her lungs. Her body arched, then softening as the intensity began to ebb. Eli gathered her close, grounding her against his chest, his touch no longer hungry, but protective. His forehead rested against hers, and in that small space between breaths, the world felt still. For a few suspended heartbeats, there was nothing but the sound of their breathing and the echo of what they shared. Only the quiet certainty that whatever came next, this—them—was worth fighting for.

CHAPTER ELEVEN
FINDING REFUGE

Upon the south-eastern wind, a dying raven glided along the invisible current. The merciful push of the breeze carried the ragged creature farther north toward the end of its purpose. Enchanted to survive without food or rest, the little bird had been made a living tool for its Master. Disheveled and weather-worn, instinct told the raven that death rode upon its wings after such a harrowing journey. Still, it pressed on, driven by magic and command, knowing only when the task was complete would the spell release it to die.

The raven broke from beneath a shroud of wispy clouds. Sunlight spilled over its sable feathers, warming its brittle body. It welcomed the heat, savoring the brief comfort like a final kindness. Its golden gaze scanned the land below as it flew. Green pines speared toward the heavens. Topaz rivers carved through dark earth. Golden fields lay barren, waiting for farmers plow to wake the soil.

Instinct urged him to descend into the woodland, and he obeyed. Dropping lower, he glided between budding maple and oak branches, narrowly evading their jutting limbs. Then he faltered. A sharp screech tore from his throat as pain stabbed through his leg. Twisting midair, he looked back. The tethered letter had snagged on a thin branch. For months the leather thong securing the small envelope had chafed against his scaled leg, rubbing it raw. The wound had festered, infection creeping beneath brittle flesh. It plagued him, yet his Master had trained him to ignore discomfort, to fly on no matter the pain.

Irritated, the raven tugged at the letter with his narrow beak, but it held fast. With a rasping squawk of frustration, he abandoned the effort and continued forward. After several more miles, the letter began to hum—a low, pulsing vibration. He recognized the sound. He had been taught its meaning. He was close. A new instinct seized him. The raven called out again, this time almost joyful. Like a moth drawn to flame, he followed the invisible lure.

Mid-flight, the winged creature tilted its head, fixing its golden gaze upon a massive two-story house below. With sudden precision, the raven done. He spiraled toward the earth in a tight descent, wind screaming past his feathers. Just before impact, he snapped his wings open and caught the air, riding into a controlled hover. He circled the house once…then again…searching for an opening. A window. A chimney. A crack in the roofline. Nothing. Then he sensed it. The owner was outside. Sleeping.

Deep in their seclusion, George and Sheryl slept naked on the back stretch of their wraparound porch. Peace settled over them in the quiet comfort of shared rest after a long night of hunting. It had become their ritual whenever the cycle of transformation ended. Earlier, they had basked in the healing warmth of the sun, letting it replace the moon's blessing with the gentle disguise of mortality. Now the morning had ripened into late afternoon. Sunlight spilled through the porch overhand in golden streaks, most of it warming George's broad shoulders. He stirred. His head rolled off his arm as consciousness slowly returned. From inside the house, the grandfather clack began its slow haunting melody. By the fourth chime, he was fully awake.

The raven hovered for a breath before settling on the white porch railing. Its claws clicked softly against the painted wood. He cocked his head to the side and saw the man's eyes were open. Compelled, the bird hopped onto the deck for a closer look. A deeper instinct stirred within its wild senses—this man was not merely human. He felt like a predator wearing skin. The raven wanted to flee. Every primal urge to screamed for it to take wing and escape. But the enchantment held. Invisible chains wrapped tight around its will and forced it to remain. Step by reluctant step, the raven crept closer. The magical tether thrummed louder in its mind, a shrill song vibrating through bone and feather alike. The sound intensified until it bordered on agony. The raven squawked in protest. Desperate for release, it jabbed its beak against the man's upturned palm, pecking sharply as if to ride itself of the cursed message bound to its leg.

"What the hell—?" George jerked awake as the raven's beak stabbed sharply into his palm. He recoiled flinging his hand back and swiping at the bird in irritation. The creature only hopped away, just beyond his reach. His fingertips barely grazed the puffed black feathers of its chest—slick and unnaturally warm. "What do you want with me, you winged devil?" George snapped, his voice thick with groggy annoyance. The raven did not retreat.

Instead, it gave a harsh, throaty squawk and lifted its leg, pecking insistently at the small leather envelope bound there. The thong had been tied tight, meant to safeguard its message through a long and brutal journey.

George pushed himself up on one elbow and watched as the raven viciously tugged at something bound to its leg A thin leather string and a pouch. Understanding dawned. "You're a messenger raven…" he murmured, a bit bewildered. For a moment he wondered if Eli had found another clever way to send word.

"Easy now," George said quietly. "Let me help before you gnaw your own leg off." Careful not to wake Sheryl, he slid his arm from beneath her head and rolled onto his side. The boards creaked softly beneath his weight as he reached for the bird. Up close, the smell hit him. Rot. The leather thong was soaked in blood and pus, the wound beneath it raw and festering. Infection had eaten into the thin scales of the raven's leg. Yellowed clots glued feathers to flesh. George grimaced, but worked gently, loosening the tie. When he looked into the bird's eyes, he saw it—the diming light of a creature kept alive past its rightful death.

"I'll make it quick," he said low. "So you can die in peace." The raven released a throaty growling reply. It seemed to relish the idea.

The moment the tie loosened and the letter passed into George's hands, the raven stiffened. Freedom. The enchantment unraveled from its bones like a fading spell. No longer bound to its Master's will, the creature belonged to itself again. With the heavy beat of its long wings, it lifted from the railing. Its inky body shrank against the sky, flying farther and farther until it became nothing more than a dark fleck…then vanished entirely. George didn't watch it long, knowing it was going to find its final resting ground. Curiosity pulled stronger. George broke the unmarked wax seal from the envelope. The crimson stamp cracked beneath his thumb, brittle flakes scattering into his palm and across the porch boards. Rolling onto his back he unfolded the letter. The script was thick. Hurried. Slightly smudged as if written with force rather than care. But it was readable. And it was meant for him.

Cronwelm,

Through the raven's eyes I have, in a manner of speaking, traveled the long and treacherous road that led this message to you. If this letter rests in your hands, then its purpose is fulfilled. My burden is lifted. The raven is freed to die. And I finally sleep. Think me not cruel. I send only the oldest of my ravens—those already perched upon deaths dark ridge. A dead raven cannot betray my location, and in their final flight they taste freedom beyond their cage. But you, George, are far from free. War approaches. All Beast Bloods who answer the Call will be drawn into it—including the sorrow-marked Eli and Roslyn. Yes, I have seen their path and what has already begun. The Holy Order of St. Michael has fallen. Its men lie dead. Its caverns crumble into ash and memory. Like poison spilled into a city well, one hand betrayed them all. Now man and beast will rise against one another for the first time since heaven touched earth. A greater evil walks behind this war. An entity of two souls. A mortal vessel housing an elder demon—one among the first chapped by the Fallen One, bearing an name of angelic origin long forgotten.

The demon within him feeds upon his hunger for Roslyn, whispering lies and fanning his obsession. I could not see beyond this veil, only the clash of two terrible desires. The visions were…difficult to endure. Each is a fire. Together, they become a weapon easily wielded and easily turned. They will find you. Nothing will stop them. Be vigilant. Keller gathers an army, strengthening them with the souls of the damned and the lost. They will become what the ancients named Sighati—Half Born in modern tongue. A legion will rise. A black tide will sweep the land, killing at his command. Hellfire will stain the soil. The sky will glow gold to horrified witnesses. Desire will burn, then hunger will follow, never satisfied. Blood will soak the withered earth. Mortals and Beasts alike will fall. And God Himself will mourn what unfolds.

This much is certain. The victor is not. For the hearts of men shift like sand. Let memory bond this legacy, for this war is but one more in a grander design. You are a keeper of what must survive beyond it. This is my prophecy, bathed in the tears of the Seven Stars and sealed in blood-wax.

-Seeker Raven.

"Jesus, Mary, and Joseph," George breathed, the words barely leaving his mouth. The porch felt smaller. He read the letter again—slower this time. Each line pressed deeper. Hellfire. Demon. Legion. Roslyn. The words didn't just sit on the page. They rearranged themselves inside him. Demon. Half-Born. Roslyn. Once more his eyes scanned the sentences and filtered through the phrase. As they caught and juggled, alarm over the unclear situation had grown, gripping his heart. He didn't fully understand how the pieces connected, but instinct—ancient and sharp—told him they did. This wasn't hysteria. It wasn't exaggeration. It was a warning. He reached the final line again. A cold surge shot down his spine. "They're coming tonight." George surged upright with a force that startled even himself. Purpose snapped into place like armor settling over bone.

"Sheryl." He nudged her with his foot—less gently that intended—urgency overtaking tact. She rolled from her stomach to her side with a sharp inhale. "What?" she hissed, eyes flashing irritation. "If this is about coffee—"

"Its war."

Her expression shifted. Sleep drained from her face in an instant. She pushed up onto one elbow, studying him. George held up the letter. "They've fallen," he said quietly. "The Order's gone." The wind shifted along the porch. It wasn't just a breeze. But a turn. George was already moving—striding inside, letter clenched in his fist. He muttered under his breath, piecing fragments together as if speaking them aloud would force them to align. Sheryl rose and followed, wrapping her arms around her bare body as a chill slid over her skin. The air had changed. She knew that wind. Death was moving. A raven's screech tore through the distance—raw, broken, final. She closed her eyes for a moment in respect to the old Gods. “Oh,” she whispered. “It’s begun.”

George heard the raven too and felt pity for the sickly creature. Although he was relieved it had finally died, he didn’t give it a second thought. He swiftly turned around and handed her the letter. "Read."

Sheryl took the parchment, scanning the heavy slanted script with swift, intelligent eyes. The ink bled thick in places. “Quill,” she murmured. “The old way. He wanted no modern trace.” Her gaze lifted. “And he used a raven.” A faint, humorless smile curved her mouth. “Of course he did.” She finished the last paragraph and the color drained from her face. “What did he mean,” she asked slowly, “that you are a keeper?” The words settled between them.

George shrugged. "I'm not sure what it means in full," he answered truthfully, “but I am sure of what we’re dealing with.” He turned sharply on his heel and headed for the staircase without another word.

Sheryl stared after him, irritation and unease tangling in her chest. “What are you doing?” she called. His voice came back steady, already moving upward. “Getting dressed.” A pause followed by the thumping sounds of drawers being slid out and shut as he looked for what he needed. “As you should too.” His boots thudded against the wood floor. “When night approaches, we send word. We call them all. Every Beast Blood who still answers to the old language.” He reached the top of the stairs and looked down at her from the landing. “And when Eli and Roslyn arrive…” His expression darkened. “they’ll confirm the rest.”

Sheryl stood still for a long breath. The air inside the house felt smaller now. Tighter. She folded the letter once more and followed him up the stairs. If the Order had fallen…if a demon walked inside a mortal shell…then tonight was more than preparation. It was an unraveling.

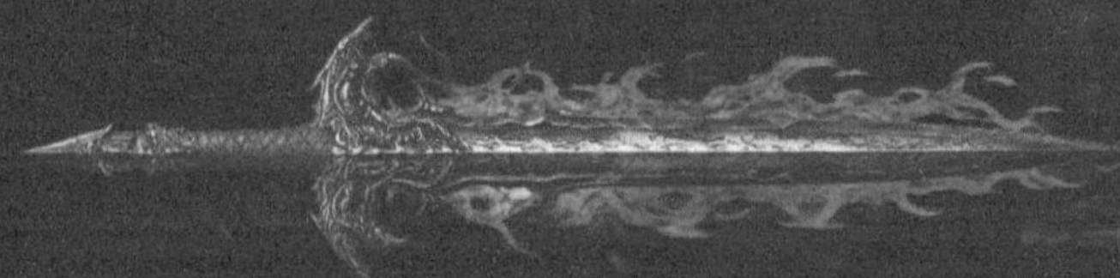

Hours passed, and night reclaimed the sky in full dominion. Not a cloud dared interrupt its endless stretch of black. Since the raven's death, a strange stillness had settled over the land. It wasn't peace nor quiet. Something heavier. As though the earth itself held its breath—alive, yet unmoving, like a widow stunned beyond tears. Even the wind seemed reluctant to speak.

Leaves shifted only when forced, brushing against one another in faint, hesitant whispers. The air had not cooled with the fall of evening; instead, it clung low to the ground, thick and unmoving, pressing against skin like a warning. The moon rose as a sovereign emblem in the heavens. Its silver light poured over the forest canopy, spilling down the trunks in pale ribbons. It caressed the grass in fleeting strokes, careful to avoid the deeper shadows pooling between the trees—shadows that felt less like absence and more like presence. Watching. Waiting.

George and Sheryl admired the night as they eagerly waited for Eli and Roslyn. Deep in their anticipation, they remained silence and routinely played chess on their front porch. Between each calculated move—or deliberate miscalculation, according to the strange rules they had long ago bent to suit themselves—their eyes drifted toward the end of the long dirt path that carved through the trees toward their home. Any moment now. Any moment, Eli would appear from the darkness with Roslyn at his side. The grandfather clock inside the house began to chime, its hollow melody spilling through the open door and into the night air. One. Two. Three. The sound carried heavier than usual.

Sheryl broke their silence after she counted each echoing notch of kept time. "Seven o'clock," she murmured, soothing the folds of her blue cotton skirt as if time itself required tidying.

George didn't look at her as he slid his bishop across the board. "You sacrificed your King," he noted, mild intrigue threading through his voice. "Even by our corrupted rules, that's a bold move." His eyes never left the dark stretch of the dirt path beyond the porch.

Sheryl studied the board, then leaned back slowly. A faint crease formed between her brows before smoothing away.

"Sometimes," she said evenly, "the King must fall so the Queen survives." She nudged her remaining piece forward with deliberate precision. "She's far more vicious." Her gaze lifted to him beneath an arched brow.

George was about to respond to his wife's dangerous undertone when movement caught in the corner of his vigilant eye. Two figures emerged from the dark line of trees. A massive black horse stepped from the forest's mouth like something conjured from shadow itself. Moonlight caught along its broad back, turning its mane into liquid ink. Eli sat tall in the saddle. Roslyn before him. George's heart dropped. It hit somewhere low and heavy inside him. His breath hitched in his throat and refused to move properly. His palms dampened against the cool iron arm of the chair. A thin, cold awareness slid beneath his skin—the kind of soldier feels before a battlefield reveals itself. This was it. The first domino.

He straightened slowly, forcing steel into his spine and air into his lungs. Shoulders squared. Chin lifted. "They've made it," he said, though it came out quieter than intended. "Finally."

CHAPTER TWELVE
UNITY

Beyond relieved at the long-awaited sight of their destination, Eli urged Maximous into a swift, steady trot down the dirt path. The stallion's hooves struck the earth with purpose, kicking up the scent of soil and crushed grass as the house loomed nearer. Unfamiliar with the secluded cove, Roslyn surveyed it with sharp, restless curiosity. Fireflies flickered around them, rising in golden spirals through the tall wisps of field grass, blinking like fallen stars disturbed by their passing. The night felt thick, watchful. Her gaze lifted to the house. Every window glowed with the warm pulse of candlelight. The light spilled across the meadow in soft rays, reflecting the dark panes like living embers. It looked less like a residence and more like a beacon. For the first time in weeks, Roslyn felt something unfamiliar brush against her ribs. Hope.

There must be many werewolves here, she thought—and the realization struck deeper than she expected. A quiet pang of melancholy tightened in her chest. Community. Safety. Something they had lost. Her eyes lingered on the white house. Its magnificent stature stretched nearly twice the size of their former home in Fortaleza. Yet this was no delicate seaside estate. This was a fortress disguised as grace. It stood enclosed from the outside world, grounded firmly in the swaying meadow that bowed at its foundation. Whitewashed columns lined the wraparound porch in perfect symmetry, their pale strength set in stark contrast against the black shutters framing every window. Brass oil lamps burned low, their golden halos steady and bright enough to watch the fields, dim enough not to invite attention. Spring flowers and thick shrubs bloomed along the perimeter, their sweet perfume carried by the evening wind. The scent softened the air, veiling the sharper smells of nearby livestock and earth. Civilization layered for wilderness. Beauty layered over survival. Roslyn swallowed. It wasn't just a house. It was a sanctuary built by those who understood war was always waiting at the edge of the light.

Breaking free from her trance, Roslyn noticed two shadows move across the porch light. Her gaze snapped toward the house. A tall man and a slender woman rose together at the edge of the grand steps, framed in gold from the oil lamps burning behind them. The light flared outward, shattering around their forms and casting their faces into darkness. They stood like silhouettes carved from shadow and flame. She strained to see their features, but the brightness blinded her to detail. Still…she knew. There was something unmistakable in the way they held themselves—steady, unafraid, waiting.

"I assume that's George and Sheryl," she murmured softly. Her eyes flicked toward the darkened windows, scanning the porch, the yard, the surrounding tree line. waiting for us. "Where are the others?"

"Others?" Eli asked quietly, his eyes fixed ahead. His ears were tuned to the smallest rustle in the grass, the faintest shift in the wind. He answered in clipped fragments so as no to break his concentration.

Roslyn clarified, her voice low. "With a house like this…how many werewolves are under their care?"

"There isn't anyone else," he replied, tone stripped of warmth. "Only them."

Her brows pulled together. "It's just us?" She kept her questions short, matching his rhythm, knowing his mind was already bracing for what waited at the porch. His gaze sharpened, a fierce light flickering behind his eyes as they closed the distance to the house.

"Tonight," he said under his breath, "yes." A heartbeat passed before he continued, "Tomorrow," he added, voice edged with something darker, "might be different."

In one fluid motion, Eli drew Maximous to a halt at the base of the porch steps. He slid down first, steady and controlled, then lifted Roslyn carefully to the ground. Her boots met the earth softly, though her hand trembled in his. With no post in sight, he released

Maximous's reins without hesitation. The black stallion remained where he stood, loyal and watchful. Eli intertwined his fingers with Roslyn's. Her palm was cool. He gave it a subtle squeeze before guiding her up the wide wooden steps toward the waiting silhouettes. The oil lamp cast long shadows across the porch, obscuring faces but not presence.

"George Crownwelm," Eli greeted, a restrained smile pulling at his mouth as he stepped forward and extended his hand.

"Eli, it's a pleasure to see you again, my friend." George said warmly, gripping Eli's hand before pulling him into a firm embrace. The reunion was brief but sincere—two warriors measuring strength through contact.

Roslyn watched the exchange with a faint smile. She knew she would be greeted next. Sheryl had not yet turned toward her, her attention still lingering on the men, affection softening her features. Taking advantage of the pause, Roslyn studied her. Sheryl's silver hair fell in a thick braid well past her hips. Though clearly aged by time, her face held a striking, almost unnatural youthfulness—sculpted and symmetrical, as if the years had chosen carefully where to settle. Her skin remained smooth, luminous beneath the porch light. Large, ice-blue eyes framed by dark lashes blinked slowly, the tips nearly grazing her high cheekbones. Power. Control. Experience. All radiated from her.

Roslyn's gaze dipped to the woman's attire—tailored, elegant, commanding in its simplicity—making Roslyn's travel-worn pale-yellow dress feel painfully inadequate. She shifted her eyes again. Sheryl was watching her now. Those piercing blue eyes locked onto Roslyn's golden ones with an intensity that felt less like curiosity and more like evaluation. Not hostility, but perhaps recognition. An unexpected impulse swept through Roslyn—sudden, visceral. To bow, lower herself, and the urge startled her. It was not fear, not exactly. It was something older. Something instinctual. A sense of dominance woven deep into blood and bone. She resisted it. Her spine remained straight, though her breath tightened. After a brief internal battle, she lowered her gaze—not in surrender, but in restraint—forcing the feeling back into its cage. Sheryl noticed.

She did not bristle at the sudden shift. Instead, something knowing flickered across her expression. She softened her posture, easing the invisible pressure in the air. A faint smirk tugged at her mouth—not cruel, but amused by what she had witnessed. Then she stepped forward.

"My name is Sheryl," she said gently, drawing Roslyn into a brief, but firm embrace. "And you must be the immaculate Roslyn." Her voice carried warmth now, layered over steel. "We've heard quite a bit about you during Eli's last visit. We were looking forward to welcoming you properly." Her tone shifted—subtle, but weighed. "Though this reunion is…far less ceremonial than we imagined.

Sheryl stepped back from the embrace and held Roslyn gently at arm's length. The pale-yellow dress hung loosely from her slender frame. Baggy and moth-eaten, it carried the faint scent of unfamiliar hands and long travel. Roslyn instinctively pulled the collar higher against her throat, attempting to shield her bare shoulders and the curve of her chest from the night air. Sheryl noticed the movement. She also noticed the sorrow lingering in Roslyn's golden eyes. Her expression softened.

"Such a delicate beauty," Sheryl said warmly, brushing a stray strand of hair from Roslyn's cheek. "No wonder Eli was so eager to rush back to Brazil." She glanced at George, amusement glinting in her eyes. "He was determined to claim you before someone else could."

George chuckled, the sound deep and genuine. His broad cheeks lifted into a grin, narrowing his eyes with fond remembrance. "Oh, he was most eager," he agreed.

Eli cleared his throat quietly behind them. At Sheryl's teasing remark, a shadow of a smirk touched his mouth—fleeting, dark. Keller tried to claim her once. He stepped forward and wrapped an arm firmly around Roslyn's shoulders. He felt it immediately—the stiffness beneath her skin. The subtle tremor she was fighting. His brow pulled tight. "*What's wrong*?" he asked through the bond.

Roslyn shook her head quickly, her expression flustered—confused, as though she were trying to untangle a riddle only she could feel.

Sheryl watched her closely. A knowing look crossed her features. "Ah," she murmured softly. "Damn the blood." She shifted her stance, lowering her hands, making her tone less dominant. "Do not bow to me in your spirit, child. You feel it because the blood recognizes hierarchy. Age. Power. It presses you to submit." Her voice sharpened slightly as she looked toward Eli. "Did you not teach her our customs? She looks like she's fighting an invisible hand at her throat."

Roslyn felt the invisible pressure ease at Sheryl's words. Her lungs expanded fully for the first time since stepping onto the porch.

Eli's jaw flexed, though his voice remained even. "Given the situation," he said coolly, "it slipped my mind." He cast Sheryl a measured look before lowering his head toward Roslyn's ear. "My apologies, love." He tolerated Sheryl for George's sake. That much was duty. But beneath the courtesy lingered something colder—an instinct he couldn't quite name. Something about her presence unsettled him, like a note in a melody slightly out of tune.

Roslyn relaxed. "It's all right, Eli," she said softly, though her mind still reeled from the sensation she had just endured. "There is much to learn of your customs and hierarchy." Her gaze lifted again—steadier now as she looked at Sheryl. "Where we come from, we were the Elders." A faint, almost self-conscious smile touched her lips. "It is… strange to feel bound by rank when you are not accustomed to bowing."

Sheryl nodded, understanding dawning easily. "Ah. Of course. You're scarcely a year into your blood. Still what we would call a newborn." She stepped slightly aside, easing the invisible pressure in the air. "It's your blood reacting to longevity. Instinct recognizes age before it recognizes character. And mine…" She tilted her head lightly. "Mine is considerably older than yours." Her gaze flicked toward George. "Though I was turned by elder blood—by him—just as you were made of Eli's. Even so, between us all, you and Eli are the younger line." A small curve shadowed her thin lips. She leaned closer, lowering her voice theatrically and shielding her mouth with the back of her hand. "Though between us…" She cast a humorous glance toward her husband. "I still look the younger of the two."

George huffed under his breath. Roslyn laughed softly, genuine now, warmth returning to her face. "I'm certain that fact pleases you both equally." Sheryl's laughter joined hers.

"Witty as well. Good." Her eyes sharpened briefly with approval. "I believe we shall get along." But even she smiled, something in her gaze measured. Calculated. Beast Bloods burned bright—and bright flames often burned fast. In the back of her mind, she knew what time eventually did to the young. And what war did to them sooner.

Hearing his name woven into their exchange, George turned fully toward Roslyn and offered her a broad, dignified smile. He gave a slight, formal bow—old-world courtesy wrapped in modern ease—and his deep voice rolled smooth as polished oak. "Mrs. Santos, it is a true pleasure to finally make your acquaintance." He straightened, cordiality lingering in his expression. "Eli has spoken of you often—and well. I am grateful you arrived safely. I can only imagine the road has not been kind.

Roslyn inclined her head politely. But Eli did not soften. The amiability drained from his face as quickly as it had come. Keller's vow echoed in his mind like a blade dragged across stone. His eyes darkened, glossing over with something colder. "We are not safe, George," he said flatly. "Not even close." The porch air seemed to thicken. "There is much to settle before anything resembling initiation can occur."

George's smile faded. "Yes," he agreed gravely. "There is much to discuss. The matter is…urgent." He glanced toward Sheryl before continuing. "Between the letter the children delivered…and the one written by Seeker Raven, we do not yet fully understand—"

Eli went still. His brows snapped together, jaw tightening. "Who," he asked, voice dropping low and dangerous, "did you say sent you a letter?"

George did not flinch. "Seeker Raven."

The name hung between them like a drawn blade. Sheryl and Roslyn exchanged no words, but both felt it—the shift. The porch no longer felt welcoming. The night air seemed to tighten around them, thick and charged. George's eyes hardened. He rolled his jaw once. Twice. A strange habit of his when thoughts aligned into strategy.

"The pieces are beginning to assemble," he said carefully. "Information is merging. And it would appear there are more factions involved than we were prepared for." His gaze lingered on Eli. "We will not untangle this in open air." Without waiting for agreement, George turned sharply and moved toward the door. "Come to my study. We will speak privately." He opened the heavy wooden door and stood aside, gesturing Eli and Roslyn through first—a courtesy, but also a silent declaration of urgency. Eli entered without hesitation. Roslyn followed, glancing once over her shoulder at the dark meadow as if something unseen lingered there. Sheryl stepped in last. George shut the door firmly behind them. The latch settled into place with a low, final click. And with it, whatever warmth remained on the porch was left outside.

As George stepped fully inside, he moved ahead of them, guiding Eli and Roslyn through the parlor with brisk purpose. Halfway across the room, he paused, realization striking him. He turned toward his wife. "Sheryl, my love—would you bring the decanters? The brandy and the wine." His voice softened slightly. "Our friends have ridden far. They must be exhausted." He glanced at Roslyn more carefully. "And likely hungry. Do we have anything prepared?"

"I'll see what can be warmed," Sheryl replied smoothly, already veering toward the kitchen. "I'll bring the drinks first."

Eli watched Roslyn from the corner of his eye. The candlelight was unkind. Her skin, already pale, had taken on a muted, ashen cast. Even the whites of her eyes looked dulled—buttery and thin, like light seen through fog. Guilt twisted low in his chest. The journey had drained her. The child had drained her. And he had pushed her harder than he should have. "If you don't mind," Eli said evenly, though the edge of concern beneath his tone was unmistakable, "bring water for Roslyn." He didn't look away from her. "She needs to stay hydrated."

Roslyn felt his gaze, and though she tried to straighten her spine, her body betrayed her with a faint sway. Sensing she was assessed in a way she did not understand, Roslyn subtly fisted the fabric of Eli's shirt and pressed closer to him. She molded against the hard plane of his body as if anchoring herself there—as if proximity alone could shield her. Sheryl's gaze lingered too long. For a fleeting, unsettling moment, Roslyn thought the woman was not looking at her face at all—but the swell beneath the loose fabric of her dress. There was something almost like… meaning in it. The baggy gown concealed the true curve of her belly, but Roslyn suddenly became acutely aware of the life inside her. Protective heat flared low in her belly.

After several seconds of her unsettling silence, Sheryl's gaze lifted abruptly. The intensity vanished. In its place, a radiant smile bloomed across her face—bright, composed, almost theatrical. Her eyes snapped to Eli. "Of course," she replied in a voice sweetened just a shade too much. "Anything you would like for Roslyn." She lingered deliberately on Roslyn's name, the syllables rolling off her tongue in a near-purr. Then she turned smoothly and disappeared into the kitchen, skirts whispering across the hardwood floor.

Before Eli could respond, George—his back already turned as he rummaged through a drawer of neatly stacked papers—answered absently. "Thank you, Sheryl." The normalcy of his tone felt misplaced. Eli did not look convinced. His arm tightened fractionally around Roslyn's shoulders. And though Sheryl was no longer in the room, the air did not feel lighter. It felt…watched.

Roslyn looked to Eli. Wordlessly, they knew George didn't notice the strange behavior his wife had momentarily presented. Eli dipped his head slightly, his mouth near her ear—but his voice did not travel through air. It moved through the bond instead, warm and low against her thoughts. "*I won't let nothing happen to you. Or our baby.*" Roslyn sighed, and let that settle for now.

"Ah. Here it is." George motioned for them to step closer to the wall of bookcases. "Just through these doors." With a firm grip, he slid apart what appeared to be an ordinary cabinet. The shelves separated smoothly, revealing a concealed doorway behind them.

Roslyn blinked in surprise. "That's impressive," she admitted. "I would have never guessed it was anything more than a wall of books."

George chuckled as he ushered them inside. "That was precisely the intention." He crossed the room and lowered himself into a deep hunter-green chair positioned near the small iron stove. The fire cast warm light across the polished wood panels and thick rugs beneath their feet. "This space was once a safe room," he continued. "Recently converted into my study. During the war, Sheryl and I stored our most valuable possessions here. Documents. Heirlooms. Paintings. Anything that we acquired over our long span of life. I have one at the lake house too."

"I would have thought no one knew of this place," Roslyn said quietly, glancing around the hidden room. "Your entire estate feels impossibly secluded."

"It is," George replied. "But the war taught us quickly that seclusion is never protection." He leaned back in his chair, hands resting on the carved arms. "It wasn't only confederates and Union soldiers looting homes. Men came in the dead of night. Desperate. Violent. Searching for anything they could take." He gaze flickered briefly toward the concealed doorway. "So I built a mechanism into the shelves. A sequence of hidden latches woven into the molding. Without the knowledge, no one could open it."

The fire crackled softly. "More than once, Sheryl and I sheltered fugitives in this room. Northerners. Rebels. Black. White. It never mattered to me what uniform they wore." His expression hardened slightly. "What mattered was the condition of their spirit." He paused for a heartbeat. "The pure were protected." A smile curved his mouth. "And the corrupted…were left to be hunted." George straightened and gestured toward a matching hunter-green sofa across from him. "Please. Sit." His voice returned to measured hospitality. "We will sort this before the Calling begins."

Eli complied. Still holding Roslyn close, they moved to the sofa together. He remained perched at the edge—tense, forward, coiled—while Roslyn allowed herself to sink into the cushion behind him. He pressed a small kiss to the back of her hand before releasing it. Then he leaned forward, elbows braced on his knees, fingers laced together tightly enough for his knuckles to pale. "George," he said bitterly, the past months flashing through his mind in brutal succession, "where do I even begin?"

George did not answer immediately. He watched Sheryl enter the room carrying a silver tray lined with crystal decanters—water, whiskey, wine, brandy—matching goblets that caught the firelight in fractured glimmers. She set the tray on the oak table between them with quiet grace and poured each drink without asking. Water for Roslyn. Whiskey for Eli. Brandy for George. Wine for herself. George waited until the glasses were in their hands before he spoke. His voice was dark and measured. "Start where it was meant to begin."

Eli exhaled slowly. He nodded once. And then he began. He told them of Roslyn meeting Keller in their youth—of trust formed, of affection misunderstood, of the first fracture of something once innocent. His voice never wavered, but his jaw tightened as he spoke of betrayal. Of obsession. Of the vow. The fire crackled between sentences. After several long minutes, he finished quietly. "It only made sense," he concluded, voice low and steady, "that we come here. We have no family left."

"This has been festering far longer than any of us realized," George said, leaning back into his chair. He looked toward Roslyn, "I'm deeply sorry for your loss." His voice lowered, sincere. "I lost a brother once. You do not recover from it. You simply learn to carry it differently." He saw Roslyn's throat tightened, but she did not speak but nodded. George's fingers brushed absently over the coarse parchment in his hand. "This aligns with the Seeker's warning," he continued. "He spoke of Keller's desire for you." He looked toward Eli. "But he also wrote of two desires."

He extended the letter. Eli took it immediately, scanning the inked lines with sharpened focus. George shifted his attention back to Roslyn. She stared into the pale surface of her water, shoulders subtly rounded—guilt settling like dust over her posture. "You acted from loyalty," George said gently. "No one could have predicted he harbored something as ancient and corrupted as an elder demon."

Roslyn lifted her gaze. There was no fragility in it now—only thought. "Now that we know what Keller is," she said carefully, "how do we know Seeker Raven is not manipulating us as well?" Her fingers tightened around her glass. "What is this prophecy is bait? What if he is leading us into slaughter under the illusion of preparation?"

The fire snapped in the hearth. Even Eli paused in his reading. It was not a foolish question.

Eli shook his head. "No. I've known Raven since I was a boy." His voice carried certainty. "My father was introduced to him by Master Percy during the reformation of the Order." A shadow crossed his features. "Percy is probably dead now. As are the others." His jaw tightened. "Keller saw to that." The words tasted like iron. Eli looked up at George. "My father would leave often to consult Raven. He never shared the full purpose of those visits, but he respected him. Trusted him."

He lowered his gaze back to the parchment. It was indeed in Raven's handwriting. "When my father died, that relationship passed to me. The Order and the Seeker became allies and part of my responsibility with aide in the reformation. His voice dropped, calculating. "Raven does not waste ink. If he sends word, it is because he has seen something that demands response." He tapped the letter with his thumb. "He sent it to you, George, because Keller has already moved." A flicker of dark realization passed through his eyes. "Keller must have sought him out at as well." Eli scanned further down the page. "He speaks of battle. It reads like scripture," he said thoughtfully. "Judgement. War. Blood. Legacy."

"It feels…biblical." George affirmed, the word lingered in the air like smoke. He scratched the back of his neck as his pressed lips curled under his teeth in concentration. "He speaks of the land withering. It's almost June. The sun has become more intense. Even the farmers are predicting a drought with the lack of water."

Roslyn felt a flutter of her child move inside her, and another twirl, followed by a kick. She shifted in her seat as a hand automatically spread across her stomach.

Sheryl exclaimed her question breathlessly. "You *are* with child. I can hear its heartbeat from here." The wild eagerness touched her eyes again and burned a feature of overzealous pleasure across her face.

George leaned forward now, attention sharpened. His eyes found Eli. He did not need verbal confirmation. Roslyn's flushed cheeks and Eli's rightened posture told him enough.

Eli slid his fingers through Roslyn's and squeezed gently. "Yes," he said protectively. "We discovered we were expecting early in our journey here."

George Exhaled slowly, casting a fleeting glance toward Sheryl. She had gone quiet. Too quiet. Her gaze was distant now, forlorn. He knew his wife could not bare children. Not even his blood could fix that. He squeezed Sheryl's hand in comfort, and turned back to Eli, whose dark eyes held his attention. "With all that you've endured, "George said carefully, "it's not surprising the growth has strained her. Stress can slow even the strongest blood." His eyes assessed Roslyn with clinical calm. "Her belly has not yet filled the fabric. How long until your time?"

"Early September," Eli answered without hesitation. His hand remained firm around Roslyn's. "She's strong enough to shift. Strong enough to hunt. But she will not stand in battle. I don't want her anywhere near it when it happens." The decision was iron. "She requires protection more now than ever. Regardless of what she may argue."

His gaze flicked toward Roslyn. She met it with a flash of defiance. Her jaw tightened. She would not undermine him in front of George and Sheryl. But the bond flared. "*How convenient,*" her voice threaded through his mind, cool and sharp. "*That you can decide that for me.*"

His response came instantly, iron beneath velvet. "*You will not change my mind on this, Ros.*" The bond vibrated with restrained force. "*I will not place you in front of that monster. I will not risk you. Or our child—which only lives if you do.*"

Her voice echoed down the bond again, louder, sharper. "*And what if you fall while I sit hidden? What then? I am capable…*"

"*This is not up for debate of your capabilities. It is a matter of strategy.*" A darker edge entered his tone. "*I will not set you in front of that monster. End of discussion.*" Eli said as he looked at her. Eyes set and jaw ticking with the pulse of his anger.

Roslyn broke eye contact, snapping her gaze away as pain flared behind her temples. The familiar pulse of a headache stirred from the mental upheaval—the cost of pushing too hard through the bond. She pressed her fingers to her brow as the bond quieted, steadying herself. "No." She whispered, but no one heard her.

George continued without pause, leaning back in his chair and dragging his palm down his stubbled face. "Of course she cannot fight," he said plainly. "It is not debatable. She's the enemy's prime target."

Sheryl looked at Roslyn but addressed the men. "She's also very young into her blood-life—"

Something in Roslyn snapped. She surged to her feet. The room felt too small, too controlled, too suffocating. She searched for space to pace but found none. So, she claimed it instead—standing tall where she was. "Enough." Her voice cracked through the study like a whip. "Stop speaking about me as if I am not present." The fire hissed behind her. "What does it matter if this is my first child or my hundredth? Why has everyone decided I am as fragile as those crystal decanters on the table?" Her chest rose and fell sharply. "I am a Beast Blood." The words rang. "I have fought, trained—and ever since the night—" Her gaze locked on Eli—blazing, "The night Keller murdered my brother. I have been dictated and directed." Her voice dropped, lethal and steady. "This is my kill. He killed my brother. My clan. I will make him suffer before I tear out his throat. He will answer to it." I swear on my life I'll do it, Eli."

The vow shuddered in the air. "I swear it." Heat rushed to her face as tears burned behind her eyes, but she refused to let them fall. She swallowed hard against the lump in her throat. The room went silent. The moment hung there—heavy and almost sacred. Geroge and Sheryl shifted in their seats as they looked at each other, clearly unsure of how to respond.

Eli moved first. Slowly. Carefully. He reached for Roslyn's hand. The slight twitch of her fingers told him he had startled her. His grip gentled immediately, thumb brushing the inside of her palm in a grounding stroke. "Ros…" His voice was quiet. Steady. Roslyn flicked her gaze onto him. And beneath the fire still smoldering in her eyes, he saw it. Fear. Fear of losing him. Fear of being left behind. The fear of surviving alone. He was all she had. He held her gaze until her breathing slowed. She exhaled shakily and allowed herself to sit again. Her hand slipped from his, but not in anger—in exhaustion.

Eli leaned closer, resting his palm at the small of her back. Slow, soothing circles. "Your fierceness," he said softly, "is more than admirable, my love." A small smile ghosted across his mouth. "And yes, I'd love to see nothing more than you tearing Keller apart." That earned the smallest flicker of breath from her.

"But I have spent these last month's shielding you so fiercely that I forgot something." His hand stilled at her spine. "In my own fear, I forgot to trust you. I forgot to consult you. I forgot you are a force in your own right. And for all that, I apologize." He shifted, turning slightly so only she could truly hear the weight in his next words. "The first child does change things." His tone grew measured. "The blood becomes unpredictable. It stretches thinner between beast and mortal." His eyes darkened slightly. "It will demand more from you. It will make you feel…almost human at times. And as the birth nears, you will weaken." His thumb pressed gently into her lower back. "Not because you're incapable," his voice cracked as he pleaded through his confession. "But because you are everything."

Before Eli could continue, George spoke—calm, steady, unflinching. "There are loopholes to immortality," he said evenly. "But none of them cheat death. We are only immortals to the humans because we can out-live them, but death comes for all who walk this earth. Beast Blood or mortal—it makes little difference when life is being created." His gaze moved to Roslyn. "It is the price of carrying an immortal child. Reproduction among our kind is rare for a reason. It demands balance—and the balance is fragile." He folded his hands together. "The child draws strength from the mother faster than she can replenish it." The fire cracked. "Some women have withered down. They feed the child until there is nothing left and their hearts give out." Silence followed that for a heartbeat before George swallowed a drink of his whiskey and continued. "It is what makes this…precarious." George leaned forward slightly. "And Keller." His tone sharpened. "He wants you." His eyes hardened. "What will he do when he learns you are carrying a child—and that you are most vulnerable? If you step onto that battlefield, every man and woman there will divide their focus between killing the enemy…and guarding you." George's tone firmed. "And that division could cost us the battle."

Eli nodded slowly. He looked at Roslyn. "So much can go wrong," he said, voice roughened. "Not just for you. For all of us who answer the call."

Roslyn inhaled deeply, but the sweet applewood smoke that burned in the small iron stove scraped against her throat. The scent that had once been comforting when they first walked into the room now felt suffocating. When she spoke, her voice wavered. "Then where do I go?" The question hung fragile and raw. "If I become so…weakened…where am I to be sent? Who protects the child and me if I am not with you?" Her eyes watered now, springing hot as they trailed down her cheeks. "Through blood and fire. Through everything." Her voice broke softly. "Together."

Eli exhaled hard through his nose. "We will figure that out. That's why we are here. I know you're afraid for me." His hands tightened into fists before relaxing again. "But you will go far from the battlefield. Somewhere hidden. Guarded." He inched closer, "Keller wants you badly enough to kill me." The admission hung there. "He may take my life," Eli said quietly. "But he will never take you. As long as my heart beats, I will not allow it." He paused for a moment, his dark eyes searching into hers. "A child can survive without a father."

His voice cracked on the next words. "But never without a mother. You will live," he said, breath unsteady. "If one of us must fall, it will be me."

The confession was not dramatic. It was certain. For a fleeting second, Eli was no longer in George's study. He was a boy again. Standing in a quiet house. Feeling the moment his father died was like a blade through the bond. He remembered the way the grief hollowed his mother—how she starved herself of life, how she wept in her sleep. How one morning she was simply…gone. The letter she left behind and the smell of her body burning in the field as she had set herself aflame. His soul broke that day. For a moment he saw Roslyn in that place for a heartbeat—empty-eyed, fading. His throat closed. He blinked hard and forced the image away.

Roslyn felt tears rolling softly down her cheeks as her voiced cracked lower than a whisper. "Seven, Eli." She swallowed. "Since I was seven years old… you have been there." Her fingers curled loosely into her lap. "You became everything I needed. My rock. My shield. My closest friend." Her breath hitched on the emotion. "My love." She looked at him fully now. Her voice thinned as a sob escaped her throat. "It is losing the part of my soul that only exists because you do." She sniffled and ran her fingers over her wet cheeks as she dried them of tears. "I don't know how this ends," she continued, fragile but honest. "And I am terrified of what will remain of me if you are not there."

Eli's chest rose slowly. "You and I share that fear," he said quietly. His tone was resolute. "That is precisely why you must go." The words did not soften. "The moment danger breaches the line, you leave. You do not hesitate. You do not look back." His hand tightened around hers. "You go far from it. If I live… I will find you." The statement carried no doubt. "If I do not," his voice roughened slightly, "you live." His thumb pressed against her knuckles. "You live for our child. You live for yourself." He leaned closer, pressing his forehead to hers. "You live for you. Do you understand me?" Softer now. But no less firm. "You will live." The words were hard, born of love sharpened by inevitability. The room fell silent and heavy with the weight of a future none of them could outrun.

George's gaze drifted toward the embers in the stove. He felt Sheryl's thin hand tighten around his arm—a subtle signal of shared understanding. He saw it all clearly now. The two before him were not merely frightened. They were exhausted. Grief-stricken. Angry at fate itself. They had been forced into prophecy before they had time to comprehend what that meant. George inhaled slowly, his voice was calm and grounded. "Listen to me." He looked at Eli and Roslyn. "Regardless of how this unfolds…you will not face it alone. Thriving is not about avoiding loss. It is about enduring it—and refusing to let it define you."

George felt the shift in the night. Time was narrowing. The Calling was near, and the clans will be out. "The facts are before us," George continued, shifting into strategy. "While awaiting your arrival, I drafted several defensive measures. There is one plan we can alter." He leaned forward slightly. "You may withdraw from the immediate battlefield and remain within proximity." His eyes flicked to Eli. "She will be guarded. Concealed. Shielded by wards no one outside this room knows exist." A slight tightening of his mouth. "And no one will know where to search, but those who are in this room."

Eli's hand tensed around Roslyn's. "Perfect," he said.

George leaned forward in his chair. "I can show you." His tone shifted—no longer consoling. Commanding. "Remove the glasses. Clear the tray." The order was crisp. Sheryl moved first, collecting the crystal goblets and silver decanters without comment. Eli rose halfway to assist, sliding the oak table free of obstruction. George reached beneath the lip of the table. There was a soft click. The center panel rotated inward and split cleanly down the middle, revealing a hidden compartment below. He quickly ordered as he reached the table. Roslyn's breath caught. Inside lay tightly curled scrolls bound in leather ties and folded parchment stacked with careful precision. George withdrew them swiftly. The papers unfurled across the tabletop—a large map of Michigan inked careful detail, accompanied by smaller hand-drawn schematics of surrounding towns, forested routes, rivers, and rail lines. Dashed trails cut through the parchment like veins. X-marks. Ink blots. Encircled clearings. Supply routes. Fall back points. Even hidden elevation markers.

In unison, Eli and Roslyn leaned forward over the table, hovering close enough that their shoulders nearly brushed George's. The firelight flickered over the maps, casting moving shadows over inked paths that would soon run red. George's voice lowered—steady, precise. His finger traced a projected movement line. "This is what I have constructed so far. We have a tunnel system here." He tapped a darkened mark near the southern edge of the state, and began to explain the plans.

CHAPTER THIRTEEN
FLAMES TO THE BEAST

The hours slipped by like wind through tall grass. Twilight thinned and night deepened. Fleetingly, a second breath of life sprang forth when the moon entered full rise once again. The pale orb sat upon its invisible throne, pouring silver dominion across the land, and began to call court all those who were marked to answer.

Roslyn's breath hitched. The Calling struck her like a blade drawn across nerve and bone. It tore through her chest in a sharp, visceral surge. She jerked her head up from the table, fingers gripping the edge as instinct flooded her veins. It was the beginning. Her eyes snapped at the others. They were already looking at one another. No words were needed. They all felt it. It was time for Calling and the converging of clans. The clutching fingers of reality crawled over their spines and charged the air to an even higher elevation. George stood first. Slow. Measured. Eli rose a heartbeat later. His spine flexed as though something ancient inside him stretched against mortal constraint. His shoulders rolled back. His chest expanded. The shift had not begun—but the beast was awake.

Eli turned back to Roslyn and extended his hand. "Up." She placed her palm in his and he lifted her smoothly from the couch, faster than she expected. His grip lingered a fraction longer. "Are you ready?" he asked, not just to her, but to all of them. His posture had shifted completely. He demeanor was that of a warrior, readying for battle.

"Let's go rally the others." George stepped through the doorway, the Calling already tightening beneath his skin. A sharp pulse of pre-shift pain rippled through his spine—a reminder that flesh would soon yield to fur.

"Sheryl, love." He reached back, taking her hand, guiding her into the hall. Without slowing, he began issuing instructions. "Eli and I will call the others. You and Roslyn go east—to the lake house." His voice was steady, tactical. "Call the others along the way and tell them where to go. Me and Eli will remain here to receive them." He stopped in the corridor, turning back toward them. "Stick to the plan." His finger tapped the side of his head, as though pointing to the map still burned in their minds.

George's gaze softened when it reached Roslyn. Her golden eyes were wide—luminous in the lamplight, still carrying the sting of prophecy and impending shift. A fatherly weight pressed against his chest unexpectedly. "Can you keep a steady pace?" he asked her gently, concern flooding his tone.

Roslyn steadied herself as the first tightening cramps rippled through her limbs. Muscles coiled beneath her skin, anticipating fur and bone reshaping beneath the moon's pull. She was tired. More tired than she allowed them to see. But she lifted her chin. "I can." The baby fluttered beneath her palm—a soft, answering tremor. Pride flared in him—fierce and unyielding. In two strides he was in front of her. He caught the front of her dress and turned her toward him with sudden urgency. Before she could speak, his arms wrapped around her and his mouth claimed hers—hard, desperate, lingering. As if carving the moment into memory. He held the kiss longer than his body allowed. A violent jolt cracked through his chest. He growled, gritting against her lips as his ribs began to shift—the first fracture of change. He tore himself away, breath ragged. The placed his forehead against hers. He memorized her—every fleck of gold in her eyes, every tremor in her breath. The way her pulse ticked in the hollow of her throat. She searched the black depths of his gaze, waiting for words. None came. He could not trust his voice. Without speaking, he turned and stepped through the threshold of the open door and went out into the night.

The bond stretched, thinned and then became nothing. He closed her off again. She pressed against it and it was a solid void. There, but empty space that merely existed. In the wake of it, she barely registered George brushing past her to follow him. The night swallowed them both. Silence pressed in. Roslyn stood still, stunned by the abrupt severing of closeness. She wanted to call him back. To demand one more second. Its not like they haven't been apart before, but this time…it felt so final. She swallowed the ache down. Tears threatened again, but she refused them. She turned the Sheryl. Her mouth opened to ask, she didn't know. Only a raw, scratchy sound escaped her. She lowered her gaze and shook her head instead. Holding herself together.

Sheryl understood Roslyn's sorrow and began to comfort her. She stepped closer, her voice lowering. "I understand loss," she said softly. "When life grants you only one true love—" She stopped. The words cut themselves off. Roslyn's trembling lips, the fragile shine in her eyes—it was too much. Sheryl straightened abruptly. For a fleeting second, a flicker of an old, haunting wound rose to the surface. Then it vanished. "This is not the hour for grief," she said, voice guarded and controlled. "It is time." She turned toward the corridor, already feeling the strain against her bones. "We transform, and run directly to the lake house." Sheryl turned and walked away, leaving Roslyn to reluctantly to follow behind her. And she followed, head bowed and heart heavy.

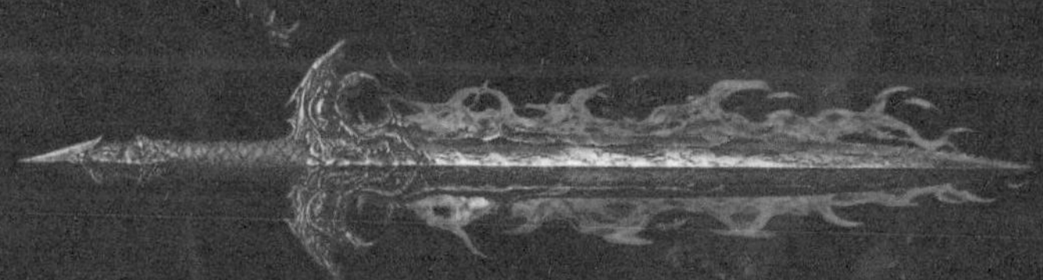

Shaking the last remnants of human flesh from his ebony fur, Eli lifted his massive head and cast his glowing eyes across the field. He found her instantly. Distance meant nothing. Roslyn stood beneath the moon like a shard of winter—her white fur luminous against the dark meadow. The light clung to her, making her appear almost celestial. Untouchable. He watched the subtle dip of her shoulders before she forced them back into place. Even as a Beast, he knew her tells. He had hurt her. He knew it. He had seen it in her eyes when he turned away without a word. She would never understand how deep his love ran—so deep it frightened him. So deep it was his only weakness. That was why he hadn't spoken. Goodbyes were too final. Too real. If he let himself say the words sitting in his chest, he might not have been able to walk away. So, he chose silence. He chose distance. He chose to let her think him cold. Better she resent him. Better she believe him hardened. Because if this night ended in blood and prophecy fulfilled, he would not leave her clinging to warm, final memories that would rot into grief. Hope, when shattered, was more lethal than hatred. In his own brutal way, he was protecting her. Even from himself.

He watched Roslyn turn her head. Just once. A quick glance over her shoulder—searching and send a quick glance his way. The look in her luminous eyes made something inside his massive chest lurch. Then she disappeared into the thick wood line beside Sheryl. Gone. Eli exhaled slowly, a heavy breath steaming into the night air, as if he could expel the ache with it. He turned—and found George already standing several paces behind him. Watching. Seeing too much. Eli considered walking away. But George Crownwelm was not a man who let truths rot in silence.

"Out with it," Eli growled, not bothering to soften his tone.

"Why are you distancing yourself from her." His voice was steady, but sharp. "I've watched you since the moment you arrived. United for her. Detached for yourself. You are preparing her for your death."

"Because I am going to die," Eli replied just as bluntly and with cold acceptance.

George was taken back. He briefly shook his head as if to clear his mind to find some logical explanation with his statement. "Says who?" His tone cracked with incredulity.

Eli turned and began walking toward the edge of the woods. George followed. "Who says you're going to die, Eli?" His voice rose now, edged with command. "Seeker Raven?"

"No," The single word carried weight.

Getting irritated, George pushed further. His patience was more than thinned. "If not him, then who?"

Eli stopped. The forest breathed around them. The moonlight cut silver across his black fur as he turned slowly to face George. He held his gaze. Then he let the burden slip free. "I will have a son."

"How do you know that?" George asked quizzically.

Eli's eyes darkened as he sighed. Pride and grief warred inside his chest. "I wasn't told. I was shown." The field seemed to still around them. "I saw my son as a man." His voice thickened with emotion. "I knew it was him. He carried my strength. My build. He was everything I am and everything I am not." He swallowed. "And he had Roslyn's eyes. Her heart." He paused for a beat. "But he was alone. Not physically." He shook his head once. "It was…a feeling. A hollow around him. As if something had already been taken." Eli continued. His brows furrowed as his snout snorted, a bitter breath left him. "Then they said I was blessed. Blessed to see him now." His eyes burned again. "Just like how I overheard my father telling my mother how he had a vision of me grown before he died. A week later he was gone. A month later, my mother followed."

Silence pressed between them. The night was already heavy and charged. This thickened the balmy air to nearly unbreathable. George studied him carefully.

George stood silent, intrigued by this information. Then he probed a little farther. "Who's they, Eli?"

Eli glanced toward the moon as he did that night on the boat. He recollected that night perfectly and he began to speak of his encounter that had haunted his thoughts for so long. "It was our first week on the ship. We waited until the mortals slept before going above deck. I always checked first. Always." His eyes darkened. "Roslyn and I learned to go to the farthest part of the upper deck—near the rail—to transform. It was the most remote corner. The wind was loud there, and the spray of the ocean was constant. The water washed the blood from us. Any trace of where we were…disappeared into the black." A faint exhale escaped his snout. "But that night…someone was already there." The moonlight silvered his fur as he described it. "The crescent moon caught on a cloak. Dark blue. Heavy. Draped over a thin, angular frame. It hung wrong. The cloak didn't move," Eli said. "Not with the wind. Not with the sway of the ship. The sea spray passed through it. The rain poured through it. The figure never shifted." His voice lowered. "It should have frightened me, but it didn't." He shook his head once. "It felt inevitable." He glanced back at George, but his eyes were still far away. "I almost turned back. I should have. Then it spoke. It had called my name. They never turned around. Just stared looking out at the ocean."

"What did you do?" George stepped closer, his interest sharpened.

Eli's gaze locked onto George's. "I answered. I stepped toward him. Time… unraveled. It didn't move the way it should have. Each second felt like a grain of sand falling in isolation. And then I was there. Right behind the figure." He lifted his hand unconsciously as if reliving it. "I reached for the cloak." His fingers flexed. "The silk was real. And that is when he turned." Eli's eye burned brighter was he spoke. "The world disappeared. There was no deck. No ocean. No wind. Only light. His face…I can't properly describe it." He stopped briefly, remembering. "Golden hair. And his eyes, seemed older than the sea. Then his wings unfolded. They were massive and so white with light, it was blinding. They stretched higher than his head and blocked out the moonlight, making it their own. I had never seen him before…and yet I knew him. Ramiel." The name felt heavy in the air. "One of the seven." Eli's chest rose and fell slowly. "My breath left me, but I did not need it. My thoughts emptied. There was only him. His green eyes bore hard into mine. He lifted his hands. I saw he held a bronze lantern and an ebony dagger within his steady hands. He raised both into the air. Then he spoke." Eli's jaw tightened. "I remember every word. The words echoed in Eli's head, but he kept them to himself.

I saw you long ago in a vision granted to your father. I pity your bloodline. I offer you the same blessing bestowed upon him. Blessed to see my vision before death and fire consume you. Eli continued. "He cast the lantern and the dagger onto the deck." Eli's eyes flickered. "And the world ignited. I saw myself dead. Keller standing over my body. That fucking smile twisting across his smug face." Eli's voice roughened. "I demanded to know how. He said a sacrifice needed to be made…for something greater to live." The bitterness in his tone sharpened before it softened once more. Quiet and solemn. "And then I saw him. My son. He was grown. Strong. Alive. He stood unbroken and healthy. And I understood." The words nearly tore from him. "My death secured his life."

Silence swallowed the clearing for several moments before his hollow words filled the air. "When the vision ended, I was on my knees. He was gone. The ocean returned. The wind. The empty deck. All was as it should have been." Eli exhaled through his teeth. "And I had to walk back below. To Roslyn. To hold her. To tell her everything would be fine." His voice hardened, scathingly he spit out the words. "Knowing it would not. That kind of knowledge is cruel." He looked at George again. "But I know she survives because I saw our son grown. In that I've found acceptance and peace."

George's long silver fur blew in the warm wind. He stood in silence for several long moments as he took deep breaths in and looked up to the moon, shaking his head slightly before he looked back at Eli. "I am rendered speechless, Eli," he finally admitted. "This is beyond us. If an archangel has intervened—" He exhaled slowly again. "This exceeds bloodlines and vendettas." His voice carried the weight of his heavy heart. "I don't know what to say."

Eli's words were sharp. "Don't say anything. I understand my purpose. And now that I know heaven itself stands behind this…my life is worth giving." His anger deflated some as demand coaxed his words. "But only if my son lives. Only if Roslyn survives." His voice fractured slightly. "I will never hunt beside him. Never teach him how to track by scent. Never see him through his immortal sickness." His jaw clenched as he pushed the words through. "Never stand there when he shifts for the first time and feels what it means to become something more." The ache sharpened. "But Roslyn will. And if mercy allows it…perhaps I will see it from wherever I am sent." Then his gaze hardened into something resolute. "What I need from you, George, is your word. Care for them. Teach them. Help her raise my son in our ways. There is no one else I trust." He stepped closer. "Promise me you will protect them. Guard their names with yours."

He began to stumble over his words as his inner turmoil raged. "I will do my damn best to change my fate, but if I fall, I do not want enemies finding loose ends." His voice dropped. "They must never be hunted for this prophecy that echoes in my bloodline. I am the Beast that must die to end the era of the corrupt order once and for all. Flames to the *Beast*." The wind shifted through the trees. Eli's words were final. They were a command. "Promise me."

George stared at Eli for a long moment. The weight of what had been said settled over him like a frost. Shock dulled his usual sharpness. But he did not waver. He gave one hard nod. "I promise." The word carried iron.

Relief moved through Eli's chest like released tension from a drawn bowstring. He exhaled slowly. He glanced once more at the moon. "Then let's get on with it."

George stepped forward, aligning himself beside Eli. Two dark silhouettes beneath silver light. He drew in a deep breath. His chest expanded fully. Then he released it. The howl that tore from him was raw, the pitch was harsh, urgent, and commanding. It did not sound like a Beast Blood, but something older. The sound cut through the night and rolled outward in widening circles, striking trees, hills, and water. It carried code hidden within tone—a pattern only those attuned would understand. The final not thinned into silence. The forest held its breath. Seconds passed.

"Do it again," Eli pressed.

"Wait." George didn't look at him. Then—from the treeline to the north, a pack answered. They mirrored the pattern. Then moments later, another answered from farther east. Then another. Farther still. Then Sheryl's call returned to him echoing and spreading the message farther into the forest and hills. They sound layered. Spreading. A chain reaction.

Eli's ears twitched as he calculated distance. "That one came from across the lake." His voice carried disbelief. "That's over fifty miles.

After a few moments, a close group of wild forest wolves began to mimic the same drawn-out howl that George had initiated. Seconds after the first pack had completed their howl, another group sounded off and were farther from them. As well as another group that was even farther away.

George nodded, and replied. "If Keller's men are near, they will hear only the forest wolves howling the call to arms for us." His silver-blue eyes gleamed. "But our kind hears instruction." Another wave of answering howls rippled through the land—rhythmic, intentional. Miles of territory ignited with sound. Hundreds of miles. Across forests, fields, and hidden dens, elder wolves shifted course. Answering and moving. The message was clear where to gather. "Now we wait." He brushed past Eli, satisfaction calm and contained. "Let's patrol the perimeter before the clans arrive."

CHAPTER FOURTEEN
RALLY CRY

June 1st, 1881

Upon suggesting they split to cover more ground, Eli volunteered for the northeastern perimeter of George's vast estate. George took the southwestern post without argument. The distance suited Eli. After everything that had unfolded, solitude felt necessary—like drawing a steady breath after nearly drowning. He passed the abandoned servant's house, its windows dark and hollow, long untouched by life. Ivy crawled over the stone like a slow reclamation. No laughter had echoed there in years.

Beyond it, the garden opened in lavish quiet. He moved along the stone pathway, the pads of his feet patterned softly against the aged mortar. Massive blossoms spilled over manicured beds—roses heavy with perfume, peonies drooping under their own velvet weight, foxglove and lavender swaying in the evening breeze. Marble statues stood in silent witness, their expressions frozen in serenity that mocked the storm brewing beyond these walls. The stable loomed ahead. Inside, Maximous shifted contentedly in a hey-filled stall, unaware of war or prophecy. Eli slowed. Beauty pressed in around him—carefully cultivated, orderly, controlled. A world preserved. And yet it felt fragile. Like glass waiting for the first stone.

Some statues bore the hardened faces of men who had known war—jaws set in eternal defiance, brows carved into permanent severity. Yet one made him slow. He stopped before a weather-worn figure of a long-haired woman cloaked in stone. Within the folds of her mantle, she cradled a newborn to her breast. Two chubby-cheeked children clung to the hem of her gown, craning to glimpse their sibling. Their small mouths were shaped in laughter, frozen in frolic. It should have been serene. It wasn't. Something in the scene unsettled him. He studied the woman's face more closely. Her lips curved faintly upward—but her eyes. The sculptor had not given them joy. They held a depth that did not match the smile. A quiet grief hidden beneath devotion. Eli's gaze dropped to the square stone base. EVE.

The name stirred something unresolved yet offered no clarity. He remained there a moment longer, trying to understand what he felt—then let it pass. White peonies clustered thickly around the pedestal, their heavy blooms spilling over the edge of the pathway. Petals brushed against his leg as he shifted. Their fragrance rose warm and sweet in the evening air. He drew it into his lungs, holding it longer than necessary. A striking thought made him realize this would be the last time he would see the transition of spring fade into days of summer. Then, Fall will eventually arrive, and soon he would be buried within the earth. Warriors were not promised seasons. They were promised purpose. *A sacrifice for the greater good. A necessary price for the longevity of my bloodline.* He told himself dutifully and to rid himself of the emptiness he was feeling.

"Eli!" George's howl cut through the night, sharp with triumph.

Eli's ears snapped upright at the sound. He pivoted instantly, catching the direction of the call from the western edge of the estate. Without hesitation, he launched forward—clearing the stretch near the servant's house in long, powerful strides. Gravel scattered beneath his paws as he veered sharply around the porch corner. He slid to a halt. The moonlit yard had transformed. George stood at its center—broad, steady, commanding. Before him, the forest breathed. From between the trees, they emerged. They trickled from the forest, one by one at first. Then in clusters. Then in a steady, unbroken current. Werewolves of every shade and size—silver, sable, russet, ash, coal. Scarred veterans. Lean hunters. Towering brutes. Their pelts caught the moonlight in shifting waves as they flowed from shadow into open ground. They did not speak, but they assembled. They gathered in disciplined silence. Hundreds of eyes gleamed beneath the moon, fixed forward, waiting.

Eli rose to his hind legs, towering now in his full height. His shoulders squared as he began striding toward George, his presence no less formidable. The call had been answered. "What do you think, Quicksilver?" Eli asked, voice low but edged.

George waited until the last wolf slipped from the tree line and joined the mass before responding. "Three hundred and fifty-seven, so far," he said with a sigh, "And that is including us" His silver-blue gaze swept over the assembled ranks. "Most that are here are lesser wolves. A handful of Elders and Alphas. Raw strength, but undisciplined." He flexed his shoulders some as a shiver raised the hair down his back through his tail. "They are trainable. With direction they will become savage killers." He lifted his head slightly, listening to the distant forest. More were on their way. "It's a stronger turnout than I anticipated for these parts. Whatever waits ahead…it seems we are not without favor."

Eli gave a curt nod as he coolly marveled at the sight. He heard all that George said but began to calculate the odds and favors of this war. "His numbers sit near a thousand," Eli said coolly. "But ours are worth more." He stepped forward, gaze hardening. "One our ours could equal fifty of his mortal men." His eyes narrowed. "That puts us eight hundred ahead in strength. And that's before the rest answer." The faintest hint of a predator's satisfaction flickered through him. "For now," he concluded, "the advantage is ours."

"That's if they survive their weapons and fire and tar long enough to reach the mud pits," George countered, watching another Beast Blood slip past and take its place among the ranks. "And that's assuming Keller hasn't found a way to turn the men like him."

Eli didn't flinch. "Then we adapt," he said assured, stepping forward. "We outthink them. We outlast them." He looked over the crowd. "Our people will survive. And they will fight." There was no boast in it. Only decision. We'll make damn sure of both."

George studied him for a moment. Then he nodded once toward the crowd. "Then bind them together, Eli. Make them follow you into battle."

Eli nodded. He saw hundreds of glowing eyes looking at him in wonderment, skepticism, and blankness. He saw their moonlit forms as still as statues as they waited. Liberating a hot breath from his snout, he rolled his shoulders, straightened his posture, and readied himself to rally the recruits. He let his presence settle over them first. When he spoke, it was not from the throat. His words were cast clear, sharp, and impossible to ignore.

"I am Alpha Eli Andre Victor Santos, the Second." His voice carried—not shouted, but projected through bone and blood. "I was named for my father. A man who lived one thousand and forty years before fire swallowed him whole on the Atlantic. A Thogagi boarded his ship, masquerading as crew member waiting for his moment." A low growl ripped through the gathered ranks. "The creature succeeded." Eli's eyes hardened. "The mortal survivors spoke of madness. Of cruelty. Of a thing that delighted in violence." He inhaled once, steady. "The night my father burned, I lay in bed gripped by immortal sickness. A boy. By dawn, I was Alpha."

He saw the crowed shift as they listened, he continued. "I transformed for the first time and inherited a throne still warm with my father's blood." Silence tightened. "I let anyway." His shoulders squared. "I hid my people from the Ebony Hunters before the reformation. I guided our young through their first kills. I built homes. I built sanctuary." His voice dropped lower. "We lived in peace." The words cracked with emotion that was still so raw in his chest. "Until five months ago." His eyes flashed with moonlight. "I was betrayed by the commander of the Ebony Knights—declared my clan a blight." A collective rumble stirred the wolves. He let that sit. No embellishment. No dramatics. Just truth. "They had ordered to have my clan, my people executed. Most of my clan had burned!" His roar split the night. "Women, children—my men—warriors." The wolves stirred, claws digging into soil. "And I stand before you because peace does not protect us." His gaze cut through the crowd. "Alliances forged in promises of sanctuary no longer protect us." His voice dropped—controlled, dangerous. "Our combined strength does!"

The ranks erupted. Thoughts slammed into him through the bond—disbelief, outrage, suspicion. Hundreds of voices colling at once. The noise ricocheted through his skull like shrapnel. He did not recoil. He absorbed it. "Your shock is mine," he thundered, silencing several voices at once. "Your disbelief was mine." A ripple of hesitation moved through the pack. "Most of us with old blood ties knows the Order." Murmurs shifted. "Some of you were told they were myth. Some of you swore oaths beside them. Some of you fought beside them to thin the evil among their ranks and mortals." His jaw flexed. "The bonds are severed." The words landed like a blade. "Corruption has rotted through their barracks. The Holy Order of St. Michael has fallen."

Eli heard the gasps, the growls and continued. His eyes burned and his voice dripped in conviction. "No balance remains. And the one who commands their broken remnants stood over my brother-in-law's burning corpse and vowed revenge." Another uproar detonated.

"You spill lies!" a female voice snarled from somewhere deep within the mass. "My clan is protected by Seeker Raven's sigil. I have proof!"

"This is madness!" another barked. "You use myth of a legend to marsh us to slaughter."

Another responded in the crowd. "It's not a myth. Before Seeker Raven, the Order slaughtered my great-grandmother's clan."

"What proof do you have?" A male, with copper-colored fur and dark green eyes, snapped his teeth and growled while he shouted his inner voice at Eli. "What proof do you have, Alpha?" The challenge hung heavy. Testing. Measuring him. Eli did not snarl back, He stepped forward. And the ground itself seemed to shift beneath him.

George stepped forward before Eli could answer. "I am Elder George Crownwelm." His voice did not rise, but it cut through the chaos. "But most of you know me by another name." He paused for a beat. "Quicksilver."

The effect was immediate. Murmurs died mid-growl. Heads lowered. Several wolves instictvely shifted their stance. Reputation traveled faster than scent. Yet one voice—sharp, mocking—pierced the quiet.

"You're not Quicksilver, old man! Half of the bloods in the northern territories have claimed to be the phantom wolf—."

George vanished. One blink. That was all it took. The lesser wolf was on his back before he understood he had moved. George's hand clamped around the light-brown throat, pinning him to the earth. Claws pressed just enough to break skin. Gasps rippled outward as the crowd moved away from the scene. George lowered his head close to the wolf's ear. "I am law to mortal men," he said softly. The softness was worse than shouting. "I am judgement to the half-born who slip through our territories." His gripped tightened. Not crushing. Promising. "You know peace, because of *me*. I am the order of the north." He hissed. "I know the scent of corruption. I know the sound of lies. "His silver-blue eyes swept the crowd while he held the wolf suspended between dignity and death. "And I deliver justice with a speed that leaves to time for regret." He released him. The lesser collapsed, coughing, scrambling back into the mass. A female greeted him, his mate, and began to nuzzle his neck, licking the hurt away in comfort as he glared at George and Eli.

George continued. "I stand with Alpha Eli Santos" He stepped back into place beside Eli. "You would be fools not to listen." Thoughts no longer ricocheted wildly—they moved in low murmurs now. Wolves learned toward one another, conferring in tight clusters. Fear had shifted into consideration. George met Eli's gaze briefly. A nod. Authority had been secured. Now the floor belonged to the Alpha again.

Eli stepped forward. When he spoke, the bond darkened. "Flames to the Beast." His inner voice became darker, deeper as it fluctuated in tone. "Flames to the Beast." The words rolled through him like distant thunder. "My brethren…those words were spoken long before any of us stood beneath this moon. They were not myth. They were warning." His gaze swept across the mass. "They were passed down because those who came before us believed this night would arrive. You are not here solely because I called you." His words gritted, "You are here because you have felt it. Beast Bloods have fallen. Mothers. Sisters. Daughters. Wives." He swallowed once, steadying his emotions that burned raw. "Brothers. Son. Fathers."

The last word nearly caught but he forced it through. "Husbands." The bond trembled with restrained grief. He could feel Roslyn push against the mental door he had raised again. "They take. They infiltrate. They burn. And they believe we will remain divided." His teeth bared. "They believe wrong! Countless perished then," Eli growled, his voice rolling through them, "and twice as many since we allowed fear to push us from out power."

Eli could feel the aura of the crowd turn in his favor. Their eyes held experience; their heads nodded in agreement and their hearts churned their blood faster. They were starting to band together. He could feel it deep within his soul. He continued and grasped their attention further. Eli snarled and snapped as he continued. The hair raised on the back of his neck while he barred his teeth. "I will fear death no longer. I will not live bowed to it. I will fight—until fire consumed my flesh—for what is right. Will *you* live today only to cower tomorrow?" A rumble spread. "When they want to take from you. Coming for your homes? Dragging your families into the flame? When your newborns are torn from your arms?" His voice cracked like a whip. "Will you watch?" Growls answered. "Will you kneel while an Elder demon commands mortal mobs to finish what he began?"

"No!"

The roar erupted before he could demand it. Eli seized it. "We were scattered!" The ground vibrated beneath them. "We were broken!" Claws struck soil as some scratched at the ground. Others snarled and snapped through there growls. Teeth bared and eyes glowed with power. With unity. They were becoming one pack. Eli stepped forward until he was surrounded by the pack. They began to respect him. "Not anymore," Eli roared. "Not tomorrow." The word barked from him and hit like a hammer. "Now!"

Howls and yips began to emerge from the crowd. "And I stand before you not only as Alpha—" His voice dropped into something primal as he growled, "but as a warrior willing to die beside you. For you. So the Order will finally fall and no one will hold power or corruption over us again. We will not be managed. We hold the power now. Flames to the *real* beast!" He looked around as their hearts beat as one. "Who stands with me?"

The answer came like thunder. Howls shattered the stillness. The trees trembled beneath it. Even the earth seemed to inhale with their unified cry. Eli let the sound rise—crest—become a living force. Then he split it cleanly. "Flames to the Beast." The chant struck back at him, stronger. "Flames to the Beast." The words rolled outward, crashing through the forest in waves of devotion and fury. Eli's gaze locked with George's. Silver-blue met black. Approval passed between them without need for speech. Before them stood no longer scattered clans, but one pack. Their voices rose again beneath the full moon, raw, and relentless. Before Creator. Before witness sky. Before whatever darkness dared answer. "Flames to the Beast!"

CHAPTER FIFTEEN
OF GODS AND GENERALS

As the army dispersed to savor what little freedom remained, Eli turned to the leaders that stepped forth for further command. They stood firm beneath the moon. "For the months to come, you stand in co-command." He directed with no flourish. Just decree. "You will earn trust—with each other and with those now under your watch. His gaze moved from one to the next. "George and I remain higher in authority. The situation requires it. No apology. "But your roles are not secondary." His tone sharpened. "You are the pillars that will hold this army upright. You govern by the ancient laws. Not the private codes of your former clans. Equality is a must. Treat each male and female as if they were your blood-kin. Protect them. Drive them. Correct them." His voice lowered, colder now. "Weakness breeds death. And we cannot afford either weakness or foolishness."

Silence, but understanding passed through the leaders. Several even nodded. "If you grow lax in your duty—" His black gaze did not waver. "You will be corrected." He did not need to describe how. "The example will be public." A final pause. "Do you understand?"

"We understand." Eli gave a slight nod. "I expect you to hold yourself to the same standard we do. None of us stand above these laws." His tone steadied—less fire now, more steel. "Strength. Unity. Purpose." Each word struck distinctly. "This is what will keep our hearts beating as one now and when battle comes. "We fight together. We endure together. We die together." The wind shifted with the rise of an approaching storm. The smell of water filled the air. "I will question each of you now. I need your strengths. Your weaknesses. Your experience. Am I clear?"

"Yes." The response rose automatically. Except for one voice. "Clear enough…General." The title carried edge. A challenge. The male stepped forward slightly from the line. Broad-shouldered. Confident. His eyes held Eli's without flinching. "Your urgency is understandable. You fear for your mate." A quiet ripple passed through the other commanders. "And your unborn son." The male continued on without accusation, but almost observantly. "I would do the same." A slight tilt of his head. "If my wife were hunted by a friend turned Thogagi, I would summon ten thousand armies."

Silence settled heavy. Shocked someone knew him so intimately it was too close for any comfort. Eli snapped his head to look to his left. He locked eyes on the large blue orbs of the werewolf who held challenge in his gaze. He stepped past George without breaking stride and approached the newly appointed Elder pair at the far end of the line. He assessed the female first. Slate-gray fur. Lean frame. Black shadowing radiating from her green eyes like war paint spread to her perked ears. She was dainty compared to her burly mate. Nevertheless, she looked as if she could hold her own when push came to shove. She did not lower her gaze now. Then Eli shifted to her mate. In his beast form, the man was every bit as tall as Eli, but twice the size of his mountainous frame. The stranger's fur was a dark smoky blue, which complimented his royal blue eyes. He looked deeply into the male's face and suddenly understanding struck him. "You're an Inceptor."

The stranger fidgeted slightly, not in nervousness, but in anticipation. He tilted his head slightly. "Good eye. Noticed the split pupil, did ya?"

Eli felt auspicious to have an esteemed warrior respond to their call. "You're a rare breed," he said. "A gift. And a risk." A flicker of something passed through the Inceptor's eyes. "You kind cannot remain within crowds too long." Eli's voice lowered. "Not without consequence." The air tightened. Inceptors—few were born in a century. Fewer survived their own minds. Their souls did not stay anchored. They fractured. Slipped. Returned and changed. Sometimes torn. Sometimes not fully whole. Madness was not myth among them. It was probability.

The massive wolf's jaw flexed slightly. "You are well-informed."

Eli held his gaze. "I make it a point to understand every weapon that stands beside me. Man or beast."

The Inceptor's lips curved faintly. "Seclusion is discipline," he replied. The man remarked firmly, but with a twinge of despondency. "I saw *everything* I needed to trust your leadership."

Eli noticed the hidden meaning and knew the wolf had seen what the angel showed him on the boat. It brought a grim tone to his voice and soured his disposition. A grim shadow darkened Eli's expression. He stepped closer until their muzzles nearly touched. A growl rumbled in his throat. "What is your name?" he asked.

"Talos." The wolf replied without hesitation.

Eli growled again, eyes narrowing, "Then hear me, Talos, I've accepted what was shown to me." The admission was sharp. "I will fight until the last breath in my lungs proves it wrong. You will keep what you saw to yourself. This is not a lost cause."

Talos didn't flinch, but studied Eli further with understanding. Your bravery boarders on defiance," Talos replied calmly. "Tis the mark of a true warrior."

There was no insult in it, but Eli held his stare a moment longer, then broke the tension himself with a nod. Then, asking firmly, "Where do you hail. Those markings—the black around your mate's eyes, the smoke in your coat—that it northern blood. You hail from the dominion in the far north?"

Talos's eyes squinted slightly in approval as he nodded. "We dwell in the forests of the Great North, but my blood hails further than you've likely traveled," he replied. "The frost lands beyond the lake country." I am Talos Wolfgram. Elder by blood and age. Last living remnant of my great-grandfather's Viking line." His gaze fell upon his mate for a moment before he looked back to Eli and George. "We thrive in our solitude in the greater part of the country still unseen by mortal eyes. A Thogagi would die from the bitter cold before they could ever reach us." He looked to his side again, "My wife, Sizrra. She is younger than I—She's a Shadow Wolf of the Rockies." A faint hint of pride stirred in his tone. "She scouts unseen. She kills without waste. No blood trails. No sound. When she strikes, they're finished."

Eli regarded them both briefly, cutting off any personal undercurrent before it could swell. "It's good we called on such disciplined blood." His tone shifted from intimate to tactical. "With your dexterity, you and your mate will serve in the outer defensive ring. No one breaches our perimeter unseen." He held Talos' gaze. "You will begin scouting rotations immediately." Then without turning his head, he shouted, "Quicksilver."

George stepped closer, silver-blue eyes assessing Talos and Sizrra in one swift sweep. "A fitting placement," George replied evenly. "If they are what they claim to be, the outer ring will never falter." He shrugged, adding, "And if they aren't we will know quickly."

Eli gave a curt nod. "After the first full month of training, you will select your own perimeter unit. Once your watch is secured, you will command the hunting parties."

George hollered down the line. "Any others among you possess prior battle experience, intelligence work or strategic planning?" His tone cut across the remaining leaders. "Speak now."

A male eagerly stepped forward and turned to them. In the moonlight, his fur illuminated to a rich brown and his light turquoise eyes glowed in an eerie starkness. He was tall, but thinner compared to the others. He spoke with a well-educated mind, and his inner voice sounded reserved as if he spent more time with books than people. "I…I am Professor Andante Hartman. I have not commanded a warband before. I have never faced a Thogagi in open combat." His turquoise eyes lifted. "But I have lived six centuries embedded among mortals. I study patterns. Systems. Power structures, and historical war strategies." He stepped forward half a pace more. "I know the history of the Holy Order. I was allied with their sanctuary after Solomon's

Reformation. I answered this call because it is my duty." His voice dipped as he looked back at the crowd real quick locking eyes with a female who had three adolescents with her. Their fur all the same chestnut brown as they played around their mother's legs.

Andante looked to Eli to stake his place within the ranks. "I also understand the history of the Holy Order. I had made an alliance with the sanctuary before they decided to summon the surrounding outposts south during the Solomon's Reformation. I answered the call because it's my duty to do so. As we all know, there are worse things to experience than the pain of death. Especially when it is your own you're worried about. My daughters and wife—"

"That is enough, Andante." Eli cut in." Their eyes held for a moment.

"I know the art of war." Andante finished quietly.

Talos tilted his head slightly. "A soul hungry for battle," he observed.

Andante continued, calmer now. "For five hundred years I have studied it. "If you understand what a man fights for, you can predict where he will strike first."

Intrigued, Eli carefully listened intently as he questioned, "Then what's his next move?"

Andante didn't hesitate. He smoothly continued. "If I'm reading this correctly, your clan was targeted not without reason. He's not waiting. He's readying himself and the army." He released a slow breath, "He will test our numbers. Send lesser forces first. Probe for weaknesses. Draw you into overconfidence." His eyes sharpened. "He believes you will respond emotionally. He will expect you to move your strongest piece too soon. If this were chess—"

Talos huffed faintly. "Why is war always compared to chess?"

Andante looked at Eli and shook his head once. "Humor me," Eli said.

Andante inclined his head. "The Thogagi is not reckless. He will send expendable pieces first. Pawns. Then his bishops and knights—specialized weapons, arcane tactics." His gaze lifted slightly. "But in the end, he is still the king—limited in movement and vulnerable once exposed—trying to get to your side of the board." Andante stepped forward, talking with his hands as he looked at the mental war board that he could only see before him. "But in this game, he's missing a highly valuable player. The queen. And when positioned correctly, a queen ends a war faster than any other piece on the board because all eyes are turned on her."

Eli gritted his teeth and growled low in his chest. Stillness pressed in before Eli's voice cut through it—controlled and coiled with danger. "You assume my queen will be placed in play."

Andante met his gaze for a moment, flinching slightly. "I assume the enemy already believes she will be."

"No." Eli snapped with authority and iron in his tone. "I will not gamble her life nor the life of our child."

Andante didn't argue. "I understand," he said quietly, processing that information.

"I'll do it." The voice was soft, almost swallowed by the night."

Heads turned as the female stepped forward again. She straightened her spine. "I'll take her place," This time her voice was firm and an octave louder than before.

Eli's gaze swept over her in a single assessing pass. Brown fur. Earth-toned. Leaner frame and yellow-blonde eyes. "It won't work," he said evenly. "You bear no resemblance to my mate."

The female held his stare. "Does the Thogagi know what she looks like when she shifts?" The female asked with a tone as if she already knew the answer.

Eli's tension eased some as her point was well established. "No," he admitted. "She has always remained at my side during Callings. When we fled, he was not present. She was never separated from me or the clan long enough to be studied."

The female nodded once as her voice carried the logic through. "Then he does not know. He expects her there. Especially if he believes her to be a weakness of yours." With a slight lift in her chin, she said, "Let him. I draw him in. You position me. You strike. Or I strike. Either way, he dies and the Order alongside of it and we can be free from this part of our long, drawn history."

"It's sounds like a good addition to the plan, Eli." George chimed. He looked at the female. "Your name?"

"Holly Skuleye." She stood steady beneath the scrutiny. "Elder. Made of the blood. I lead a clan of cavern." She added in with an air of pride, "They follow well."

Speaking again, Andante stepped in carefully. "We now have structure." He nodded toward Talos and Sizzra. "Outer security." Then to George, "Combat refinement." Then he nodded to Eli. "You are the pivot and she—" he gestured subtly toward Holly. "She is the lure."

George watched Eli carefully. The army was forming around his will. "Thoughts?" He asked.

Eli's gaze remained lowered for a long moment. Calculating. If Keller believed Roslyn was vulnerable, and believed that he was desperate, then his overconfidence could be his undoing. "The lake house is isolated," he said quietly. Then he raised his head, eyes sharpened. "Stone foundation. Limited approaches. Dense tree line to the north."

George's silver-blue gaze narrowed slightly. "You intend to draw him there? Where we just sent our Sheryl and Roslyn?"

Eli did not hesitate. "We draw him where we choose." His gaze swept across the estate—the tall pines, the flowering maples, the meadow grass already brittle in the dry wind. He inhaled once. "You can feel it. The air is denser and dusty. This season will bring a drought." He looked back to everyone and added, "And we are not going to sit in a forest that can be turned into a pyre."

George nodded once, replying, "Their weapon is fire. No trees to torch. No canopy to trap heat."

"Then we take away its strength," Eli countered.

Talos stepped forward slightly. "We build mud trenches along the shoreline. Keep our warriors coated and heavy with mud." His blue eyes gleamed. "Spike trenches between land and water. Funnel them where we choose. He heard George give a short approving grunt.

Holly spoke carefully. "If he hunts by scent, we can give him what he wants. I can carry your mate's trace."

Andante added, looking at Eli. "Not her scent alone." All eyes turned." Andante's mind was already moving. "How long did it take you to travel here?" Andante asked.

"We moved cautiously. Masked everything we could. It took longer than necessary. Why?" Eli questioned.

Andante nodded, "What if we used the drought to our advantage? With drought, scent lingers. No rain to erase it." He looked at Holly. "We create a controlled trail." His gaze moved to Talos. "You'll know where to place your scouts and outposts for lookouts." He looked back at Eli and Holly. "You lay the trail into our trap." Silence held the space before a moment before he added in, "He will suspect deception," Andante continued calmly, "But suspicion still requires pursuit. If he believes he is close enough, he will commit." Another low rumble of approval echoed low, but from Talos this time.

"Predators like them overextend when they smell blood. It could be his downfall. Usually is of gods and generals. The enemy thinks he's both."

George folded his arms. "And when he commits, we close the jaws."

All eyes shifted to Eli. This was no longer a theory. It was becoming doctrine, waiting on the final word. For a moment he said nothing. The weight of command settled heavily on his shoulders. The plan was sound—but something was missing. An escape. "We cannot trap ourselves against the water," Eli said at last. "If the battle turns, we must be able to withdraw and regroup." His eyes flicked between them. "We need a tunnel." He saw a few brows lift. "From here to the lake house. Beneath the ground. With our strength," he continued, "we could dig it in weeks. Split the labor among teams. Rotations day and night. Start from both ends and meet in the middle."

George's eyes narrowed as he calculated the distance. "That's roughly about fifteen miles—"

Eli cut him off. "Can it be done?" He pressed. The question hung in the air like a challenge. The silence was deafening for a moment before Holly's voice rang through. Her claws sank into the soil, carving deep groves through the earth. "With my clan," she said firmly, "it can." She lifted her gaze. "We are cavern dwellers. We build systems like this all the time."

That was all Eli needed. A low rumble rolled through his chest as he nodded. "Then we have a plan." His eyes hardened with resolve. "Let us end this once and for all."

CHAPTER SIXTEEN
THE HALL OF DAMNED SOULS

Temple ruins of The Holy Order of St. Michael
Fortaleza, Brazil

Keller stood over another failed soldier, disbelief hardening his features. The man's lifeless green eyes were frozen wide, still holding the terror he had suffered before death finally showed him mercy. His mouth hung open, locked in the shape of a scream that seemed to echo off the stone walls. Blood seeped steadily from his eyes, nose and ears, dripping onto the wooden table that had been converted into a crude holding rack. A black mist rose from the corpse—the shattered remnant of the damned soul that had been forced into the body. It spilled into the air like smoke before a sudden flash of light consumed it, erasing it from existence.

Keller's fury flared hotter. He roared and kicked the chamber door open so violently it slammed against the stone wall. His boots thundered down the corridor as he strode toward the Sabbath Hall. His jaw clenched, muscles twitching as his mind tore through the events of the failed ritual.

Earlier that morning, Keller had been informed that out of the thousand men gathered, a quarter had failed to receive the souls of the damned. The report had left him enraged. Determined to secure one more successful conversion, he waited. Hours passed as he stood in the shadows of the ruined hall, watching the sealed trick door that led to the deeper corridors. At least it opened. A lone soldier stepped through, clutching a missive meant for Keller. The man never saw him. Keller moved the instant the door closed behind him. He seized the unsuspecting soldier, wrenched his arms behind his back, and bound his wrists together before the man could even cry out. Then with brutal force, Keller drove him forward through the tunnels, forcing him toward the deeper chambers of the underground compound—the sections still usable for their needs.

As Keller forced the bound man down the corridor and into the great hall, the newly converted soldiers did not speak. They did not move. They simply watched. Black, beady eyes, followed Keller and his prisoner with slow, unsettling focus. One by one their necks tilted, joints creaking as they tracked the movement across the chamber. The hearth fires crackled behind them, their flames reflecting in those dark eyes like embers trapped beneath glass. The prisoner twisted violently in Keller's grip.

"Help me!" he shouted hoarsely. "Brothers—help me!"

No one moved. The man's pleased faltered as he studied their faces. Whatever humanity had once lived behind their eyes was gone. Only something cold remained. The firelight gleamed across their hollow stares, and the realization struck him with crushing certainty. Evil had taken root in holy ground.

"Demons!" he screamed. "Demons!"

Keller had only smiled.

They forced the struggling man into a candlelit chamber that had once served as Master Vaughn's healing room. The irony was not lost on Keller. Where wounds had once been treated, something far darker would now be born. The possessed soldier waiting inside moved without hesitation when Keller gave the order. He turned the surrounding tables, gathering the ritual instruments laid out across the wood. Behind him, Keller hauled the captive forward and slammed him onto the wooden platform. The man thrashed violently.

"What are you doing?" he shouted. "Let me go!"

Keller ignored him. He pinned the soldier down with brutal efficiency—one hand crushing the man's throat, the other forcing his legs against the table to stop kicking. The possessed soldier returned to the platform, the ritual items clutched in his hands. Keller lifted his gaze to meet the creature's blackened eyes. Then he gave a single nod.

Keller watched closely. He wanted to witness the final conversion himself. Following the ritual John had taught him, the possessed soldier moved with precision. He retrieved a small vial of Keller's tainted blood from the table and poured the thick, black liquid into a wooden chalice. The blood settled like dark sludge at the bottom. He then lifted a dagger and dipped the blade into the blackened mixture until the metal glistened red. The struggling man screamed and thrashed against Keller's grip when the solider seized the man's face and forced one green eye open.

Holding the blood-slick blade above the wide pupil, he let the gungy drops fall. "See the darkness," he whispered. Blood dripped into the eye. The man shrieked. "I can't see! I can't see!" His eyes rolled wildly before turning into pale, milky orbs. Without hesitation the knife was dipped into the chalice again, coating the razor edge with more of Keller's blood. He grabbed the man's chin and lifted the blade toward his face. But the prisoner twisted violently, knocking the soldier's hand aside as he thrashed from side to side.

Growing irritated with the man's struggling, the possessed soldier waited until the prisoner began shouting for help again. The moment the crying came, he struck. He jammed four fingers into the man's mouth and forced the jaw open with brutal pressure. The dagger hovered above the wide throat. Slowly the soldier tilted the blade. Dark blood dripped from the metal onto the man's tongue before sliding the blade clean against it. "Speak the darkness," he commanded, and withdrew his fingers.

The prisoner gagged and coughed as the acidic blood stained his teeth as he screamed again. His face turned red from how hard he screamed, body arched and veins protruding from under his skin. Then the words began. They spilled from his mouth in a broken mixture of his native tongue and something older—something harsh and guttural.

The language of the Nephilim. His soul fought against it. But the blood was already spreading through him, tainting flesh and spirit alike.

The soldier dipped the blade once more into the chalice and left it there as he turned back to the man. Grabbing the collar of the prisoner's thin black tunic, he ripped the fabric apart in a single motion. The cloth tore easily, exposing the man's heaving chest and trembling stomach. The prisoner's mind was beginning to fracture. Savage impulses stirred beneath his skin as the tainted blood spread through him. He threw his head to the side and struggled to lift it, forcing his blurred vision to focus on Keller.

"Please, Commander…" he rasped in the moment of his clarity. "Let me go—" The words died in his throat. The blood showed him the truth. What stared back at him was no longer a man. Beneath Keller's skin was something ancient and unholy. It stirred, and when those inhuman eyes locked onto him, terror consumed him. His screams tore through the chamber and echoed down the stone halls.

The possessed soldier pulled the dagger from the chalice. Blood clung thickly to the blade. He pressed the metal against the man's chest, just above the heart. The entryway for the soul. Slowly, he began to carve. The blade opened flesh in shallow, careful strokes. Blood flowed immediately, running down the man's chest and stomach in ribbons, mixing with the crimson coating the knife. Two vertical slashes. Then a horizontal cut crossing them both. The marks formed twin inverted crosses. Without a pause, the solider began carving again. Starting from the left point of the symbol, he etched the lines of the pentagram into the bleeding flesh. When the shape was complete, he dipped the blade back into the chalice. From its edge, he let a single drop of demon blood fall onto each point of the mark. Thirteen in all. The soldier spoke the final words. "Receive the darkness." He reached for a bowl beside the table and seized a handful of coarse salt. Without hesitation, he pressed the grains deep into the man's bleeding wound. The reaction was immediate. The prisoner screamed as the jagged crystals bit into the raw flesh of the carved symbol. His back arched violently against the wooden platform.

Unmoved, the soldier turned and retrieved a bottle from another table. The clear liquid inside sloshed softly as he removed the cork. The sharp scent of alcohol filled the room. He tilted the bottle and slowly poured the liquid over the wounded mark. Agony tore from the man's throat as the mixture burned through the wound, dissolving the salt and cleansing the gaping brand. Blood thinned and ran across the wood beneath him. When the bottle was empty, the soldier set it aside. Then he reached for a nearby candle, lowering the flame to the carved pentagram. Fire caught instantly. The burning alcohol ignited in a sudden flare, and the searing heat fused the ritual mark into the man's flesh. Smoke rose from the cauterized skin as the brand sealed itself into his chest.

Deep within Keller's shadowed mind, John watched in silence. He could feel it. Unholy power and presence gathered in the air like lightning before a storm. The candlelight flickered violently as the dark pulse moved through the room, rising and falling like the beat of a monstrous heart. The veil was open and a vessel was ready. From the corners of the chamber, shapes began to emerge. Black figures peeled themselves from the shadows, twisting and stretching into thin, darting forms. Dozens became hundreds, filling the chamber in a writhing swarm that swallowed the candlelight. The room dimmed beneath their presence. The prisoner saw them. They circled above him. Around him. Their shrill, piercing cries filled the chamber as they clawed at the air, fighting for the body bound beneath them. The branded flesh and blood made him a vessel. An empty gate waiting to be claimed. One by one the dark entities surged forward, colliding and tearing at one another as they tried to force their way inside him. They passed through his body in violent bursts of shadow, each ripping away fragments of his life. The law among them was simple. First kill. First claim.

The prisoner's throat had grown raw from his useless screams. Each time one of the vile souls forced its way through his body, it felt as though swords were being driven through him from the inside out. A freezing cold followed every intrusion, bursting through his flesh where the shadows passed. His strength was fading. Life was slipping away. His body convulsed violently as the darkness tried to claim him. Still, he resisted. An immoveable fragment of his soul clung desperately to reason and faith. It fought against the demon blood poisoning his veins. It fought against the writing entities clawing for dominion over his dying body. He would not surrender. For a moment the language of the fallen slipped from his lips, forced there by the ritual and the corruption spreading through him. But then something inside him broke free. The man pushed through the demonic syllables clawing at his tongue. With the last of his mortal will, he reclaimed his own voice. At first it came as a low, choking growl in his throat. Then gathering the final remnants of his strength, he lifted his head and cried out to the heavens.

"God!"

The word echoed through the chamber. For a heartbeat, the darkness recoiled, screeching and hissing as they took to the shadows before they swarmed the room once more like flies. The man's strength finally gave way. His head sagged against the wood as breath rattled in his chest. In a broken whisper only meant for the Creator, he spoke one last time.

"Forgive me."

A blinding light suddenly burst through the stone ceiling, pouring into the chamber like a spear from heaven. It engulfed the man's dying body. Keller and the possessed soldier recoiled instantly, turning away as the brilliance seared their eyes. The radiance burned against their pale flesh, forcing them back from the table. The shadowed entities shrieked in fury. Their piercing cries echoed through the chamber as they scattered, retreating violently into the corners and recesses of the room. The ritual had been broken. Pain surged through the man one final time as the demonic blood had been pulled from his body. Streaming like black smoke from his eyes, ears, nose, throat. Blood began to trickle in streaking rivers along his bronze flesh. The pain was fading. The coldness was gone.. The screaming voices were gone. The darkness that had clawed at this soul had vanished. The prisoner—the final solider—looked directly into the descending light. A faint smile touched his cracked, dry lips. Beyond the brilliance he saw something the others could not—freedom waiting within the warmth of that radiant beam. Divinity had come for him. With trembling effort, the man lifted a blood-stained hand toward the light. His lips moved as he whispered something meant only for the one who had answered his call. Then his body shuddered. Life slipped from him like a final breath. His arm fell limp as he collapsed back again on the wooden table with a hollow thud. The light vanished as suddenly as it had appeared. Darkness reclaimed the silent chamber. Keller and the soldier turned back toward the table. The man lay motionless. Dead.

"He was weak. Like the others," John remarked as they moved down the dim corridor.

Keller's jaw tightened. "We needed his soul to hold on long enough for the entity to take root. Without a living vessel, the spirit cannot anchor itself." His voice lowered, thick with frustration. "Is my army enough to face the Beast Bloods? What if their numbers exceed ours?" He heard the echoes harshly through the passage of his mind of John laughing, deep and mockingly. Keller stopped walking. Fury flashed across his face. "This is no laughing matter, demon." In his mind's eye, Keller could see John's smile widening.

"You're afraid," John said, amused. "All this power… and you still quaver." John began laughing again.

Keller bristled, his anger and voice rising in conjunction. "Do not mock me."

"*You* mock *me* with your fear, pestilent mortal!" John's voice exploded inside Keller's skull. The force of it drove Keller to his knees. Pain vibrated through his bones as the demon's presence filled his mind. "You still fail to understand what the circles of Hell truly are." John's tone shifted suddenly—calm, terrible, absolute. "In Hell we are not born warriors. We are forged. We are whipped. Burned. Flayed. Broken. Mended. Forced to rise and fight again. Again. And again." A low growl followed the words. "We battle each other. We battle mortals. We battle the angels themselves." His voice dripped with cold certainty. "The Beast Bloods are nothing compared to soldiers forged in the fires of Hell. Nothing compared to our fire." The demon's presence pressed tighter around Keller's thoughts. "And remember this, mortal. I am not merely a soldier. I am a Commander. My soldiers now live within your men."

"I don't see soldiers," Keller said coldly. "Only mindless shades. If this is what Hell has to offer…perhaps I have chosen the wrong side after all."

John's fury erupted inside his mind. The demon's presence coiled around Keller's heart like a tightening fist. His essence squeezed. Keller's pulse hammered violently in his chest. "Don't mock my gift!" John roared. "My kin are adjusting to their weaker vessels! They will be ready soon." The pressure tightened. "They must feed tonight. Feed them the humans who clung to their God—starting with the one who just died." John's voice dripped with savage anticipation. "You will witness their brutality soon enough."

Keller gasped as the crushing pain intensified. "I…let it go!" Keller yelled through gritted teeth. One hand clutched at his chest as his heart pounded wildly beneath his ribs. His breath came in short, desperate bursts. "Then do not oppose me," John growled. The crushing force vanished. Air rushed back into Keller's lungs as he steadied himself and slowly rose from the floor.

"Listen carefully, mortal. We know the Beast Bloods went north. If you march the entire army along the trail taken by Eli and Roslyn, we will be exposed. I know another path. There is a river that runs that will get us there. Prepare the carrack. It will carry our soldiers as far as the river allows. From there rowboats will take them the rest of the way to the shores of Lake Erie. Our men do not require sleep anymore. But they must feed—constantly. Raw meat. Blood will restore their strength. When they are fully fed, their speed will double. They will get us there in half the time." John's tone darkened with satisfaction. "Meanwhile…we move by land. You and I will lead thirty of our finest scouts as a diversion. While the main army strikes from the east."

Keller slowly nodded as he recalled the maps and globes scattered across the walls and floor of his bedchamber. "Yes…the river system that feeds into the Great Lakes," he murmured. "It will carry us through the waterways toward Like Erie." His lips curled faintly. "Farmland. Lumber towns. Settlements scattered along the banks." A dark satisfaction crept into his voice. "Our soldiers will feast along the way. The mortals will die…and their blood will strengthen our ranks."

John's voice slithered through his thoughts. "Are you ready to feel the glory of it?" A pause. "To claim Roslyn as your own….and take vengeance upon the man who stole her from you."

The words settled deep into Keller's mind. His eyes darkened. "More than you could ever know."

"Then gather the dead," John snarled. "Give them to our soldiers. Let them gorge." A pause lingered in Keller's mind. "Tonight…we march. And we will own the world." The words ignited something dark within him. Keller turned and strode down the corridor with fierce determination, heading for the great hall where his army waited.

CHAPTER SEVENTEEN
APPROACHING DANGER

September 3rd, 1881

Marching through the steep mountainsides of Virginia, Keller and John led a small scouting force of thirty well-equipped soldiers across the brutal terrain. Through rain, wind, night, and day, they marched with little rest. Every few days the orders were given to feed. The soldiers obeyed with savage eagerness. For miles they scattered into the wilderness, hunting and stalking anything that breathed—wildlife or human. When the hunt ended, each returned to camp clutching their prize. They crouched apart from one another, hunched over their kills like feral beasts. Their black, beady eyes darted nervously as they guarded their meal. Once satisfied no one would challenge them, they fell upon the carcasses with violent hunger. They tore into flesh with gnarled hands, ripping through hide and muscle. Blood spilled freely as they forced their mouths to the wounds, drinking greedily from the struggling bodies beneath them. Bones cracked. Organs spilled. Flesh was devoured raw and dripping. Though they had advanced beyond the earliest stages of conversion, remnants of their primitive nature still clung to them like rot.

When it was time to move again, they left with their hunger satisfied, their strength restored, and lifeless bodies rotting in their wake. Each soldier carried several oversized sacks of oiled leather filled with gunpowder, tinderboxes, and jars of flammable oil. Alongside the volatile cargo, every man bore weapons—swords, bows, and arrows—each blade and shaft coated in oil, waiting for a spark to send flames racing along the steel.

Standing in a scattered ray of late afternoon light, a scout positioned atop the hill searching the terrain ahead. Suddenly he shouted to Keller in the native, guttural tongue of the fallen angels. "Commander! I've spotted another dried blood mark!" He crouched low, studying the ground. Large footprints pressed deep into the disheveled leaves. "It looks as though he staggered over the debris of this rotten stump," the scout continued. "Then fell into this tree. The wound smeared across the bark."

Keller stomped toward the scout and dropped onto his haunches. Running his fingers across the rust-colored smear, he inhaled deeply. The scent was unmistakable—Eli. "Good," he snapped. "Move ahead and watch for more markings." The soldier obeyed immediately, moving forward along the trail. Sniffing the air and overturning leaves and rocks as he tracked carefully through the forest. Keller remained crouched, studying the bloodstain. Roslyn had been here. He closed his eyes and inhaled deeply, catching the faint trace of her scent clinging to the leaves around the smear of blood. He held his breath, holding the scent for so long his lungs burned with spent air. He released a shaky and slow breath. He was eager to finally reach her…yet something about this felt too easy. Yet he was so close to her to give up now. His pulse quickened. The thought dragged him inward.

Keller shivered as dark pleasure flooded his mind. Images of Roslyn rose vivid, consuming, and intoxicating. He could almost taste her lips. Almost feel the warmth of her skin beneath his hands. He imagined his teeth slicing into her beautiful flesh above her breasts. Her stomach. She would moan for him with every incising prick as he watched little torrents of blood run down her little perfect body. He would lick every trail clean, taking every drop as he ran his tongue over her body. Kissing the pain away before he did it again. He would watch her heal only to do it again. She would find pleasure in the pain he planned to bestow on her. Keller imagined how tight her pussy would be for him. How soaked it would be, waiting for his cock. And it will be him. Not Eli. Soon he would wear Eli's face. He would speak with Eli's voice. She would believe it was her husband who held her. All the while it would be him.

John would inhabit Keller's broken body and command the Ebony Knights, while Keller lived eternally inside Eli's form—untouched by age or death. A new order would rise from the ashes of the old world. Cities would burn. Kingdoms would crumble. And when Roslyn watched everything, she knew fall to ruin, she would turn to him for comfort. He would be there. Waiting.

John fed Keller more lies, savoring the twisted, lustful fantasies he had planted in the mortal's mind. Each one pushed Keller closer to the end John required. Keller had always been a temporary vessel. When the moment was right, John would sever the loose ends. And that moment was approaching. Initiating the next stage of his design, the demon moved quickly, knowing they were in Eli's territory. A soft whisper began to coil through Keller's mind. The words slipped through his thoughts slowly, each syllable thick and deliberate, luring him into a haze. "Surdi… caeci…velut mortui. Anima somno. Tactu mimicum metit…"

Keller shook his head as he stood up. Alarm setting a racing course through his body. "What…what are you doing to me, demon?" Keller muttered, his voice thick and unsteady.

John continued. "Nolite audire sermonem meum… usque vigiliae consurges percusserit." The incantation flowed like dark honey, pulling Keller deeper into a fog he could not fight to control.

"S…stop it. Fuckin'—" Keller commanded groggily. Head spinning as if he had drained too many tankards of ale. Sweat beaded across his skin. His stomach churned violently. He understood the Latin. That was the worst part. The meaning echoed through his mind even as the spell tightened around his soul.

Deaf…blind as the dead.
The soul sleeps.
Mimic the touch of the angel of death.
Do not wake…until my command is spoken.

When the final word was spoken, Keller's resistance vanished. His soul slipped away in the deep recesses of the body without the strength to fight back. John seized control. Keller's pale eyes darkened, the color draining away until only deep, consuming black remained.

For the first time since entering the mortal world, John held complete command of the body without Keller's thoughts clawing at the edges of his mind. The silence was invigorating. He felt alive. More alive than he had in centuries. Yet the mortal soul lingered somewhere within the flesh. Keller's spirit would eventually poison the vessel, weakening him. When the time came, John would abandon the body and take the mortal soul with him. Keller would die as a man. And his spirit would be dragged screaming back to where it had begun. Hell. He just needed him to think he was in control in the meantime.

John shook his head. "Not again," he muttered to himself. "This tumor will be removed soon." He lifted his gaze toward the sky. Orange, pink, and blue streaks bled across the fading daylight. Within a few hours the night would rise, and the new moon would claim the heavens. The wolves would sleep in their brief liberation from their transformation. Since the face of the moon would be blackened, it could not Call to them. John looked forward again, though his attention was fixed beyond the forest around him. He reached inward to the fragment of the power his Master had placed on the witch that had summoned him to this realm eons ago. It pulsed low and faint, but it was still there. Their bond was unused for quite sometime, but it remained strong. Steady. But the witch was clever. More powerful than he had first suspected. She had concealed her face and masked her true location behind layers of arcane wards. No matter how deeply he searched through the connection, he could not see her. John snarled, his lips curling slightly. For now, she remained hidden. He ran his tongue over his dry bottom lip, wetting it as he reached toward the bond.

Speaking flatly and with quiet authority, John reached out through the bond. "Hello, little Witch." Silence answered him at first. But he felt her. The jolt of surprise raced down the bond with the quick smoothing of it into cold indifference. She wasn't alone, he sensed. She was careful—always careful. Yet, she had bound herself to him long ago. No matter how well she hid, she could never fully escape him. His voice slipped through the connection again, darker now. "It's been a long time, love. Did you miss me? I imagine you must have…even while playing house with the dogs. Tell me. Does his cock stretch you like mine—"

"What do you want?" Her reply snapped through the bond like a whip.

A faint smile pulled at the corner of his lips, "Guess who has finally found a body again. It's not without fault," his tone dropped into a mocking, guttural rumble, "but you'll enjoy it. You always did enjoy what I could do, no matter the body I wore."

"I don't care," she shot back. "Leave me along. I..I don't want to see you."

John teased, "Oh, but I want to see you. Come now, little witch. It's hardly my fault that *you* cast me into this fucking body. Did you think you would get rid of me so easily?" His voice hardened. "We are bound. Original Sin, remember? We created and destroyed something beautiful together that night."

"Rape isn't beautiful, Incubus. You took everything from me. From us." For a moment he felt the tremor in her voice before she forced it steady again. She swallowed the lump of bile that clogged her"I rebuke you in the na—."

John laughed. "Did you forget?" he purred. "You had already forsaken Him the first night you tasted what I offered?" His voice slid through the bond like a snake. "You couldn't resist. You never could avoid the temptation. The delicious, poisoned apple between your lips. You couldn't get enough of me. Every sweet, devouring—"

"Go to hell," she growled.

"Been there. Done that, little witch." John replied calmly. "And I have no intention of returning." He paused, "I plan to remain here for a very long time."

"And you need my help," she said dryly.

John sneered, "Yes."

"No." she hissed.

His anger flared instantly. The pressure of his presence surged through the connection like fire. "Listen carefully, little witch," he said, his voice dropping to a deadly whisper. "You can meet me…or I will find you myself." The threat hung between them. "I will tear apart everything you've built. Everyone you hide behind. I *will* burn and pillage your world and drag you back to mine by your goddamned hair. The choice is yours. You can either meet me tonight or by dawn I will have found you. I will wake you in your sleep, holding you down and taking what is rightfully mine. Over and over while your man-beast lays dead next to us. Do you want that again?"

There was a long pause that broke with a sob. Before her voice, sunken and small, whispered back. "I will meet you. Tonight."

John smiled. "Good. Wait for my call." The connection faded, the bond dimming into silence.

Sheryl gasped as the link broke. The world rushed back into her senses all at once—the shouts of warriors training, the rustling of birds overhead, the dry whisper of autumn wind moving through the clearing. And the frantic pounding of her own heart. Masking the turmoil inside her, she kept her expression steady as she glanced around the garden where she had been gathering herbs and vegetables. The plants were beginning to wilt under the season heat. Quietly she began whispering ancient words under her breath. A warding charm. Old magic meant to conceal her path and mislead those who hunted her. She would need it to leave without being tracked to where she went.

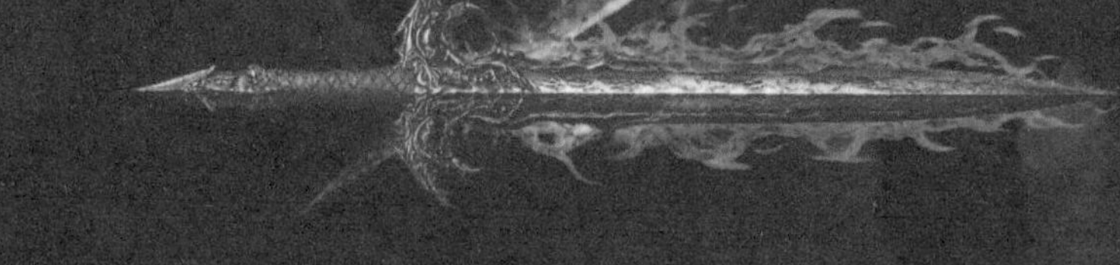

On the final night of the new moon, the sky lay empty of light. Only the stars shimmered faintly against the vast blackness above. Hidden within the shadows, John sat upon the largest of the bordering sarsen stones that jaggedly lined the coast of Lake Erie. Since the moment he had arrived, he had been brooding over what must be done—and what could be accomplished in the little time that remained. His soulless black eyes remained fixed on the dark water as it shifted and whispered against the shoreline. Keller's soul still slept within the body. For now, John was alone with his thoughts.

Able to see clearly in the darkness, John surveyed the shoreline. He heard the flutter of mosquitoes, the quiet slosh of the water against the rocks, and the rustle of dried leaves shifting in the trees. John sneered at the world around him. He stepped down from the rock and approached the black water. Crouching low, he extended a single finger and touched the lake's surface. Slowly, he stirred the water. The small circle beneath his finger began to heat. Then it boiled. The heat spread outward in widening ripples. Steam curled into the night air as violent bubbles burst across the surface. Within moments, fish began rising from the depths—belly up and lifeless—floating in the wake of the spreading heat. John watched them with amusement. A small act of destruction. A petty insult offered to the God who so carefully cherished His fragile creations.

"You were always like a child with ants and a magnifying glass, Evod," Sheryl said mockingly. "So, this is your new vessel?"

A ghost of a smile pulled at the corners of his mouth as he turned his head. He remembered every detail of his little witch, even down the to sound of her voice. There she stood beside him, motionless in a black silk robe. Her hood shadowed her face, but he knew her eyes were fixed on the water—and the mass of boiled fish floating upon the surface. He rose slowly to his full height. "I've often wondered," he said calmly, "if God truly loved the world…why did he make everything in it so utterly defenseless?" His gaze slid over her with predatory interest. He licked his lips. "Remove your hood."

Sheryl looked at him again from beneath the shadows of the robe. Because she was bound to him, she saw him as both the demon and the mortal shell that he wore. His true self shone through, like a phantom overlay to the mortal casing. He towered nearly seven feet tall, thin, scaled skin a dark blood red. His limbs were long and powerful, his ribs faintly visible beneath the stretched flesh of his chest. Two twisted horns crowned his head, and his eyes were black as the lake beside them. When he spoke, dark fangs flashed between his lips. His thick cock hung low between his legs. Its length covered in soft scales the same reddish black of his skin, and ridged, with veins and small groves. They engorged while it erected watching her. He inhaled slowly; a rumbling hum of pleasure released the breath as he studied. He was an intimidating and cruel creature, but Sheryl did not flinch. She gave him a small nod. "I see more than you think, Evod."

The words had barely left her mouth when he lunged. His hand closed around her throat, lifting her slightly from the ground as his grip tightened. His voice dropped lower, darker. "Do you *like* what you see?" His tongue traced slowly across the side of her face as he leaned closer. "Remove. Your. Hood." Her slender neck slightly within his grasp to draw in a breath that he threatened to close off completely. Quickly, she reached up and grasped the edges of the hood. Then she pulled it back. "Let me go, Evod," she hissed, venom thick in her voice

The moment he saw her face, he released her throat and stepped back, laughing darkly. "Tell me this," he said, studying her. "When the world is finally cleansed by my Master's power…will you be left behind again?" He smiled widened. "Or will you finally come home with me?"

"I will never be yours," she spat. "I belong to no one. I swear I will send you back tonight and end this—for you and your master."

John laughed as he began circling her slowly. "Swear to who?" he mocked. "Will you fall to your knees and crawl back to him? After everything you've done?" His voice sharpened. "Murder. Lust. Witchcraft. Fucking demons to breed the—"

"Silence demon!" she cried as she shut her eyes to focus, trying to block him from playing with her mind with his words.

He shook his head and clicked his forked tongue. Then his expression shifted—calculating and cruel. "Perhaps you would rather hear about your sons." He leaned closer, his voice dropping into a whisper beside her ear. "They burn in my fires, little witch." He saw her cringe against his biting words. They struck her heart, twisting like knives and causing her pain. He continued, "I hear them scream. And it is...such a pleasurable sound when they call for you."

Sheryl's eyes widened at the mention of her sons. For a moment something wild flickered behind them, but it vanished as quickly as it appeared. Her voice dropped with conviction, "My sons made their choice," she replied coldly. "And I do not fear you." Her gaze raked over him. "You speak as if you're still immortal. You are bound to a human vessel. You are as vulnerable as a babe in a wolf's den. Whatever fragments of power you still cling to in this realm doesn't compare to who I have become."

Evod's expression darkened. His clawed hands flexed, the urge to seize her delicate throat rising again. For a moment he nearly gave in to it. But the larger plan stayed his hand. "I am *bound* to this festering human," he said coldly. "And I intend to be rid of him." He took a slow step toward her. "In less than two days, there will be war. The mortal whose body I inhabit will lead my army against the Beast Bloods." His black eyes gleamed. "This man desires only one thing. A Beast Blood female named Roslyn. He wants her husband dead. The thought consumes him—every waking moment." Evod's lips curled into a thin smile. "When the time was right, I offered him a bargain."

Sheryl remained silent, watching him carefully. "I convinced him to give me this body in exchange for her husband's," Evod continued. "Once the Beast Blood dies, I will take his form…and the mortal will have Roslyn through it. Oe so he thinks."

Surprise flashed through her veins, but she smothered it before he could sense it through their bond or see it on her face. "That's awfully caring of you, demon," Sheryl said dryly. "But it has nothing to do with me." The sarcasm was unmistakable. Creatures like him knew nothing of compassion—only hatred, ruin, and endless hunger to corrupt whatever they touched. And Evod had been the architect of her own downfall. That alone was the reason enough to deny him. What were Eli and Roslyn to her, after all…other than temporary distractions from a much older war?

He bared his teeth in a snarl and struck her across the face. "Fuck who you are!" he roared. "Never speak to me in that manner!"

Sheryl staggered slightly but did not fall. She raised her hand to her cheek. When she pulled away, her fingertips were slick with blood. Four deep gouges burned across her skin where his claws had torn her flesh. Already she felt the wounds knitting closed. Tears stung her eyes, but she forced them back. The pain only fed the fury rising in her chest. Her breath hitched once—then she screamed at him. Her scream tore through the night, and the wind stirred across the dark lake. "I know what you want," Sheryl shouted. "And I know what your master wants." Her eyes were wild with fury. "You expect me to transfer Keller's soul into the man he kills. Then your power will unleash fully inside your vessel, and you will be free to retrieve the Spear of Destiny and rule the army for him." She lifted her chin and straightened her shoulders. "No." Her voice rose into a rasping scream. "I will not let you thank this world from me. It's mine!" She pointed upward as she drew in a hard breath. "He is not here. I am. I hold the power now, and I will not waste it on either of you. You will live with this soul…and you will die with it." She turned sharply to leave, but Evod moved faster.

Hurriedly, Evod grabbed her wrist while she turned away from him to walk away. "You *will* help me, or I'll kill you, now!" He snarled through barred teeth ready to rip her throat out with his hands.

"*Lit-eh- Ro!*" Sheryl screamed. She thrust her hand forward and struck his chest. A blazing beam of white heat burst from her palm and tore straight through him. Flesh and blood exploded across the rocks and sand, hot droplets spattering her face. Evod's body hurled backward, a smoking cavity blasted through his chest, before crashing into the black waters of the lake. Sheryl didn't wait to see if he rose again. She gathered her robes and skirts and ran.

Maximous waited where she had tied him to a nearby tree. She worked the reins free in seconds, swung into the saddle, and drove him forward into the dark forest. Branches whipped past as the horse thundered through the night. Her heart pounded in her ears. Adrenaline burned through her veins. Now, she understood. The final pieces of the plan had fallen into place. Evod's master wanted two things. The genocide of the Beast Bloods…and the Spear of Destiny. Sheryl's hands tightened on the reins. It's been him all these centuries. Rage trembled through her. She would not have it. If anyone was meant to claim such power, it would be her. And she did not need a dagger to do it. She snapped the reins again, leaning low over Maximous's neck as they raved deeper into the forest.

Bleeding and mending, Evod dragged himself across the wet sand. The effort drained what little strength remained in his stolen body. When he finally collapsed, his face struck the ground with a dull thud. Pain surged through him like liquid fire. Black blood poured from his mouth as he choked and gasped. His lungs struggled to knit themselves back together after the witch's blast. For several long moments he could not breathe. Still…he lived. Evod trembled, cringing as the agony rippled through his body. Fury hotter than the fires of Hell burned inside him. At last his lungs restored enough for a ragged breath. "I. Will. Kill. Her." He rasped through clenched teeth. A deeper voice echoed around him through his mind. He recognized it instantly.

"We need her. And you're failing me."

Evod stilled.

"She possesses the resurrection spell. I have the Grail. All that remains is the Spear…and the invocation."

"But, Master…" Evod croaked. "Her ambition rivals ours. Is there another—"

"There is no other!" the Master thundered. "After you kill them, gather what remains of the army and bring the witch to me. I will break her if I must. I will force her to destroy the human anvil. Then she will serve us willingly."

Evod cough violently, more black blood staining the sand. Slowly, he nodded. "It shall be done…my Master."

CHAPTER EIGHTEEN BIRTH OF A BLOODLINE

September 4th, 1881

As she quietly shut and locked the door to the third-floor library, Roslyn released a deep breath. She leaned back against the elaborate oak carving of the door, its design depicting the Tree of Knowledge. A morbid—but fitting—symbol for a room like this. Massive floor-to-ceiling shelves of dark oak crowded the walls, packed tightly with hundreds of books. More than any mortal could ever hope to read in a single lifetime. Out of habit, she scanned the cozy chamber. It was empty. Relief washed through her. She sent a quick, silent thanks heavenward before pushing herself away from the door and savoring the rare silence. For once, she was alone.

The chapel was rarely empty. Others were always inside—praying, lingering in the quiet comfort of the space. Because of that, the library had become the only room that remained unoccupied. Most days she slipped away unnoticed. It was easy when the trainees came in from the exercise yard every other hour. When they flooded the halls in loud groups, Roslyn would use the commotion as cover, hurrying up the stairwell before Eli—or anyone else—could see her attempting such a climb in her advanced stage of pregnancy. Once inside the library, she could finally escape the suffocating anxiety that followed her through the days. Locking the door behind her, she shut herself away within the dark teal walls of the room. Sometimes she tried to distract herself. She would read. Or sit quietly and daydream, forcing her thoughts toward anything other than the air of death that seemed to hang over everyone in the house. But it rarely worked. No matter how hard she found herself clutching her swelling belly as tears spilled down her face, whispering silent prayers into the empty room. It was impossible not to think about it. Since the moment Eli and George had arrived with the horde of Beast Bloods, the house had been filled with nothing but talk of war and death. And when her thoughts turned to Eli…she couldn't finish them.

She shook her head and pushed herself away from the plush turquoise furniture arranged in the center of the room, several feet from the cobblestone hearth. Despite the many comfortable seats scattered throughout the library, she always returned to the same place—the wide chair before the bay window that overlooked the eastern side of the property where the lake glittered in the evening sunset. Fatigue weighed heavily on her as she moved across the room. Her growing child made every step slower now. She drew in a steady breath and carefully made her way toward her favorite spot. Halfway there, a sharp cramp seized her stomach. Roslyn gasped and grabbed the back of the couch and squeezed. She steadied herself. Pain twisted through her abdomen, forcing her to pause. With her free hand, she cradled the underside of her swollen belly and stood still for several moments, breathing slowly as she worked through the sudden wave of discomfort.

Eli sat on the edge of his chair in the darkened corner of the room, ready to rise at a moment's notice. From the shadows, he watched his wife with wide-eyed concern as she worked through another wave of pain. He tensed, prepared to go to her. After a few moments he saw her body relax, and she began slowly shuffling toward the window seat again. Only then did he allow himself to ease back slightly. Still, he watched her carefully from across the room—careful enough that she wouldn't notice him there. If Roslyn knew he was hiding in the library, he would lose the rare privilege of seeing her in these quiet, unguarded moments. She looked beautiful. Health and life seemed to radiate from her now, a stark contrast to the fragile woman she had been months ago. Her curls were thicker, catching the soft evening light from the window. Her flawless skin glowed faintly, a sheen of sweat glistening as the head of the house deepened with the lingering drought. Eli grimaced slightly. He should have opened a window before she arrived. But he had wanted to be in place first—ready for the moment she inevitably broke his rules and climbed the stairs on her own. At least she and the child were well. Both were strong. Thriving.

Since the night they had recruited the clans, an unspoken tension had festered between them. Neither of them had been the same since that night. Whenever Roslyn saw him enter a room or pass by, her entire demeanor would change. She would fall silent until he was out of sight. Sadness lingered within her. Anger burned quietly within him. When their eyes met, neither would speak, yet their expressions said everything—and nothing—at the same time. Inevitability they would turn away from one another, each retreating into foul moods that lasted the rest of the evening. The others always sensed it. The tension between them filled the room like a storm waiting to break, and one by one the others would quietly leave.

Eli knew there was still deep love, fierce and undeniable between them. They denied themselves the comfort of each other, despite the overwhelming urge to simply reach for another. Yet, he still refused to open the bond, and she refused to share the same anything with him. By now, it was more than pride keeping them apart. Across the room, Eli watched as Roslyn lifted the hem of her loose gown, gathering the fabric high along her thighs so she could settle more comfortably onto the window seat and maneuver around her swollen belly. A faint smile tugged at his lips. His son was growing strong inside her. Already the child demanded space within her womb, full of restless life. Pride swelled in his chest. Yet with it came a sharp ache of longing. He wanted nothing more than to cross the room, take her into his arms, and never let go. But Eli only ground his teeth and remained where he was. He knew her reaction would not be acceptance. Only another quiet rejection.

Roslyn pressed her back against the wall and settled into the corner of the window seat. She lifted her legs from the floor and tucked them to the side, gathering the loose fabric of her gown beneath them. With the thin cotton lifted her from her skin, the cool air of the room finally reached her. The relief was immediate. The dress stretched tightly over the curve of her belly. She looked down and rested a hand upon the mound. Instantly the child kicked—hard. Pain shot up into her ribs and a sharp jolt stabbed through her pelvis. Roslyn winced.

"Ow—my lord, child…you are active tonight," she murmured softly, forcing sweetness into her voice despite the ache. She turned her gaze toward the window. Below, the clans filled the training yard. Warriors clashed in controlled combat as they practiced the techniques George, Eli and the other seasoned fighters had spent months drilling into them. What had once been scattered, inexperienced clans had begun to move with discipline. Days of brutal training had hardened them. Now they fought like soldiers. Roslyn searched the yard carefully as the groups began to disperse. Her brows furrowed. Eli was not among them. She rubbed her belly absentmindedly and spoke to the child again, her voice hoping it was settle him despite it being tinged with worry.

"It's evening…where has your father been today?" Her eyes drifted back toward the fading light outside. "It's almost time to transform."

Eli smirked as he listened, leaning forward slightly. *Sitting right here*, he thought. *Keeping an eye on you.*

Roslyn continued scanning the land beyond the window. Her gaze drifted across the farming fields below. She remembered the day Andante had led her and the others through an invisible maze after one of their transformations. They had been forced to move carefully, placing each step exactly where he instructed. The fields were now riddles with hidden trapdoors and mechanisms designed by Andante and a few others. It had taken nearly two months to finish building them. Beyond the fields stretched the surrounding forest, where their scouts and hunting parties remained hidden. Talos and Sizrra stayed there with the warriors they had chosen and trained, constructing small housing forts high within the trees.

Roslyn sighed. Her golden eyes narrowed slightly as her brows drew together in troubled thought. She looked down at the mound beneath her hand. "My darling child…my baby." Her voice faltered as she reached for the right words. "I…I'm just—" She exhaled slowly, struggling to continue. "There is so much happening in the world around you," she whispered. "While you lie safe and warm within my womb, your father is preparing for war." Her gaze drifted back toward the training yard below, searching for him again. He was nowhere to be seen. Roslyn's attention returned to her belly. "Any day now the scouts will howl that the enemy has arrived…and then all hell will break loose." Her fingers tightened slightly against the curve of her stomach.

"There is no doubt in my heart…your father…he will face Keller himself, all to save the lives of the others." Tears welled in her eyes. "I have such a horrible feeling."

Eli arched a brow as a lump of emotion clogged his throat. His dark eyes were rimmed with tears that he held back. He clenched his jaw so hard he thought he would shatter his teeth. He listened further.

Roslyn spoke again, forcing down the knot of anxiety twisting in her stomach. "I know he's only trying to protect us…all of us." Her voice cracked. "But I'm afraid. So afraid of the unknown…and of the thought that your father could die because of me." The words finally broke her restraint. Tears spilled freely down her cheeks. Her soft sobs shook her shoulders. She sniffled, wiping the tears away with her trembling fingers, but more followed. "I know I shouldn't think like this," she whispered." But how could I live forever without him?" Her gaze fell back to the curve of her stomach. "Since we were young, it has always been him and me. That was our promise." She paused, crying softly for a few moments before gathering enough composure to continue. "And now there is you." Her hand rested gently over the mound of her belly. "You are part of us…a creation of our love." A sob caught in her throat. "If he were to die… how could I ever look at you and not see him?"

Roslyn leaned forward until her forehead touched the cool glass of the window. Then she covered her face with both hands and cried into her palms. "How can I be weak and so selfish…when you need me more than ever?" She sobbed.

Eli was already out of the chair, stepping from the shadows. He cast aside his doubt and crossed the room toward his wife. In a few long strides he reached her and, in one fluid motion, wrapped his arms around her—gentle, yet firm enough to tell her it was time for their silence to end.

"Where did—" she gasped, but she saw him shake his head. He said nothing. He simply gathered her against him and lifted her carefully to rest in his lap, against his chest. Roslyn sagged into him. Eli cupped her face in his hands, his fingers resting softly along her hairline. Her eyes were still closed as she leaned into his palm, tears spilling freely as she tried to speak. "Eli, I'm—"

He silenced her with a soft kiss. Words were not needed. He had already heard enough—her fears, her thoughts, the quiet pain she had carried alone for so long. She had tried to remain strong, searching for hope in a situation that seemed doomed from the start. But it had become too much for her to bear by herself. And he knew he had only made that burden heavier by closing off the bond. Limiting access to his very heart. Now she was finally breaking. And she needed him. The truth was…he needed her just as much. His arms tightened around her as if he feared she might vanish the moment he let go.

He brushed a light kiss across her closed eyes, tasting the salt of her tears. Then he kissed her cheeks, feeling the soft warmth of her skin before finally claiming her lips. The kiss lingered. For a moment he poured everything into it—his love, his longing, the passion he had kept locked away for far too long. Reluctantly, he drew back and pressed a trail of gentle kisses along her neck before resting one against the curve of her collarbone. At last, he found the courage to speak. "Roslyn," he murmured softly, "I will always love you with all of my heart. With every fiber of my soul—it is yours in all forms. Man. Beast. Ghost. I am always yours." He paused, his voice thick with emotion. "I'm sorry for staying away from you for so long. I thought…I thought it would make things easier for both of us." His hand drifted down to rest over the swell of her belly. "But watching you…watching our child…" He shook his head slightly. "I couldn't stay away anymore."

Her tears had stopped, though a trace of sadness still lingered. Roslyn sniffled softly as she lifted his head from her shoulder, where he still pressed lingering kisses against her skin. She looked directly into his eyes, her lips trembling with emotion. In a breathless whisper she said, "I love you with all I am…and more." Then she kissed him hard, wrapping her arms around his neck to keep him close. Eli slid one hand to the back of her head, cradling it in his broad palm, while his other arm slipped beneath her to steady her weight. He refused to let the moment break. Without separating from her, he guided them slowly toward the large couch. Carrying her. Carefully, he lowered her onto the smooth satin cushions and pulled a pillow down from its upright place to support her.

Outside, the last traces of daylight had faded beyond the horizon. The room settled into a warm, ember-like glow as night fully arrived. Eli opened his eyes and looked down at her. In the soft light of the oil lamps, she seemed almost luminous. Her lips were swollen from their kisses, her eyes still reddened from tears—but behind them burned a fierce, living fire as she watched him. Roslyn searched his eyes for a moment longer, the worry still lingering there. Then she relaxed beneath him. Her fingers slid into his hair as she pulled him closer, pressing her forehead against his. "I was afraid you would keep pushing me away," she whispered.

Eli closed his eyes briefly, regret flickering across his face. "I thought I was protecting you," he admitted quietly. "But all I did was leave you to carry to the fear alone."

Roslyn covered his hand with hers, guiding it softly against the place where the child had kicked moments before. "Our child already knows you," she said faintly. "Every time you speak…it moves."

Eli smiled softly at that. He looked into her eyes, and his voice became a low, heady growl, "I'm going to make love to you, Roslyn." He lifted the hem of her gown and slid her short pantaloons down her legs, letting them fall to the floor. His hands followed the length of her legs, fingers trailing slowly along her thighs until they rested against the curve of her hips.

Roslyn's body arched beneath his touch as his hands drifted over the round swell of her belly. Then suddenly she stiffened. Her expression shifted—something uncertain, almost fearful. "The baby, Eli—" she began.

"It will be unharmed," he reassured her softly as he nibbled kisses on her neck. "It's perfectly natural to be together—"

"No, Eli!" She said suddenly, her voice sharp with alarm. "The baby—I think my water broke!" She pushed against his chest and struggled to sit up, staring down at herself.

Eli placed his hands between her legs, feeling the fluid soaking through the couch cushion. The lower part of her gown was drenched, the darkened fabric clearly marking where the fluid had spread. "Oh my god," he breathed in disbelief. "He's on the way." Eli got up from the couch and strode toward the door. Forgetting she had locked it, he pulled the brass handle off from its casing.

"He?" Roslyn snapped her gaze up to him.. Panic crept into her voice as another contraction tore through her. "Oh my god," she ground, clutching her stomach as the pain tightened around her again. "Where are you going? Please don't leave me." Fear crept into Roslyn's voice as the reality of labor set in.

Eli paused at the door while the handle slipped from his grasp, falling to the floor. He turned back to look at her. His calmness was almost unnerving. "I will never leave you," he said resolutely. "I'm only going to get Sheryl. When it comes to this I trust her with you—and with our child."

Before Roslyn could respond, he was already gone. The door closed behind him. Roslyn sank back against the pillow, squeezing her eyes shut as another wave of pain rolled through her. "Fuck, this pain." Her voice rose as she pleaded desperately, hoping her prayer would somehow be heard and answered. Another contraction tightened through her body. She felt the start of the shift claw at her chest. Roslyn forced her eyes open and turned toward the window. The moon was rising. A cold realization washed over her. "Oh…God."

Eli rushed out of the room and thundered down the stairs. He moved quickly through the main halls, searching for George or Sheryl. She was nowhere to be found. The urgency of the situation began to crush in on him. "Sheryl!" he shouted down the hallway. From the back of the left-wing parlor, George answered. He rose quickly from his chair the moment he saw the panic on Eli's face, pushing past several people who had been gathered in conversation.

"What is it? George demanded. "What's wrong?"

Eli didn't hesitate. "Roslyn is in labor in the upstairs library. I need Sheryl. She's the only one I trust to handle this. Where is she?"

George's jaw dropped as the realization struck him. His eyes shot toward the staircase. "Oh my god…she's going to transform while in labor."

"Not if it happens quickly," Eli replied grimly.

George ran a hand through his hair as he thought rapidly. "Last I knew, she was outside taking the scraps from dinner to the fertilizer pile—"

The front door burst open. Sheryl rushed inside from the night air, crossing the foyer at a run before skidding into the hallway. "I heard my name." she called breathlessly. "I'm here. What's wrong?"

Eli quickly grabbed Sheryl's hand and pulled her toward the winding staircase. As they rushed upward, he twisted his head back toward her, speaking in short, breathless bursts. "Roslyn's in labor. Her water broke in the upstairs library. She needs you—now." He heard her gasp.

Sheryl's eyes widened. "Oh no!" Turning back down the stairwell, she called to George with sharp authority. "We have less than an hour until the Calling. Pump water into a large pot and place it on the stove in the kitchen—warm it, not boiling. Bring me clean linens from the closet in the washroom, and a bottle of your moonshine." Her voice hardened. "I must get that child out of her before we transform." She pointed toward the others gathering in the hallway. "Out! Everyone outside. Ready yourselves just in case."

George nodded immediately. "Got it!"

Sheryl hurried ahead of Eli up the steps. She lifted the hem of her skirt so she wouldn't trip as she climbed. Halfway up, she glanced back. Eli followed close behind, his jaw set hard, his black eyes burning with tension. Sheryl steadied her breath and spoke to him firmly. "I need you to be strong, Eli. She was strong enough to carry your child. She'll be strong enough to birth it." Her gaze softened slightly. "We've done everything we could to keep them both healthy. It's…it's in…Gods hands now." The last words slipped out quickly, almost unwillingly. Before Eli could respond, she turned away and pushed open the library door, rushing inside.

Eli didn't answer. He had heard her—but the words barely reached him through the storm of his thoughts. Fear gripped him too tightly to speak. Many mortal women died in childbirth. A Beast Blood female wasn't any different. If Roslyn died…if his son died…his world would collapse into a darkness so complete he would walk into battle and let Keller kill him so he could join his family. He had months to accept that he might die in battle. But never this. Never the other way around. Eli closed his eyes for a moment in silent prayer before stepping inside. *Please. Spare her. Spare them both.* Yet even as the prayer formed, bitterness crept into his thoughts. Perhaps this was the design all along.

Reaching the threshold, Eli pushed the door open. Sheryl knelt between Roslyn's parted legs while Roslyn panted through clenched teeth. Sweat soaked through her gown as moonlight poured through the window behind her. Roslyn caught sight of him. She blinked, as if unsure he was really there. "Eli," she breathed before another contraction ripped through her. Her head fell back against the pillow as she screamed, the sound tearing through the room while her muscles tensed and flexed.

Sheryl glanced up from her examination. "She's nearly ready. The baby's starting to descend." She quickly looked around the room. "But I have nothing to lay the child in once it arrives, and George isn't back yet."

Eli was frozen. The room felt distant, unreal, as though he were watching everything happen from somewhere outside his own body. "I…" His voice came out quiet and stunned. "I made a bassinet. For them. For our baby." He knelt beside Roslyn and brushed the damp curls back from her face, hoping to cool her skin. His fingers trembled as he tucked the hair behind her ear. He pressed soft kisses against her forehead, desperate to offer some small comfort. Roslyn looked up at him. He saw her eyes softened. "You did?" Her voice was small and breathless. Eli gave her a small nod. "I did, baby."

Sheryl's expression warmed with surprise. She nodded approvingly. "Then go get it. It's almost time." She glanced between them. "They'll want to meet their father while there's time."

Eli looked at her, the meaning of her words settling over him. In this moment, he was becoming a father. Pride and fear twisted together inside his chest until he could hardly breathe. Too many emotions flooded him at once, mixing into something overwhelming. He turned back to Roslyn. "I'll be right back, love."

"Please hurry back, Eli!" Roslyn called after him as he was already halfway through the doorway. The door closed behind him.

Sheryl immediately turned her full attention back to Roslyn. "Don't worry," she said calmly. She noticed the oil lamps she had lit before dusk were burning low. Moving quickly around the room, she adjusted the wicks until the flames brightened and filled the library with warmer light. "I need more light," she said as she worked. "I have to see what I'm doing." Sheryl turned up the last oil lamp, but the lighting was still too dull. She hurried to the hearth. "I know it's already hot in here, but I need more light."

She didn't wait for Roslyn to respond. Grabbing a stick from the wood box beside the mantle, she dipped the end of the flame of an oil lamp until it caught. She shoved crumpled paper from the tinder box between the stacked logs and pressed the burning stick into the pile. The fire caught quickly, flames licking upward as the dry wood began to burn. Sheryl turned back toward Roslyn. "How are you doing, girl?" she asked briskly. "Are you ready to start pushing?"

Roslyn stared at her, wide-eyed and confused. "I…I don't know how to do that." Another contraction slammed into her before she could say anything more. Her body tightened as she drew in a sharp breath, panting through clenched teeth. For the final wave she held her breath until the pain crested and passed. A small cry escaped her as she released a strained puff of air. "This hurts," she gasped. "The pain is worse than transforming."

"How many are you having?" Sheryl asked as she dragged a large rectangular ottoman in front of the couch and pressed it firmly against the edge.

"One, I hope!" Roslyn blurted, eyes widening as panic flashed across her face. She thought Sheryl meant children.

Despite the tension of the moment, Sheryl let out a brief laugh. "It's rare for a Beast Blood to have twins," she said as she guided Roslyn into position. You're almost certainly having one." She helped Roslyn stretch across the couch, lifting her legs and bracing them over the ottoman. "I meant your contractions," Sheryl clarified calmly. "How close together are the pains?"

"Oh, God…they're really fucking close together," Roslyn gasped as another contraction seized her body. She screamed as the pain tightened through her stomach and back.

"When did they start?" Sheryl asked quickly, trying to calculate how much time they had. If the child did not arrive soon, Roslyn could transform during labor. The shock alone could distress the baby enough to still it inside of her.

"Yesterday morning," Roslyn cried as another brutal wave of pain tore through her body. Her stomach clenched again, forcing the air from her lungs. Instinct took over. "I feel like I need to push," she panted, panic creeping into her voice. "Down there…I feel like I need to push."

At that moment the door burst open. George and Eli rushed in carrying the supplies. Sheryl glanced up at them. "Good. She's been in labor since yesterday. This baby is ready to come now."

"Will the baby be here before the Calling?" George asked as he dropped the supplies near the door. One by one he handed them to Sheryl as she reached back to take them, quickly setting up the space around her.

Eli set the small bassinet where he stood before rushing to Roslyn's side. He sat beside her and brushed a soothing hand across her forehead, feeling the sweat that coated her skin. He looked into her eyes. She shook her head weakly and squeezed them shut. Suddenly she grabbed his hand and clamped down with brutal strength as a violent contraction tore through her. She pushed and screamed. "Jesus Christ, Ros—!" Eli gritted through clenched teeth as he felt his fingers crack and grind painfully in her grip. He didn't pull his hand away. He kept it exactly where it was meant to be. If his hand was nothing in comparison to the absolute hell his mate was going through birthing their child. He welcomed the pain. If she had to endure it. He would deal with any pain she inflicted onto him.

Sheryl lifted Roslyn's gown over her knees, letting the fabric gather at her waist as she examined her. "Alright," she said quickly. "I see the head. The baby's crowning." She could feel the Calling beginning to tug at the edge of her senses—the ancient pull stirring deep in her blood—but she forced it aside. Time was running out. "Roslyn, listen to me," Sheryl said firmly. "Just a few more strong pushes and it will be over. Your baby will be born, and you can transform without worrying about harming it." She looked up at her. "Are you ready?"

Roslyn tightened her grip around Eli's hand. Her fingers flexed, crushing his already aching knuckles as she gathered her strength. She nodded her head fiercely. "More than you could ever know.

"Good," Sheryl urged. "Then push!"

The Calling surged again, clawing for Roslyn's attention. It snapped through her body like a bolt of pain, demanding obedience from the blood that ran in her veins. She knew she didn't have long before it consumed them all. Another brutal contraction racked her body. Roslyn bared her teeth and pushed with everything she had.

"Push! Push again, Roslyn!" Sheryl commanded, her hands poised and ready. "Don't you dare give up now!"

Roslyn felt the pressure build—then suddenly release.

"Here he comes!" Eli exclaimed through clenched teeth as Roslyn's grip tightened around his hand, crushing his fingers even harder and snapping a few more in the process. He didn't care. He watched as the baby's head burst free, the rest of the small body following in one swift motion. Eli's breath left him entirely. For a moment he could only stare at the fragile, beautiful form of his son. Sheryl caught the newborn carefully by the shoulders, guiding the slick body safely from the birth canal. He was here. Eli gazed wordlessly as tears rolled down his face. Their tiny boy in Sheryl's arms released short, fitful cried that filled the room. Eli looked back to Roslyn and kissed her softly before turning his attention back to the child. "Our son," he whispered hoarsely, extending his arms to receive his first born.

"George—rip a strip from those linens and wet it with the warm water," she said quickly… "I need to clean the baby and Roslyn." Then she looked down. The newborn wailed loudly in her arms, full of life. A smile spread across Sheryl's face. She lifted the plump child slightly so Eli and Roslyn could see. "A boy," she said softly. "Congratulations. You have a son."

Roslyn leaned her head back against the couch and released a trembling breath. "Eli…look. A son. We have a son." She turned her head to see him better. "You knew," she said softly through a sniffle. You had a feeling, and you were right."

Eli laughed through a broken sob as emotion clogged his throat. "Yeah," he murmured. "Something like that." He and George exchanged a brief knowing glance.

Sheryl nodded and rose from the front of the ottoman, shifting aside to give Eli room. Carefully—yet with eager hands—Eli gathered the whimpering infant into his arms. The newborn's body was still slick with blood and birth fluids, already drying into a sticky warmth against Eli's shirt and bare skin. He didn't care. All he could think about was the tiny life cradled against his chest—and the miracle that he had lived long enough to see his son born. He studied the child with awe. Chubby arms and legs. A head full of dark brown hair. A small, frantic heartbeat that fluttered wildly beneath fragile ribs. The baby released soft, trembling cries as he encountered the strange new world around him. Eli lowered his face closer and gently touched the infant's tiny clenched hand. "My son," he cooed.

The deep rumble of his voice startled the newborn, and the little boy sniffled in confusion. Eli chuckled softly, his heart swelling. "I bet I sound different now that you're earth-side." The infant squinted, struggling to focus his newborn vision. Weakly, he turned his head to the side until his gaze drifted upward toward Eli's face before his eyes went crossed and he closed them again. For a fleeting moment, the baby's lips curved into the faintest smile. Something inside Eli broke open. His chest tightened painfully as devotion, love and fierce protectiveness flooded through him. Without thinking—driven by pure emotion—he spoke. "My firstborn and heir." He brushed a finger gently across the child's cheek. "From this moment, and for the rest of your immortal life, you will be known as Gabrio Bade Santos-Mackley." His voice softened. "Santos, so those you trust will know who you truly are." His gaze hardened slightly. "Mackley. Your grandmother's maiden name…to hide you from those who will become your enemies." He looked down at the child again, pride shining through the tears still clinging to his lashes. "You will grow strong. Noble. You will become the hope of our people." He leaned closer, resting his forehead briefly against the baby's. "You are the legacy of everything your mother and I are."

For several quiet moments, no one spoke. They simply sat together, absorbed in the fragile miracle before them. Love and relief filled the room like a warm tide. Sheryl cleared her throat gently, breaking the silence. "I'm sorry to interrupt," she said, "but the Calling is still approaching. It would be wise to feed the baby while you still can." She glanced between them. "There are mortal women who came with their husbands and children who not yet of the blood, but are still clan-protected. They've volunteered to serve as wet nurses while you're in beast form—if you're not comfortable holding him in your furs and claws just yet."

Roslyn looked at Eli, uncertain.

Eli gave a small nod. "It is up to you," he said softly. "But it's common practice among our kind. That's where the saying '*It takes a clan to raise a child*' came from.

Roslyn hesitated, then nodded faintly. "O…okay. But let me be the first one."

Eli looked at Roslyn, his eyes soft with admiration. "You amaze me, love," he said gently. "You did this." He glanced down at the baby. "Are you ready to hold him?" Roslyn nodded, tears rising in her eyes as she reached for her son. Eli carefully lowered the child into the crook of her arms. She pulled the newborn close to her chest, cradling him with one arm while her other hand moved to the top buttons of her nightgown. Slowly, she loosened them, slipping the fabric aside until one breast was exposed. With a small adjustment of her shoulder, she guided the baby closer. Instinctively, the newborn found her nipple and latched. Roslyn felt the sudden pull as he began to suckle, the tingled warmth of milk releasing as her body responded. A soft laugh escaped her through lingering tears. "It's…fascinating."

George smiled as he poured the bloody water from the small pot into the hearth stirred the fire with a poker. "Looks like your natural motherly instincts are taking over, Ros." He gave her a quick wink before setting the cauldron on the stone platform beside the fireplace. "We're going to get ready for the Calling," he added. "And give you some privacy." George glanced toward Sheryl. "Come on, love." Sheryl nodded silently and followed him out of the room. The door closed softly behind them.

Roslyn returned her gaze to Gabrio, watching him nurse. "Gabrio…it fits him so well." When she looked up again, she saw Eli standing beside her, holding a small wooden bassinet. Her brows lifted slightly. "Eli…you made this beautiful crib?"

Eli's chest swelled with pride as he set the bassinet gently near her feet and knelt beside it. "I made it for him," he said quietly. "For both of you." He brushed a hand across the polished wood. "We don't have much of our own yet. But this is a start. Our child's first heirloom.

Roslyn nudged the bassinet gently with her foot, watching it sway softly. "You made this?" she asked in quiet disbelief. Her eyes traced the elegant curves of the polished wood that formed the headboard, footboard, and rails. Carved into the wood above where the baby's head would rest was their clan's crest. She studied it closely. The symbol of their house stared back at her: a seven-headed water serpent pierced through the chest with a sword, surrounded by a clash of fire, water and curling smoke. Two wolves stood on either side of the three-horned shield, holding it upright with an angel above unfurled a scroll bearing the name SANTOS in old lettering. Beneath the design, their family motto was carved: *Fight strong. Live forever.*

"You carved our crest on it," she whispered, careful not to disturb Gabrio as he continued to nurse. Her eyes softened. "I love it, Eli. *He* will love it. It's perfect." Gathering herself, she lifted her gaze to him again. "Always bound."

Eli smiled and leaned forward, pressing a soft, lingering kiss to her lips. "In this life and the next," he vowed. For a moment, the world felt still. He listened to the gentle breathing of his son, and allowed himself to rest in the quiet reconciliation between himself and the woman he loved. Then the twisting pain struck. Sharp and sudden, it rippled through his entire body. The Calling. Eli drew a slow breath as he felt it settle deep in his bones. He saw Roslyn wince too. Taking a deep steady breath, he sighed. "It's time," Eli murmured quietly. "The waiting is over."

Roslyn looked at Eli with clear disappointment, knowing the moment had ended far too soon. If the pain coursing through her body had not been growing worse by the second, she would have held her son forever. "But what about Gabrio?" she asked reluctantly, her voice tight with unwillingness to be parted from her child even for a moment.

A sudden knock sounded at the door. Before either of them could respond, George stepped through the threshold with a small girl beside him. "I brought her, Eli." Standing next to George was a dark-haired girl who could not have been more than ten years old. She was thin, with large green eyes and remarkably straight posture. Her long brown hair was tied neatly at the base of her neck, revealing the graceful line of her small shoulders. In the soft lamplight, she looked like a delicate mixture of Talos and Sizrra. She wore a simple blue cotton dress and stood quietly beside George, hands folded in front of her.

Confusion crossed Roslyn's face as her gaze moved between Eli and George. "I don't understand."

Eli spoke gently. "She's the middle child of Talos and Sizzra. She hasn't transformed yet, but they believe next year Mother Moon will accept her into the blood." He glanced toward the girl. "She will watch Gabrio while we transform. Once the Calling ends, you'll be back with him."

The little girl stepped forward slightly, her voice small but steady. "I am qualified, Mrs. Santos," she said politely. "Mother and father trust me to care for my three brothers who are all younger than ten."

Curiosity and caution mingled as Roslyn addressed the little girl. "Where are your brothers now, my dear, if they're entrusted to you?" The girl lowered her head slightly, as though the question had embarrassed her. Roslyn immediately wondered if she had been too harsh, but she waited patiently for the child answer. When the girl spoke, her voice carried and surprising calmness—an old wisdom that seemed far beyond her years.

"I am twelve," she said. "All of my brothers have already transformed before me. I was with them only a few days ago at my aunt and uncle's cottage until Sheryl came to fetch me—with my mother's permission, of course." She straightened a little as she continued. "She needed someone to watch and care for your child while you and your husband answer the Calling. Mr. Santos and Mr. Crownwelm thought it would be wise to have more hands caring for the baby until morning." The girl gave a small shrug. "Children this young sleep most of the time anyway. It shouldn't be difficult. Just a little boring." She lifted the book she had tucked under her arm. "That's why I brought something to read." Her eyes drifted toward the towering shelves surrounding them. "…Or perhaps I will have much more to choose from."

Roslyn glanced toward Eli with visible uncertainty. "Her mother allowed her to come into a war camp?"

Before Eli could respond, the girl spoke again. "It's for the greater cause," she said simply. "I understand that. And so does my mother. It takes a clan, Mrs. Santos."

Roslyn looked up at Eli, a faint glimmer of amusement in her eyes. "So I hear." She sighed softly. "You thought of everything to make sure we were okay, didn't you?"

Eli met her gaze without hesitation. "You are my world," he said quietly. "And I am your shield."

Roslyn gently unlatched Gabrio from her breast and pulled the nightgown back into place over her chest. With one hand she finished fastening the buttons before slowly rising from the couch. Cradling Gabrio carefully in her arms, she walked toward the little girl. She bounced him gently and kissed the tiny tip of his nose. A small smile touched her lips. But when she looked at the girl again, the smile faded, replaced by a careful, measured expression. "What is your name, young miss?"

"My name is Helena," the girl replied confidently, meeting Roslyn's golden gaze.

"Helena," Roslyn repeated, committing the name to memory. "Helena, this is Gabrio. I'm going to trust you with him tonight." She looked down at her son. "He and I have been through a lot this evening."

Helena spoke before Roslyn could continue. "I know, Mrs. Santos. Many of us were gathered outside the house. We could hear your screams across the yard." She lowered her voice slightly. "We prayed for you. All of us did. Even I sent a few prayers to Heaven for your safe birthing." She hesitated shyly. "Then we heard the baby cry…and many of us cried too."

Roslyn glanced at George. He gave her a reassuring nod. Turning back to Helean, Roslyn offered a grateful smile. "Thank you for your prayers." Her expression became serious again, but softer now. "But if you are to care for Gabrio tonight, I need more than your best. Stay sharp. Stay alert." She glanced toward the door. "I'll be outside."

Helena nodded solemnly. "Yes ma'am. I understand."

Roslyn straightened slightly and gestured toward the hallway. "Please go downstairs. I'll bring Gabrio and follow you." Helena turned and walked out obediently. George followed close behind. Then Roslyn. Eli watched them leave through the doorway. After a moment he sighed deeply and closed his eyes. Sending a prayer heavenward, he whispered, "Thank you for letting me live see my son." Basking in the moment for a few seconds more he stood there, then bent to lift the small bassinet from the floor. Carrying it carefully, he followed them into the hall and pulled the door closed behind him.

CHAPTER NINETEEN DEATH HOWLS

September 5th, 1881

Stepping from the ring of his discarded flesh, Talos flexed his newly mended muscles and rolled his shoulders. Turning his head to the right, he saw the forty Beast Bloods who had transformed alongside him. Some shook out their thick fur, ridding themselves of the last remnants of their mortal skins, while the others stood waiting for their next command. "Spread out and hold your posts," Talos ordered. "Keep your eyes sharp." The warriors scattered at once, racing back to their camouflaged tree huts that formed a wide ring around the property. Two Beast Bloods occupied each of the twenty platforms, giving them a clear view across the surrounding forest.

Standing watch along the eastern edge, Talos turned his attention is Sizrra. She stood perfectly still, her gaze fixed on the endless stretch of the woodland before them. But Talos knew she was looking farther than that. Beyond the trees lay the dark waters of Lake Huron—the distant lands of their homeland. Sizrra's body was tense, coiled like a drawn bowstring. Her ears twitched at every shifting current of wind. The air rushed through the forest in restless gusts. Something about it felt wrong. Sensing his gaze on her she finally spoke into his mind. "Someone…something it out there. I can feel it."

Talos knew what she meant. He could feel it too—the slow, crawling sensation along the nape of his neck. The trees swayed restlessly, their branches pulsing with a silent warning to those connected deeply enough to hear it. Even the wind had turned cruel, whipping grains of sand from the cracked earth and scattering them through the forest. For more than a month nothing had stirred beneath the cover of the night. Most of the wildlife had either migrated or died from the lack of water and food. Aside from the distant drone of insects and the restless wind, the land had remained empty for miles. Talos had spent centuries learning to read the signs of the world around him. He knew what this silence meant. This was the hour when death rode upon the wind. It waited patiently in the shadows, gathering the souls it would soon claim and carry to judgement. The wind thrashed violently through the trees once more, its howl cutting through the forest. Talos did not need further confirmation. The old signs had never lied to him before.

I'm going to check it out," Talos said quietly. Without another word, he closed his eyes. He emptied his mind of though and shut himself away from the sounds of the world. Seeking complete stillness, he drew inward and gathered the essence of his soul. It pooled slowly within his chest. A tingling spread through his body and the fur along his spine lifted. Pale, translucent wisps began to coil around him, weaving through the air like drifting smoke as his concentration deepened. Talos released a slow, measured breath. Then suddenly—his eyes snapped open. His soul burst free from his body in a flash of glowing white vapor, leaving his physical form standing rigid and unmoving behind. The spirit took shape as it rode the wind: the fierce outline of a wolf's head leading a trailing mass of shifting mist. Carried by the rising gusts, Talos's soul surged higher and farther, leaping from current to current across the dark waters of Lake Huron. It sped toward the distant Canadian shore.

From where his spirit rode the wind, Talos scanned the dark waters below. There was no immediate sign of demonic presence. But instinct warned him the search was not finished. To cover more ground he divided his soul. The vapor that formed his spirit rippled and split apart. From the drifting mist, several smaller wolf forms emerged, each carrying a fragment of his essence. They followed the larger alpha shape that led them. Then, like hunting wolves breaking formation, they scattered across the sky. Each spirit ranged farther over the lake, spreading wide to sweep the surrounding waters. Through their shared senses, images flickered across Talos's mind. Dark shoreline. Silent forests. Empty water. Then the faint orange glow flickered against the black horizon. Talos's spirit snapped its focus toward it.

"I see something," he reported coldly. "Fire. Over thirty miles from the Canadian shore."

Sizrra stepped forward. She had been waiting for confirmation.

Talos willed several of the scattered wolf spirits to regroup with the alpha, forming a hunting pack one more. Together they rode the night wind, gliding silently across the dark sky as they turned against the current to sweep the area again. Lowering toward the distant glow, Talos focused on the lone flame below. Then another torch flickered to life. And another. Soon more than a hundred flames burned through the darkness. Their light revealed the faces of the men who carried them. Keeping his spirit concealed, Talos drove his soul pack forward, slipping through the gathering like a silent storm. Once more he divided his essence. White streaks of vapor split away from him, scattering across the mass of soldiers. The spirits darted between them, weaving through the marching crowd. Talos saw everything through their shared sight. Mud-streaked faces of half-demon men. Armor dulled with grime and spattered with blood. Cold, hollow expressions. And their eyes—the windows of the soul. Talos's split pupils widened. There was no mortal essence behind those eyes. Only demons.

Grimly, Talos spoke. "It's them. They're heading this way. Armed—and carrying leather sacks filled with explosives." Having seen enough, he summoned his scattered soul back to him. In a flash of white vapor, the fragments raced across the sky and slammed back into his waiting body. The force of it made his muscles tighten as his essence settled once more within his chest. His strength returned in a rushing surge. Talos turned to Sizrra. "It's time," he said coldly. "We fight. We avenge our people—and secure our future with their deaths."

A flicker of trepidation stirred in her chest. But it lasted only a heartbeat. Years of training smothered the feeling before it could grow. Fear was acknowledged only long enough to be mastered. Then it was gone. She straightened, ready. "I'll give the signal." Sizrra turned the dark forest and drew a deep breath. Then she lifted her head and released an long, piercing howl. The sound carried across the lake and through the trees—the warning that the enemy had arrived.

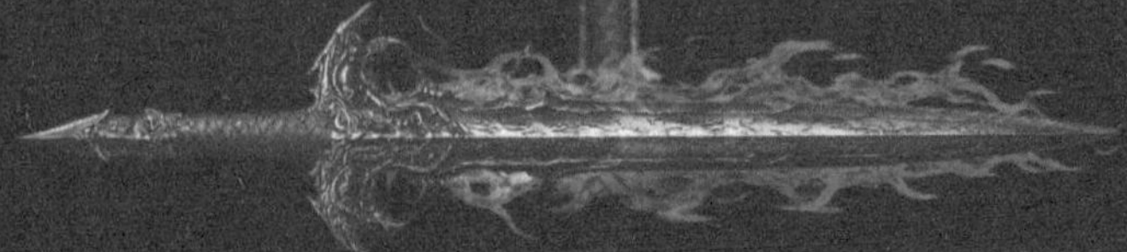

Eli, Roslyn, and everyone else turned toward the eastern woods. Sizrra's warning howl tore through the stillness of the night, echoing across the open fields like a blade cutting through silence. The signal spread instantly. Warriors scattered to their positions, racing to prepare for the oncoming assault of the Thogagi's army.

"They're coming." George snarled, glaring toward the tree line. "They're coming from the east, not the south."

"Eli stood rigid, listening. A second howl rose above the first—Talos's voice carrying across the wind. Eli translated the coded call immediately. "There numbers are smaller than expected," he said grimly. "We nearly match them." After months of preparation, the moment had finally arrived. He turned toward Roslyn, fear rushing through his body. She hadn't moved. Her wide eyes stared at him filled with fear as well. She whispered into his mind. "Gabrio." It was all she could say.

Eli rushed to Roslyn and pulled her tightly into his arms. He buried his face against her neck, holding her as if he could shield her from everything that was coming. When he spoke, his voice left no room for argument. "Take Sheryl, Helena, and our son and get to the cellar. The tunnels are finished. Head back toward the main house. Keller won't know you're there. He pulled back just enough to look into her eyes. "This house is solid brick—it won't burn easily. Once you reach the cellar, find the painting of the woman overlooking the sea. Andante built a hidden door behind the canvas." His grip tightened around her arms. "Use the escape tunnel. Run to the safehouse and don't look back. Don't come back for anything." His voice hardened. "I mean anything. Do you hear me?" His chest felt as if it were splitting apart. "I will find you again. I swear to God—but you must not come back here."

Roslyn nodded, fear swallowing her words. She refused to say goodbye. Something deep inside her recoiled from the thought, as though speaking it would make the separation final. A sickening weight settled in her stomach.

Eli saw the hesitation in her eyes and pulled her close again. "This isn't goodbye," he whispered. "I am with you, wherever you go. Always bound to you and our son. In this life…and the next." With visible effort, he forced himself to let her go. He turned to Sheryl. "Take Roslyn inside." Then he froze. Something had caught his attention. Facing south, Eli stepped forward instinctively, placing himself between Roslyn and the distant darkness. His eyes locked onto a point along the tree line. He waited.

George moved beside him. "What is it?"

A shape emerged from the forest as if it appeared from the shadow itself. Then another. Eli's eyes widened as he saw Keller sprinting across the field, thirty Ebony Knights fanning out beside him with torches in hand. "Keller!"

George's answering howl split the night. "Everyone—in your positions!"

"Sheryl!" Eli shouted. "Get Roslyn inside. Get my family to safety!"

Sheryl didn't hesitate. She seized Roslyn's hand and pulled her toward the house. "Now, Ros!"

Roslyn resisted for a heartbeat, her eyes locked on Eli. Then she heard it—the frightened wail of Gabrio crying inside the house. That was enough. Without another thought, she ran, growling. Sheryl was on her heels as they dashed through the front doors.

Eli watched them disappear through the doorway. Only then did he turn back toward Keller. Fury burned through him. The man looked just as deranged as the day he had stood watch over Leonardo's burning grave. Eli scanned the approaching enemy. Keller's soldiers were spreading across the field like a rising tide. He began issuing orders immediately. "Talos and Sizrra will have the shoreline," he said sharply. "They'll handle those trying to cross the water." He looked to George. "George—stick to the plan." He saw George give a curt nod, already preparing to move. Eli turned to the four Beast Bloods standing ready beside him. "Jasper. Solomon. Talon. Colt." The massive wolves—all black-furred with eyes of different colors—snapped their attention to him. "Two of you flank left." Eli ordered. "Two flank right. George runs center." He pointed toward Keller's advancing troops. "Open the oil bellies, circle behind their line, and wipe them out." His voice dropped into a cold growl. "Kill them all." His gaze fixed on Keller. "But leave him to me."

Eli stared across the field. Behind Keller, he could see them—faint flashes of the demon lurking within him, and the twisted lesser souls that animated the Ebony Knights running at his side. They were grotesque things. Decrepit. Vicious. Creatures that reeked of rot and hellfire. Eli held his ground, waiting. He wanted them deeper in the field. Closer. He flexed his hands, claws at the ready. He snapped his teeth in anticipation, a low snarled rumbling in his throat. The fur along the back of his neck rose.

"They're getting closer," Jasper growled, adrenaline burning in his veins.

"Not yet," Colt said calmly. "We must wait for Eli's say."

Keller and his men pushed forward. Closer. Closer. Eli watched them reach the center of the barren field—the exact place he hand been waiting for. Then he bared his fangs. "Now!" He howled.

George burst into a full sprint down the center of the field. The others moved instantly. Eli followed close behind him as they left the yard and charged toward Keller. Colt and Jasper veered sharply to the left, breaking from the pack, while Solomon and Talon darted right. The four wolves raced past the advancing line of Ebony Knights, slipping wide around them before cutting inward to circle behind their enemy. With the moon only a thin silver in the sky, their dark fur melted into the night. They moved like shadows. Undetected. George, however, was impossible to miss. The pale moonlight spilled across the open field and reflected off his silver-gray coat, making him blaze against the darkness and he thundered toward the enemy. He was the bait. And the only target the Knights could clearly see charging straight for them.

Keller bared his teeth as he charged toward the approaching werewolf. A cruel grin twisted across his face. “Looks like we have our first kill, men!” His voice dropped into a snarl as he fixed his gaze on the silver Beast Blood charging toward him. “Come and get me, beast!” Without breaking stride, he barked another command. “Knights—draw your blades. Aflame!”

Steel rang through the night as swords slid free from their sheaths. Enchanted fire burst along the blades, bathing the charging soldiers in flickering orange light. Keller tilted his head slightly, glancing to his left. Then it happened. One of his men vanished—pulled violently out of formation along with the silver wolf. Keller frowned. Another knight disappeared. He spun his head to the right just in time to see two more bodies ripped from the line—dragged screaming into the darkness. Keller skidded to a halt.

"There circling around you!" John barked. “Shield circle—now!.”

Keller roared to his men. “Stop!” The night exploded with screams. His men shrieked as unseen jaws tore into them. Keller heard the wet choke of blood flooding their throats, the snap of bones beneath crushing bites. The darkness around them had come alive. And it was feeding. “Shit!” Keller snarled, fury replacing his surprise. “Circle me! Now!” His men closed ranks rapidly, forming a tight defensive ring around him. They stood shoulder to shoulder with flaming swords raised, staring into the surrounding darkness where swift shadows flickered just beyond the firelight. Keller rolled his wrist slowly. A sphere of hellfire blossomed within his palm. The flames writhed and pulsed as he lifted his arm back and hurled it across the field. “Come out, beasts!” he screamed mockingly.

The fiery orb streaked through the night sky before slamming into the earth with a violent explosion. Jasper and Talon leaped away just in time, clearing the blast as fire erupted outward in a roaring wave. The flames devoured everything they touched. Driven by the wind, the fire spread across the dry grass, dancing wildly in the night as it grew higher, hotter, and more alive.

Breaking away from the wall of fire, the wolves regrouped. Talon led the charge, with Jasper, Colt and Solomon racing close behind as they surged back toward Keller's defensive ring. Talon struck first at the shield circle. He launched himself at the unsuspecting half-born knight, slamming into the soldier with enough force to knock several others from their feet. The fallen knights scrambled desperately to rise. They were too slow. Each Beast Blood seized a victim with brutal ease. Talon made quick work of the man beneath him. His jaws tore through the rotting flesh, shredding muscle and sinew until bone gleamed beneath the blood. Dark gore soaked his black fur as the soldier bled out across the dirt. The man went still. Talon howled as he spun, searching for his next kill—and ran straight into a blade.

Shhhunk! A flaming sword drove upward beneath his throat, punching through flesh and bone. The demonic knight twisted the hilt cruelly as the blade buried deeper. Talon's body jerked violently. The knight shrieked in savage triumph, reveling in the kill.

George saw Talon—the first of them to die—and released a thunderous roar. He darted past a raging soldier just as the man's flaming sword slashed through the air where George had been standing moments before. George vaulted over Talon's burning body as the knight ripped his blade free from the corpse. Without slowing, George crashed into another half-born knight and sent the man sprawling to the ground. Before the soldier could rise, George lunged forward, clamping a clawed hand around the creature's throat and dragging him away from the thick of battle. George loomed over him. The knight snarled up at him with a remorseless grim. In one savage strike, George raked his claws across the man's torso. Armor split. Flesh tore open. The knights insides spilled out in a gruesome cascade. George lifted the dying body and hurled it aside. The corpse slammed into the ground with a clang of armor and a wet, final thud.

Out of the corner of his eye, Colt spotted another knight charging straight for him. The half-breed came in with wild fury. At the last second, Colt dropped low and seized the man's leg. The knight shrieked as Colt yanked him off his feet. With brutal force, Colt swung the soldier downward and smashed him into the ground. The man's body bent grotesquely as his upper half slammed against the earth. Still gripping the leg, Colt jerked the knight upward again and slammed him back down. The half-born thrashed wildly, clawing at the air, snapping his teeth as he tried to rise. He never had a chance. Colt lifted his foot then brought it down with a stomp. Bone cracked beneath the crushing weight. The knight's skull collapsed, and the body went instantly still.

As Jasper finished quartering the knight pinned beneath him, he lifted his head with a detached arm clenched between his teeth. Blackened blood dripped from his snout as he dropped the severed limb onto the ground. Rising to his feet, he spotted one of the knights breaking from the defensive circle as Keller shoved him out of formation to go fight next. The demon charged, screaming, sword raised high. Jasper followed the knight's line of attack and saw the intended target. Colt. Colt stood with his back turned, looming proudly over the demon he had just crushed. Jasper moved instantly. With a powerful burst of speed, he stormed forward and intercepted the knight before the blade could reach Colt. The knight rolled across the ground and sprang back to his feet, swinging wildly. The flaming sword carved burning arcs through the air as it slashed again and again. Jasper twisted and dodged the rapid strikes as the half-born pressed its attack. Then the blade found its mark. The burning steel tore across Jasper's chest. The hot edge sliced through his thick pelt and sank deep into muscle. Jasper roared in pain. Fury stormed through him. He swung a massive backhand that struck the half-born across the face and sent the creature stumbling. That was his mistake. Jasper struck. His long, hooked claws raked across the knight's face and punched straight through the skull. A wet, choking scream tore fro the man's blood-filled mouth, shrieking through Jaspers sensitive ears. Without mercy, Jasper drove his other hand into the knight's abdomen, ripping it open. Entrails spilled free as his claws pushed forward through the man's body. With one final motion, Jasper seized the creature's throat and squeezed. The neck snapped with a sickening crack. The screams stopped instantly.

Keller was nearly the last one standing. He scanned the battlefield and watching another knight fall, dragged screaming from the defensive circle to meet the same fate as the others. His eyes flicked across the field. Eleven knights remained.

"I'm taking over!" John roared inside Keller's mind.

"You can't, remember? You are weak from the stunt you pulled a few nights ago!" Keller squeezed his eyes shut as his body began to twitch. The brown field was littered with bodies of his men. "I will win, demon!" Keller snarled. He rolled his wrists fluidly, summoning the power that gathered within his palms. From the light of the growing flames, he could now see the shifting silhouettes of the camouflaged Beast Bloods moving through the smoke. "I'm going to kill you all!"

Fire burst from his hands in a violent stream of white-hot flame. The blaze raced across the dry field, devouring the brittle grass. Keller spun in savage delight, casting fire over the bodies of his fallen men. The flames caught quickly—fueling the inferno. Then the fire found another target. One of the black-furred Beast Bloods. Solomon. The flames wrapped around his leg as he tore into another half-born. Keller laughed maniacally as the wind surged and fanned the fire higher. The flames leapt across Solomon's fur. Within seconds he was engulfed. Solomon roared in agony, thrashing wildly as the fire spread across his body.

Eli's eyes widened at the sight as he downed another knight. For a heartbeat, the flames twisted into something else. Solomon was no longer Solomon. He was Leonardo. Burning. Eli's stomach dropped as terror surged back into him. Then reality snapped into place. The illusion shattered. Rage exploded through him. "No!" Eli roared. "Save him!" He dug his claws into the dirty and launched forward in a furious sprint toward the burning wolf. His howl tore across the battlefield. "Open the water traps!"

Jasper heard Eli's command as the others dodged the spreading flames and seized the last of Keller's remaining men. He sprinted to the small iron lever hidden along the field's edge and yanked it down. Metal groaned beneath the strain. Then the earth moved. A hidden gate dropped open as sections of the ground collapsed inward, revealing the carefully prepared traps beneath the field. Pits of muddy water and black oil yawned open across the southern side of the battlefield. From above, the terrain would have looked like a chessboard—alternating squares of water and fire.

Eli's eyes snapped back to Solomon. The wolf staggered through the flames, his fur still burning as he fought desperately toward the nearest water pit. For a moment, it looked as though he might make it. Then his legs failed. Solomon collapsed at the edge of the pit. Unmoving. Eli's chest tightened as he watched. The great wolf did not rise again. With a slow, final tumble, Solomon's charred body slipped over the edge. Loose dirt followed him down as his lifeless form slid into the murky water below. The flames hissed and died where the burning fur touched the surface.

Keller nearly fell with the collapsing earth. The ground beside him caved inward as another sinkhole opened, and he leapt back just in time to keep from sliding into the muddy pit below. When he steadied himself, he realized he stood alone. Three Beast Bloods remained, grouped together across the torn field. He didn't need to see the rest. He could hear it. Behind him, the last of his chosen thirty screamed as a werewolf hurled him into a flaming oil pit. The man's cries were brief before the inferno swallowed him. The wolf that shoved him followed moments later—dragged into the flames buy the same blaze. Despite it all, Keller smiled. He lifted his chin proudly, reveling in the destruction around him. "It's too late," he said coldly. "I have already claimed all your lives!" He spread his arms slightly savoring the moment. I am Thogagi now. The demon feeding from my body will see to it that every one of you dies."

Keller stepped forward. Something cracked beneath his boot. He glanced down. A charred limb from one of the fallen Beast Bloods crumbled beneath his weight. Keller sneered. He spat on the burned corpse and deliberately ground his heel into the remains before lifting his gaze back to the three massive wolves before him. He waited for their reaction. There was none. Only cold, unblinking stares and the low, rumbling growls vibrating deep in their throats.

"I gave you power!" John bellowed inside Keller's mind again." Use it!"

Keller's jaw clenched as anger rushed through him. With a sharp motion, he sheathed his steel blade and drew the cursed silver sword from across his back. The wolves shifted slightly at the sight of it. That alone brough a thin smile to Keller's lips. He began pacing slowly before them, swinging the blade lazily with practiced ease. "Fools," he called out mockingly. "Do you not hear my army against yours?" He stopped and leaned forward, raising a hand dramatically to his ear as if listening to the blood-curdling cries and howls that rang throughout the night in a chorus through the hum of the flames around them burning so high that night became day. Then Keller burst into hysterical laughter. His eyes flashed white. The shift was immediate. Keller's body stiffened as a guttural scream tore from his throat, the veins in his neck bulging beneath his pale skin.

"It sounds like I'm winning this war!" the voice roared. For a moment, John held the body. "You will kneel before me, my army and my blade. Death-bringer." Then Keller pushed back. He dragged the swords top across the ground as he paced again, the silver blade grinding against the dirt. With a flick of his write, the blade lifted and sang through the air before leveling toward the wolves. Keller stood still now. His voice dropped lower. Darker. "I will spare you all," he said coldly, "if you bring Eli and Roslyn to me." His gaze searched the shadows around them. "I know they're here." The blade pointed directly toward the three Beast Bloods. "Bring them to me…and I promise I will call back my army."

"He's carrying a cursed blade. You can feel the energy draining from it just by him holding hit," George said grimly, never taking his watchful eyes off Keller. "A sword like that is bound to its master until the master's dead."

"Then we kill him after we disarm him," Jasper replied.

"It's not that easy." George countered. "If he cuts us, even once, it will steal our soul right out of us. And belongs to the wielder. I've only read of such weapons in some of the ancient texts I've come across. I have no doubt that's what it is." He looked toward Eli. "How do you want to go about this one? I can phantom next to him and try to disarm him."

“And we can all try taking him together.” Jasper said.

“No.” Eli’s voice carried finality. “I don’t want anyone getting near that blade.” The others looked to him. “We give him what he wants.” Eli knew the only way to lower Keller’s guard was to let him believe he had already won. "Jasper." Jasper turned his head toward him. Eli met the young-blood’s dark hazel eyes. "Get Holly." Jasper gave a curt nod and disappeared into the darkness.

Across the field, Keller saw the black wolf break from the pack and run into the night. “Good,” Keller shouted. “I see we're in agreement!" He laughed crudely, savoring what he believed was victory. "Then there was three."

John’s harsh voice echoed inside Keller’s mind, beginning as a whisper before rising with anger. “Something is wrong, mortal. You’re too busy playing God with my gifts to use that pathetic head of yours.”

George glanced back at Keller and saw the man’s head snap violently to the side as the Thogagi argued with himself. He knew the mortal was speaking with the demon inside him. George leaned closer to Eli. “This is it,” he said grimly. “The defining moment of destiny.”

Eli nodded, scanning the inferno spreading across the field. Behind him, demons and Beast Bloods clashed at the traps and warriors held the enemy at bay. Small explosions erupted across the battle fields as Andante’s buried land mines—packed with shards of metal and gunpowder—detonated beneath the growing head of the fires. The battlefield had become a vision of hell on earth. And in its center stood Keller. The flames swirled around him, reflecting off the cursed blade in his hand. The only thing missing was blood dripping from its edge.

Eli’s black eyes reflected the firelight, mirroring the cold resolve within him. There was no room left for fear. No room for doubt. Only strategy. Only death. Only the duty to end this. He looked at George and gave a small final nod. “If this don’t work, and I die before he does,” Eli said quietly, “let my body burn, and go to Roslyn. I know my wife. She will come to try to get me. He might use my death to lure her out.” George said nothing. Eli continued. “Don’t leave anything to chance." He glanced once more at the battlefield. "As for Keller and his army—burn them all just as he burned our people. Kill every single last one." Eli paused several moments before he added. "And George. Thank you, brother. For everything." Without waiting for a reply, Eli turned and walked toward the burning field. Toward Keller. There was only one thing left he intended to do. Kill him.

Keller saw a massive, black-furred Beast Blood walking toward him through the firelit field. He swung his sword in a full circle before settling into position, the cursed blade poised and ready. The creature's calm unsettled him. Eli walked steadily through the open ground as the wind shifted and the flames crept closer, shrinking the battlefield around them.

"Who do we have here?" Keller asked scathingly.

"Eli presents himself to you at last. Consider it your reward—a chance to reclaim what was meant to be yours all along. Kill him and take his mate. Just as I promised." John's voice lowered into a dangerous whisper. "But remember our deal. Break it, and I will take everything from you."

Keller sneered as he licked his lips. "I remember our deal perfectly," he muttered. "I will not fall by his hand." His eyes lifted to Eli. The great wolf stopped several yards away. Firelight danced across Eli's dark fur rippled in the firelight as fury glinted in his black eyes, his stance low, balanced and ready. Prepared for war. Prepared to kill. For a moment, the battle faded behind him. They studied one another while the war raged around them.

CHAPTER TWENTY
FLAMES OF HELLFIRE

With a battle cry, Keller raised his sword and charged. He moved with unnatural speed, his body blurring as he rushed toward Eli. Eli stepped calmly aside. Keller thundered past him—but Eli dodged, refusing to let the man circle behind him. Snatching Keller by the back of his chain mail, Eli's claws dug through the metal and into the scarred flesh beneath. With a violent jerk, he hauled Keller backward. The Thogagi crashed to the ground. Without effort, Eli dragged him across the dirt and threw him back to the very spot where he had begun his charge. Eli stood silently before him once more. Waiting. Ready.

Keller snickered through his wheezing cough as he forced air back into his lungs. Then something in the distance caught his eye. One of the black-furred Beast Bloods was approaching, guiding another wolf toward them. The one was smaller. Its chestnut-brown fur shimmered in the firelight—almost the same color as Roslyn's hair when sunlight passed through it. The wolf's frame was slender. Delicate. Female. The realization slithered through Keller's mind. *Roslyn.* He lifted his head and inhaled deeply, catching the female's scent on the wind. It smelled like her. A groan of pleasure escaped his lips as he breathed in again, savoring the intoxicating mixture of smoke, blood and her scent drifting across the battlefield. It fueled him. A wicked smile spread across his face. "Hello, Roslyn, my love," he called out softly. "Ready to come home to where you belong?"

Eli growled low and foreboding. Keller's eyes flicked back to him. "So," he rasped. "I finally get to meet the great and holy Eli Santos…and in front of his…mate." He rose slowly to his feet, steadying himself. His gaze moved between Eli and Roslyn. Something about the moment felt wrong—but he ignored the unease. "You're the monster who took my life away!" Keller shouted. His voice broke into a furious scream. "And now I'm going to take yours!" Keller lunged forward again. At the last second, he twisted left—feinting—before driving the cursed blade toward Eli's side.

Eli roared as he slipped past Keller's thrust. The cursed blade sliced through empty air. In one fluid motion, Eli pivoted and slammed his massive palm against the back of Keller's head. With his other hand, his claws raked downward—tearing across Keller's face and dragging deep across his throat. Blood burst free in hot streams. It slickened Eli's hands as he seized Keller by the collar of his ebony chain mail and lifted him clear off the ground. With brutal strength, he hurled him across the field.

Keller crashed across the dry ground, skidding through dirt and ash before landing near the encroaching ring of flames closing around the battlefield. The flames crackled close in Keller's ears.

"Get up!" John snarled inside Keller's mind. "Don't let the fire take you!"

Keller felt the scorching heat licking at his face as he lay on his stomach. The deep wounds Eli had inflicted were already knitting themselves closed. The flesh mended rapidly of the fire close to his face as he slid across the dry field on his stomach. The deep wounds Eli inflicted were already clotting, mending rapidly, leaving only drying blood and dirt behind.

Rolling onto his back, Keller kicked his legs beneath him and sprang upright. Rage surged through him. His vision tunneled. A furious scream tore from his throat. "I will not be bested by you, Eli!" You are weak compared to me—and my power!" Energy exploded from his body. Blue-white streaks of lightning cracked through the air around him like living veins of electricity. Keller slammed his wrists together, stabilizing the raging current. Then he spread his hands. Bolts of lightning burst outward in rapid succession, tearing across the battlefield as they shot toward Eli.

Eli leaped from his position just as a bolt of lightning struck the ground where he had been standing. The explosion tore dirt and stone into the air. Dropping to all fours, Eli sprinted along the shrinking perimeter of the battle field as the encroaching fire closed in around them. Keller pursued him relentlessly. Lightning cracked from his hands in wild bursts, the bolts slamming into the earth behind Eli in chaotic succession. Explosions followed him. Chunks of dirt and shattered rock rained across his back as he ran. Eli roared with each blast. Sparks from the spreading lightning licked across the backs of his legs, sending searing pain and numbness through his muscles. His nerves faltered under the electric shock. He stumbled. The he dug his claws deep into the ground. The sudden pivot sent him spinning back toward Keller. With a savage roar, Eli lunged.

The force of his charge slammed into Keller and drove them both across the scorched field. In the chaos of the tumble Eli seized the opening. He clamped his massive jaws around Keller's throat. Fury exploding from him. His fangs sank deep into the flesh of Keller's neck, piercing the pulsing veins and scraping against the bone of his spine. Then Eli tore. With a violent jerk of his head, he ripped Keller's throat open. Eli released him and leapt back from the struggle. Keller's body continued rolling across the dirt before finally coming to rest on his back. His white eyes stared blankly toward the heavens. The face that had once twisted with hatred was now empty of life. Blood poured from the gaping wound in his neck and soaked into the thirsty earth.

Eli slowly rose to his knees. Then to his feet. The feeling returned to his legs as the last tremors of lightning faded from his nerves. His eyes never left Keller's body. Beyond them, the raging inferno closed inward, shrinking the field into a tightening circle of fire. Through the flames he heard them—the victorious howls of his people. They had won. They killed them. And they cheered for him for killing the Thogagi. For killing Keller. Still cautious, Eli stepped closer to Keller's corpse. He stood over him. The wound in Keller's throat still bled slowly into the scorched earth, feeding the pool of blackened blood around the body. The white eyes stared upward, empty. No presence. No life. To be certain, Eli slashed a claw across Keller's chest, cutting through armor and flesh. He waited. Nothing. No reaction. No fresh blood. Eli released the breath he had been holding. Relief flooded him. He had survived. He was spared.

For a brief moment he allowed himself to believe it was over. He stepped back from Keller's body, almost in disbelief. For so long he had prepared himself for death after the night he had never imagined any other outcome. Now the war was finished. The man who had nearly took his world lay at his feet. Everything he had locked inside his heart broke free. Eli lifted his head and released a long, thunderous howl of victory that rolled across the burning battlefield. The surviving Beast Bloods answered his cry across the field. Not wanting to question the miracle of his survival, he turned away from Keller and started toward the nearest water pit, hoping to escape the encroaching fire. His thoughts rushed ahead of him. Roslyn. Their son. Their Gabrio.

Behind him, Keller's blood stopped flowing. The pool around his throat began to draw slowly back toward the wound. The fire around Keller bent inward. Not from the wind—but toward him. Bowing. Keller's eyes flickered. In a blur of movement, his hand shout outward. Eli froze mid-step. An unseen force seized him. Keller rose slowly from the ground, hatred blazing in his eyes. With a violent rise of his hand, he lifted Eli into the air. Then slammed him back into the earth. Before Eli could recover—Keller drove the cursed blade forward. The sword pierced through Eli's back. It shuddered as it pierced him. As if the weapon itself had been waiting. It's blood-slick edge burst through his chest. The hellblade drank. In an instant—Eli's life was gone.

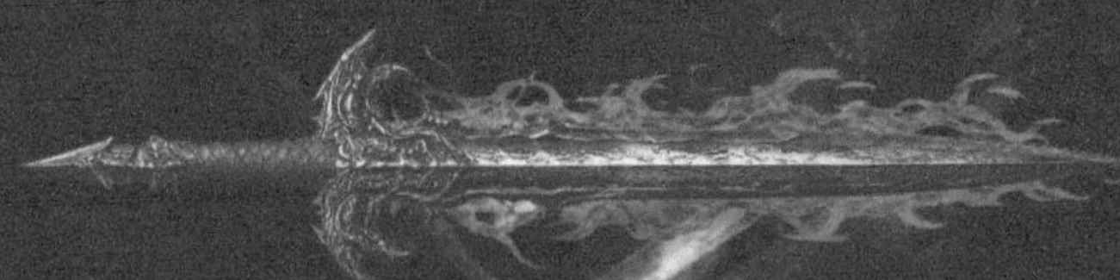

Roslyn suddenly sucked in a sharp breath inhaling the dust from the dark tunnel. A guttural roar tore from her throat as she doubled over, clutching her stomach as if a blade had been driven straight through it. Sheryl and Helena stopped walking as they looked back. Gabrio began to cry instantly at the sound. Helena rushed forward, lifting him from the crib and cradling him tightly as she tried to soothe his frightened wails.

"What's wrong?" Sheryl shouted, rushing toward Roslyn. "What is it?"

Roslyn looked down at her stomach. There was nothing there. No wound. No blood. But the pain—the pain was real. It twisted deep inside her, sharp and violent. Her eyes rolled white and the vision took her. She saw the blade. Wicked. Aflame. Coated in Eli's blood as it tore free from his body. Roslyn began to gurgle on her emotions as she watched helplessly.

"Eli!" She cried. "He's dead!"

Keller stood before him now. His pale skin was smeared with blood, his scarred face warped and melted into something monstrous. His eyes were black—empty—and his jagged teeth stretched into a grotesque smile. He was speaking. Roslyn could hear him—but it sounded distant, distorted, like his voice was echoing from beneath deep water.

"Did you think I'd die like a mortal, Eli?" Keller moved suddenly. He turned and suspended Holly into the air before he hurled a ball of hellfire. Roslyn saw her. Frozen in place. The fire struck and it consumed her instantly. Flames wrapped around her body as she burned, screaming, like a witch bound to a stake.

"Did you think I didn't know that was an imposter?" He snarled.

The connection shattered. And in that instant—she felt it. Eli's life leaving the world. Gone. Her vision snapped back. The cellar. The people around her. The cries of her child. Reality rushed back in—but nothing felt the same. Shock crashed over her, followed by a wave of immediate, unbearable heartbreak. It felt as if her own soul had been severed in half and burst into a supernova of blinding agony. She was both dead and alive. Grief struck so violently it stole the breath from her lungs. All she could do was scream. Roslyn threw her head back, and a howl of pure agony tore from her throat. Panic seized her. She needed to get to him. She needed to see for herself. She couldn't think—only act. Her eyes darted wildly around the cellar, searching for the way back out.

Sheryl spun around. "Don't go, Roslyn!" She shouted. "You can't save him now. Think of your son. He's all that matters right now. Think of him!"

Roslyn froze for a single, fragile moment—as if clarity pierced through her hysteria. "I *am* thinking of my son," she snapped. Her voice broke, rising with fury and grief. "Eli failed!" she cried. "Eli failed,—and Keller is still alive. Holly is dead too…." Her voice faltered into a whimper. "And Keller won't stop, Sheryl. He won't stop until he has me—every part of me." Her chest heaved. Tears streamed freely, but her eyes hardened with resolve. "I'm tired of running," she said, her voice trembling but firm. "I can't hide forever. And with Eli…" She choked on the words, forcing them out. "I will not give Gabrio a life of fear…now that Eli's—" The word wouldn't come. It lodged in her throat, thick and suffocating. Her gaze shifted to Gabrio in Helena's arms. A sick, twisting dread coiled in her stomach—knowing he might lose both parents tonight.

"With Keller's death, my son will be safe," she said, quieter now, but unwavering. "I have to ensure that." She stepped toward Helena and sank to her knees. Her heart shattered with every passing second. She studied her son—his small, fragile body wrapped in a thin blanket. Reaching forward, she pulled Helena and Gabrio close, nuzzling into them, pouring every ounce of love he had left into him. Through grief. Through agony. She gave him everything that would last a lifetime. "I will always be with you," she whispered. "I love you more than life itself."

Then she tore herself away. She swallowed her sobs, replacing them with something sharper—colder. Hatred. Roslyn straightened, her voice numb with terrifying certainty. "Eli said it takes a clan…right?" Her gaze snapped to the cellar doors—barricaded, splintered and fragile. Before Sheryl could react, Roslyn lunged forward. With a surge of desperate strength, she tore at the makeshift blockade and slammed her body into the wooden doors. The wood groaned, splintered—then gave away as she forced herself through into the firelight night beyond.

"Roslyn—no!" Sheryl shouted, racing after her and reaching out—but she was too late. Roslyn was already gone. Sheryl staggered to a halt, breath catching in her throat. Panic flared—but instinct took hold just as quickly. She turned back. "No…no…" she whispered, shaking her head before her voice rose again, breaking. "What about your son? What about Gabrio?" But the cellar swallowed her cries.

Swallowing her grief, Sheryl moved fast. She crossed to the wall, tore the framed painting free and revealed the hidden passage behind it. "Helena—go. Now." Helena stood frozen, wide-eyed and trembling, clutching Gabrio tightly in her arms.

Moments later, George burst through the opening Roslyn had just torn open. "Sheryl!" he called. He scanned the room—Sheryl at the wall, Helena with Gabrio. No Roslyn. His stomach sank. "Where's Roslyn?" he demanded, panic breaking through his voice.

Sheryl turned to him. "She ran. Eli's dead, Keller's still alive—and she went to him. What do we do, George?"

" Jesus Christ!" he swore, scanning the chaos around him. Firelight flickered violently as Beast Bloods rushed past, fleeing the spreading inferno. His jaw tightened. "I might not be able to protect her," he said grimly, "but we can protect her son." He reached out for Sheryl's arm, urgency sharpening his tone. "Move," George barked. "The tunnel exit will be engulfed before we've reached it. This whole damn state could burn with how dry the land is. "We head for the Canadian coast—Talos and Sizrra are leading the way now, and asked me to get Helena to them." Sheryl didn't hesitate. She waved Helena forward. "Go—stay with me." Helena rushed through the threshold, clutching Gabrio tightly against her chest. The moment they emerged from the cellar, chaos swallowed them whole. Flames roared. Smoke choked the air. Beast Bloods scattered in every direction as bodies of both man and beast surrounded them. Helena screamed as Maximous barreled past her, nearly knocking her to the ground in his desperate flight from the fire. George moved instantly. He lunged forward, scooping both Helena and Gabrio into his arms before she could fall. "I've got you," he said steady but urgent.

Sheryl pressed in at his side, one hand braced against Helena's back, the other shielding Gabrio. "Stay close," George ordered again. Together, they pushed forward through smoke, through fire toward what little safety remained.

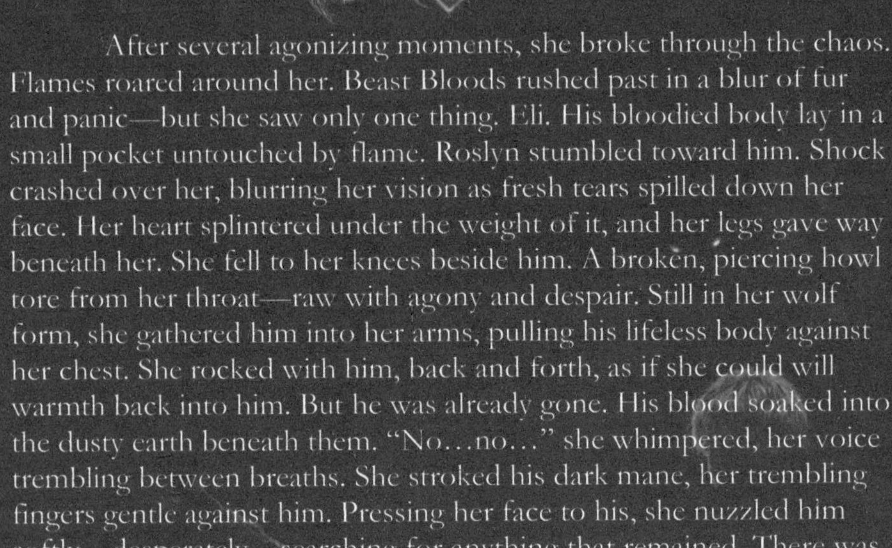

After several agonizing moments, she broke through the chaos. Flames roared around her. Beast Bloods rushed past in a blur of fur and panic—but she saw only one thing. Eli. His bloodied body lay in a small pocket untouched by flame. Roslyn stumbled toward him. Shock crashed over her, blurring her vision as fresh tears spilled down her face. Her heart splintered under the weight of it, and her legs gave way beneath her. She fell to her knees beside him. A broken, piercing howl tore from her throat—raw with agony and despair. Still in her wolf form, she gathered him into her arms, pulling his lifeless body against her chest. She rocked with him, back and forth, as if she could will warmth back into him. But he was already gone. His blood soaked into the dusty earth beneath them. "No…no…" she whimpered, her voice trembling between breaths. She stroked his dark mane, her trembling fingers gentle against him. Pressing her face to his, she nuzzled him softly—desperately—searching for anything that remained. There was nothing. The bond was gone.

"There you are," Keller said, his voice low with dark satisfaction "I've been looking for you… love." His presence crept up behind her. Then his voice cut through the chaos—loud, jagged, filled with twisted pride. "It should have been me," he snarled. "You were always meant to be mine, Roslyn." He stepped closer, boots crunching against scorched earth. "I have started a war with God for you," he continued, his voice dark with obsession. "I've slaughtered in your name. Burned everything in my path—just to have you. Everything I destroyed…was for us to rebuild together." A warped smile pulled at his lips. "I'm the one who proved my love." His voice dropped—quieter now, more dangerous. "I will love you better than he ever could."

At his words, anger unleashed up her throat. Roslyn dug her claws into the earth and forced herself to her feet. "You could never love me the way he did." Slowly—reverently—she leaned forward and lowered Eli's body to the ground. The soft thud that followed was final. Permanent. It fed her anger. It sickened her. When she straightened, she towered over Keller by several feet. Firelight danced in her golden eyes, reflecting the inferno closing in around them. She stepped toward him. Slow. Intentional. Each movement heavy with pain—and purpose. "You are disease," she said, her voice low and seething. "Rotting through everything you touch. Perverse. Twisted. Corrupt." Her lips curled. "I was a fool to save you." A growl rolled deep within her chest, thickening with every word. "Once, I called you friend…but now—" Her eyes burned into his. "I loathe you. For what you are. For what you've done. For what you've become." Keller's expression shifted. Hope. Twisted, delusional hope. He nodded slightly as she drew closer—mistaking her approach for something it was not. She could've laughed—wild, unhinged—but there was nothing left in her now but rage. She was death. And he would be her only victim. "And I am going to end you."

John's voice lashed through Keller's mind. "Kill her! Grab Eli's body. She's going to betray you." The demon clawed for control, but something held it back. Something stronger. Keller ignored him. "Kill her—now! She'll ruin everything we've built!" John burst through He had learned how to overpower him that night by the lakeside—the night they had nearly died. And he would not lose control now. Not when he was so close. A sharp pain split through his skull—but he held fast. His focus never left Roslyn.

"It's okay," he called softly. "Come to me, Roslyn." He extended his hand toward her, palm open—inviting. "We'll rebuild the world together. Just us. "I'll love you until my last breath."

Roslyn towered over him. In his twisted pleasure, Keller began to relax. In his delusion, he believed he had tamed her. That she had come to him. That she was his. He was wrong. Knowing her son was safe—knowing he would live—Roslyn lunged. A violent roar tore from her as her jaws found his throat. They crashed together, and fell into the inferno. Flames swallowed them whole. Fire tore across Roslyn's body, devouring flesh and fur alike. She did not scream. She did not fight. She accepted it. Held him there. Forced him with her. Keller's screams shattered the night. They twisted—warped—as John surged through him in terror.

"What have you done?" the demon shrieked. The fire answered. It consumed them both. Burned through flesh. Burned through bone. Through soul. For one fleeting second, Keller's scream was his own. Then even that was gone. The flames roared higher. Roslyn's body gave way at last, collapsing into the blaze. Nearby, Eli's still form was taken next—fire curling over him, claiming him, joining them in the same consuming end. The inferno surged outward. What had begun as destruction became something else. A cleansing. The battlefield vanished beneath it. Blood burned away. Death erased. Sin reduced to ash. The fire spread for miles—driven by wind, by drought, by something that felt almost…divine.

For three days, it raged. Relentless. Unstoppable. Hell itself upon the earth—until the rain came. And silence followed.

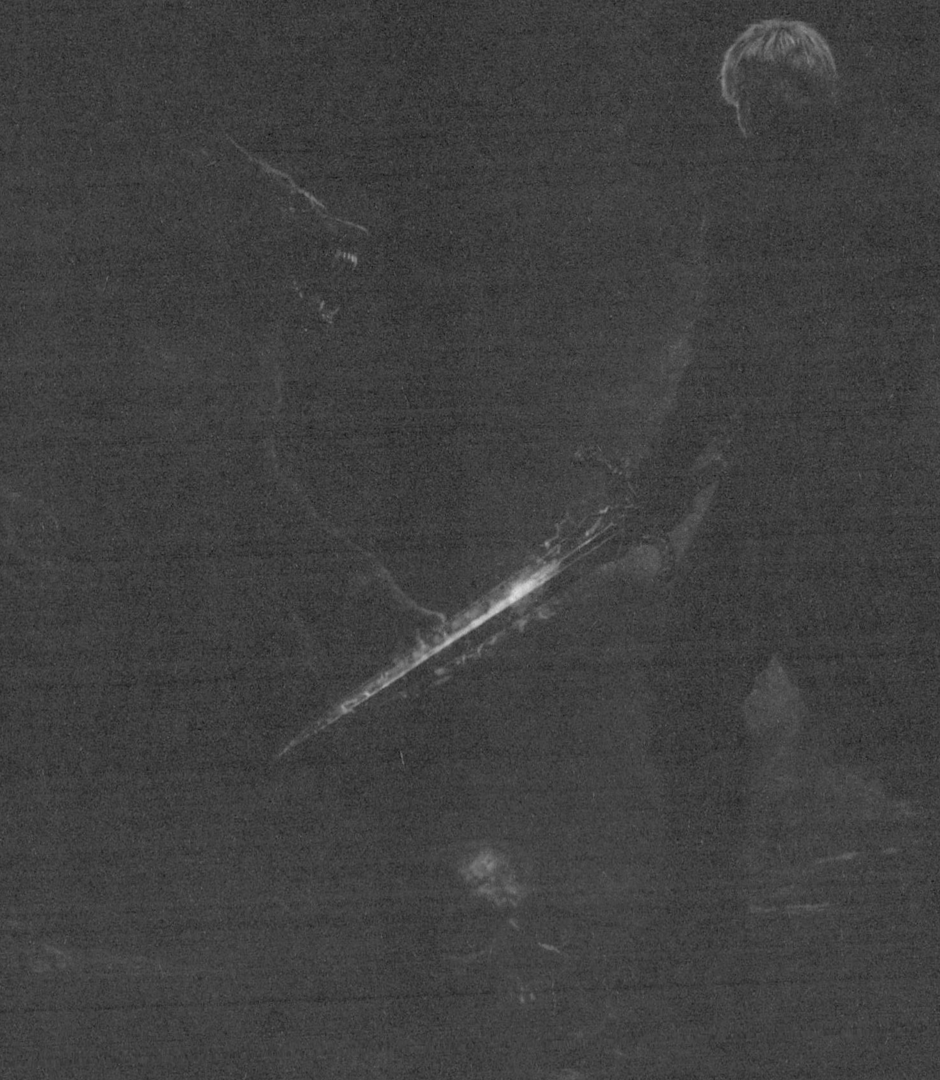

CHAPTER TWENTY-ONE
A KNOWN STORY RETOLD

OCTOBER 15TH, 1899
EIGHTEEN YEARS LATER

"The mortals never knew what that day truly was. The blaze had spread so far—so wife—they saw it in other states. A strange, golden-yellow glow lit the sky and bled across the land. Ash and soot choked the sun, turning day into something dim…unnatural. They called it the Great Thumb Fires. Said it started with a lightning strike deep in the forest. Said the drought and wind carried it."

George scoffed, his gaze drifting across the vast stretch of land before him. "Lightning may have sparked it," he said quietly, "but it wasn't the cause." His voice hardened. "Keller was the cause. His army. The demon. He paused. "And it cost us. Innocent mortals. Beast Bloods. Families torn apart. Children left without parents. Wives made widows." A heavy silence settled between them. "But it had to happen," George continued. "It forced us together. What we did that day—what *they* did—stopped something far worse." He turned his head slightly, his voice lowering with quiet reverence. "Your mother…no matter how hard Eli tried to protect her—she chose to fight." A faint, humorless smile etched his lips. "They are heroes." He added in. "We held the line. We fought the army. But in the end…" he exhaled slowly, "they did what had to be done. They gave their lives so the rest of us could keep ours."

George finally looked over at Gabrio. Grown now. A perfect reflection of both of them. Gabrio looked at George, his dark brows drawing together over golden eyes—so much like his mother's.

"So…this house..." Gabrio began. He glanced around—the white wooden porch, the pale brick walls warmed by sunlight. His gaze drifted across the open yard, now stripped of trees, but thick with lush grass. Beyond the gentle dips of land, Lake Huron shimmered under the light. He took it all in—imagining what once stood there. Fire. Blood. War. "….all of this was spared from the fire?" he asked, though it sounded more like disbelief that a question.

George nodded, rocking slowly in the wicker chair. "Yeah," he said. "Like the Creator laid a hand over it." He exhaled through a faint smile. "For what we did…for what *they* did." His tone shifted—firmer now. "We were meant to stop them. The Half-Breeds. The Half-Born. That's why I raised you the way I did."

Gabrio ran a steady hand through his thick black hair, his eyes drifting toward the old horse tired to the dark blue carriage. "And Maximous…" he said. "That's how we still have him? You found him here after the fire?"

George let out a low chuckled, the memory catching him. "Not out here," he said. "Basement." He shook his head, smiling wider. "Damn thing was down there eating through the whole pantry. Vegetables—everything." A breath caught in his chest, softer now. "I was so relieved…I didn't even think. Just grabbed him, buried my face in his neck and—" he huffed a quiet laugh, "cried. Then laughed." He looked at Gabrio again. "Your parents…" he said quietly, "they were something else."

Gabrio nodded, a small smile flickering across his face—then fading. His expression tightened again. "So many years," he said, voice lower now. "Wondering. Hating. Taking it out on everything around me…" He looked back at George. "Why tell me now? You could have told me sooner."

George stopped rocking and leaned forward, clasping his hands together. His gaze settled deep into Gabrio's searching eyes.

"The crest on your crib—the one still in the basement," he said, "that's not just decoration. It's who you are." He held his gaze. "It speaks of your blood. Your lineage. What you will one day become. No matter what name you use…no matter where you go…you will always be a Santos." He leaned back slightly, but his voice remained firm. "And now—you're a man. You know our ways. You understand enough to choose your own path." A faint smile touched his lips. "You have everything your father built—his businesses, his wealth. Power. Opportunity." His tone softened. "But more than that…you have their story. And that will guide you, if you let it." George paused. "One day, when you have children of your own, you'll tell them about their grandparents. And you'll do it with pride." He looked at him fully now. "You are their legacy, Gabrio. A good man. A noble one. I have no doubt you've made them proud…and you'll keep doing so."

Gabrio nodded slowly, absorbing every word. But the questions in his eyes didn't fade. They deepened. George noticed—and let out a short laugh. "What?" he said. "What now? What haven't I already answered?"

Gabrio smirked faintly, though it didn't quite reach his eyes. "I'm trying to process it all," he admitted. "It's… a lot." He exhaled, gaze drifting out over the land. "But the legacy part…" he continued, quieter now. "My grandfather. My father…" He hesitated, searching for the words. "What about me?" He looked back at George. "What will I become?"

George's expression shifted. He turned his gaze outward, jaw tightening slightly as he considered the weight of the question. "You know," he said slowly, "we're never given more than we can carry." He paused. "But if we are…" he looked back at Gabrio. "Then remember what you're fighting for. And you carry it anyway." His voice steadied—firm, grounded. "With courage. With duty. With honor." Gabrio turned his eyes back to the land—but something in them had changed. They didn't just reflect the world anymore. They were beginning to shape it. And George saw it. Something greater. Something inevitable. Something coming.

"Come on gentlemen. Time to head home," Sheryl called as she secured the last suitcase to the back of the carriage. Tomorrow is the day of the Rite."

George and Gabrio rose from the rocking wicker chairs and made their way down the steps. Gabrio climbed into the carriage without hesitation. George lingered a moment, glancing between him and Sheryl, a soft smile touching his face. "It's the least we could do," he said. "For Eli and Roslyn. And all those who fought that night. Isn't it, love?"

Sheryl returned the smile. "Always." She paused, almost as an afterthought. "Helena is with child," she added. "Her first."

George let out a quiet breath as he climbed into the driver's seat. "How time flied," he murmured. He glanced back over his shoulder, making sure Gabrio was settled. "Ready?" he called.

"Yeah," Gabrio answered "I'm good."

Sheryl stepped up beside George and took her seat. A faint, knowing smile curled at the corner of her lips—something unreadable flickering in her eyes. "I'm ready," she said.

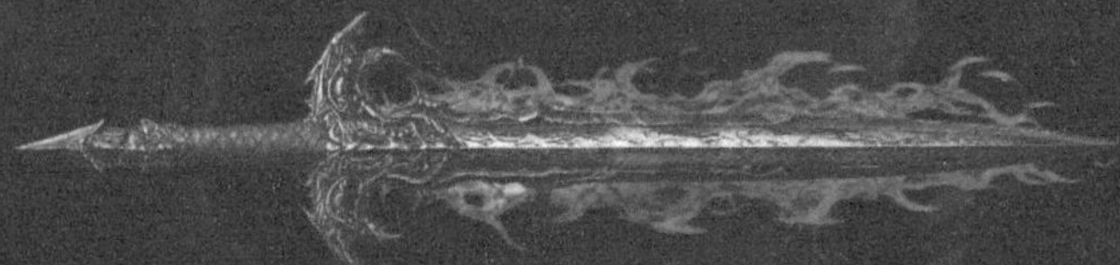

He stood at the edge of the woods, concealed within the thick line of trees. His gaze followed the carriage as it rolled away—lingering not on the men, but on her. Draped in ice-blue satin, her black wool cloak pulled tight against the breezed. He watched her laugh. Watched her settle beside the older man. Her husband. Watched her leave. His jaw tightened. Eighteen years. Eighteen years he had lingered in the shadows—watching her, tracking her, learning her every movement. Waiting. His teeth ground together as hatred coiled tighter within him. He could have moved now. Could have ended her. But he didn't. Not yet. He needed what she had. As the carriage disappeared beyond the bend, he walked away to grab his horse and follow their trail.

EPILOGUE

May 1, 2008

Homebound

Gabrio's nerves were stretched to their limit as he walked the familiar train beneath the moonlight. The forest loomed around him—overgrown, unchanged. His body remained coiled, teeth clenched as anticipation tightened in his chest. *It's been too long. Nearly ninety years. I shouldn't have come back like this…not without warning. I should have told them.* His gaze moved constantly, scanning the path ahead, the shadows between the trees. He tired to steady himself by focusing on what hadn't changed since his youth. Fireflies still flickered deep within the brush. Frogs and crickets filled the night with their layered chorus—an old, familiar rhythm. Once, it had been calming. Now, it wasn't. The sound twisted in his ears—too sharp, to chaotic—until it became a restless, grating hum. He knew it wasn't the forest. It was him. His thoughts were too loud. Everything else followed. Still, he moved—quick, controlled—burying the tension beneath practiced calm.

As he drew closer to the clearing at the end of the trail, the tension inside him tightened further. He dragged a hand through his long black hair, then shoved both hands into his pockets. A deep breath filled his lungs—the warm summer air expanding his chest before he slowly released it. The scent hit him instantly. Drawing closer to the opening at the end of the trail he felt himself growing even more anxious; he stuffed his hands in his pockets after he ran them through his long black hair. Earthy. Familiar. Unchanged. It stirred something deep within me. Comfort and sorrow. For years—before he left to explore the world, before he tried to outrun the memory of his parents' brutal end—these woods had been his entire world. He knew every inch of them. By day, he ran wile with the other children like him—laughing, playing, living. By night, he hunted beside them, chasing game beneath the same moonlight that now followed him. He had loved this place once. So much that he had asked George and Sheryl to hold the memorials here—in the meadow beyond the open field. They had agreed. And ever since, they always had.

Even then, everyone who knew him had seen him the same way—the legacy. Nothing more. He had been born in the shadow of destruction and blood, a living remnant of the 'Heroes of Hellfire.' Over time, their pity had become unbearable. Worse still—the way it shifted. From sympathy to expectation. To something close to worship instead of leadership. He knew what they wanted from him. What they believed he would become. But he didn't want that power. He didn't want to lead before he knew what that even meant. He didn't want to be a Clan Master like his father, and that's why he left. He didn't even let anyone know he was going. Not even George.

He needed to experience a life where no one knew his past—where no one expected him to be anything more than a man. And for a time, it was freedom. Real freedom. But it came at a cost. Loneliness. He had his share of women—more than enough when desire called—but he never let any of them stay. A few weeks at most. Long enough to forget, but never long enough to matter. Too many left heartbroken. He felt some guilt of it. But they would have never understood him—not after the illusion faded. Not after the truth of him settled in. Friendships fared no better. He never made them. Never allowed them. And eventually, even freedom began to feel empty. Like a life half-lived.

When he had taken all he could from the world beyond the clans, something shifted within. A quiet knowing. It was time to return. Time to begin again. *Maybe I'll build a house in the this meadow…right beside these woods.* The thought came honestly, but it tasted bitter. Because for the first time…his future felt uncertain. So naturally, he was nervous. He didn't know what time had changed—or how he would be received after so many years away. Open arms or cold resentment. The latter felt more likely. He wondered if they would even recognize him. He had stopped aging not long after he left. Forever twenty-five. Back then, he had been lean—almost scrawny. Not anymore.

A brisk wind swept through the opening at the end of the trail, carrying with it the scent of the clans—distinct, layered, alive. Laughter and merriment followed. Then music—guitars and tambourines weaving together in lively rhythm. And beneath it—
the noise of someone unfamiliar to him beginning to sing. Like a flash of lightning, Gabrio's thoughts vanished. Worry and doubt dissolved as her voice took hold of him. It was more than lyrical. It *pulled* at him. Held him. Before he could think, he was moving. He rushed the last few steps, crossing the threshold into the meadow. Firelight flickered across gathered figures. Clans mingled freely around scattered pits, their faces glowing in the warmth.

Gabrio moved through them unnoticed, scanning each face. No one he recognized. Relief flickered—then faded. He felt it settle in instead. Distance. He didn't belong here anymore. The voice grew louder. Closer. Hauntingly beautiful, wrapped in a rough, smoky twang that made it feel both raw and irresistible. Drawn forward, he passed a large, billowing tent. Now he could hear it clearly. His gaze snapped toward the sound. And there—there was no mistaking her.

Gabrio's heart stuttered. She stood center of it all —eyes closed, singing as if nothing else in the world existed. And for a moment…nothing else did. He was consumed by her as she was by the song. She looked almost unreal—like something pulled from a dream. Bright white flowers were woven through her ebony hair, soft against the dark strands, framing her luminous, creamy skin. Her lips, flushed gentle rose, parted with each note, her voice spilling out with raw, effortless beauty. He couldn't look away. The way she moved—subtle, rhythmic—her hand tapping lightly against her hip as she kept time with the music. The white fabric of her dress swayed with her, catching the firelight, shifting with every motion like a whisper against her form. Everything about her drew him in. Not just her beauty—but something deeper. Something he couldn't name. Something that held him there, rooted, watching. Rosy pink lips parted and revealed her perfect white teeth and a promising pink tongue. His eyes devoured her as she tapped her hand on her curved swaying hips to keep time. The way her body shifted the white flowing sundress in a swing made him want to see what laid underneath the almost see-through material.

"Her name is Esmeralda, son. Quite the sight, isn't she?"

Gabrio turned at the familiar voice. "George—" Emotion hit him all at once. His chest tightened, and his eyes glassed as he stepped forward wanting to embrace the man who raised him. However, he held out a hand instead. "I'm sorry…Judge."

George let out a soft breath, his voice thick with feeling. "No, no, Gabrio." He grabbed his hand and pulled him into a firm embrace. "Don't be." He gave a small, reassuring chuckle. "You needed to go. We understood that long ago. You had to find your own way. Even if it took longer than expected." He added with the faintest hint of a scolding tone.

Relief flooded through Gabrio, sudden and overwhelming. He held on tighter—longer than he meant to. Years of guilt, of uncertainty, of imagining this moment and fearing it…all of it melted away in the warmth of that embrace. George had always been that way. Never lingering on what was broken—only on what remained. Gabrio finally pulled back, a wide, genuine smile breaking across his face—something he hadn't felt in a long time. Home. He turned his gaze back to the meadow—back to her. "She's…more than beautiful," he said quietly. "I don't think words could ever do her justice."

George smiled knowingly in reply. So—this was it. Gabrio had finally met his match. And here, of all places. Home. The song ended. Music faded. Applause rose around them. Gabrio watched Esmeralda smiled—bright, stunningly—before her gaze drifted out across the crowd. Then—it found him. Her expression shifted. Joy…to stillness. Something deeper clicked for her. Her crystal-blue eyes widened as recognition sparked between them. Her breath caught—just slightly—but it was enough. Enough for him to see it. To feel it.

George clapped a firm hand against Gabrio's back, laughing under his breath. "I won't keep you from her any longer," he said. "We'll catch up tomorrow." His voice softened. "I'm just glad you're home, son." And with that, he turned and walked off, a quiet chuckle following him into the night.

Gabrio's smile came slow. Unguarded. Real. Esmeralda's answered—soft, shy. Her gaze dipped, lashes brushing against her cheeks…then lifted again, settling only on him. As if the rest of the world had fallen away. Something shifted inside him. In that instant, he knew a love like none before. She was his future—his world—the reason fate lead him back home. With her, he could conquer the impossible, face the inevitable…love her until the stars themselves fell from the sky. And for the first time—he didn't un from it. He embraced it. He stepped toward her. "Hi," he said. "My name is Gabrio Santos." And for the first time—it meant something.

If this story carved itself into your bones, if you felt the fire, the ruin, the love that refused to die—then do not let it fade into silence.

Leave a review. Speak of what you witnessed. Let the world feel it too. Stories like this survive because readers like you give them breath.

And if you're not ready to leave this world behind—if something inside you still lingers in the ashes…then you already belong with us.

Join M. A. Levi and the other Beastlings on her socials. Steep deeper into the shadows. Gain access to exclusive content, unreleased scenes, future books, ARC opportunities, and the secrets that were never meant to be found.

This is more than a story.
This is a world.
And it is waiting for you.

M. A. Levi is the author behind dark, emotionally intense stories that explore love, trauma, devotion, and the shadows that shape us. Known for blending gothic atmosphere with raw, character-driven storytelling, Levi writes worlds where beauty and brutality coexist—and where survival is its own kind of magic.

When not writing, Levi creates immersive journals and creative works through the brand **Worlds Within**, a space devoted to self-reflection, imagination, and healing through storytelling.

Flames to the Beast is the first installment in **The Beast Series**, a dark fantasy saga of prophecy, bloodlines, and love forged in fires.

www.ingramcontent.com/pod-product-compliance
Lightning Source LLC
LaVergne TN
LVHW030918080826
845145LV00013B/2955

9780692793657